Praise for *Without A Trace*

'Involving, sophisticated, intelligent and suspenseful –
everything a great crime thriller should be'   Lee Child

'A gripping, twisty police procedural – fans of the Kate
Daniels series will love this one'   Shari Lapena

'Mari Hannah has a rare gift. She can write compelling, page-
turning suspense with the very best, but she adds heart to
every page. Kate Daniels is a character to cherish, and Mari is
a writer at the very top of her game'   Steve Cavanagh

'With a cast of compelling characters and a chilling plot,
Without a Trace sets off at a cracking pace from page one and
never slows down'   Rachel Abbott

'Mari Hannah is in the uppermost echelon of British crime
writers and *Without a Trace* demonstrates why. It's her best
book yet – compelling, emotional and intricately plotted with
a procedural authenticity few can match. A stunning novel'
          M.W. Craven

'I loved it – both compelling and incredibly moving'
          Elly Griffiths

'*Without A Trace* is a deft blend of emotional drama and
crime procedural that kept me hooked to the very end. Mari
Hannah has a talent for writing about the light and dark of
life, and creates characters who feel so realistic they almost
pop from the page'   Adam Hamdy

Mari Hannah is a multi-award-winning author whose authentic voice is no happy accident. A former probation officer, she lives in rural Northumberland with her partner, an ex-murder detective. Mari turned to script-writing when her career was cut short following an assault on duty. Her debut, *The Murder Wall* (adapted from a script she developed with the BBC), won her the Polari First Book Prize. Its follow-up, *Settled Blood*, picked up a Northern Writers' award. Her Kate Daniels series is in development with Stephen Fry's production company, Sprout Pictures. Mari's body of work won her the CWA Dagger in the Library 2017, an incredible honour to receive so early on in her career. In 2019, she was the Programming Chair for Theakston Old Peculier International Crime Writing Festival and was awarded the Diva Wordsmith of the Year.

Also by Mari Hannah

WITHOUT A
TRACE

MARI
HANNAH

ORION

An Orion paperback

First published in Great Britain in 2020
by Orion Fiction,
This paperback edition published in 2021
by Orion Fiction,
an imprint of The Orion Publishing Group Ltd,
Carmelite House, 50 Victoria Embankment
London EC4Y 0DZ

An Hachette UK company

3 5 7 9 10 8 6 4 2

A CIP catalogue record for this book
is available from the British Library.

ISBN (Paperback): 978 1 4091 9237 4

Typeset by Input Data Services Ltd, Somerset

Printed and bound in Great Britain by Clays Ltd, Elcograf S.p.A.

MIX
Paper from
responsible sources
FSC® C104740

www.orionbooks.co.uk

For Mo
With love, always . . .

1

Autumn, 2014

Kate needed to be calm but was struggling to process the scene facing her. In a major incident suite unfamiliar to her, the names of passengers and crew of a missing transatlantic aircraft were being uploaded in real time onto an enormous electronic screen, the plane disappearing from the radar around a hundred and fifty nautical miles short of New York's JFK. Having driven through the night at breakneck speed – almost three hundred miles from her Northumbria base – she was in no fit state to take it in. Dripping wet in the doorway of the Metropolitan Police's Casualty Bureau (Aviation Security Command), Kate was counting down the seconds until it was time to sell a pack of lies that would give her access to an investigation that was well outside her jurisdiction.

DS Hank Gormley glanced sideways. His SIO's face was ashen as she took in the mayhem, physical and audible. Phone lines were hot, personnel jammed into every available space, traumatised by their task. On the journey south, he'd been constantly on the phone, checking the net for updates, consulting press colleagues, an information-gathering exercise he fed to Kate as the miles flew by. The missing flight was breaking news. Predetermined emergency telephone numbers had gone live on TV and radio within fifteen minutes of notification that a plane had been lost. A designated contact centre had been set up, manned round the clock by trained call-handlers from Met Police and other forces – all this replicated in New York.

Kate checked her watch: almost ten a.m. Nine hours earlier, when Hank told her that Jo Soulsby's flight was missing, the glass she was holding fell from her hand, shattering as it hit the deck. Symbolic. She was in bits, her breath coming in short, sharp bursts. She stumbled into his arms, the only prop she could cling onto. With her father's coronary and life-threatening, emergency surgery a matter of hours old, she'd half-expected a death today – if that was what this was – but not Jo. Never Jo. Jo was vibrant and full of life, a skilled professional and loving mum. A survivor. Maybe she hadn't travelled after all – maybe it was all a mistake.

Hank remained silent. Kate hadn't cried, not when he'd shared the news, nor on the drive south. She was too numb. He knew her well enough to see beyond her professional persona. She was deeply distressed, trying to keep a lid on it for his sake. Jo was more than a colleague to both of them. Kate was in denial, unable or unwilling to accept that she was missing. There was a deep affection between the three, a camaraderie that was hard to come by, even by MIT's standards. Hank couldn't reject the notion that Jo might have changed her plans. Detectives didn't write people off on the balance of probabilities. He'd attended enough accidents to know that people who were deemed to be aboard a bus, a train or travelling in a car were sometimes not among the casualties. That improbable hope died in his head but stayed alive in his heart.

What was taking so long? Fifteen minutes ago, Kate had asked to speak to the Gold Commander. He hadn't appeared. On the other side of the room, two men were deep in conversation, one of them making his mouth go, an arrogant stance. He glanced her way, deeply suspicious of the stranger who'd blagged her way into the Casualty Bureau, in no hurry to hook her up with the man she'd come to see. Locking eyes with him, Kate held her bottle, the enormity of what she was about to do feeling like a heavy weight in her chest. In her head, she replayed Hank's attempt to comfort her in that grim hospital corridor back home. She'd never forget the panic that flashed across the face of her second-in-command. Hank was in shock, too, battling hard to keep his composure so that she could fall apart. She was damned if she would.

Hank eyed the Met detectives. The cocky bastards turned their backs, making the Northumbria officers wait. If they took any longer, Kate would lose her cool. He wouldn't put it past her to march over there and intervene – and it wouldn't be pretty. She looked smaller somehow. Grief did that to people. She appeared to have her shit together but you never knew in situations like these. Had he been able to summon words of support, they would have been woefully inadequate. She was on leave with no authority to pull this off and no hope in hell of doing so. She needed her mettle now. He could only hope that she knew what she was doing and why she was doing it.

It hit Kate then, the enormity of a situation she wouldn't have thought possible a few hours ago settling in her gut. She focused on the man approaching, a detective with a confident presence, an arrogant swagger. He was late forties. Tall. Fit. Unfriendly eyes. A brave face was required. The cause of the lost flight – deliberate or accidental – would be determined by others in due course. So traumatised was she by either scenario, she didn't answer when Hank asked what her plans were. She didn't look at him either, though she expected his condemnation for going off-book. Kate had one focus. She had to find out for sure if Jo was on that flight.

2

'DS Blue. Can I help you?' An aggressive stance.

Instinctively, Kate knew he wasn't the Gold Commander she'd asked to speak to. Proffering ID, she said: 'Detective Chief Inspector Kate Daniels, Northumbria Police, Murder Investigation Team.' She thumbed in Hank's direction. 'This is my 2ic, Detective Sergeant Hank Gormley. We'd like to offer you any assistance we can.'

'Northumberland is a long way off, ma'am.' The Met detective glanced at the wall clock – 09.59 – then at her. 'You must've been motoring.'

Kate sidestepped the comment as if it were of no consequence. She didn't have time for small talk. He needed a nudge, a credible reason why she was sticking her oar into business that was outside her remit as a murder investigation SIO. 'We have reason to believe that our force profiler, Josephine Soulsby, was on board Flight 0113. My guv'nor has been in touch.'

'Really? That's news to me.'

No wonder. It was a downright lie.

Kate's frustration grew. Blue was clearly suspicious of her motives. 'DS Blue . . .' She fixed him with a steely gaze. 'Are you questioning my authority?'

'No, ma'am. I'm just making the point that we've had no word from your force—'

'You take all calls personally?' A pause. 'No, I didn't think so. Has it occurred to you that his offer hasn't filtered through yet?'

'That's entirely possible.' Blue gestured to the mayhem going on around them, a resigned shrug. 'As you can see, we have our hands full. In the last few hours, we've received thousands of calls from concerned friends and relatives. In the wake of Hillsborough, BT recorded half a million via the Sheffield exchange. Only a small percentage of which got through to the Casualty Bureau—'

'Yeah, we're from the sticks, not outer space,' Hank said. 'You're busy. We get that. Do us all a favour and save the history lesson.'

'Leave it, Hank. I'm sure DS Blue didn't mean to insult us. We don't want to fall out before we get our feet under the table.' Kate refocused on the Met detective. 'Excuse the northern bluntness. Hank meant no offence by it. In his cack-handed way, he's making the point that we're up to speed on HOLMES 2.' HOLMES was the acronym for the Home Office Large Major Enquiry System on which the enquiry would be run, the number signifying the fact that it was second-generation.

'None taken,' Blue lied. 'But in case you didn't know, we normally put out a formal request for help, if we need it—'

Kate's tone hardened. 'Up north, we're proactive, Sergeant. I suggest you check your call log. As I said, we've come a long way. We're here to help for the foreseeable future.'

Hank's eyes were on Blue, his expression inscrutable. He didn't need telling that the police had learned by their mistakes, nor that forces nationwide could now pool resources to assist at peak times in cases like these. Blue met his gaze, hinting that the Northumbria detective duo had had a wasted journey, considering that calls could be input from all points in the UK, transferred electronically to the home force via an updated computer system.

A momentary stand-off.

The two detective sergeants were about to lock horns. Kate kept her composure, allowing them a moment to finish their game of blink first. Tuning them out, she thought about the high level of calls the Casualty Bureau had already received.

There would be more. Many would be duplicates. Experience had proven that to be the case. Among the callers listed, Jo's sons from a former marriage would figure there somewhere: Thomas and James Soulsby.

In the early hours of the morning, prior to leaving Newcastle, Kate had grabbed some clothes from home and woken Tom, the oldest, before he heard the news on TV, then called on James in Sheffield to repeat the process. She made the South Yorkshire city in ninety minutes, topping a hundred miles an hour for most of the way on dry, empty roads, Hank urging her to stick to the speed limit, not because she might get pulled over, but because she was in shock, a situation guaranteed to slow her reactions.

She wouldn't listen.

Bad news was best conveyed face-to-face, not over the phone. Kate didn't offer any likelihood to either lad that they would see or speak to their mother again. Although she chose to keep the faith on that subject, it would be cruel to give them false hope. They were both shattered, James taking the news much worse than his older brother. The exchange unnerved her, made worse by the fact that, for them, this was déjà vu.

Kate had been the lead detective in their father's violent death.

Hank had interviewed James in the course of the enquiry into the shooting that ended his father's life. The lad Kate had since come to know as laid-back – much like his mum – had a very different temperament then. Belligerent was how she'd describe him. He made no secret of the fact that he didn't rate his father, before or after death. Consequently, he was high on the list of suspects, a murder his mother had later been wrongly accused of. Kate had worked tirelessly to prove her innocence, putting her job on the line in order to do so, and now she was digging her own grave at the Casualty Bureau, risking her career all over again. All that distressing history came flooding back, though it seemed a lifetime ago. And now, this . . .

How much more could one family take?

How much could she?

Kate wondered if James remembered the day she'd broken the news of his father's murder or if it was all a blur, a jumbled recollection that he hadn't properly taken in at the time, an event he'd blocked out since. Even now, hours from receiving reports of the plane's disappearance, Kate was struggling to recall the exact words Hank had used in the hospital corridor with her own father hanging on by his fingernails in a ward not far away.

Cowardly, Kate had let the breakdown in communication between herself and Jo go without a mention to either Tom or James. If they had questions to ask, she'd answer them truthfully, but not today. She'd already handed them enough grief to cope with without adding to it. It was James's likeness to his mother she found particularly difficult. Emotional: open and honest. Physical: ashen hair, identical pale blue eyes.

That image made her want to weep.

3

Having taken care of the distressing revelation to Jo's sons – almost, but not quite, a death message – Kate abandoned all thoughts of her leave period. She was state zero, off duty, with no authority in London, but she wanted in on the action so she could investigate Jo's whereabouts, exhausting all the possibilities before she gave up hope, unwilling to accept anyone else's word for it. Hank was staring at her, wondering what the hell she was playing at. In order to support her, he'd gone AWOL without permission. No doubt he'd be looking to dissuade her from getting involved.

He could think again.

Kate hadn't ordered him to accompany her to London. He'd volunteered, as he always did when she was about to commit professional suicide. It wasn't the first time she'd gone over to the dark side, but it may very well be her last. She was thinking on her feet – moment to moment – one step at a time. She hadn't consulted him on the drive south, but she needed him onside. If anyone could get her through this, he could. Left alone, she'd go into meltdown. Hank was so much more than a competent and loyal 2ic; he was her best friend, in and out of the job. He might have to be dragged kicking and screaming to see her point of view now and then, but he'd never let her down, unlike the Met detective facing her.

Blue was stalling. 'Thank you for the generous offer, ma'am, but I need confirmation from your guv'nor before I take it to mine. When I get it, I'll speak to my commander and call you.'

Handing him her business card, Kate withdrew.

She knew a knock-back when she saw one.

Her eyes swept the Casualty Bureau as he moved away.

Met personnel were going about their business with professional detachment, something she'd always prided herself on, except things were different now. Today, no officer held the same status as yesterday. Today, like Blue, they appeared hard-arsed, unable or unwilling to offer her instant answers – precisely what she was after. She took it on the chin. There was no comfort for law enforcement nor for the families of victims at times like these. Despite her extensive training, Kate was dying inside, ill-equipped to deal with the urgency of a major incident due to her close connection with someone on board that fateful plane.

As she made for the door, she pulled out her mobile, pressing the speed dial number of Detective Chief Superintendent Philip Bright, head of the Criminal Investigations Department, Northumbria's most senior detective. She needed his help.

If she had to beg for retrospective authorisation, then so be it.

His new PA picked up. Kate asked to be put straight through. The woman was intuitive; the fact that there wasn't time for niceties didn't faze her. She wasn't affronted by it. What some saw as unfriendliness, the woman who kept Bright's motor running recognised as Kate's preoccupation with her job.

Seconds later, the line clicked.

'Morning, Kate. How's your old man?'

It was a good question. One Kate had no answer to. Pushing open the door, leaving the Casualty Bureau, she took shelter from the relentless rain beneath the portico, sucking in a lungful of much-needed fresh air. Her mouth was dry, head pounding. How she handled the next few minutes was crucial.

'He's fine,' she said. 'I'm not.'

'What's wrong?' He knew it was serious.

It didn't surprise her. They had known each other forever.

9

Her voice sounded wobbly, even in her own head. The man on the other end had been her mentor since she was nineteen years old. He was the detective who'd moulded her; the man to whom she owed everything. In one way or another, every commendation and successful resolution of a case she could trace back to him.

She found her voice. 'You've seen the news?'

'Yeah, dreadful.'

'Guv, Jo was booked on that flight.' It was hard to say her name.

It wasn't often that Bright was speechless. It took a while for him to respond. 'I don't understand . . . I thought you two were off to Crail.' He was referring to the tiny fishing village Jo loved so much in the East Neuk of Fife in Scotland, their cancelled holiday destination. He may as well have pointed an accusing finger.

'We broke up. Her decision, not mine.'

'Because of Atkins? Oh, the irony . . .' Kate had recently been outed to her team by her nemesis and former boss, DCI James Atkins. Bright had jumped to the wrong conclusion. 'That snake will get what's coming to him—'

Kate cleared her throat. 'He had nothing to do with it.'

'Then why?'

'What can I say? I was a rubbish partner.'

'You weren't.'

'Jo wasn't prepared to play second fiddle to the job, Phil. She couldn't hack it and I don't blame her. She ended it, cancelled our plans and booked a trip to New York.' Kate felt compelled to explain that their relationship boiled down to moments like these, that her decision to keep the union a secret for fear that she wouldn't reach her full potential if it became common knowledge; because of someone else's homophobia; a callout from Control taking precedence over their plans. 'If only I'd listened—'

'That's the nature of the job, Kate. This is no time for

10

recriminations. Neither is it your fault—'

'Isn't it?' Her tone was bitter. 'Jo was sick of lame excuses that didn't stack up. She deserved more. She thought, hoped, that I'd put her at the top of my agenda just the once. Our work asks too much sometimes. I may never have failed you, but I certainly failed her.'

Kate locked eyes with Hank.

He thought so too.

He looked away through a curtain of rain. When he'd found out about the split, he was gutted. He'd played peacemaker for a while, hoping that the situation would resolve itself, as it had done many times before. Aware of Jo's decision to take off without her, Kate knew different. Hank was angry, believing that she should have made more of an effort to rescue her failing partnership. That was her time. That was her moment. And now that moment had passed.

4

It took a split second for the terrible truth to dawn, a moment more for Bright to offer condolences Kate didn't want to hear. Even before Atkins's spiteful intervention, motivated by jealousy, an attempt to disgrace her, Bright had known that Kate and Jo were an item, still very much in love. Discretion personified, he'd kept it to himself, believing that who Kate slept with was her business and no one else's. His feelings for his favourite DCI were deep and unconditional.

'Stay where you are,' he said. 'I'll come over.'

'No, guv, I'm in London . . . at the Casualty Bureau.' Kate held her breath, bracing herself for a verbal backlash. 'I want an in and you're how I get it.'

'That's not going to happen.' There was no hesitation. 'Get your arse home now. That's an order—'

'I'm on leave—'

'And off duty,' he reminded her. 'Step away, Kate. There's nothing you can do. You know that as well as I do. Stand down and let them do their jobs—'

'I've offered my assistance.'

'On whose authority?'

There was a pause.

'I'm begging you, Phil.'

'Seriously? Incidents like this run and run—'

'I'm aware, but I'm not the only SIO on the force. The North-East won't descend into anarchy if I'm not around. I was once arrogant enough to think that it would and look where it got me. I need your support.'

'And you'll have it as soon as you get here.'

'No! I do this or I resign.'

'Start typing.' The dialling tone hit her ear.

12

'Damn him!'

Hank was on the verge of saying something. A call to her mobile cut him off. Taking the device from her pocket, she prayed that her guv'nor had reconsidered. She should've known better. Bright didn't respond to threats. It wasn't Jo either – much as Kate hoped it might be. She'd called her several times and received no response.

The display screen showed the name Fiona Fielding.

Kate didn't take the call.

Hank eyed her phone. 'Who was that?'

'Fiona.' She didn't add, *the woman who shared my bed two days ago, believing that my relationship with Jo had finally run its course*. How ridiculous that now sounded. Nor did she need to explain who Fiona was. The three had met during a previous investigation. An artist of international standing, Fiona had been a witness in the case of a missing girl whose portrait she'd painted years before. The two women had remained friends.

'If you're about to launch headlong into a fishing expedition, as I suspect you are, maybe you should talk to her,' Hank said.

'Why?'

'She was one of the last people to see Jo before she left Newcastle, Heathrow-bound, the very person who told you she was flying to JFK and delivered the news to me that the plane had fallen off the radar.'

Hank was right – Fiona might have insight to share.

The sequence of events that led up to Jo's departure was highly significant. It was vital to gauge her mood, any conversations she may have had, any lingering doubts over her travel plans. Casualty Bureau personnel wouldn't be investigating that. Their sole focus would be the passenger manifest, collating information of persons missing presumed dead, recording the details of loved ones. The aircraft went down on the other side of the Atlantic. Homeland Security – a cabinet department of the US federal government – would deal with everything else, aided by air accident investigators, British and American, all desperate to establish cause: pilot error, devastating mechanical failure or technical fault, explosion on board or another mindless act of terrorism. Kate would help in whatever way she could, though how she would go about it when US agents were in the driving seat was less clear.

'Maybe I should call Fiona,' Kate said. 'Wait in the car.'

She watched him walk away, head down. It wasn't that he didn't like Fiona. He believed, wrongly, that she was complicating Kate's fucked-up relationship with Jo. Before Kate made the call, she took a moment, remembering a conversation she'd had with the artist. The day before yesterday, Fiona had turned up at Kate's house uninvited. She wasn't in, but Jo was standing outside when Fiona arrived. Jo had told her that she'd come to return her door key, asking her to pass it on to Kate. Revealing her travel plans to Fiona was proof, if it were needed, that her relationship with Kate was over. The coast was clear. Over and out.

Fiona wasn't buying it.

Her voice arrived in Kate's head. 'There's time to catch her if you hurry.'

Kate hadn't hurried. Reeling from their last meeting, she'd done nothing to dissuade Jo from running away to America. She'd let her go, convinced that in a few days she'd reconsider, that they would kiss and make up, an arrogant assumption she bitterly regretted now. She'd seen the end coming and taken no action whatsoever. She'd simply buried herself in work as a diversion from their split. Then, with her investigation almost wrapped up, an admission of guilt in the bag, she'd had the audacity to send Jo a text to try to put things right . . .

The case won't be long. We're not far away. There's

time. We still have the booking and you're off for ages. I'll be able to disappear for a week before I sign off on the murder file.

Jo's answer was short and to the point:

> Enjoy Crail – I've made alternative arrangements.
> Please reconsider.
> I've made my decision.
> I love you.

Jo didn't respond and Kate knew why. Her text had fallen short of an apology for letting her down. It was grossly unfair and condescending. The great detective was free now. Fall in step while you have the chance. Was it any wonder she got no reply? Kate had known then that she'd blown it.

5

Aware of Hank's interest, Kate tapped in a number on her mobile phone and turned her back on him. Fiona answered on the first ring, as if she'd been sitting by the phone waiting patiently for the call.

The artist was rattled. 'Oh, thank God! Kate, are you OK? I'm so sorry. The minute I saw the news, I knew. I don't know what to say. I've been calling you. If there is anything I can do, ask.'

Kate had no words.

She liked Fiona. She was an amazing woman, a strong woman and great conversationalist, a free spirit in every sense of the word. She believed that marriage was an unnecessary institution, that monogamy was too lofty an ambition for most people. Consequently, she had neither the need nor inclination to tie herself to one person. Maybe that was the attraction. A relationship with her was never going to get heavy . . . but she wasn't Jo.

She'd never be Jo.

Kate missed the first half of her apology . . .

'I couldn't bear to be the one to tell you, so I rang Hank.' Fiona's anxiety was almost palpable. 'I had to be sure you had company when you heard the news. I called on you in the early hours but the house was in darkness. Are you there? I won't come over if you need to be alone. I would too in your position, but I want you to know that you don't have to cope with this alone. I'm here if you need to talk.'

Kate tried to speak but no sound came out.

Fiona filled the silence. 'Kate? Are you still there?'

Kate cleared her throat. 'Yes, and I need you to be honest with me—'

'When have I ever been anything else?' Fiona back-pedalled, begging Kate to forget what she'd said. Solidarity was called for, not taking a pop at one another or picking up on insults that weren't really there. She apologised again. 'I have no idea why I said that. I'm such an insensitive cow sometimes.'

Fiona was a lot of things: relentless flirt, laugh-a-minute escort, but never insensitive. Telling her that, Kate moved on. 'Listen, no matter how brutal it might sound, how hurt you think I'll be by it, you need to be straight with me now. Did Jo give you any indication whatsoever that she might change her mind about her trip to New York?'

'No, quite the opposite – but then that's not surprising, is it?'

Kate knew what she meant. The minute Jo caught sight of Fiona getting out of a taxi, she'd have jumped to the conclusion that the artist was there by invitation. The thought that a misconception like that may have sealed her fate was sickening. Panic squeezed the breath from Kate's lungs. What did Fiona know? In the face of competition, Jo wouldn't want to convey the impression that she was in two minds.

'When you got out of that taxi, you said that Jo was about to push her key through my door.'

'She was. Well, I assumed she was.'

'Assumed?' Suppositions were not what Kate was after. 'Jo had a key to my place for a reason, Fiona. Is it possible she was about to let herself in? She often did if we'd fallen out. I'd come home and find her cooking dinner—'

'Are you suggesting that I chased her away?'

'No . . .' Kate stepped aside to allow more staff to enter the Casualty Bureau. 'Just hoping that she had an ulterior motive for being there, that perhaps she wanted to talk things through.'

'Kate, don't do this to yourself—'

'Is that a euphemism for clutching at straws?'

'You said that, I didn't.'

'Yeah, well right now, straws are all I have and mine are of the short variety. What else do I have to cling onto? Never, ever think that I'm blaming you. There's only one person at fault here and we both know who that is. Did Jo say how long she'd be away?'

'No. Why is that important?'

Kate was asking herself the same question. Except, deep down, she knew the answer . . . A fortnight, a week, a day, an hour, was too long a time to be away from someone you loved. If Jo was in two minds about ending their relationship, she'd have planned a short trip, a few days to calm down and reconsider. A longer journey meant that she'd finally made the break, and Kate couldn't accept that.

The enclosed yard was filling up, detectives abandoning cars in every available space, keen to get inside and start work. From the car, Hank used his hands as winders, urging her to get a move on before they were blocked in.

'I'm not sure,' she said finally. 'It's probably academic. Thanks for the help. I'm hanging up now. I've stuff to do—'

'Kate, call me. Day or night. I mean it. I'm here if you need to talk.'

Kate's voice was small, like a desperate child who'd lost her favourite toy. 'I have to find her.'

'I know . . . I know.'

Kate hung up, tears pricking her eyes. She blinked them away, for fear that she would crumble if she allowed herself to feel, unable to cope with sympathy – Fiona's, Hank's or anyone else's. She would rise above her emotions, find her detective persona and then find Jo, dead or alive.

6

As Kate walked towards the car, an image of the Lockerbie bombing forced its way into her thoughts. The twenty-first of December 1988. Two hundred and forty-three passengers, sixteen crew and eleven victims on the ground wiped out in the worst terrorist incident on British soil. Kate had talked to officers who'd been in the Northumbria control room at the time. They were inundated with distressing calls from people who'd found pieces of the fuselage, seats, luggage and other wreckage of Pan Am Flight 103 strewn over two thousand square kilometres, some not far from her family home.

Given that Flight 0113 had pitched into the sea, there would be less recoverable wreckage. From the moment it left the radar, US emergency response teams had swung into action: police, search and rescue teams, crash scene investigators, comms units, press and public relations. In the UK, HOLMES was eating data, constantly being fed by a dedicated team of professionals who'd work round the clock until they were stood down.

Kate reached the car, unsure where to go next or what her intentions were. The car park was jammed with emergency vehicles. It was debatable if she'd ever get out, a miracle that the gate officer had let them in in the first place. He almost didn't, until she showed her warrant card and told him to get the hell out of her way. Ignoring his questioning look, Kate climbed in, wondering if they'd be that lucky second time around.

One thing was certain . . .

She'd be back . . .

Hank too.

A moment of deep sorrow passed between them. They had been colleagues for years, dealing with every kind of human misery, but nothing compared to this. Whatever was coming, they would deal with it together, as they always had, following the evidence. First they had to find it.

'What exactly did Bright say?' Hank asked.

'He said no.' Kate pushed wet hair out of her eyes, the better to see him. Pulling her seat belt across her chest, fastening herself in, she had only one question on her mind: was Jo on that aircraft? Turning the engine over, she apologised for dragging him into what would develop into a shitstorm. 'You want out, Hank?'

'Did I say that?'

'You don't have to do this. I'm not asking you to put your job on the line for me.'

His eyes flew to the gear lever, her left hand clamped around it in a vice-like grip, so tight her knuckles were white. Gently, he placed his hand over hers and gave it a supportive squeeze.

She turned her head away, unable to look at him.

Selecting first gear, she pulled out into heavy traffic, heading for Heathrow Terminal 5. They didn't speak again – at least not to each other. Kate managed to stem the silence with a spur-of-the-moment call to the hospital to check on the condition of her father.

On the coronary care ward, the duty sister came on the line. Her tone was at best unsympathetic, at worst indifferent. She made it perfectly clear that Ed Daniels wasn't out of the woods and deserved a visit. The fact that Kate had other priorities – an emergency of her own to deal with – went over the nurse's head. Miss Judgemental would brook no excuses.

One final shove from her. 'He's been asking for you.'

'He knows I'm away,' Kate said.

'That's not my impression.'

Semi-conscious, he hadn't remembered. 'Please tell him I called.'

Kate hung up.

Her father was recovering in one of the finest heart units in the country surrounded by medics trained to keep him alive. At Hank's insistence, she'd spoken to him briefly before she left the hospital, fudging an explanation as to why she was going away. An injection of realism was not an option for intensive care patients.

If he'd looked into her eyes, she'd never have been able to cover her grief. It suited her that he'd been out of it. She'd been hiding from him for years. When she'd finally had the courage to be honest about who she really was, he'd thrown it in her face, her relationship with Jo another stick to beat her with. Kate would never live up to his idea of what a good daughter should be – and then there was her choice of career.

His disapproval wasn't new.

Even in his precarious medical state, the selfish git was hardly able to form a sentence and yet he'd managed to summon up the energy to put her in her place. Unbelievable. When Kate told him about her relationship with Jo, he'd shown no interest, just pushed her away. So that was it. When her mother passed away, so did Kate's support. She'd been left alone, struggling with her identity.

Her father had no right to pry into her life.

Not now.

Or ever.

He'd been against their relationship from the get-go, his condemnation overt and unwarranted. He refused to listen or even talk about it. Prior to his operation, Ed had shifted his view of Jo slightly, for his own ends. While Kate was tying up her murder investigation, Jo had covered for her, visiting her old man daily, going that extra mile to make her life easier. A captive audience on a hospital ward, her father had no choice but to suck it up and get on with it. His hand relaxed as he slipped away to the comfort of sleep. Kate had taken one last look at him, wondering if this would be their final conversation.

7

'Now turn left,' the satnav advised.

Sensitive to her plummeting mood, a mixture of anger, regret and deep sadness, Hank swivelled in his seat to face her. 'Stop the car and let me drive.'

'I'm fine.'

'No, you're not. You must be exhausted.'

'I said I'm fine.' She wasn't.

He took a bottle of water from the door's side pocket, unscrewed the top and handed it to her. She took a sip and passed it back, balking as the unthinkable manifested itself firmly in her head, a mortuary the size of an aircraft hangar, full of bodies, or bits of them. On one side of the structure, a red door stood slightly ajar. In her mind's eye, Kate pushed it open, peered inside and came face-to-face with a mountain of personal belongings: passports, wallets, clothing and toys being sifted and labelled by forensic teams. This was her very own disaster movie.

As they arrived inside Heathrow Terminal 5, Hank received a call. He slowed, lifted the phone to his ear and took a few strides out of Kate's hearing. She imagined he was explaining to his wife why he might not be home for several days or even weeks. He'd not spoken to Julie when he'd gone home briefly in the small hours to pack. She was asleep and he didn't wake her. He'd left a message. Julie was used to playing second fiddle to Kate.

Hank hung up, bad news by the looks of it.

Kate's stomach somersaulted.

'What now?' The question was a toss-up between a beg and a bark.

'That was Lisa.' He was referring to DC Lisa Carmichael, a young detective in Northumbria's Murder Investigation Team. His uncharacteristic hesitation didn't bode well.

'Today would be good,' Kate said, impatiently.

'I had her check Jo's phone with her service provider.'

Kate could see from his expression that the outcome was not what she was hoping for. She braced herself, imagination in overdrive. A million thoughts rushed through her head: those agonising calls received by friends and relatives during the atrocity of 9/11; people on the ground hearing details of an emerging drama in real time through terrified voices; stabbings, mace attacks, all eyes on the cockpit. She couldn't bear the thought of Jo dead; the thought of her alive and suffering, trying to call her kids, was even harder to take.

'And?' It came out like a whisper.

'It was switched off here and hasn't been turned on since.'

Kate steadied herself. 'That's perfectly understandable—'

'Only if she boarded that plane.'

'Not necessarily.'

Hank looked at her, searching for an explanation he couldn't find. In his opinion, there was no other way to call it.

Kate disagreed.

On the face of it, Jo was dead, but without hard evidence Kate refused to accept it. Her name might appear on the passenger manifest, but it would take the recovery of her personal belongings, sight of that tiny tattoo on her left thigh or the penny-sized mole beneath her right breast to convince her.

'Kate?'

'Shut up. I'm thinking.'

He backed off, hands in the air like he was facing a pistol, frustrated by her failure to see sense. There was a valid explanation for Jo's lack of communication that didn't involve her being on that plane.

A slim chance was still a chance.

Hank might think that Kate was mad but he was wrong. She glared at him defiantly, feeling the need to explain her thinking. 'Jo wasn't talking to me, was she? And it's not unusual for her to switch off totally. Remember when she went to Thailand? There was a reason I didn't go with her. She'd booked into a Buddhist retreat, seeking solitude—'

'She never said.'

'On my advice. Can you imagine the reaction from a group of hairy-arsed coppers if she had? They'd have laughed her out of the station. She'd never have lived it down. My point is, no one understands the psychological impact of stress more than she does, nor how to treat it. I've known her to go for days without consulting her phone on holiday. She calls it "disengaging", the only way to have a proper break. She's always banging on about it, asking me to do the same. When she was with me, she wouldn't even take her mobile. Tom told me that she'd be away a while and that he didn't expect to hear from her.'

'Kate, you can't read too much into—'

'I'm not! Maybe she was relieved of her phone. It happens.'

'I know you want to believe that, but—'

'But what?' Her eyes were dark. 'I'm overreacting? Off my rocker? Is that what you think?'

'Did I say that?'

'You didn't have to. It's all over your clock. I'm on top of this, so back off.'

He stared: *let's not do this.*

Unable to let it go, Kate swept her hand out. 'Use your bloody eyes. A flight takes off here every forty-five seconds. Seventy million passengers pass through the airport every year. Six thousand-plus CCTV cameras and still this place is pickpocket heaven. Do you know how many people lose their mobiles here every day?'

'No.'

'Neither do I, but the ones they find are auctioned off. That should give you the scale of the problem. Those that are stolen must run to thousands. Do the maths.'

His objections brushed aside, Hank wound his neck in, knowing there was no point arguing when she was like this – and that suited her. Kate took out her phone, swiped right and tapped on an image of Lisa.

Moments later the phone was answered. 'DC Carmichael.'

'Hank tells me Jo's phone was switched off at Heathrow and hasn't been used since.'

'That's right. Guv, I'm so—'

'Get on to EE,' Kate said. 'Quick as you can. Tell them to keep checking. I want an update every hour.' That way, she knew Carmichael would stay in touch. 'And while you're at it, get in touch with Santander. I want to know if her bank account has been, is being used.'

'Consider it done. Is there anything else I can do for you, guv?'

'No . . . Actually, yes. Swing by Jo's house for me. If she was heading for the airport, she probably jumped on the Metro, but I'd like to know if her car is still parked outside. Failing that, have someone check the airport car park. If you find her vehicle there, have a word with the booking office to see if she prepaid and, if so, for how long.'

'I'm on it.'

'Thanks.'

'Guv?'

'I know, Lisa.' Kate hung up, cutting off her sympathy.

Pulling at the collar of her shirt, feeling nauseous and dehydrated in the dry atmosphere of the terminal building, Kate turned on her heels, striding off in the direction of airport security, keen to talk to anyone who'd listen. She wanted irrefutable documented evidence that Jo had boarded that plane. She wouldn't stop until she got it.

Security staff were naturally cautious when she showed ID from a police service that was not the Met, insisting that she was a representative of the Casualty Bureau even though she wasn't.

One phone call to verify her ID and she was sunk.

The young security officer stared at her for what seemed like an age. He had longer hair than was appropriate for a man in uniform. His goofy teeth and gold-rimmed specs gave him the appearance of a geeky student, not someone whose job it was to deal with safety issues, or cope in an emergency within the boundary of Terminal 5.

'Do you guys never talk to each other?' he said. 'The information you're asking for has already been sent electronically to you and the US Federal Aviation Authority.'

'I know,' Kate bluffed. She was ready to punch his lights out. 'What I'm after is physical evidence to back it up, so stop buggering about and get it for me. This is a major incident involving foreign nationals. We have the FBI, Homeland Security and Uncle Tom Cobley breathing down our necks, so boarding cards will do for starters.' She held a hand in the air, cutting off his objections. 'And before you tell me that they're mostly digital, we want the audit trail of those, too.'

8

Crushed by the news that Jo had passed through airport security, Kate felt her world tilt, a door of hope slamming shut. Jo was through the last checkpoint, on her way to the hydraulic airbridge connecting the terminal to the plane. Kate imagined her waiting patiently as a queue built up, chatting to fellow passengers, unaware of the drama ahead.

Fighting hard to keep her composure, Kate stared at the woman who'd delivered the confirmation. 'Was her boarding pass scanned?'

'I believe so, at departure gate B34 at 16.04.' The woman glanced at the iPad in her hand. 'According to the passenger list, she was one of the last to board.' She looked at Kate as if she were a toddler who'd lost her mummy and needed careful handling.

She did.

Breathe.

Concentrate.

Kate loosened the neck of her shirt, feeling as she always did in airports, frustrated, overheated, anxious, keen to get her journey over and done with. In the aftermath of the plane crash, with no explanation on cause – whether terrorist-related or due to engine malfunction – travellers were agitated, suspicious of anyone they didn't like the look of. Understandable when the place, inside and out, was crawling with armed police toting semi-automatics and extra security patrols. Officers deployed to reassure the public sometimes had the opposite effect, particularly for those for whom flying was a necessity and not a pleasure. Security staff were carrying out more checks than usual, using dogs to sniff out explosives. The press were badgering people about how confident they felt flying in the light of what had happened yesterday, making matters worse.

Kate wondered how many travellers had abandoned their plans today.

The voice of the woman she'd been talking to interrupted her thoughts.

'I can check to see if she actually embarked if you'd like me to, Inspector.'

Kate turned to face her. 'That would be helpful.' A thought occurred. 'You said Ms Soulsby's boarding pass was scanned at 16.04.'

A nod.

'Wasn't the flight due to take off at four?'

'There was a bit of a hold-up.'

Kate's heart leapt. 'Hold-up?'

'Around twenty, twenty-five minutes, I think.' A slight shrug of the shoulders. 'We were rushed off our feet. You might think flight crew work hard. Well it's not all beer and skittles for ground crew either. That could explain why the lady you're asking about didn't go through until later than expected. We don't call passengers until we're given the go-ahead to board. I'm not sure what was going on—'

'Then hazard a guess,' Kate said abruptly.

The woman's eyes flitted between the detectives, finally landing on Kate. 'It could have been any number of things. There were two no-shows. If they had checked luggage, it would have been removed.'

'Tell us something we don't know.'

Hank intervened before war broke out. 'We'll need specifics, Miss . . .?'

'Reynolds . . . Daisy.' She smiled. 'It's possible that someone presented as too drunk to board, became ill, or there was an administrative error on the passenger manifest. It doesn't happen often but no system is perfect.'

'Look, Daisy, we're not here to play guessing games,' Kate

28

said. 'We need to get to the bottom of this as soon as possible.'

'I'm sorry, but you'll have to talk to Adriana Esposito.'

'Who is?'

'The person in charge of ground crew. I've not seen her today. Our rosters cross over, so it may be that she's not in. You want me to call someone?'

'No, but thanks for the offer. DS Gormley will track her down.'

Hank made a note of the name.

'Pick-up central,' Kate said under her breath.

'Excuse me?' Reynolds looked oddly at Hank.

He shrugged: no idea.

Kate was someplace else, too busy to explain, wrapped up in a memory she was desperately trying to unravel. Something surfaced but didn't click immediately into place. It continued to slosh around inside her head, refusing to be still, like a revolving roulette ball keeping a hopeful casino punter waiting.

She glanced at Hank. 'Jo's words, not mine.'

And still he was clueless.

Her eyes sent him an unspoken message: *get rid of Reynolds*.

Hank threw Reynolds an awkward smile 'Thanks, Daisy. You've been very helpful. Could you give me your contact number so we can get back to you if we have any further questions?'

She gave him what he wanted, took the hint and walked away.

Before he had time to ask what was going on, Kate's mobile rang.

'It's Bright.' She tapped the red 'Decline' button. There were more important things on her mind than round two with her guv'nor. Hank's disapproval was instantly on show and she reacted to it. 'If he's not with me, he's against me. His choice.'

'There'll be consequences.'

'Yeah, my days are numbered. I'm not sure I care. If he's

29

looking for my resignation, he can have it.'

'You don't mean that. Why don't we sit down?'

'I'm fine standing.' The imaginary roulette ball stopped dead in a pocket. 'After Jo left Newcastle, I called her several times for work-related advice. She was angry with me and didn't pick up, so I rang the airport, asking them to put a call out over the public address system for her to contact the nearest information desk. Thinking that my old man had kicked the bucket, she rang me, offering to fly home immediately. She was right here in the departure lounge and she wasn't alone. Someone spoke to her while we were talking. A man.'

'Pick-up central—'

'Precisely. Jo told him, in no uncertain terms, to sling his hook. I want him found.'

'Why?'

'Don't question my judgement, Hank. I know what I'm doing.' Kate regretted her harsh tone immediately. 'I'm sorry, I didn't mean to bitch at you. Maybe Jo thought twice about being so abrupt and apologised to him. You know what she's like. She hates conflict. She's too polite for her own good sometimes. If she had any interaction with that man, good or bad, I want to know the details.'

'It's a hard ask. And who will we get to do it?'

'Work it out.'

'You can hardly ask Maxwell—'

'Why not?'

'Want a list?'

Hank had a point. DC Neil Maxwell was the office Lothario, the least productive member of their Newcastle-based Murder Investigation Team. He got all the shit jobs, the ones no one else wanted. 'Needs must,' Kate said. 'He's shown signs of improvement lately and deserves credit for that. Besides, do you have a better plan?'

'Bright will go nuts if you tie up Northumbria resources—'

'Not if he doesn't find out.'

'You trust Maxwell to keep his mouth shut? You are losing it.'

'It's a risk I'm prepared to take. Clear it with Robbo.'

Back at base, Detective Sergeant Paul Robson was in the driving seat, holding the MIT together in their absence. Had Hank been available, he'd now be acting up as DI – his big moment – but he was prepared to forgo that opportunity in order to support her.

Kate was fond of both men, but Hank deserved it more.

He raised an eyebrow. 'You think he can hack it?'

'Temporarily, yes.'

There was a reason Hank had asked the question. Like everyone else, policemen and -women were fallible. Robbo had been through some very dark times in recent years. He'd fallen from grace, had been marginalised by his colleagues and disciplined for cocking up a major investigation. It acted as a wake-up call, forcing him to explain himself.

It had been painful to watch him disclose an addiction that no one in the office was aware of, one that almost ruined his life. It took courage to face the team head-on with his deepest, darkest secret, that for months he'd been gambling away money he didn't have, the worry over it affecting his concentration. Despite the bad choices he'd made, with help he had managed to overcome his addiction, repairing damaged relationships at home and at work, renewing his commitment to the MIT. Witnessing his comeback from the brink of disaster was like meeting an old friend after a prolonged separation.

Kate was very proud of him.

She reassured Hank. 'You'd have been my first choice.' He knew that, but still he wasn't happy. His concern prompted her to push him on the subject. 'You know something about Robbo that I don't?'

'No, Kate. He's doing fine.'

'Your words don't match the expression on your face.'

'OK, I'm not entirely convinced he's ready to run a major

incident but I'm not about to rubbish the guy to make myself look good.'

'There's nothing going on at home that he can't handle. We'd have heard about it if there was. Besides, his acting up hasn't been formalised.'

Hank dropped the subject in favour of the one they'd been discussing a moment ago. 'You do realise that it could take weeks for Maxwell to check out the CCTV.'

Kate had to think about that one. 'Maybe not . . . as I said, Jo responded to the airport public address system, That narrows our search down to information desks. How many can there be? If we can find out which one, we can track Jo's movements to the moment she called me and hopefully identify the sleaze who was trying to hit on her.'

'I still think you need to rein it in. If Bright gets wind of this, he'll have your badge and mine along with it.' Hank's mobile rang. He took it from his pocket and checked the display. 'Speak of the Devil.'

'Not interested.'

'Fine.' Hank gave a disparaging look. 'I hope you don't mind if I am. I have a wife and a kid and I want to keep my job.' He walked away, pressing the phone to his ear, expecting a lecture.

9

'Guv?'

'How is she?' Bright sounded more concerned than angry.

Hank looked across the busy terminal building. Kate was standing where he'd left her, stock-still, looking daggers at him. Though above average height, she struck a diminutive figure today, shoulders down, eyes pleading with him to end his call and get on with the job of finding Jo. Gone was the dogged determination she was known for, that air of authority she carried off with such composure. 'Use your imagination, guv. She's in chunks. Don't worry, I have her back.'

'A hospital case then?'

If the situation hadn't been so serious, Hank would've laughed. He didn't. Kate was risking everything. *Why now?* was the question he was asking himself. Why not when Jo was still breathing.

Bright swore loudly. 'She won't budge?'

'I'm not seeing any evidence of it.' Another check on Kate. She'd turned her back on him. Hank detected a slight movement of her shoulders. She was either weeping or taking a deep breath, steeling herself for more misery to come. If Jo were dead . . .

He didn't want to go there.

'Then you have a problem,' Bright barked. 'I thought she had more sense than to throw everything away on a long shot—'

'You taught her everything she knows, guv.'

Bright ignored the dig.

He knew that whenever Kate was in trouble, Hank stepped up to watch over her. In the last few years she'd broken all the rules: failing to disclose a possible motive for murder;

she'd slept with a witness; crossed force borders to interview a suspect who'd died running away from her; and now she'd lied to DS Blue that she had authority from the head of CID to be in London. If there was a job to do, she had no shame.

Bright might moan about her methods, even bollock her from time to time, but faced with similar circumstances, he'd have done exactly the same. He couldn't help himself any more than she could. He was the one who'd encouraged her to go the extra mile. Her success reflected favourably upon him.

Had he forgotten that?

Hank took his job as protector seriously and had no intention of withholding his feelings on something this important. Bright or no Bright, it was time to talk man to man, with no regard to rank. 'Cut her some slack, Phil. She's hurting. Imagine if it was Ellen on that plane.'

'It's not.'

'No, it's Jo. You know what she means to Kate.' Hank paused before delivering a blow he knew would find its target. 'You've been there yourself, guv. It's time you remembered who was there for you.'

Bright didn't react to the low-baller. His first wife had been injured badly in a horrific car crash and never fully recovered. Stella had since died and Kate had been their guv'nor's rock throughout a difficult period of his life.

There was a beat of time when neither man spoke.

Hank was first to end the deadlock. 'I can't leave her, Phil.'

'You mean you won't?'

Hank lied. 'If you order me, I'm on the next train—'

'Book your ticket.'

Hank bridled. It was unwise to argue with Bright. Those who had were now pounding the streets of Sunderland, on ten-hour shifts, wearing itchy blue uniforms. Nevertheless, he pushed on, hoping to dissuade Northumbria's finest from ordering his departure from the capital.

'Will you at least hear me out?'

'No, you hear me. In case you've forgotten, I'm responsible for the whole of the CID. As of now, you're acting up in Kate's absence. I wouldn't blow your first opportunity to do that if I were you. It's make-your-mind-up time—'

'Can't you use Robbo?'

'Oh, believe me, if you dick me around any longer, that's exactly what will happen. He's itching for the opportunity to show what he's made of, and he'll do a fine job, but you've earned the right. You want to give it away without a fight?'

'No, but—'

'Then don't let Kate sideline your career as well as her own. She has no business poking her nose in where it's not wanted. Tagging along on this particular goose chase is foolhardy. Take my advice and concentrate your efforts on bringing her home.'

'Short of knocking her out, that's unlikely to happen. I agree that her actions were unorthodox—'

'You can say that again.'

'Guv, give me a break. Think about it. With me here you have half an eye on her. If you order me home, you don't. She's flying solo. I pity anyone who gets in her way.'

10

Hank didn't mention what had been said on the phone. It didn't take a genius to work out that it involved a reprimand. Kate thanked him for taking the flak, then turned her attention to the length of Jo's trip and how she might have booked it, online from her home computer or with the travel agent she regularly used in Newcastle. She'd taken two weeks' leave. A long weekend to get away was one thing. A fortnight's trip to the Big Apple was something else entirely, requiring more of everything: planning, money, clothes.

The thought hit her like a brick.

'Hold luggage,' she said.

Hank looked at her, nonplussed.

'Come with me.' Grabbing his arm, she charged off in the direction of the BA information desk, giving him an explanation as they moved through the terminal. 'If any hold luggage belonging to Jo was loaded onto that plane, it means she boarded too. If it wasn't, she might have bailed at the last minute and been escorted landside—'

'Kate, slow down! You're not thinking straight.'

Hank stopped walking and waited for her to do the same. She pulled up sharply, ready to deflect another row. Hank was a practical copper not given to hare-brained theories. As her professional partner, he'd played a big part in her life, giving her the benefit of advice on complex cases. As in any partnership, they had argued their points of view, sometimes agreeing to disagree, but they had learned to compromise and, for the most part, come to an accommodation they could both live with. She hoped they could do that now.

'Mind if I inject some realism into the discussion?' he asked.

Kate rolled her eyes, a sigh.

'*If* is a very big word, Kate. If Jo changed her mind, why haven't we heard from her? She'd know you'd be tearing your hair out. Whatever was going on between you two, there's no way she'd let that happen. I'm with you all the way, you know that, but don't let your emotions cloud your judgement. Jo's flight from Newcastle International was the first leg of a longer journey. Her luggage would go directly to her ongoing flight.'

Kate couldn't argue. Jo wouldn't have handled her luggage at Heathrow; it would've been booked through for her. She'd not have seen it again until she reached JFK, a fact Kate would never have missed had she been firing on all cylinders. Her silence was an acknowledgement that Hank was right.

Wiping her face with her hand, she forced a nod, letting him know that she understood.

'I need to get my shit together, don't I?'

'You're in shock . . .' He dropped his head on one side. 'You're not a machine. You're human. At least I think you are. What you need is to eat and rest—'

'How can I rest?' She looked away, thoughts all over the place.

This was precisely why she needed him. She had a tendency to push herself to the limit. Without him she'd have burned out years ago.

She checked her watch: one o'clock.

Staring at the dial transported her to that dim hospital atrium, twelve hours ago, to the point where Hank had turned away from a vending machine with an expression that broke her heart, mobile in hand, tragic news on the tip of his tongue. Kate couldn't allow herself to dwell on that moment.

'You're right, of course. If Jo decided not to travel at the last minute *and* checked hold luggage at Newcastle airport, they would have taken it off at Heathrow. No passenger, no bag.'

'Agreed, but—'

'Perhaps that was the reason the flight was delayed.'

'You can't assume that.' Hank shook his head. 'From where I'm standing, you're twisting the evidence to suit your point of view. Can't you see that?'

'So humour me. We never got to the bottom of it, did we? The answer to this lies at home.' Ignoring his scepticism, Kate called the incident room.

Carmichael picked up.

'Lisa, it's me again. I know how busy you are, but I need you to do something for me. I can't order you to do it, but before you decide, I should tell you that Bright is on the war-path, so feel free to turn me down.'

'What do you need?'

'Confirmation of Jo's travel plans.'

'No problem. There's nowt going on here. I'll take a rest day.'

Kate felt her heart swell. Lisa was an exceptional detective: intuitive, quick-witted, naturally bright, with the ability and potential to follow in her footsteps. For her, nothing was too much bother. She was at the very core of the Northumbria team. Apart from Maxwell, who'd been forced on Kate by Bright's deputy while he was on leave – suffice to say he no longer held that post – squad members had been hand-picked by her and vetted by the most senior detective on the Northumbria force. Carmichael was as much Bright's protégé as Kate was.

Shame he wasn't supporting her now.

'I need every last detail,' Kate said. 'Including exactly how long Jo planned to be in New York and, crucially, whether or not she booked hold luggage – anything and everything you feel is relevant. Send me her booking form as soon as you have sight of it and I'll take it from there.'

'I'm on it, boss.'

The line went dead.

'Now will you take a break?' Hank pleaded.

'I have another "if" for you,' Kate said. 'If Jo was counted in, I want the names of everyone on duty airside that day.'

'Kate—'

'Do it! We can hardly ask the captain, can we?' Kate closed her eyes, then opened them again. She cradled her hands in front of her face, forefinger resting on her chin, like she was praying. 'Please, Hank. I need to know.'

He gave a fatalistic nod.

From that moment on, she knew that Bright luring him to their Northumbria base was unachievable. If Kate had been injured on duty, her 2ic would've been the first to pull on the Kevlar and head out to find the bastards responsible. She was injured now – maybe not in a life-threatening way – but injured all the same. Hank was her backup, faithful sidekick and loyal sergeant. He was in for the long haul.

11

Kate sent Hank off to find the ground staff whose job it was to count passengers from the air tunnel and onto the flight. While he was gone, she arranged for an escort to take her airside, making the journey to Gate B34 without him. The boarding lounge was empty when she arrived, a flight having just taken off, another not scheduled for a while yet. As her escort departed, Kate sat down in quiet contemplation, hands folded loosely in her lap, eyes scanning rows and rows of empty seats, an unmanned desk, a view through the window of an aircraft being readied for take-off, the slight whiff of aviation fuel. She had no sense of Jo having passed in transit through the featureless, functional space a matter of hours ago.

Moments later, two ground crew emerged from the corridor, strangely at odds with one another. There was none of the joie de vivre from the more senior of the two females, of the type Kate had come to expect of personnel skilled in the art of interaction with tourists and businessmen and -women taking off to who knows where. No swagger. No carefree exchange of pleasantries – even when the younger clocked Kate sitting there and whispered conspiratorially to her mate from behind a cupped hand.

Kate stayed put, observing them closely as they crossed the room: high heels accentuating legs that walked long distances, iPads, smart uniforms, half-smiles that made her realise that they knew who she was – more importantly, why she was there.

Her ID would remain in her pocket.

Kate continued to observe as they began getting ready for the next planeload of travellers. The younger woman was talking non-stop, in a heightened state of animation Kate took for morbid curiosity. She'd seen more of that than she could stomach in a lifetime. Most of what she overheard was to do with the press, the increased police presence and the agitation of the travelling public.

The older of the two appeared visibly shaken as her eyes homed in on a child's abandoned teddy on the desk. Dropped, Kate assumed, by a boarding passenger, not yet transferred to the lost property office. The thought that it might have been left behind by one of the children on Flight 0113 almost made her tear up.

Unaware of her colleague's distress, the junior crew member set down her papers, still gassing at a hundred miles an hour, a flash of whitened teeth visible between red-painted lips as she spoke. Word travelled like wildfire in places where tragedy struck. The longer the girl talked, the louder she became. 'They're reporting small amounts of wreckage floating in the sea—'

The older woman gave her a look that shut her up.

'Is that breaking news?' Kate's stomach rolled over. She wanted the girl to say no; that what she'd said was supposition on her part, not something she'd picked up from an indiscreet police officer or security guard. 'Sorry, I heard a little of what you were saying.'

Nodding, the young woman didn't stop for breath. 'We just fought our way through a media scrum in the admin block: TV, radio and newspaper journalists. They're all there, squashed together like sardines, putting the bite on everyone in uniform.'

Kate's response was matter-of-fact. 'That's their job.'

'Well, they should do it more sensitively,' the older one snapped. 'There are family members here, relatives in distress who have no place else to go. They're looking for help, not here to answer questions. The press have no bloody respect.'

Despite the validity of her objections, Kate tuned her out.

In her job, she'd learned to tolerate the media. In the age of technological advances, submitting copy before the next deadline was more competitive than ever. Information made the world go round. And with social media almost always ahead of the curve, it was everyone's business nowadays. Quick or dead was the name of the game if you happened to be a journalist.

'Where are you getting your information?' Ordinarily, Kate would shy away from uncorroborated accounts, unhappy with anything other than the official version of events. On this occasion, she was as desperate for intelligence – any intelligence – as her hack counterparts. She'd take anything she could lay her hands on. It took all her resolve to focus on the woman now talking.

'The US Navy reported the coordinates to the British Aviation Authority. There's little doubt that all aboard 0113 are lost.' A manicured nail smoothed an arched eyebrow, pencilled in with the precision of an artist, below which were overly made-up eyes, camera-ready should anyone be interested. 'It's OK for management. They don't have to face a worried public. I asked for compassionate leave but it was refused. Bastards. They should try smiling when flight crew are lost.'

'Serena, stop!' The senior crew member's tone was harsh. 'The detective has work to do and so do we.'

Get on with it or ship out was an attitude Kate understood. Her profession made few allowances for feelings either, even though her colleagues were queuing at the door of the force psychologist at HQ. Put simply, to feel was to fail.

12

Kate took her leave as the first passengers arrived at the boarding gate at around three thirty, picking up her escort as she entered the corridor. As she negotiated the flow of travellers coming the other way, her phone rang, a number she didn't recognise.

Jo?

Hope wore a cruel face sometimes. Pressing to accept the call, Kate lifted the device to her ear, a breathless 'Hello?' the only word she could manage.

'This is DS Blue, Casualty Bureau. Your guv'nor has been on the blower. My commander can't imagine why you thought he'd already been in touch. He wants a word.'

Shit! Kate stopped walking.

'Is now a convenient time?' Blue asked.

It was a warning shot from the Met detective. Was he giving her the opportunity to reschedule and get her story straight? If so, he was a good egg – one for her Christmas card list – but she knew nothing about him. That was enough to make her wary of anything he said. Still, she could do with an ally. An insider was essential to anyone working off-book.

'It's fine,' she said. 'Put him through.'

'Keep your hands in your pockets. He bites.'

'Thanks for the heads-up.'

Seconds later, a man came on the line announcing himself as Detective Superintendent Waverley. He sounded gruff, officious and distinctly unhappy. Wondering how much Bright had told him, Kate held her nerve.

'Good afternoon, sir.'

'Let's dispense with the niceties, shall we?'

Not a good start. 'Sir?'

'I've had a call from your guv'nor. Bright seems to have a lot of time for you. He wants you to assist with this appalling tragedy and to use the experience as a training exercise. There has to be an operational benefit for you being here, over and above the fact that your profiler was aboard.'

He knew.

'Listen carefully. Whatever your agenda, whatever game you're playing with Bright, it stays in Northumbria. I'm not interested in your motivation, much less your internal politics. However, I could do with all the help I can get – for as long as I can get it – especially from a detective of your calibre. For now, you and your lapdog are in.'

As the Senior Identification Manager or Gold Commander – 'Gold' as he was known to his Met colleagues – Waverley was in overall charge, the linchpin of the Casualty Bureau. It was his job to assess the level of assistance required from outside of his home force. Even so, Hank was a bonus Kate wasn't expecting.

'Thank you, sir. DS Gormley is a fine detective, the very best—'

'Don't thank me,' Waverley bit. 'If it were up to me, you'd both be facing Professional Standards for neglect of duty. You may have Bright tied around your little finger, but we do things differently down here.'

'You've never met my guv'nor, sir.'

'And I have no wish to. From here on in, you play by my rules. Is that clear enough for you, Daniels?'

'Perfectly.'

The use of her surname and not the rank that went with it was designed to put her in her place. It hadn't worked. Kate was lucky to have Bright as a guv'nor; he was tough but fair. Some senior officers were cowards who ruled by fear and testosterone-fuelled intimidation. Kate had been handling guys like him since she was nineteen years old. If 'Gold' turned out to be one of them, he'd need careful handling, but then so did she.

She was almost beside herself, desperate to ask him for an update on the fate of the stricken flight. In the end, she held off; far better she make her way to the Casualty Bureau and ask someone less prone to tension than Waverley. Maybe Blue would give it to her straight. Whether she was ready to hear the confirmation voiced was another matter entirely.

'You go rogue on me, Daniels, and you'll be heading out under police escort. We have a difficult task ahead. There's no room for prima donnas here. And . . .' Waverley paused for effect. 'When you've found what you're really looking for, you can take your DS and piss off north.'

The call was ended abruptly. Kate blew out her cheeks. Texting her thanks to Bright, promising to call him soon, she set off to find Hank.

13

Adriana Esposito, the woman whose job it was to count passengers into the tunnel for Flight 0113, was off duty. A part-time worker, she wasn't due at Heathrow for another three days, a frustrating delay the detectives could ill afford. Securing her number, the DCI called her immediately. Esposito didn't answer. Leaving a message, Kate hung up, slipped her mobile in her pocket and left the airport bound for the Casualty Bureau, this time allowing Hank to take the wheel.

As they drove through street after unfamiliar street, the radio was dominated by reports of the crash. Every commentator was speculating on cause. Though the cause might be in doubt, the result was indisputable: a catastrophic loss of life.

Kate listened carefully. In the US, the Federal Aviation Administration (FAA) were pursuing every possible line of enquiry. Actions had been raised to establish when the aircraft was last serviced and by whom, how much fuel it might have on board when it disappeared from the radar. The list went on. Every tiny detail would be picked over and analysed, starting now. It would appear that the press had already made up its mind: this was no tragic accident, but terrorism.

'No group has claimed responsibility,' the BBC World Service presenter said. 'We will update you as soon as we can . . .'

Kate turned off the radio.

A big sigh.

She wondered how her depleted team was coping without a Senior Investigating Officer at the helm. The incident room would be like a rudderless ship, but that cut both ways. She needed them as much as they needed her. Every one of them would now be aware that she was in deep shit with senior officers at either end of the country and totally spent; that she was dealing with a personal drama and was not where she ought to be – at her father's bedside – or wandering down the cobbled streets of Crail with Jo as she'd planned. More was the pity. Instead, she was in denial, heartbroken, committing one transgression after another, risking everything she'd worked for on a long shot.

Never in her life had the stakes been so high.

Bright may have given in to her demands earlier than expected, paving the way for her to assist the Casualty Bureau, but that didn't mean he'd forgiven her for interfering in another force's major incident or putting Jo before her job, just once.

It had been a long time coming.

Kate owed her guv'nor and he'd be sure to collect with interest. She'd kicked aside the rule book without a thought for the consequences. There would be some. She could count on it. Bright would try to impose his will on her. Jo was gone. Move on. No point living in the past. That was the philosophy he lived by, the one he'd expect her to follow. In the past, his advice had taken her far. Now she found herself resenting it. Rejecting it. Her drive to be the very best detective – to live up to his rigorous standards – had robbed her of a home and social life.

Her choice, but now she wanted those things . . .

She wanted Jo.

Kate was being unfair. It wasn't all Bright's fault. Yes, he'd championed her, sharing his considerable experience in order to prove that good detectives didn't come ready-made like TV dinners. Anyone who rose to the top had to do the hard yards and work their way up the greasy pole. Before Jo blew into her life, Kate had sucked up his praise, swept along in his wake, keen to prove her worth. She was the chosen one – the golden girl – the officer tipped to succeed him one day. If she could change her present situation, she'd hand over every last commendation and Chief Constable's compliment she'd ever earned. They were nothing compared to the day she met Jo at that party, the split-second realisation that she'd found her soulmate.

14

The Casualty Bureau's function was administrative: to collect, disseminate and process information to aid the investigative process; to manage misinformation, too. Parallels could be drawn between a major incident and a major disaster; the latter being run without a criminal offence at its heart. The aim was to trace, log and ID the individuals involved. To reconcile, in this case, missing passengers and crew of Flight 0113 with casualty survivor records.

Leaving Hank to introduce himself to the troops, Kate went to find Gold. Waverley wasn't in his ops room so she sought out DS Blue instead. She wanted to thank him for covering her arse. Like any good detective, he'd been in touch with the MIT in Newcastle in order to get the low-down on her and to establish her interest in what was, technically, none of her business. Robbo had filled him with enough detail to keep him happy, but not before contacting her.

So far, the Northumbria DS was playing a blinder.

Blue stood up as she entered. He was surprisingly relaxed given the mayhem he was dealing with. Someone had to stay cool. Kate was glad that he was a man not easily rattled. She felt surprisingly at ease in his company, as much as she was able, given that Jo's name was on his list of casualties. Some coppers were like that, but something about him didn't ring true and she decided to reserve judgement until she got to know him better.

'The name is Fraser, guv.' He proffered a hand. 'Welcome to the madhouse.'

It was a firm handshake. 'What exactly is your role here?'

It was important to establish who was who.

'Casualty Bureau Manager.'

'That's quite a responsibility. Good to meet you properly.'

Arms crossed, sleeves rolled up, Blue reminded her of Bright: immaculately dressed, good aftershave, strong jawline and deep-set eyes. He gestured to a chair, waited for her to sit, then did the same.

Nice manners – if trying a little too hard.

Kate crossed her legs, eyeing him across the desk. 'What do we know?'

'The plane was a Boeing 777. It took off half an hour later than scheduled at 16.33 hours BST. Due to land JFK at 18.55 hours. Routine flight. Radar tracking was normal. Ditto cruising speed. The last radio communication with the pilot raised no concerns. Then it simply disappeared off the screen.'

Kate couldn't make sense of why it should matter, but she needed to know exactly where and when the passengers, crew and on-board security personnel met their fate. In time, families of the bereaved might wish to visit the spot where their loved ones died. The middle of the Atlantic Ocean would make it difficult – but not impossible. If Jo was on that flight, Kate would be among them.

'Forgive my ignorance, but did 0113 go down in US airspace?'

A shake of the head.

'When did the radar lose it?'

'17.52 local time.'

'So, dark?'

'Not when it went down, but by the time the US Navy responded I would have thought so.'

'How many fatalities?'

'Twelve crew, two security staff and three hundred and two passengers – men, women and children – three hundred and sixteen in total, the majority British and American, plus citizens of eleven other countries.'

Kate managed to contain her reaction. She didn't verbalise her horror or argue with the number of casualties quoted. It would make her sound like a fantasist, rather than a detective whose watchword was realism. Her plan was to persuade Blue to feed her the information she required. If he refused to come across, she'd switch to plan B.

'Could've been worse,' he said.

Kate couldn't imagine how.

'The flight was nowhere near capacity,' he added.

He wasn't to know that she had a friend in the Air Accidents Investigation Branch who dealt with civil aircraft accidents and serious incidents within the UK, its overseas territories and crown dependencies. Although the plane had gone down outside of that geographical airspace, the department would automatically have offered assistance and expertise to their counterparts in the US. Rob Clark would be keyed up and able to help her. Now she came to think of it, he might be able to do even more than that.

She parked that thought. 'What are we doing for the families?'

'Not our remit, ma'am.'

'I didn't say it was, but someone needs to take care of them. I gather the press are all over them.'

'Airport administrators are prioritising a safe place in a hotel where relatives can wait, with counsellors and, if required, ministers to help them cope with the unfolding situation.'

'Good. Lack of information is a killer at times like these. No pun intended. The families are facing a long wait.'

'You were close to Jo Soulsby?'

Kate wasn't expecting that. Blue didn't know the half of it. Every time Jo's name was mentioned, Kate's heart broke a little more. Blue was searching her face, waiting for an answer that came as a nod.

'I'm sorry for your loss. Does she have family?'

'Two sons, Thomas and James.'

'They've been informed?'

Another nod. Kate wanted him to stop digging. She couldn't countenance the idea that Jo was among the casualties. If she did she'd fold for sure. Quickly, she changed the subject: 'Are we talking technical fault or terrorism?'

'Too early to say.'

'Can't they tell from the data log?'

The Met detective said nothing.

'C'mon, Fraser. I need to know.' And still he hesitated. 'Look, I won't quote you to Waverley or anyone else. Just tell me what the ACARS system transmitted prior to the plane falling off the radar.'

'You're well informed.'

'I read the newspapers.'

The ACARS acronym stood for Aircraft Communications Addressing and Reporting System, a digital data link for transmitting messages between aircraft and ground stations via satellite or airband radio. It had many functions: picking up faults or abnormal events during flight, inexplicable loss of altitude being one.

Kate sifted all the possibilities of what might have happened to Jo's flight: pilot error; disastrous technical problem; act of terrorism – bomb or surface-to-air missile strike; sabotage – a timed detonator on board – or, God forbid, a suicidal pilot. At this stage nothing would or could be ruled in or out.

All options were open.

Earlier in the year, a Malaysia Airlines flight (MH370) had gone down somewhere over the Southern Indian Ocean, west of Australia. No wreckage had yet been found and the search had been called off, but the mystery remained. And in July, another Malaysian airliner was shot down over eastern Ukraine killing everyone on board. Those two events aside, the Triple Seven was considered to be one of the safest aircrafts in the sky, having notched up eighteen million hours of flying.

Right now, it didn't feel like that to Kate.

She inhaled, bit down hard, eyes on Fraser. 'No SOS or emergency signal code?'

He shook his head. 'No, but at thirty-seven thousand feet it's unlikely to have been a surface-to-air missile, according to those I've spoken to.'

'Any loss of speed or altitude?'

'No. I gather the plane was on automatic pilot at the time.'

'So, the crew and presumably the passengers weren't aware of a problem?'

Blue shook his head.

'That's a blessing, I suppose.' Kate imagined an underwater beacon sending out the location of the black box, a major search underway. She looked Fraser in the eye, a plea on her lips. 'Any emergency squawk code or distress call to the military?'

'Look, I'm aware that you have a staff member on board. I'd like to put you out of your misery, but—'

'Let's get one thing straight – my involvement isn't personal.' Like hell it wasn't. 'How can I help unless I'm fully up to speed on what's happening?'

Blue apologised for overstepping the mark. 'Aviation experts suspect a bomb. It went down in an area where there was radar coverage – military and civil. The plane just stopped transmitting. US air traffic control tried but couldn't raise the captain or first officer. The US Navy was all over it by dawn. The wreckage – such as it is – has yet to be identified but there are no other reports of aircraft missing within a thousand miles of the coordinates the Ministry of Defence received from American Intelligence, confirmed by Homeland Security.'

Kate walked to the window and looked out, her resolve fading. Aviate. Navigate. Communicate. That was a pilot's mantra. It seemed that, in this case, they could do none of that in order to get themselves out of trouble. On autopilot herself, Kate was trying to process what she'd been told and yet hang onto the last dregs of hope. DS Blue gave her a moment to gather her thoughts. He thought she'd lost a colleague. Any copper knew what that felt like. Jo may not have been police 'family' but she was still one of them, a team player, as good as any.

Better.

Unwilling to give up on her, Kate swung round to face Blue. 'The HOLMES Casualty Bureau was activated immediately?'

'Standard procedure. All units fully deployed as soon as we heard. There's less of a risk at your end of the country. Down here we have to be ready 24/7.' He didn't need to tell her this major incident could go on for months. And they still might not find out what had happened.

15

The Premier Inn close to Heathrow and Junction 4 of the M4 motorway was basic but convenient, a place for Kate to shower and lay her head – no more, no less – but she had slept badly. Over dinner last night, she'd picked at her food in a restaurant Blue had recommended. She hadn't asked him to join her. Hank was the only company she required, the only one who understood where she was at right now. He could eat for England but had barely touched his jalfrezi. The onion bhaji he'd eaten would have sufficed.

A bad sign.

Kate had looked across the room to where other diners were enjoying themselves. Jo would have liked it there, the instrumental music floating in the air transporting her to a land far away, one full of colour, heat and energy: Mumbai's Marine Drive, a Goan beach, the Taj Mahal; a land of tigers and peacocks – all places she'd put on their bucket list.

For ten minutes, Kate had watched Hank push another piece of chicken around his plate. He wasn't often stuck for words, but then she hadn't been very good company. She was numb, drained and unresponsive, her mind in disarray, the events of the day too overwhelming to keep track of.

She loved Hank like a brother. There wasn't a man alive she loved more, and that included her father. Although Hank had never ever let her down, it had been easier to talk to Fraser Blue about the investigation than to him; Hank felt her pain, he was too close to her, and more importantly, to Jo. Close meant emotional. Emotional sapped strength and rendered people ineffective. No-brainer. They needed to focus, not crack up. But when she'd queried his mood, he'd launched a verbal attack, telling her that Jo was on that plane because

Kate had put her there, because *she* wouldn't know a good thing if it ran up and bit her. Kate couldn't remember paying the bill or leaving the restaurant. All she could think of was what he'd said and the expression in his eyes as he said it.

Across the room, her abandoned suitcase seemed to poke fun at her. It had sat on the floor of her bedroom at home for days waiting to be filled. Jo had asked several times if she'd packed for their trip to Scotland's east coast. On the eve of their holiday, stressing about a murder enquiry, not to mention her father's medical condition, Kate had telephoned her, for no other reason than to hear the sound of her voice.

Talking well into the night, Jo had taken her by surprise by bringing up the subject of Ed Daniels, prepared to forgo the holiday so that Kate could spend time with him during his recuperation. Initially, Kate was horrified by the suggestion. Why should she lift a finger to help? But Jo being Jo had managed to talk some sense into her. Next morning, difficult though her relationship with her father was, Kate had offered to cancel her holiday and look after him, only to find that she was surplus to requirements. A nurse was on standby to spring into action the minute he was discharged – someone he could stand the sight of, most probably.

The olive branch she'd offered had been pushed aside.

Kate had buried herself in work instead.

And now, as she lay in that grim hotel room, her row with Hank replayed in her head. He'd been right to challenge her. She alone was responsible for abandoning Jo at the eleventh hour. No one forced her to do it. It was her decision. When he'd found out that Kate was about to let Jo down, knowing full well that she'd be at home researching where they might eat and what landmarks to visit, Kate saw for herself what it meant to him to see them off on holiday together. Just like in the restaurant, he went ballistic, unable to hide his disapproval, criticising her for not caring enough, for fucking up her life again.

Kate skipped breakfast and went for a run, a way to avoid Hank until she was ready to face him. She showered and dressed, calling the hospital to check on her father even though he didn't deserve it, briefing Bright on progress, checking in with Robbo and Carmichael, then texting Hank when she was ready, asking him to meet her downstairs, without mentioning their harsh exchange the night before. It would be impossible to concentrate without him onside. They might have an in at the Casualty Bureau, but they had to be careful around Waverley and his team. Duty would drive them on; an obligation to Jo, not Queen and country.

Her Majesty could wait.

As they headed for her car, Kate kept her tone light. 'I spoke to Tom this morning.'

'How was he?'

'Better than expected given the circumstances. He'd just collected Nelson from Emily's.' She didn't need to explain that Emily was an old friend, Nelson Jo's adorable chocolate Labrador. Hank was well acquainted with both. 'Tom said he needed the company and James is heading north.'

'They're not coming down?'

Kate shook her head. 'I advised them not to. They'll kip at Jo's place until they hear, one way or the other.'

'Wise move. I'd hate to think they were hoping for a quick result. They do realise it could be years before we receive a positive ID? Months more before we're in a position to inform next of kin?'

'Yeah, they're in the picture. Don't worry, Hank. It might not always seem so but they're close. They'll support each other, and so will we . . .' Blipping the car doors open, she climbed in. When he did likewise, she swivelled round to face him, right forearm resting on the steering wheel, left elbow on the backrest of her seat. 'There's no one I'd rather have here with me. You know that, right?'

'Same here.'

'Hank, I owe you an apology.'

'You owe me nothing. It's me who should be sorry. I was out of order. I had no right.'

'You had every right.'

'How you treat Jo is none of my business.'

'It needed saying, but let's draw a line under it.'

'Kate, all I want is for you to stop torturing yourself—'

'Hank, don't . . . I know you think I'm mad but please don't take my hope away. It's all I have left, the only thing that'll keep me going. I won't, I can't accept that she's dead until I have unequivocal proof – and we're a long way from that. In my position, you'd feel the same. Bear with me for a while longer. For what it's worth, I wish I'd listened to you. I'll never forgive myself that I didn't.'

16

Mid-morning, Kate and Hank knocked off for a break. They took it in the refectory – posh Met-speak for the canteen. Despite the fancy name, the space was no different from the grim bait room they were used to at their Newcastle base. Kate's belly growled with hunger. She bit into an apple she'd half-inched from the hotel breakfast table on the way back from her run. It wasn't fresh and she threw it in the bin. Ordering a bacon roll, she ate it too fast and felt bloated afterwards. It was unlike her to whinge, but she did it all the same . . .

'I'm no connoisseur but this coffee is dreadful. How's the tea?'

'Like piss.' Hank pushed his mug away, his eyes shifting to a point over her left shoulder. 'There's a cooler over there. You want water?'

'Please.'

He went off to fetch some, returned moments later, handing her a paper cup as he sat down. Swallowing a gulp of liquid, he used his tongue to remove sandwich debris from his teeth. 'Now are you going to tell me what you hope to gain from helping the Casualty Bureau?'

Kate brushed crumbs from the edge of the table with the back of her hand, an avoidance tactic. 'They need our expertise,' she said casually.

He narrowed his eyes. 'And we're doing our bit, but it doesn't answer my question. Let me rephrase. What specifically is going through that head of yours?'

'We have access. That's a start.'

'Access to what?'

Hank was clever. He too had been mentored by Bright, but wanted nothing to do with promotion. He was happy in the rank of detective sergeant – the exciting end of murder investigation – and had never shown an interest in moving up. But, with Robbo now in temporary charge up north, Kate couldn't help wondering if he resented missing out.

'C'mon,' he said. 'You need to give me something to go on. You can't expect me to follow you over the cliff without knowing why I'm committing hara-kiri.'

Kate grinned. 'And there was me thinking that was your role in life.'

'Maybe the question I should've asked is: where do we fit in? Or perhaps: what will we be doing in our own time, given the remit of the Casualty Bureau is mind-numbingly boring? You and I both know they'll be receiving intelligence and feeding the machine. Nothing more.'

He'd got that right. Casualty Bureau personnel were mere collators of information on a massive scale. It was time to level with him. 'And while they're seeking, receiving and in-putting that information, they'll not be looking at individual cases or watching what we're doing, will they? We're now bona fide members of the bureau with IDs to prove it. Do you really think that the shower at Heathrow know what our brief is supposed to be? Because I sure as hell don't.'

'So, we'll operate under the radar in our spare time in the hope that we learn something about . . .?' He left the question unfinished.

'By day we help out,' she said. 'By night, we'll play it by ear. I need to know if Jo was on that plane.'

'You know she was.'

'No, Hank. She showed a boarding card. That's not the same thing. She may only have been yards from the cabin door, but, until we know for certain that she crossed the threshold, I'm begging you not to write her off. Are you in or out?'

He seemed conflicted.

'Hank, if you have something to say, out with it.'

'I don't want to push my luck.'

'Push away. Do what you've always done. Challenge me. Ask your questions. I'm not as fragile as I look.'

'You have a plausible explanation as to how Jo missed that flight?'

'To be honest, no.' How could Kate convey what she was thinking without making Jo – or herself – sound predatory? Knowing that he wouldn't understand, she went for it. 'Look, Jo and I were both very upset when she ditched me. She'd made it perfectly clear that we were at the end of the road. I took Fiona to bed to get over her.' Startled by the revelation, Hank glowered at her, on the verge of another emotional outburst. Never a pretty sight. She raised a hand, cutting him off at the pass. 'I know, perhaps not my best decision, but mine to make, not yours.'

'Why are you telling me this?'

'Because I keep thinking about the guy she spoke to at the airport. I need to find him and talk to him. OK, I need to question him. I'll interrogate the bastard if I have to. Only then will I know if she continued the dialogue after I hung up.'

He'd second-guessed where she was heading. 'You think they went off together? You said he was a creep.'

'*She* said he was. She was in a foul mood. He may not have been on the prowl. He could have been Mister Nice Guy for all I know, perfectly amiable, respectable and lonely. She was, too, don't forget. Don't we all do daft things when we're upset? Lonely people need comfort, too.'

17

Eight years earlier

Kate turned to look over her shoulder. Her friend Janet Crozier smiled at her, a woman Kate had never seen before standing by her side – a modern tuxedo, slim trousers, high heels. She was almost identical in height to Kate, with deep blue eyes.

Janet turned her palms face up and brought them together, providing a bridge between her two guests. 'Jo Soulsby, meet Kate Daniels.'

Kate smiled a hello. 'Janet and I go back a long way.'

'Stop that!' Janet said. 'You make me sound ancient.'

'Nice to meet you.' Jo, the stranger, had a wicked smile. She held out a hand, long slender fingers. Icy-cold. Her eyes were on their host. 'Sorry I'm late, Jan. I had an issue at home.'

'Nothing serious, I hope.'

'Nothing I can't handle.'

Sounded like a domestic to Kate.

'Can I get you both a drink?' Janet said. The doorbell rang. 'Bugger. Will you help yourselves?' She eyeballed Kate, a scary face. 'I hope this isn't one of your lot, darling. My new neighbours aren't really party people. Between you and me, they're a complete and utter pain in the arse.' She leaned in to Jo and said, 'Look after Kate for me. Gary's had a few too many. He thinks he's in with a shout.'

Jo smiled. 'I noticed.'

'Nothing I can't handle,' Kate mimicked her.

'Be honest!' Janet laughed. 'You get it all the time.'

She rushed off to answer the door, grabbing a full bottle of bubbly from the table; a peace offering, Kate assumed. She cast an eye around the living room. Most of the party guests were couples. She'd only come to make up the numbers and would rather have been lifting a pint with Hank, or watching TV with her jimjams on, her hand in and out of a bag of Revels.

'Do you?' Jo said.

Kate was on the back foot. 'Do I what?'

'Get it all the time.'

That was a double entendre if ever Kate had heard one. Her grin graduated to nervous laughter. 'Janet has an overactive imagination.'

'Nothing wrong with that,' Jo said. 'It's not true?'

'Not as often as she's led you to believe.'

'Welcome to my world.'

'Who has the time?'

Jo bit her lip, an expression that said: *we should make time*. They chatted for a while over wine and nibbles, a frisson of excitement developing between them. A short time later, Kate excused herself, heading for the bathroom. She glanced at her reflection in the mirror as she walked in.

Was she reading this right?

When Kate returned to the living room, she was disappointed to see Jo in conversation with another woman, smiling politely at something she'd said. Confusion reigned. Kate was sure she was getting signals, but perhaps she was seeing something that wasn't there, something she hoped *was* there.

A ripple of excitement ran down her spine as Jo returned to her side. None of the guests was paying them any attention. When Kate dared look again, Jo flicked her eyes in the direction of the offending and rather inebriated guest who'd been bothering Kate when Jo arrived at the party. He was being dragged away by a larger man.

Jo lifted her glass. 'Never trust a lawyer. They're a bloody liability.'

Kate smiled with her eyes as well as her mouth. 'You're not

a legal eagle yourself? Most of Janet's cronies are.'

'Heaven forbid.' Jo didn't offer an alternative occupation and Kate didn't pry, though she was dying to know everything about her. She didn't have a clue why. 'Nothing I can't handle' sounded like baggage, but – try as she might to discount her as anything other than a friendly sort – Kate knew something inexplicable was happening. She didn't quite know what, only that it was good and special and exciting and lightning fast.

She couldn't describe how it made her feel, even to herself, but was drawn to Jo's mouth when she spoke, the way she threw her head back when she laughed – really going for it – nothing forced or put on. Everything they talked about was interesting and fun. They'd take cinema over TV. They liked fast cars, good food, theatre, music. They enjoyed short city breaks, but also longer holidays by the sea that offered peace, quiet and the chance to be at one with nature.

The list went on and on . . .

At a quarter to midnight, with the party winding up to a crescendo, the noise level increasing, they found a place where they could be alone, adjourning to the garden with a bottle of wine, the din of someone singing Whitney Houston's 'I Wanna Dance With Somebody' drifting out through the patio doors.

Jo was grinning. 'I don't think she'd impress Simon Cowell.'

'Who'd want to?'

In the house, they had managed to contain their attraction to one another. In the isolation of the garden, Kate sensed the possibility of . . . she didn't know what, only that it brought a rush of blood to her face, a physical urge deep inside, a sexual tension enhanced by the fact that she wasn't in a position to act on it.

Janet's guest was driving her wild.

For a while, Kate and Jo had the space to themselves, but their private party ended all too soon. They were called in for Janet's birthday cake, a speech from the new man in her life, Nigel. Then back outside for fireworks, whereupon Gary – the drunken lawyer – seized his chance to move in for a second hit.

Behind him, backlit by lights rigged in a weeping willow, Jo was mostly in silhouette. As she moved closer, her eyes twinkled in the firelight, a wry smile that seemed to say: *get rid of this idiot*. Surrounded by partygoers, Kate had a brief vision of her lying in bed, naked and sweaty. The fantasy – because that's all it was – was short-lived on account of Gary's continued antics.

Still, the image made Kate's heart beat faster.

Clenching his fists, Gary turned them palms up and held them out to Kate. 'I confess, I'm a sexual predator. Slap the cuffs on and take down my particulars, officer. In fact, forget the interrogation. Let's go straight for the punishment.' Snorting at his own pathetic chat-up line, he tripped, lurching forward, practically nose-diving into Kate's cleavage.

She held him off, bored now.

And where was Jo?

A cool hand rested on Kate's shoulder – one woman protecting another was her first thought – the gentlest of touches. Nothing about the gesture felt awkward. Quite the opposite. The hand moved slowly to the nape of her neck, barely noticeable, but a thrilling sensation all the same. Kate struggled to breathe as a cool, slender finger stroked her bare skin. Feather-light. Exquisite.

She didn't turn around.

A fellow guest with a pronounced Geordie accent intervened. 'C'mon, Gary, that's enough, man. You've had your fun. If I were you, I'd leave before you get more than you bargained for. Kate deals with arseholes like you all day. Give her some space, eh?'

The hand was lifted as Gary shrugged off the man.

'Did you hear that, Kate? They want me to piss off home.'

'Why don't you do that?' she said, locking onto Nigel. 'Do us all a favour and call him a cab.'

As he made the call, Janet was falling over herself to apologise as other friends managed to wrestle Gary away and propel him through the garden gate. Watching him go, not wanting to put a damper on the party, Kate rolled her eyes to the rest of them amid hoots of laughter and leg-pulling. She wanted them gone so she could be alone with Jo. Kate imagined her standing behind her, equally as impatient.

They too would leave the party . . . and then what?

Kate thought she knew.

'What a prick.' Nigel was far from happy. 'Are you OK, Kate? I'm so sorry. I wouldn't mind, but he wasn't on the guest list.'

She answered with a shrug. 'In my line of work, it comes with the territory.'

'He won't remember a thing tomorrow.'

'Oh, he will . . . when I remind the dozy sod.' Kate held up her mobile, pressed play on the Voice Memos app reproducing Gary's chat-up line, then switched off the recording. 'I'll keep that in case he ever makes Home Secretary, then it'll be my ringtone.'

Everyone fell about, including Nigel.

'You're such a sport,' he said.

'It was that or deck him.' She turned, expecting to find Jo standing behind her, enjoying the banter. She was nowhere in sight. She'd vanished into the night leaving Kate baffled and in a state of utter despair.

18

As Kate made her way along the corridor towards the Casualty Bureau, Hank touched her forearm, stopping her from pushing through the double doors leading to the open-plan, no-expense-spared incident room. He leaned in, almost a whisper. 'You're going to have to spell it out for me, Kate. I still don't get why Jo would be interested in the guy she spoke to at the airport.'

Kate stopped walking and turned to face him. 'Why not?'

His eyes widened. 'He's a bloke—'

'Oh, for God's sake. What century are you in? She was married to one, remember?'

'Are you telling me she's bi? She loves you.'

'And I love her, even though I took Fiona to bed. Don't judge me, Hank. Despite what people think, I'm not a machine. I needed someone. Anyone. Actually, that's not fair. Fiona is a wonderful woman. And spare me the black looks. Coming from you, they won't wash. It's not like you never shagged anyone behind Julie's back, is it? And you weren't even separated. In fact, as I recall, she was pregnant at the time.'

'I didn't know that—'

'And that makes it OK? You were married, Hank. I'm not. Neither was I in a relationship at the time.'

He looked away.

He'd made a mistake years ago and been caught in a hotel room with a hooker when his wife turned up unexpectedly to surprise him with the news that they were expecting their first child. It certainly was a surprise. Their marriage survived, though trust had been an issue since.

Feeling bad about dredging it up, Kate apologised. 'What I

said was uncalled for. Hey, think about it.' A half-smile. 'For once, we're agreeing with each other. A quick screw is one thing. Love is something else entirely. Even Julie knows that. And, apart from the information desk clerk we've yet to trace, the guy Jo met is the one person we know of that she had any direct contact with at the airport. Who knows what went on afterwards?'

'You're weird, you know that?'

'But nice.' She made a crazy face.

'Sometimes.'

'No one's perfect.' Kate was grateful that he hadn't taken offence and was genuinely sorry for having upset him. She checked the corridor, making sure no one was earwigging on their conversation and dropped her voice. 'Look, whichever way it goes for Jo, if this case turns out to be terrorism – and that's the way it's looking at the moment – we're going to help nail the bastards responsible.'

'That's not going to happen. US authorities will be all over it.'

'Agreed, but if there's an airport employee that conspired to down that plane, he's ours. Don't breathe a word of this to anyone, but my request to view airport CCTV was signed off. I've asked their security bods to send it directly to Maxwell.'

'Signed off by whom?'

'DS Blue.'

'How the hell did you manage that?'

'He's the Casualty Bureau Manager.'

'That's not what I meant and you know it.'

Kate shrugged a shoulder. 'He likes me.'

'He doesn't know you.'

'He'd like to change that.' Kate's expression was coy.

'So, you infiltrate the Casualty Bureau on a false premise, lie to everyone but me, then use your sexuality to gain a pe-cuniary advantage.'

'That's about the size of it.'

'Incorrigible.'

'Needs must.' She held his gaze. 'What can I say? I have no morals and an agenda no one – bar you – is aware of. If the job had required me to invent a legend on an undercover operation, I'd have done it without a second thought and with your full support. How is this any different?'

'It is—'

'Not to me.'

'Is Blue aware that you played him?'

'I don't give a toss. I intend to use every weapon in my armoury until Bright hauls me out of here. Our home base is quiet now. If that changes, our days are numbered. We have to work fast, Hank. Waverley is suspicious and looking for an excuse to send us packing. If the shit hits the fan, we're history.'

19

No one knew Jo like Kate did. At one time they had been inseparable, Kate so smitten she couldn't bear to be out of her sight for any longer than a few hours. They had met again when Jo walked into the incident room and introduced herself as Northumbria's new criminal profiler, rendering Kate speechless. From that moment on, they shared everything, except a home and those bits of their past that deserved to remain there. Everyone had dark secrets. Jo had been Kate's.

I think we're done.

Kate had taken refuge in Fiona's arms after Jo's decision to split, and now she wondered if Jo's emotional response been similar. Had she screwed a stranger for the hell of it, because she could, in order to feel alive? After Hank's negative reaction earlier, Kate didn't voice her thoughts a second time, merely tossed them around in her head, hoping that Jo had gone off with the man she'd met at Heathrow, thereby saving her own life.

Hank's question nibbled at the edges of a scenario he'd scripted like a deadly piranha: why hadn't Jo called? Kate could offer no rationale for that. The news of Flight 0113's disappearance was at the top of the press agenda, the subject of every headline worldwide. The tragedy had been spoken about by families across every breakfast and dinner table, by colleagues in offices and strangers on public transport. Unless Jo was in a monastery with no contact with the outside world, she must've heard.

Falling into the chasm between optimism and realism, Kate was losing faith, floundering in a sea of doubt as she caught Hank's eye from across the room; a flash of encouragement for her to keep going. It was as if he'd read her mind and seen her head go down. Even though he believed she was chasing rainbows, he'd support her until they had the proof she so badly needed. He already thought that she and Jo were two crazy bitches without the sense they were born with. He'd never understood their on-off relationship.

For fear that he might read something into her facial expression, Kate turned away. In her head, she and Jo weren't mad, just madly in love, two women who enjoyed physical contact, women for whom sexual pleasure was as necessary as breathing. Sex was a great release after a row, or the loss of a loved one, whether by death, divorce or separation. It was natural. Obligatory, almost. A rebirth.

Kate felt no shame for her actions.

No regret.

Taking a walk outside, she punched Fiona's number into her mobile, for no other reason than to talk to someone who fully understood not only the complexities of her relationship with Jo, but the strength of it, even at the times when they weren't together.

The ringing tone stopped, the artist's phone switching to voicemail. Kate didn't leave a message. What was there to say beyond the fact that she was losing the will to live, slowly and painfully, as each hour passed?

Shaking herself free of rising pessimism, Kate made another call. Carmichael answered immediately. It was good to hear a cheerful voice.

'Any update from EE, Lisa?'

'Still no joy, boss. The phone is switched off. No calls in or out.'

'What about Santander?'

'No movement on her account since Jo left Newcastle, though she'd made withdrawals a couple of days before: three hundred quid on two consecutive days. No US dollars, all sterling. By the way, her car is parked outside her house – I checked.'

'Any news on her travel plans?'

'BA said she booked through a local firm.'

'Hays Travel, Acorn Road?'

'How did you know?' Carmichael tripped over herself to apologise.

Of course Kate knew. The agency was right around the corner from her house, not much further from Jo's. It's where they booked the majority of their holidays together.

'Lisa, it's OK. I take it the travel agent is closed today?'

'Yeah, I've tried calling the keyholder but she's not picking up. I'll forward Jo's booking form as soon as I have it. By the way, Robbo sends his love. He was wondering if you'd been getting his texts.'

'Yes, thank him for me.'

'He's worried about you.'

'How's he doing?'

'He's fine.'

'And Maxwell?'

'Really well. He volunteered to come in.'

'On a Sunday? I'm touched. How far has he got with the CCTV?'

'He's about a third of the way through. Heathrow sent him footage thirty minutes either side of your suggested timescale in case your calculations were out. Within an hour of receiving the footage, he nailed Jo at the information desk. It's a question of tracking her movements through the airport now. That's trickier, different cameras are involved. He'll get there. It'll take time.'

Kate thanked her and hung up.

Moments later, a video clip arrived from Lisa via email. She was such a good cop. Level-headed, with a maturity way beyond her years. Taking a deep breath, Kate pressed play and the footage started to roll, a busy airport information kiosk the location on view. Her heart skipped a beat as Jo walked into shot, leaning in to ask a question. The image was slightly out of focus but not so blurred that Kate couldn't make the ID.

Definitely Jo.

No doubt about it.

It made Kate's heart ache to see her standing there, listening intently, straining to hear what the woman behind the counter had to say against the hum of the travelling public, a concerned look on her face as she received Kate's message to get in touch urgently.

Pressing pause, Kate stared at the image, praying that their subsequent conversation, albeit work-related, had given Jo cause to alter her plans to travel to the US. Three thousand miles was a bloody long way to go to prove a point.

Kate replayed the image one more time. On first viewing, she had eyes only for Jo. On the second run-through, she saw something she hadn't picked up on: a tall businessman arriving to Jo's left. He didn't speak, to her or to anyone else, but, as she walked away, he seemed to lose interest in talking to the information clerk and wandered off in the same direction. Now Kate had something.

20

Adriana Esposito came to the door wearing sports gear and a towel round her neck. As the name suggested she was of Italian descent. She lived in a fifth-floor studio apartment in High Point Village, a contemporary block complete with swimming pool and spa. Close to Hayes and Harlington railway station in the west London Borough of Hillingdon, it was only a few miles to the airport and a short hop to Paddington.

Esposito was mid-to-late thirties, petite in stature with smouldering eyes, olive skin and a mass of dark hair worn half up, half down. She had no need for make-up and wasn't wearing any. She offered the detectives a cup of coffee, which they accepted. Neither had managed to grab a decent drink all day, just an insipid mug of something that tasted vile. Queues at Heathrow were a mare, staff facilities at the Casualty Bureau no better than any force canteen Kate had ever had the misfortune to frequent.

If you want proper coffee, ask an Italian.

A crucifix swung loosely from Esposito's neck as she bent over and slipped off her trainers. Tucking her feet beneath her, she curled up in a sumptuous white leather armchair, the Grand Union Canal shimmering in the moonlight behind her through floor-to-ceiling picture windows. All very nice, but Kate hadn't come to admire the view.

Rejuvenated by caffeine, she was about to cut to the chase when Esposito morphed in Kate's mind into an image of Jo in the same relaxed pose, then shifted to one of her strapped into her seat belt on the plane, treating herself to a glass of wine, reading a novel, enjoying the journey. Unlike Kate, who flew because it was necessary to get from A to B, Jo loved flying.

She saw it as part of any holiday, not the means of getting to her chosen destination. In Kate's head, Jo put on her specs, turned a page of her book, took a sip of wine, before checking out white fluffy clouds through the cabin window. She could watch those all day.

'I'm so sorry I couldn't see you before nine,' Esposito said. 'Dance class.'

'Not a problem,' Hank said.

Don't mind us, Kate thought. Carry on having fun, why don't you? Nothing that important happened yesterday. A plane fell out of the sky. So what? There are plenty more where it came from. Through the bitterness, Kate was vaguely aware of Hank making the introductions and getting down to business. She tried to shake the sarcasm free and concentrate, but Jo was still there, boarding an aircraft bound for New York.

Dropping her head, Kate took a moment to regroup. If she allowed herself to get sidetracked, the images in her head would fast-forward to the point at which a terrorist made himself known, or a radio announcement was broadcast to passengers by a concerned captain struggling with a serious technical fault. Such a horrifying prospect scuppered her resolve, squeezing the remaining dregs of hope out of her, rendering her ineffective. She preferred to think of Jo with her eyes shut, earphones in, listening to music, unaware of the unfolding situation.

Music was their passion.

The sound of Hank's voice made Kate look up. He was staring at her, aware that she hadn't been paying attention. His eyes sent a message: *if you insist on being here, do your bloody job.* Kate tried to stem her agony. Hank's angry expression changed to one of concern as he realised she was in trouble, an unprecedented loss of control, behaviour unbecoming a police officer in the company of a witness. It had never happened in all the years he'd known her.

'Are you OK?' Now their host was staring at Kate. 'Can I get you some water?'

Covering for his SIO, Hank turned to Esposito. 'Sorry, Adriana, it's been a long day. My boss has many balls in the air. Can you repeat what you said a moment ago? Then we'll be on our way. We have your number if we need more.'

'Of course.' Esposito focused on Kate, no doubt aware that the detective chief inspector had missed everything she'd said. 'I was telling your sergeant that there were a couple of passengers who didn't board.'

Kate's heart almost stopped.

In control now, she prayed that Esposito – a woman who so obviously appreciated style – would remember Jo. Removing a photograph from her bag, Kate passed it to her. 'Was this woman one of them?' Her hopes faded as the Italian shrugged, unable to make the ID.

'I'm sorry. We see so many people.'

Kate probed further. 'But there were two missing passengers?'

'Yes.'

'Both women?'

'I think so.'

She thinks so?

'This was your last shift at work and you can't recall? Please look again.'

Esposito took the photograph, another shake of the head. 'As I said, she's unfamiliar to me.'

'For God's sake! You're part of airport security. How the hell do you people sleep at night?'

'Kate!' Hank apologised on her behalf.

The Italian was already responding. 'I sleep very well, Detective.' Esposito fiddled with her crucifix as if it might protect her from the unfriendly copper sitting in her living room. Affronted by Kate's outburst, she tapped the image in

76

her hand. 'I don't remember seeing her. Do you recall every member of the public you come across?'

Kate's frustration grew.

What planet was this woman on?

An idea occurred.

Jo looked very different depending on the mood she was in or what she was doing. Sometimes she was made up. Often she was not, especially if she was on the move. If she wore her hair up, people tended not to recognise her. In the picture she was dressed for a business conference: smart suit, hair tied back, make-up on. Travelling she'd be wearing casual clothes, hair down, not a shred of make-up in sight.

Poles apart.

'I'm tired.' It was a heavy hint that Esposito wanted the detectives to leave.

Hank stood up. 'Kate?'

'Just a moment longer . . .' Remembering the video she'd received from Carmichael, Kate bent down and rummaged frantically in her bag. It took a moment to find her mobile, a moment more to access the clip and play it for Esposito. In it, Jo was dressed in jeans and a T-shirt, hair loose. 'Now do you recognise her?'

Suspicious of the DCI, Esposito glanced at Hank.

He explained: 'This lady is a close colleague, a very dear friend of ours. She's particularly close to DCI Daniels. They've known each other for a very long time.'

Don't overdo it, Kate thought.

Esposito got the message but the response was the same. Still, if the Italian was right, and two women failed to board Flight 0113, it was enough to keep the dream of finding Jo alive.

21

'Are you trying to throw your career down the pan?' Hank said as they got in the car and buckled up. He was seething and didn't try to hide it. 'Because if you are, you're going the right way about it. What the hell happened in there? You're more diplomatic with the unsavoury prigs we normally deal with. You didn't give Esposito the lickings of a dog. The woman didn't know where to put herself.'

'OK, so I was out of order.'

'Apologise to her, not me. And do it quickly. She's probably calling Waverley as we speak.'

Kate looked up at Esposito's flat, hoping he was wrong, unwilling to climb down despite the risk. 'She's a professional. She should act like one.'

'Did you really say that out loud?'

Kate shot him a dirty look. 'You've got to admit she was a bit flaky—'

'And you weren't? She lost colleagues too, don't forget. You have no idea how close they were—'

'Yeah, she's so upset she had time to fit in a fucking dance class. Wait here, I'll fetch my ballet shoes.'

Hank stifled a grin. 'You need to take it gently, Kate. She's wondering why you're so interested in one passenger and not the other three hundred and fifteen souls on board. If she repeats that, it won't look good on your CV. Waverley will throw the book at you.' He paused. 'Maybe our witness isn't as stupid as she makes out. She might have other interviews lined up.'

'What do you mean?'

'I think you know.'

She did know and it stung.

Hank said it anyway. 'Why would Esposito talk to a mouthy copper who gave her a hard time when she can tell her story to someone more sympathetic, possibly even get paid? You said yourself the press are all over airport staff. Do you want her shouting her mouth off about a Geordie polis treating her like shit in her hour of need?'

'Oh, pleeease.'

'I mean it, Kate. All she has to do is turn the tears on. Journalists would love that and so would a certain Gold Commander looking to burn you. All I'm saying is—'

'I know what you're saying,' Kate snapped. 'You're as subtle as a brick.'

'And if Esposito embellishes her experience—'

'Then she'd be lying.'

'People do, for all sorts of reasons, and sometimes it gets them in deep shit. If Tony Blair can fabricate weapons of mass destruction to impress a US president, Gina Lollobrigida can make you look bad for the hell of it. If you ask me, she was enjoying the attention. Probably wants her name in the papers, her rather gorgeous face on TV.'

'Noted,' Kate said.

They parked the car at the Premier Inn, then walked out onto the main road, turning right past a Costa Coffee house. Kate felt revitalised by the chilly evening air and the exercise. Her run that morning seemed light years away. Crossing the road, they went left into a wide avenue where north–south carriageways of a private estate were separated by a strip of neatly cut grass dotted with mature trees. When they didn't find the pub they were hoping for, they returned to their hotel resigned to a sandwich and a beer.

Hank paid the barman and carried the drinks to a vacant table that was semi-clean. He set the beers down, pulling off his scarf. 'Did you manage to get hold of Maxwell?' he asked.

'No.' Shrugging off her coat, Kate hung it on the empty

chair, her cheeks burning from being in the warm. 'Thanks for reminding me. I'll try him now.' She drew out her mobile and dialled Maxwell's home phone number. The detective constable picked up almost immediately, his demeanour uncertain.

'Boss? Is that you?'

She picked up her beer. 'Isn't that what it says on your phone?'

'Yeah, I'm just not used to you calling so late in the day.'

There were reasons for that. One: he was well down the pecking order. Ordinarily, she'd call the whole squad before him. Two: he lived alone and was always shit-faced before ten. Kate checked her watch: it was twenty past the hour. The thought of his alcohol intake – she'd stop short of calling it dependency – made her question the wisdom of utilising him for such an important job. But where CCTV analysis was concerned, he'd found his forte. In the words of the song, or as good as, no one did it better.

'Neil, I know you're state zero but are you sober?'

'I'm a teetotaller me, on or off duty.'

She could almost hear the grin. 'Great. Now listen carefully. Lisa sent me the clip of Jo at the Terminal 5 information desk. There's a tall guy standing to her left. He doesn't speak but wanders off after her when she leaves the counter. Tomorrow morning, when you're checking the CCTV, keep an eye out for him. I want to know if he's trailing her. It may be the same guy Jo mentioned when we spoke on the phone.'

'I'm on it.'

'Thank you.'

'Anything else?'

'No . . . yes, you did an excellent job today. I appreciate you coming in on your rest day. I won't forget it.'

'It was nothing. Are you OK?'

'With guys like you in my team, how could I not be?' She hung up.

'Did you just say what I think you said?' Hank was sporting a full-on grin.

'He deserves it. He found Jo.'

'I know. Lisa texted me.'

'I've been thinking,' Kate said.

'Does it hurt?'

It was a tired joke and she didn't laugh. 'I have a serious point to make, so open your ears and pay attention. The police service isn't the only organisation paring back and cost-cutting. Airports are no different. Baggage handlers are paid peanuts and probably have ten jobs to do where they once had five. If an incendiary device got onto that aircraft, someone put it there. They could be the key to this whole affair, whether secreting a bomb on board or allowing a suicide bomber to stow away in the landing gear. Security breaches do happen. Remember the fifteen-year-old who flew from San Jose on the wheel of Maui-bound Hawaiian Airlines flight? He survived, virtually unharmed. Then there was the Romanian guy found in the wheel bay on a flight to Heathrow from Vienna, another so-called miraculous escape from the jaws of death. Lucky for him, the plane was cruising at lower altitude because of bad weather. He gambled with his life in order to reach the UK, but that's a hop compared to a transatlantic flight. To escape persecution, you'd take a chance, but we're dealing with a very different scenario – a bomb-toting terrorist won't give a stuff about survival. All they care about is murdering as many as they can get away with and die a martyr. Once they're ready to detonate, BOOM. Job done.' Kate shivered involuntarily. 'We need to investigate security breaches.'

'And how do you propose we go about it? It's not yet a criminal case.'

'Deep down, you and I know it soon will be.' If there was one thing they were good at it was apprehending villains who needed locking up.

Hank took a long pull on his beer, then set it down on the table and crossed his arms. 'You have a plan?'

'Unformulated.'

'Involving Blue?'

'Not this time.'

'What then?'

'Nothing illegal or sneaky. Quite the opposite. If I can swing it – and I think with my credentials I can – it'll open doors and we might learn something to our advantage.' She lifted a hand, cutting off an attempt to cajole her into disclosure. 'Leave it with me. As soon as I know anything concrete, I'll fill you in, but first, we need to establish if Jo checked in hold luggage at Newcastle.' Kate was praying she hadn't.

22

A plane had gone down in the Atlantic Ocean. Jo might have been on it. Thomas and James might have lost their mother. There was no comfort to give, no scene to secure, no body to recover, all tasks Kate excelled at, practicalities that would keep her occupied. She couldn't deny hard evidence. Jo was on the manifest. Booked to fly. The pencilled line beneath the question _Had she?_ held no authority. It had been written so faintly it was barely legible.

Proof! Kate scribbled on her notepad.

She needed something tangible, more than the scan of a boarding card or a name on a list. She required DNA; a recognisable part of Jo's body; her purse or other personal effects; the Omega watch Kate had given her one Christmas – the one she never took off. Nothing else would do.

Kate stood, pulled on her coat, heading for somewhere less public to make the confidential call she'd been reflecting on all morning. In the corridor, she made sure the coast was clear and pushed open a fire escape door that wasn't properly secure. The mystery as to why that should be was solved the minute the smell of nicotine hit her senses. Smokers had collared the outside space in order to feed their addiction. Fresh smoke wafted up from below causing Kate to peer through the holes in the steel platform beneath her feet to see who was hiding there.

The guilty smoker looked up.

Kate shook her head. 'You're well and truly busted, mate.'

'What can I say?' Hank began to climb the stairs to join her, his weight shaking the structure, a sheepish expression on his face. They had both stopped smoking years ago, making a pact never to light up again without consulting the other.

Using all four fingers in line Kate beckoned him forward. 'Give! And if you're going to lie to me, make a better job of it next time. I knew you were up to no good when you left me. Sly bastard.'

'Takes one to know one.'

'In my case they call it astute.' It was nice to see him smile. 'C'mon, hand them over.'

'Don't give me a hard time. And whatever you do, don't tell Julie. She'll kill me if she finds out. She likes the new me rather than the one who used to smell like an ashtray.' Like a kid caught behind the school bike sheds, he handed her the packet of Marlboro, fully expecting her to crumple it up and head for the nearest bin.

She was checking to see how many were gone.

'What the hell,' she said, tapping one out, lighting up. She coughed as the smoke caught her throat, then took another couple of drags to make sure she didn't like it.

Hank took a last pull on his own before extinguishing it on the handrail, turning to leave. 'This time I really do have to go.' He pointed at her cigarette. 'Bin that. It doesn't suit you.'

'You neither.' She crushed it under her boot.

Hank eased himself inside, pulling the door to behind him.

Left alone, Kate took out her mobile and rang Tyneside Hospital's intensive care unit. She needn't have bothered. She received the same bland statements every time: little change, recovering relatively well, Mr Rai will be in to see him later. Of course, he would. Her old man had undergone ten hours of open-heart surgery. She left a message and then made that all-important call to her friend Rob Clark. His extension rang out for what seemed like an age. Kate was about to hang up and go inside when he answered with a cheery: 'Rob Clark speaking.'

'Rob, it's Kate . . . Daniels.'

'Hello, stranger! How long has it been?'

'Too long. I need to talk to you urgently.'

'About?'

'Not something I can discuss over the phone. I'm in the area. Why don't we have dinner? My shout. I'll come to you. Are you still in the same house?' He said he was and she rang off. If anyone could help her cause, Rob could.

23

Last time Kate and Jo travelled through Heathrow Airport, they had gone for a meal at Gordon Ramsay's Plane Food and made the boarding gate with minutes to spare. Kate took Hank there, treating him to something that didn't involve bread or pastry. It was time they began looking after themselves. She ordered Caesar salad, pancetta, anchovies and soft-boiled egg. He'd gone for the steamed sea bass, crushed minted potatoes, courgette pesto. While they could both have murdered a G&T, non-alcoholic drinks were the order of the day. As soon as he'd finished eating, Hank put down his cutlery and studied her, a worried expression that made her nervous.

Her mobile rang.

She checked the screen. 'I need to take this, it's Rosemary Taylor.'

Hank knew how important the call was. Kate's dream of finding Jo depended on the answer to one question: did her bag go on that plane? Because if it did, and didn't come off again, she was sunk.

Their collective ignorance surrounding the baggage-handling system was disconcerting. Their detective brains could only function in terms they understood, a chain of evidence passing from person to person, signed for at every stage. Kate had spoken to Taylor in order to clarify matters and had been waiting for an answer.

She lifted the phone to her ear. 'DCI Daniels.'

'Inspector, I have news. You want it over the phone?'

'No, I'll come up.'

'You know where to find me.'

Kate ended the call, eyes on Hank. A deep breath. 'Stay put.'

Leaving him to pay the bill, she went in search of the elevator. As she raced through the terminal, dodging travellers, mentally crossing her fingers, she hoped that Taylor's news would go her way.

Any second now . . .

Their last discussion replayed in her head as Kate moved towards the lift. 'This is not a trick question but a general one,' she'd said. 'I'm curious. In your experience, does luggage ever manage to find its way onto or off a flight without being entered into an airport baggage system?'

'It shouldn't happen.'

From anyone else, Kate might have thought they were being deliberately evasive but, the first time they had spoken, Taylor had gained her trust. She knew she'd get a straight answer.

'Could it, theoretically speaking?'

'Everything relies on computers, Inspector. They go wrong. Millions of bags are lost or mishandled globally every year.' The woman had been talking sense. No matter how good the system, human error and computer glitches were a fact of life in most organisations. HOLMES wasn't infallible by any stretch of the imagination. And that's where they left it.

Kate jabbed the button for the lift. Nervously, she watched it begin a slow descent, her mind in turmoil. Last time Jo had visited New York was on a shopping trip. She'd checked hold luggage, a suitcase that was practically empty, a few old clothes that she intended to wear and discard so she could buy new kit to bring home. Kate prayed that she hadn't done it this time around.

Stepping into the lift, she pressed the second-floor button, her foot tapping impatiently as the door closed. When it opened again, she rushed off to find Taylor, arriving almost out of breath at the rendezvous point, unable to contain her anxiety.

Taylor's expression was hard to read.

'Tell me,' Kate said.

'No hold luggage checked through from the Newcastle flight for passenger Jo Soulsby.'

Kate covered her mouth, stemming the scream waiting there. Taylor gave a smile of encouragement, as if she knew that this was a momentous outcome, one that the DCI had been hoping for. The first three words of that brief but perfectly formed sentence echoed in Kate's head . . .

No hold luggage.

No hold luggage.

Her heart almost leapt from her chest. There was still an outside chance that Jo had changed her mind about flying. This was the best news ever. Her focus switched to the sheet of paper in Taylor's hand.

'Are you absolutely sure?'

Nodding, the woman handed over a document supporting what she'd said. The image of that flimsy form would stay with Kate for the rest of her days. It offered an element of hope, a lifeline that led to Jo.

24

Ignoring the lift, Kate thundered down the stairs. She wanted Hank to be the first to know. She was close to tears by the time she caught sight of him across a moving sea of bodies, armed police among them, more than yesterday, deployed to reassure the travelling public. He was sitting where she'd left him, talking on the phone. She weaved her way through the crowds towards him.

Sensing a presence, he looked up, ending the call. From the petrified look on his face, he'd jumped to the wrong conclusion as to which way it had played out upstairs.

He stood up. 'What's wrong?'

'Absolutely nothing.' Kate's bottom lip quivered as she spoke. 'No hold luggage.'

His response was half-hearted, as she knew it would be. That was OK. A true detective, it was his job to be sceptical. It was a long shot that Jo didn't board 0113 but, right now, Kate was happy to play the naive civilian, the airheaded optimist, the dreamer. Any role would do. She couldn't keep the smile off her face and was clinging to the only life raft she had.

She cut the caution he was about to deliver. 'I know it's not much, but to me it's everything.'

Her mobile rang again.

The call ended before she could wrestle the device from her bag.

In such a precarious position – on a massive high – Kate panicked in case Taylor was ringing to tell her it had all been a terrible mistake, then relaxed when she saw that it had been Carmichael calling.

The phone was still in her hand when an email arrived, subject: Hays Travel Itinerary. Clicking on the attachment,

Kate found an unremarkable holiday document, complete with confirmation of a booking in Jo's name. She was going to New York for ten days – the Ritz-Carlton, Lower Manhattan, near the waterfront with a view of America's most iconic symbol of freedom, the Statue of Liberty. She and Jo had been there before.

I think we're done.

No, Kate thought. They were far from done if this was where she was intending to stay. The smile slid off her face as her eyes focused on one item listed on the itinerary. Her stomach heaved as she read it again, unable to take in what she was seeing, not wanting to. Her sudden intake of breath raised Hank's stress levels to an all-time high.

'Kate? What is it?'

Unable to speak, she handed him her mobile.

His face paled as he read the document.

In silence, he handed it back.

Punching in Carmichael's number, Kate lost her voice at the very moment her young DC picked up. Her eyes found Hank's. 'I can't do this.'

He took the mobile from her, clearing his throat before speaking. 'Lisa, Kate's tied up, but she received your email and there seems to be a discrepancy. A moment ago, she was told by staff here that no hold luggage arrived at Heathrow for Jo's onward journey. The travel itinerary you sent says different.'

Aware of the implication, Carmichael hesitated. 'All I know is that Jo booked and paid for one bag as hold luggage. It's on the receipt.'

'So I see. The question I'm asking is, did it actually go on?'

'That's what I was told.'

Kate was in pieces as Hank pushed Carmichael for a straight answer. 'Is it possible that she didn't use her allocation, that she paid for it, then changed her mind in favour of carry-on?'

'I guess so. I'll check it out.'

'Do it now. Hang on, I need a word with Kate.'

She didn't hear what he said. Her head was down, imagination in overdrive. She pictured Jo at Newcastle International Airport check-in desk, hold luggage being lifted onto the conveyor belt to be weighed, ID tags attached, the luggage disappearing through a strip curtain. Grabbing the device from Hank, she lifted it to her ear.

'Lisa, it's Kate.'

'Guv, this is very worrying, but even if a bag went on here, the fact that it didn't arrive with you is meaningless.' Carmichael sounded rattled. 'It could have been loaded on the wrong flight this end. It happens more than you might think. Unless it went on but wasn't entered correctly. You sure the error is not at your end?'

'I don't know, Lisa. I bloody hope not.'

Hank was trying to attract her attention.

Kate asked Lisa to hold so she could consult with him . . .

'If Jo checked luggage in at Newcastle and it arrived at Heathrow but she subsequently changed her plans, she'd have attempted to retrieve it.' He said. 'If that's the case, there's bound to be a record of it somewhere.'

'Go!' As he did so, Kate returned to her phone call. 'Lisa, get back to me. I want to see that luggage going on. Grab the CCTV and send it.'

Hanging up, Kate found a quiet, relatively empty corner of the building and slumped down on a seat. Three days and she was no further forward. It was time to acknowledge, if only to herself, that if hold luggage went onto the New York flight, then so did Jo.

25

Kate was pinning her hopes on an error in the baggage system. She reviewed the facts she'd been presented with. Jo had booked hold luggage – that much was clear – but none had been recorded at Heathrow, according to Taylor. It was a devastating blow, a nauseating piece of a much larger jigsaw, for Kate personally and for Northumbria MIT who were so fond of Jo. For the first time since Flight 0113 had vanished, the DCI felt her hopes slipping away. The chance of Jo's survival had been slim. It was now infinitesimal.

A horrible thought emerged.

Kate's mind raced yet again through the probable cause list: terrorism; catastrophic engine failure; suicidal pilot; bird strike, like the one that brought down US Airways Flight 1549 in 2009, an Airbus A320-214 flying from New York's LaGuardia Airport forced to ditch in the Hudson River, saving the lives of the 155 people on board. She discounted a bird strike immediately. It wasn't credible at the altitude of Jo's flight, unless . . . There was always a flip side. Could the aircraft's computerised instruments have been transmitting the wrong data?

Kate tried to separate fact from supposition. Reliable information was hard to come by at such an early stage of any investigation, never mind one on a scale of this magnitude. Earlier in the day, she'd overheard someone say that, assuming it hadn't blown to bits in the air, it would take a few minutes for a plane flying at thirty-seven thousand feet to reach ground level – a horrendous length of time if you were awake and knew what was coming.

Those poor passengers.

Kate imagined the crew yelling at everyone to brace for

impact, panic and prayers, sobs and screams; the aircraft gyrating wildly as its pilot lost control; oxygen masks dropping down from the console above their heads, everyone wishing that they had paid attention during the in-flight safety demonstration. Kate would – if she ever flew again.

Of the believers among them, Kate visualised people crossing themselves, offering up a final prayer to whichever god they worshipped. Kate liked to think there would have been heroism from flight crew and passengers had a terrorist made him or herself known. The fact that Kate hadn't imagined Jo in the centre of the mayhem was down to sheer doggedness.

She wasn't there.

She wasn't.

Kate had no idea what happened to bags in transit from one flight to another, only that Carmichael was right. Many never arrived at their intended destination. Did they have a special sticker attached to identify the onward flight? Could it have come off? It could, she decided. Anything was possible. A damaged bag might have been held back; a suspect bag seized by customs officials.

A series of scenarios rushed through her head, confusing her but also driving her on. For every question raised there was a counter-argument. Where humans were involved in any process there were bound to be mistakes. How many times had Kate almost sent a confidential report to the wrong person? A click on the wrong name in a contacts list and it would be gone in an instant. Given the millions of travellers passing daily through busy airports, anything was possible. Oftentimes, airline check-in personnel were so busy they hardly gave you a second look. They couldn't always be certain whether travellers were with someone else or travelling solo.

Every scenario she came up with only raised more questions. Which made it more important than ever for Kate to keep her date with Rob Clark.

*

He'd changed his mind about meeting at his place and called to suggest that they meet at seven thirty at the Two Brewers, a seventeenth-century inn close to Windsor Great Park and the River Thames. After her mother died, Kate had gone there with her father for a few days' break, an attempt to shake him from his grief and prove to him that life would go on without her. Whether Kate still believed in that meaningless platitude was a different matter. Her father hadn't made it to the funeral. Too upsetting for him, apparently. Didn't matter that Kate needed him by her side. Selfish sod. Now she was back at the pub, no less distressed than on her first visit.

Rob stood up as she entered, always the gent.

They kissed on both cheeks, genuinely pleased to see one another. Despite the intervening years, he looked no different from the last time they had met. Like Kate, he was a bit of an adrenalin junkie, for no other reason than to maintain a level of fitness that would see him through the exceptional demands of his job. His eyes shone with good health. After the day's events, Kate hated to think what hers looked like.

They sat down at a table already set for dinner. The inn hadn't changed. It was full of punters and big on atmosphere: weathered oak, wood floors, candlelight. Hank would have called it a real pub as opposed to a pretender. The fire in the grate gave the dining area a cosy feel.

'It's great to see you, Kate.'

'Thanks for meeting me at such short notice. I hope it's not too far out of your way.'

'Not at all.' He gave a knowing smile. 'You're lucky you caught me. I'm flying to the States tomorrow afternoon.'

She knew he would be and had to move fast.

'This place was good for both of us,' he added. 'Given the fact that you're a northerner, it was clever of you to pick it. It's bang smack in the middle of my workplace and Heathrow.'

He'd already guessed why she was there.

Kate wanted to dive right in, but what she had in mind was a bloody big ask. It would take some organisation on his part to swing it, at a time when he was most probably run off his feet. She decided to bide her time, prepared to beg if necessary. Failing that, she'd have to think of something else . . . but first, the small talk.

She pointed at his pint. 'Can I get you another?'

'I'm good, thanks. If you want real ale I can recommend a good one. Or would you prefer something stronger? They do a fine G&T.'

She could die for one. 'I'll stick to water, thanks.'

'You're on the wagon?'

'Driving.'

'Bummer.' He toasted her with his pint. 'Helen dumped me and took off to see a friend.'

His wife, Helen Clark, was born and bred in the gentle Coquet Valley town of Rothbury. Whenever the Clarks made the trip north to Northumberland, Kate made a special effort to visit them there. It was the number one destination for motor-cyclists in summer, an exhilarating ride along twisty roads in order to reach it. Riders, Kate included, loved that route.

'Shame I won't see Helen this trip,' she said. 'I'm sorry but I can't stay long.'

He looked as disappointed as he was relieved.

Kate knew why he was heading to the US and that he'd be gone for months. 'How is she?'

'Great.'

'And the boys?'

'Men,' he reminded her.

She glanced at the menu, then back at him, a smile developing. 'Yeah, I forget we all age at the same rate. They must be at least twenty-two.'

'Twenty-four and twenty-six.' He took in her shock. 'Yeah, I know. Our Jack is living overseas these days. He's a tele-communications operations manager in Singapore. Simon's at university in the middle of a PhD. Aeronautical, Maritime and Transport Engineering.'

'Blimey!'

'Don't be too impressed. I have a strong suspicion that he'd have studied the exploits of Mickey Mouse in order to remain in academia.' Rob was joking, happy with Simon's choice. 'The life suits him. Why work for a living when you can hang out as a full-time student or, better still, move up and become a lecturer?'

'No-brainer. Did I ever tell you I was going to be a vet?'

'I don't think so.'

'Yeah. I had a place at Edinburgh University. Joining the police was a last-minute decision, a shock for everyone, including my parents, especially my old man. He never forgave me . . .' Kate frowned, adding an explanation. 'He was a miner.'

'Ouch. I don't think I've ever heard you mention him.'

'That's because he's a self-righteous, hypocritical dinosaur.'

He's your dinosaur.

Jo's words transported Kate to the Coronary Care Unit after her father's heart attack. Kate was angry, for many reasons, bemoaning the fact that he'd point-blank refused to accept her for who she was. Jo had done her level best to calm troubled waters, reminding her that he was very unwell and may not survive, urging Kate to give the man a break.

Why should she?

He'd never given her one.

Kate took a sip of water.

Before Rob had a chance to query her untimely dip into the past, a waiter arrived to take their order. Kate rechecked the menu, opting to skip the starter and go straight for a main course: root vegetable tartlet, new potatoes and green beans. She didn't intend hanging around for dessert.

Rob closed his menu. 'I'll have the roasted lamb rump, please.'

'No starter for you either, sir?'

'No thanks.' He handed over his menu.

Kate did the same, waiting for the waiter to move off before resuming their conversation, or lack of it, forcing away all thoughts of her father and Jo. If she was to make her case and ask for Rob's assistance, she had to do it now, except he beat her to it.

'So,' he said. 'You wanted my ear on something too weighty to discuss over the wire. It's the air disaster, right?'

Kate nodded.

'Well, fire away. I qualify.'

He did too.

He'd been employed in the Air Accidents Investigation Branch of the Department of Transport for almost twenty years. They had met at a coroner's inquest early on in Kate's career. He was an engineering inspector then. They were both giving evidence about a light aircraft that had come down near Cheviot. Based at Farnborough Airport, he was an experienced pilot and air accident investigator. These days his role was to provide assistance and expertise on a global scale, determining the cause of incidents with the sole aim of improving aviation safety.

Kate's mobile vibrated in her pocket.

'Excuse me.' She held up the device. 'This might be important. Do you mind?'

'No, take it.'

'Lisa, what gives?' Kate listened, her eyes fixed on Rob. She tried hard to keep the frustration from her voice. 'I know she paid for hold luggage, but did you see the bag go on?' Lisa was uncharacteristically hesitant. 'Are you there now? Well, do it! That's what I asked for. If they're so bloody incompetent, you have my authority to seize the CCTV . . . No, Lisa. We don't need a warrant.'

Rob was staring at Kate, taking it all in, a concerned expression on his face. He was joining dots, filling in blanks, working out why she was so keen to talk to him. What she was asking Carmichael to do was hard for anyone, even for a maverick like her. And still Lisa wasn't playing ball.

Kate rubbed at her temples. Lisa's observations were making her head hurt. 'I'm not saying it'll be easy without one, but I need to know if she put hold luggage on that plane. Work your magic, sweet-talk them, handle them with kid gloves, do whatever is required in order to get the information. I know you will . . . yes . . . and if they give you a hard time tell them to call me directly, day or night. I'm available. Yeah, keep me posted.'

Kate hung up.

'You have someone on board?' The question didn't require an answer. Didn't get one either. A ten-year-old could have worked that out.

26

Hank sat on his bed, suspecting that the uncomfortable, wobbly chair in his hotel room wouldn't take his weight for much longer. With a better view of the TV, he flicked channels, trying to find something to watch post-watershed. Failing to find anything that floated his boat, he scrolled down to BBC News 24 where yet another so-called expert was giving an opinion on what might have caused a plane to fall from the sky. He was somewhat relieved when an incoming text message arrived, taking his attention away from the screen.

Scooping his mobile off the bed, expecting a text from Kate, he found one from Carmichael. The message was short and to the point: Are you alone? Intrigued by the question, he muted the TV and called her number. Dispensing with a greeting, he went straight for the joke on the tip of his tongue . . .

'Either you're drunk, DC Carmichael, or it's my lucky day.'

When Lisa failed to respond to his lame attempt at humour – something she always did – he knew she was in trouble.

Lisa tripped over herself to explain what Kate had asked her to get hold of and why. 'She wanted an update, PDQ – in fact she insisted – but now I can't raise her. Her mobile is switched off. I found that strange, bearing in mind her insistence that she'd make herself available—'

'She went out to meet someone.'

'So?'

Hank yawned. 'So what?'

'Her phone is always on standby. And she stressed how important it was. Even if she's in a meeting, as soon as she saw I was trying to reach her, she'd have taken the call.'

'Maybe her battery died.'

'With all that's going on? I doubt that.'

'She hasn't called me either, as it happens.'

Lisa didn't ask who Kate was with or why he wasn't along for the ride. The thought lingered, his mind wandering off up the M4 to Windsor. He had no idea of the identity of the person she'd gone to meet, or the venue; it was a rendezvous she'd kept to herself. Sometimes, she frustrated the hell out of him.

'Were you expecting her to call?' Lisa asked.

'I never expect anything from the boss . . .' Hank chuckled. 'She's an unknown quantity. Who knows what goes through that head of hers? I hoped she might give me a bell, if only to tell me she was back so I could sleep.'

'What are you, her dad?'

'Never let her hear you say that.'

'Why?'

'He's not the cuddly type and doesn't appreciate her like we do. Besides, is that any way to speak to the person writing your evaluation? It's due imminently.' He'd been responsible for Lisa's supervision since the day she arrived in the MIT.

'I couldn't give a shit about that now, Hank. I need to speak to Kate.'

'Then send her a text. She'll pick it up soon as she's done. If you get no reply and it's urgent, send it to me and I'll shove it under her door.' Hank's eyes were on the TV screen, the same images he'd seen less than five minutes ago, going round and round in a loop. 'Is there any reason you're not discussing this with me? You know you can tell me anything, right?'

Lisa didn't answer.

Hank folded a pillow in half and shoved it behind his head in an effort to get comfortable. He spoke through another yawn. 'C'mon, Lisa, I'm not as young as I used to be. It's way past my bedtime. I need to brush my teeth and say my prayers, so get to the point before I drop off. I can't help unless you tell me what's bugging you.'

'Kate asked me to acquire CCTV without official authorisation. It made me feel uncomfortable. I just want to talk it through with her before I proceed.'

Hank loved Lisa's honesty. She was well liked within MIT. Few people knew how good she was at her job. He'd made it his business to thrust her progress under the noses of those who could do her some good. For someone so young in service, no one could touch her. When it came to commitment and integrity she was in a league of her own. He could only speculate on what had shaped her ambitious personality; she had lost both her parents and the aunt who'd brought her up. There was no knowing whether it was in her genes, but she certainly had the right attitude to succeed as one of Northumbria's finest.

'She's the boss,' he said reassuringly. 'Her authorisation is all that counts. She wasn't asking you to steal the CCTV. You're a copper. You're good for this. It's within the rules to ask, so long as you do it nicely. If the airport's administrators don't want to hand it over, call Kate for further instructions.'

'That's what she said.'

'So, what's the problem?'

'I already asked nicely.'

'And they won't play ball?'

'No, it's not that . . .' She allowed the sentence to tail off. There was more to this.

A feeling of unease crept over Hank, settling right between his shoulder blades. Carmichael was acting weird and he thought he knew why. 'Have you got the CCTV already? Is that what all the cloak and dagger is about?'

'Not yet. They're considering my request and will let me know first thing in the morning.'

Hank took a swig of warm beer, the last of a four-pack he'd bought at the corner shop down the road. Crumpling the can, he threw it towards the rubbish bin, hitting the target for the third time in a row. He was worried about Carmichael. It was unlike her to be so evasive. And still she didn't elaborate. Suddenly he understood. Or thought he did. 'You don't want to acquire the CCTV in case there's something on it that the boss won't like, right?'

'Right.'

'Then send it to me and I'll talk her through it.'

'Would you?' She sounded relieved.

'Lisa, Kate's in a really bad place right now, but she's strong and she won't thank you for keeping things from her, no matter how unpalatable you think they might be. This is no time to lose your bottle—'

'I'm not. Well, OK, I am. It's just, knowing how much this means to her, I'd rather not be the messenger if it's all the same to you. I don't want to be the one to break her heart if this goes tits up, Hank. Promise me you'll be with her when she gets the news.'

'No sweat.'

'And if I can't get what she needs?'

'That won't be your fault. Kate made the decision to work off-book, not you. Relax. Whatever the outcome of your enquiries, she won't blame you any more than she'll blame me if the news isn't what she's hoping for, so crack on. And if you need a warrant, I'll contact Bright and make sure you get one.'

A pause. 'How is she?'

'I won't lie to you. She's on the floor. You couldn't knock her any further down if you used a mallet. As far as Jo is concerned, Kate would rather know than not. It's the uncertainty that's killing her.'

'I know, but every time I've tried to say something nice, she's cut me off. I feel helpless—'

'Join the club. Now put the phone down and get yourself away home.'

'How did you know I was in the incident room?'

'I know you . . . and so does Kate. She'll talk when she's ready. Be there to hold her hand when she does.'

'I will. Thanks, Sarge.'

'You're welcome.'

Hank ended the call, turning up the volume on the TV, yet another opinion on the missing flight, this time from across the pond, where distraught families gathered for news on loved ones. How the hell was he supposed to sleep now?

27

Hank checked his watch for the umpteenth time since he'd got out of bed at seven a.m. He may have put Lisa's mind at rest last night, but now he too was anxious. It was after nine and there had been no word from her yet. What the hell was keeping her? He'd breakfasted with Kate and driven her to the Casualty Bureau. She hadn't mentioned her meeting in Windsor and he'd kept Lisa's call to himself. When Kate left to call her father to tell him she'd be back as soon as was humanly possible, Hank seized his chance to text Lisa.

> Any news?
> CCTV clip came through.
> And?
> Not had a chance to check it out yet.
> Send it to me. I'll deal.
> Will do.

A second text arrived:

> Thanks Hank. X

Moments later an email arrived, complete with video attachment. Hank took a deep breath. So much depended on what it contained. As soon as he'd arrived at work, he'd looked into the possibility of Jo having made an attempt to retrieve a bag from Flight 0113. If her plans had changed, she certainly would've done so. The memo in his hand was confirmation that she had not.

There were three scenarios in play. One: Jo had not used the luggage allowance she'd paid for. Two: she'd checked hold luggage at Newcastle and it had been diverted to the wrong onward flight. Three: checked luggage had arrived at Heathrow for her transatlantic flight but had not been recorded properly.

What a shambles.

The absence of a suitcase would allow them to cling to the possibility that Jo didn't travel. The presence of a suitcase, on the other hand, together with confirmation that she hadn't tried to retrieve any luggage would mean that Jo was, quite literally, sunk.

No wonder Carmichael was fretting.

The video attachment was critical.

'Who was that?'

Hank swung round to find Kate standing in the doorway. He hadn't heard her approach. 'Jesus, you nearly gave me a heart attack.' He pulled a face. 'Sorry, that was insensitive.' His bad choice of words gave him an excuse to change the subject. 'Did you get through to the hospital and speak to Mr Rai? How's your old man doing?'

'That's two questions to my one.' Kate sat down at her desk. 'Well?'

'It was Julie.' The fib was unimpressive.

'Nice try . . .' Kate admonished him with her eyes. 'Now tell me the truth.'

Nothing got past her. Hank didn't want to say before he had the chance to view the footage, but there was no point trying to bluff his way out of it. Kate had clocked his concern the minute she set eyes on him and knew him too well to be fooled by his attempt to deceive. He had no choice but to front up.

'It was Lisa.'

'She has the CCTV?'

A nod.

Hank noticed an immediate change in Kate's body language. Instantly, she became rigid, steeling herself for more bad news. 'She hasn't looked at it,' he added quickly. 'And neither have I, so slow down and take a deep breath.' He didn't want her to think he was hiding the worst possible scenario.

'You expect me to believe that?' She was staring at him, a tortured expression on her face.

He didn't try arguing, just located the unopened email and handed her his mobile. 'Happy now?'

'You'd better upload it then.'

She walked round to his side of the desk and sat down beside him so that they could view the footage together on his laptop.

He felt tense as he carried out her instructions.

The file opened and he pressed play.

As expected, the CCTV lens was pointed directly at a busy queue in Newcastle Airport's departure hall. It took him a moment to adjust as travellers moved in what seemed like a continuous stream in the foreground, a moment more to spot Jo. She was halfway from check-in desk number 21, queues on either side of her, long straggly lines of passengers partially obscuring her from the camera.

They watched her inch forward in the queue . . .

It was obvious to both that she was pulling something. Hank couldn't see what it was but, from the angle of her arm, it looked fairly heavy. His heart was pounding in his chest as he continued to observe the line. There were travellers of all ages, mostly happy to be taking a trip to the capital, some impatient to dump luggage and be away to the bar, an occasional stressed face.

Hank could relate.

He wasn't keen on flying.

It was harrowing to watch; more so for Kate, whose eyes were fixed to the screen. There were parents carrying young babies, toddlers jostling for position, some astride brightly coloured Trunki fun luggage. The thought that some of them might have been heading for the same connecting flight as Jo – unaware that they wouldn't be returning – was sickening. The fact that the queue was slow-moving made the process all the more distressing.

Neither detective spoke for what felt like an hour but what was, in reality, a matter of ten or twelve minutes in total. Kate seemed to shrink physically as she continued to observe the queue. Hank hung onto his distress. Jo was his friend and colleague too but, if he buckled, he'd be no use to his guv'nor.

She needed him more than ever now.

In the past few days, layer upon layer of armour she'd put on during her police career had been peeled away, leaving her exposed to the same raw feelings as anyone suffering the loss of a loved one. Stripped of her confidence, she was inherently vulnerable. He hated seeing her this way and daren't imagine what kind of self-destructive workaholic she might become without Jo's hand on the tiller.

On screen, Jo shuffled forward in the queue, inch by painful inch. She seemed uncharacteristically depressed, not like someone looking forward to a break in the Big Apple, and didn't talk to anyone around her. Then the very worst thing that might happen did. She was wheeling a suitcase towards the check-in desk.

'No!' Kate's hand flew involuntarily to her mouth. 'Zoom in.' Her voice was barely audible.

Hank did as she asked.

Jo walked forward, hauling a bag onto the conveyor belt.

'Oh, thank God!' Kate locked eyes with Hank. 'It's not hers, Hank. That bag is not hers.'

'You sure?'

She rounded on him. 'I said so, didn't I?'

Relief washed over them both as Jo stepped away from the check-in desk without offering up her passport, smiling at the old lady standing by her side, so small and frail she'd been obscured from the camera by Jo and the passengers surrounding her. As the elderly passenger shuffled forward to the check-in desk, Jo retook her place in the queue.

It was like a last-minute reprieve as the executioner stepped forward to do his job but, for Kate, it wasn't enough. She watched for another minute, maybe more, until Jo offered up her passport. The check-in clerk took it from her, scanned it into the system, asking Jo a question to which she received a shake of the head.

There was no suitcase by her side.

Only when she moved away did Kate and Hank possess clear-cut verification that she hadn't checked hold luggage. Jo looked up as she mounted the escalator that would take her to the floor above where she'd pass through security. In that split second, she was staring directly into the lens of the CCTV camera. Hank froze the image on screen. Kate was undone, but the dream was still alive.

28

Hank could see and feel Kate's pain. Deep down, she knew that the possibility of finding Jo's body was zero per cent, but she was a copper and would follow the evidence until she'd exhausted every possibility. Right now, she was hanging on by her fingernails, trying desperately to find a reason – any reason – why Jo might not have boarded that plane. She was doing what any detective would do: looking into a victim's phone, her bank account, the whereabouts of her car, taking nothing at face value. Flying solo, she was risking everything on an outside chance. Bright was against her, the Met police were suspicious of her motives and Hank was humouring her. She was up against it, heading for a car crash, the hold luggage question her last throw of the dice. It would end in tears. He was sure of it.

Kate's failure to accept any version other than her own had kept her semi-sane, though she was aware that it was tormenting Hank. She only needed to look at him to confirm it. After the high of finding that Jo hadn't checked hold luggage at Newcastle, he probably thought that she'd drop like a stone if things went wrong. So far, she hadn't, but she could swing the other way at a moment's notice.

'Why the delay at Heathrow?' she said.

He looked at her as if she were completely barking.

'Remember what Daisy Reynolds said? After Jo's boarding pass was scanned at the departure gate, there had been a slight delay, confirming a late pushback of around twenty, twenty-five minutes. She was vague on cause – could have been a technical hitch, difficult passenger, illness on board, error on the passenger manifest . . .'

'All valid possibilities, I'd have thought.'

'I don't want possibilities, Hank. I want specifics.'

'Are you asking me to find out?'

'You're catching on.'

Unaware that their remit was about to change, Kate and Hank went for lunch to discuss the way forward and work out what they would like to do and what they could reasonably expect to do, given their limited scope within the Casualty Bureau. When they returned to Gold Command, trouble was brewing. Conversations ended the minute the two Northumbria detectives crossed the threshold. No one in the incident room would make eye contact. Given the meeting she'd come from, Kate stood there wondering what was going on.

An elbow nudged her arm.

'Your two o'clock,' Hank whispered.

Kate's eyes shifted to the right. DS Blue was hovering on the periphery of the room, trying to attract her attention without showing his hand. Locking onto her, he gave a slight nod in the direction of his office and was gone. 'I think Waverley noticed our extended absence. Wait here.'

'I'm not leaving you.'

'Don't crowd me, you know I don't like it.' He looked wounded. 'And don't sulk, I won't be long.'

Leaving him muttering under his breath, Kate followed Blue to his office. The Met detective didn't bother to walk around behind his desk to sit down. Instead, he perched on the end of it, feet and arms crossed, tie loosened slightly, his expression bordering on lecherous. His roving eye made Kate feel uncomfortable. You could go off people.

'Shut the door,' he said. 'You and I need to have a chat.'

'Shall I bend over, too? Your tone is beginning to resemble that of my old headmaster with a cane in his hand.'

Blue grinned.

Kate didn't.

'There's been a significant development. While you were out of the office, US Homeland Security asked for your help. In fact, they demanded it. I'm not sure why, only that their request went directly to Waverley, copied to Northumbria's head of CID, Detective Chief Superintendent Bright—'

'I know my guv'nor's name, so cut the crap or I'm out of here.'

'He must think an awful lot of you.'

'We get on. Is there a point to this?'

'You tell me.' He looked past her through the glass panel of his office door. 'Why don't we take it outside? You can confide in me over a quick pint. Maybe we could have dinner later.'

'I already have a date.'

'With whom?'

'My 2ic – not that it's any business of yours.'

Her first warning shot had gone over his head. He was unsure whether or not she was joking. The more direct she became, the more turned on he seemed to be.

'C'mon,' he said. 'You're away from home. I'm a free agent. We're going to be working together for a while. Call it southern hospitality, inter-agency cooperation or being nice. You have a problem with that, Kate?'

I have a problem with you . . .

'May I respectfully remind you that I'm a guest of the Metropolitan Police and that I currently hold the rank of Detective Chief Inspector. Unless it's different down here, I think the term you're look for is ma'am. Now, shall we start again? If you have something to tell me, get it said. I need to crack on, even if you don't.'

Slighted was the best way to describe his reaction.

Uncrossing his arms, Blue scurried off to hide behind his desk, placing a physical barrier between them, as if it might protect him from the dominatrix he'd conjured up in his head. Kate suppressed a laugh. She could never dine with a man whose suit trousers were too tight.

Not a good look.

'My mistake . . . ma'am.' Blue cleared his throat, his arrogance morphing into hostility in thirty seconds flat. 'For some reason, Waverley has sanctioned your inclusion into the inner circle of the Casualty Bureau. No holds barred. He's even providing you with an office of your own, an outside line and a computer linked to HOLMES—'

'What about Hank?'

A shrug. 'You'll have to ask my guv'nor—'

'I will.'

'Good luck with that,' he scoffed.

The internal line rang.

Kate nodded towards it. 'You'd better get that. It might be the man from Del Monte.'

Blue hesitated.

'Don't worry, Fraser, I won't tell Waverley that you've been feeding me confidential information for your own ends, dissing him behind his back – not unless he asks.'

The Met detective leaned forward, snatching up the landline. 'DS Blue.'

His eyes fixed on Kate, a smirk forming on his face as he listened.

She gathered it was the Gold Commander.

'Yes, sir, right away.' He put down the phone. 'Waverley wants you and your bagman in his office.'

She didn't bother asking when.

The answer was now.

29

Without another word, Kate left the room, feeling daggers in her back as she made for the door. Hank was loitering directly outside. He fell in behind her as she headed along the corridor, a stupid grin on his face.

'Like your style . . . ma'am.'

Kate narrowed her eyes. 'You shouldn't have been listening at keyholes.'

'You shouldn't have led him on.'

She waved away the comment. 'Needs must, Hank. I always knew the guy was a snake. Take note: any detective prepared to disrespect their boss to an outsider deserves exactly what he gets.'

'Noted.'

They fell in step.

Kate hadn't the time to celebrate the success of her plan, let alone call Rob Clark to thank him for his support. She had no idea how he'd managed to sway the American authorities so quickly and could only assume that he was well in with the decision makers. She checked her watch. No point emailing. He'd be halfway to the US by now. In a few hours, he'd pass over the fatal crash site. She imagined naval vessels in the sea below, a wreckage and body search in full swing.

They had reached Waverley's door.

Taking a deep breath, Kate gave a gentle knock and heard a muffled 'Come!' from the other side. She eyeballed Hank. 'Keep shtum, I'll do the talking.'

A cheeky nod.

Expecting a row, he pushed open the door, standing aside to let her in. Kate approached Gold as she would any senior officer, shoulders back, head held high. It was a plush office, four times the size of hers back home: a huge desk, book-shelves crammed with police and legal manuals familiar to her. A framed photograph of Waverley in full dress uniform proudly shaking hands with former Labour Home Secretary, Jack Straw, was mounted on the wall. There were no personal mementos she could see. The commander was strictly business.

Kate stared at the top of Waverley's head. 'Sir, you wanted to see us?'

Looking up, he left them both standing.

As anticipated, he came down on her royally for wheedling her way into the mix. She had no idea why he'd asked Hank along – except maybe to embarrass her. The Gold Commander had no clue what her link with US Homeland Security was, only that it existed, and probably involved what he described as 'failing to follow proper procedure'.

In other words, she'd gone over his head.

For all he knew, she'd shagged the US Attorney General, the Director of National Intelligence or both at the same time in order to secure her new-found status. Kate would never divulge her connection or mention who was involved. Rob Clark was a star. He deserved anonymity. Kate would ensure that his name was left out of any political fallout, should Waverley decide to make an issue of it. She wasn't sure if the US authorities had sanctioned Hank's help, or just hers, and there was no way she was about to ask for clarification. Rob would brief her later, even if Waverley would not, and still his motor mouth was running . . .

'I told you before. I will not put up with your interference or stand for your showboating on my watch.'

On his watch?

Who did he think he was – a US Navy Seal?

'Be afraid, Inspector. Northumberland is not as far away as you might think. One false move and you're out, Homeland Security or not.'

Kate kept it buttoned until he ran out of steam or, more accurately, ideas. There were only so many ways that a misogynist could disrespect her in front of someone he considered to be her subordinate and who she valued as a close and loyal colleague. Hank was seething but managing to curb his temper.

So far.

He'd be expecting Kate to give Waverley a piece of her mind. She held her tongue. This was the Met commander's turf, not hers. Someone with his management style wasn't about to listen to a woman of any rank. Kate had noticed that not one of his senior staff was female. Blue hadn't responded when she raised it with him.

Silence spoke volumes.

Waverley reminded Kate of DCI Atkins, a detective who had taken pleasure in baiting her at every opportunity, trying to provoke her into an argument and piss her off to the point of retaliation. When she was a young officer and he was her uniformed sergeant, he'd given her all the shit jobs, hoping she would fail.

She hadn't.

The officer she was facing now was of the same ilk. The more she resisted the temptation to argue, the more irate he became. Kate was too experienced to fall for that one. She'd crossed swords and held her own against better men.

Waverley's face was crimson.

The only way to deal with guys like him was to excel in the job, impress the hell out of them and then let them take the credit. It worked every time. The Gold Commander nodded towards the door, dismissing her. Kate turned the handle and stepped outside, Hank on her heels like a shadow she couldn't shake off, a volley of expletives spilling from his mouth as soon as they were out of earshot.

30

Kate wrestled an iron and ironing board from the hotel service cupboard near the elevator. If she was on temporary secondment to US Homeland Security she intended to go in smart with all guns blazing. The cliché perhaps wasn't the right choice, given her aversion to the Second Amendment to the United States Constitution: the right to bear arms. Every year, there were thousands of homicides, suicides and accidental deaths from gunshot wounds in America, a tragic waste of life. She was proud that UK police hadn't followed suit and never would.

While she pressed her shirt, a radio presenter gave the seven o'clock news headlines. The aircraft disaster was followed by a report that assaults on teachers were on the rise; medical staff were being sent to Cuba to help combat Ebola; older people were being advised to heat only one room in order to get through the winter; prison officers were facing the sack for blowing the whistle on the state of British jails and for highlighting soaring levels of violence.

Depressing.

She shut down the app.

Dressed in navy strides, a white shirt and smart jacket, she clipped her hair up, put on some make-up and checked her appearance in the mirror. *Add a pair of dark sunnies and you'll be channelling an agent of the FBI.* Those were Jo's words last time Kate had worn a dark suit to an inter-agency meeting. She swallowed her grief. This was for her. Whether or not she was still breathing, it was all for her.

Pleasantly surprised was an understatement when it came to Kate's reaction to her new office. Recently decorated, the smell of fresh paint lingered. It wasn't the hovel Waverley might have chosen. Quite the opposite: it was altogether nicer than the cloying atmosphere of the Casualty Bureau's incident room. She was nothing short of amazed at the size of her temporary home. Bigger than the broom cupboard she was expecting and well equipped: two desks, comfortable chairs, computer monitors, landline, printer and shredder for confidential waste. A window on the outside world was a bonus. A small posy of flowers sat incongruously on the sill.

Seriously?

Kate pressed her lips together, stemming a giggle. Hank hadn't yet noticed it. He would. And when he did, it wouldn't take him long to work out who'd placed it there – a certain Met DS who'd now be feeling a little silly and a lot miffed after his spat with her yesterday.

Served him right for being such a dick.

For the next couple of hours, Hank organised the space to their satisfaction. Kate was a woman who liked order, the type that would shelve novels alphabetically and by publication date. A bit of a saddo, really; she simply couldn't cope with mess.

While Hank was busy, she emailed Rob Clark requesting the identity of her contact in the US, thanking him for his help. The reply made interesting reading. Homeland Security Special Agent in Charge (SAC) Gabriele Torres was an army veteran and experienced law enforcement officer. Her job was complex, involving three elements: the detection of, prevention of and response to terrorist attack. She specialised in aviation. According to Rob, she was no slouch. He signed off by confirming that Hank was part of the deal.

'Thanks, Rob,' Kate whispered under her breath.

Hank turned to look at her. 'Rob?'

'My mate Rob Clark, good friend and saviour rolled into one.' She explained that he was the contact she'd gone to meet in Windsor and what he did for a living. 'He came up trumps. You're in.'

'In?'

'In . . . With me! I made it clear that we work as a pair or not at all.'

'Without consulting me?'

'Yeah, right. If I'd left you out, your pet lip would've been like another airport runway. You should be thanking me. You now have bona fide reason to be here, unrestricted access to all areas of Heathrow – confirmed by the Civil Aviation Authority and the Federal Aviation Administration. We now have a big fat US stamp of approval.'

'Would it have made a difference if they'd knocked me back?'

'It was a deal-breaker.' She made an innocent face. 'Not a whole lot, no.'

'That's what I thought.'

Hank resumed what he was doing, knowing that she'd have used him with or without authority. In spite of his casual reaction, he'd be quietly satisfied with the state of play. Leaving aside their close connection with someone on board that plane, it was an honour and privilege to be working on an enquiry of this scale on behalf of a United States security agency. He got up and left the room, telling her he'd grab them something to eat. All of a sudden he was starving.

A good sign.

Left alone, Kate reread the email still open on her computer monitor. At the bottom of his communication, Rob Clark had attached details of how SAC Torres could be contacted. Kate sent a heartfelt thank you in return, followed by an introductory message to Torres, then sat back, placing both hands flat on her desk. She surveyed the room, head swimming with conflicting emotions – sorrow, nervousness, blind panic – but also a sense of euphoria, commitment and determination. The tension drained away, replaced by the adrenalin rush of a new investigation. It was time for some legitimate detective work.

31

The briefing arrived from SAC Torres within an hour of Kate's initial contact. It wasn't yet official but there was a strong suspicion that an improvised explosive device had brought down 0113. There were many attachments to Torres's email. The gist of her report spoke to the theory currently being explored, that a suspect bag had been introduced onto the plane. It was important to concentrate on where it came from, find those responsible and shut them down.

Having offered herself up for a specific role – investigating possible sabotage by ground staff – Kate would have to deliver. In order to do that, she first had to pin down a process she knew little about. The question was: where to start when no group had claimed responsibility?

Forcing herself to concentrate, Kate slid her warrant card into the slot in her computer, logged on and brought up the access code for Heathrow Airport administration that Torres had passed on. The special agent was shit-hot when it came to laying her hands on information, even from three thousand miles away.

Kate was impressed.

Knowing she had a pro to work with, along with Hank as her wingman, made a huge difference. It didn't take long before the two Northumbria detectives were in the zone, hard at work, researching areas of particular interest vis-à-vis the point at which a bomb might have been introduced to the flight. Tapping out the word BAGGAGE, Kate pressed the return key and waited for the page to load.

A long list popped up in alphabetical order, mostly self-explanatory.

Clicking on the item she understood the least – interlining

– she quickly established that it meant the transfer of freight from one carrier to another, the belongings of passengers who'd arrived at Heathrow from feeder flights, as Jo had done.

This was exactly what she was after.

Closing down the page, Kate consulted the digital blueprint of Terminal 5 also contained in Torres's communication. A giant floor plan filled the screen. There were other pages, too, showing the flow of baggage around the airport. Finally, she was in business.

Kate had no idea how long she and Hank had been working. During their research, Fiona had sent a text Kate didn't return, then her father called. She was initially pleased that he felt up to making an approach, but the feeling didn't last. He was in no better mood than he'd been for several years prior to his operation.

While she took the call, Hank stopped what he was doing and put his feet up on his desk, affording her the opportunity to chat, a call he knew was unsolicited, an untimely intrusion she could well do without. For Hank, it was a welcome break from a discussion she was keen to finish; for her, it represented nothing more than earache. The man who'd cheated death had nothing nice to say to her.

Ending the call abruptly, she sat back in her chair, hands clasped on top of her head, her attention straying out of the window at an alien landscape that made her feel homesick for the dark skies, lush green landscape and wide open spaces of Northumberland where she'd grown up.

Hank's eyes were back on his computer screen.

'Take five,' she said. 'I feel like a brew.'

He made her one, then paid attention.

'Of seventy thousand workers employed at Heathrow, what percentage do you reckon are on the take?' she asked.

A shrug. 'The law of averages would suggest a fair few.'

'We need to get a handle on the small scams within the

terminal. Once we find the minnows, we'll have leverage with the sharks, those whose misdeeds impact on airport security.'

'Does the Met's Aviation Policing Command know what you're planning?'

'No, and I want it to stay that way. We're assisting the Casualty Bureau. That's all they need to know. Outside of Waverley and Bright, Blue is the only one with knowledge of our role change.'

'You think you can trust him?'

'Blue? Not as far as I can throw him. He's been warned of the consequences should it go any further. Anyway, forget him. He was a means to an end. We no longer need him or Waverley. We have clearance from a higher authority now.'

A few minutes later, her mobile rang.

Thinking it was her father again, Kate leaned forward, peering at the screen without picking it up, then at Hank. 'Talking of a higher authority. It's the General.' It was Hank's nickname for Bright when he was in a radge. 'Sorry, this time I can't ignore him,' she said. 'I have some grovelling to do.' She pressed to take the call. 'Guv, I've been meaning to contact you.'

'So why didn't you?'

'Hank and I have been trying to get a handle on stuff this end. I wanted to thank you for allowing us to assist Homeland Security—'

'Allow?' He spat the word out.

Kate rolled her eyes at Hank. He'd heard every word, but she put the phone on speaker so he could listen in. This concerned him too. 'Phil, I'm sorry. It won't happen again. I'm on leave, technically, but please accept my profound apology for acting without talking to you first—'

'Your default position, isn't it?'

'I might've pulled a fast one occasionally.'

'Don't push it!' His voice was louder than before.

Kate eyed Hank across her desk. He grimaced. Bright never held back if he had something to say. Worryingly, he sounded more wound up now than he had when he first found out where they were and what they were up to. There was more to this call. They braced themselves for a roasting. It didn't take long to arrive.

'Kate, I haven't got all day. You're not going to like this, but I'm withdrawing my authorisation, or should I say half of it. Homeland Security will have to do without one of you.'

'Guv, you can't.'

'There's been a development.'

He meant a murder. 'Guv, can't Robbo deal?'

'Given your walkabout, that's exactly what he's doing, temporarily—'

'So, what's the problem?' Kate cut him off. 'You're happy, he's happy. Win-win.'

'You think this is a joke, Kate? Think again. This afternoon, a guy was taken to A&E by two heavies with a serious gunshot wound to his head. He was practically DOA and died soon after. Police were called, but by the time they got there, the guys who took him in had disappeared.'

'Any ID?'

'Not yet.'

'Then what's the problem? This is bread and butter to Robbo.'

'No, I want one of you here. You have a decision to make. Drop your insane crusade or book Hank on the next plane. If you're staying put, you had better make me proud, Kate. Waverley is making his mouth go. I've spent the majority of my day deflecting questions about your conduct when, frankly, I have more important things to do with my time. I've covered for you – you left me no choice – but I don't like the feeling of my arm up my back when I make operational decisions. Put another foot wrong and you'll part company with that warrant card you prize so highly. You can also kiss goodbye to your pension, and so can Hank.'

The line went dead.

32

'Shit!' Kate locked eyes with Hank. 'This death is causing Bright a great deal of anxiety. Put it this way, it doesn't sound like a suicide. This changes everything.'

'You reckon?'

Kate didn't answer.

She'd pulled some strokes in her time but none compared to this. She was more worried now than at any point in her entire career, for Hank as well as herself. Bright may be their mentor, one they had a close and open relationship with, but he'd made it clear that they had gone too far.

'You heard him, he'll can us if we step out of line again.'

Kate could handle that. She had savings, a house that was paid for, no ties. She'd survive a lengthy period of unemployment and was well qualified to find another job; doing what, she didn't know. With her security clearance she could probably swing a consultancy for a high-end legal team. Hank had a family, a wife and kid to provide for. What would he do? The police force was his life – as it had been hers for so many years – it would kill him to have it taken away. He'd end up working as a civilian investigator or MIR indexer assisting serving officers in another force, a downward shift he'd find impossible to take.

As she raised her head, their eyes met.

Hank knew his future was hanging on a thread and was trying not to show it.

'I'm sorry I got you into this,' she said.

'Did you hear me complain? Where you go, I follow.'

'The guv'nor means it, Hank.'

'Relaaax.' He waved away her concern. 'He's blowing off steam. You know what he's like—'

'No, he's had as much as he can take. I don't have enough fingers and toes to count the rules I've broken. Taking you down with me isn't fair. Hank, I can't go back. What happened to Jo, finding her, is more important than anything. If she's dead, I don't even want the damn job. How could I carry on, knowing that it's driven a wedge between us? Every time I step into the incident room, her ghost will be there, a reminder of what I've lost. It'll never go away. It'll stay with me for the rest of my days, a dark shadow I'll never shake off. You understand, don't you?'

Kate could see that he did.

She got up and put some space between them, her focus on anything but him. When she turned around, he was staring at her with an expression that left her in no doubt that he knew what was coming.

'I'm sending you home.'

'The guv'nor's right. You are insane.'

'Hank. I won't be responsible—'

'For what? You think I'd want to stay in the fucking job if you go? It wouldn't be the same. We're a team, which means we stick together. That's what we do. Bright knows that. Hasn't he drummed it into us time and again to look out for one another? I'm sorry, but he can't have it both ways.'

'Oh, he can—'

'But he won't. He'll get over it, like he always has.'

'And if he doesn't?'

'Then we'll have to' – he made inverted commas with his forefingers – 'make him proud,' he said, a stupid grin on his face.

It was all an act.

Kate didn't even raise a smile. 'I've made my decision. You're missing out being down here. It's time to sling your hook.'

'Well, be prepared to drag my sorry arse to the airport because I'm going nowhere.' He glared at her. 'You can't pull me in, then push me out when it suits. I'm not Jo!'

Kate recoiled. 'Fuck off!'

Hank palmed his brow. Shamefaced, he stood up and took a step forward. Kate stepped away, retreating like a wounded animal to lick her wounds. The world was going on as normal on the other side of the windowpane. Inside, hers was falling apart.

Hank spoke to her back. 'Kate, I'm sorry. I was angry, I shouldn't have said that.'

'Why not? It's true . . .' Slowly, she turned to face him. 'Of all the things you might have said to persuade me to change my mind, you've finally had the guts to give it to me straight. Well, job done. Message received and understood. Now piss off before I lose my temper.'

'Kate, be reasonable.'

'Go on, get out!'

He stood his ground. 'You think you're the only one who needs answers? In case it passed you by, Jo is my mate too. And even if she wasn't, there are hundreds, possibly thousands of people out there affected by this tragedy. Their loss is as important as ours, the case more serious than a stiff in the morgue back home. Like it or not, you're stuck with me.'

'What makes you think I want you?'

'I know you do.' He dipped his head on one side, a sorry face. 'You do, don't you?'

She almost cried. 'Of course, you idiot. Why else would I be trying to protect you?'

Not for the first time, her 2ic gave her a brotherly hug. 'I'm an idiot. Forgive me? I can't, won't let you cope with this alone.'

'If you stay, it could cost you.'

'I'm prepared to take that risk.'

33

Alone in her office, Kate stared out of the window at nothing in particular with Hank's words and Bright's angry warning ringing in her ears, grateful that she could still call herself an SIO – or even a police officer. Her guv'nor's validation meant a lot. Hank's unconditional support meant more. She'd be lost without these two men in her life.

She sat down, turning her attention back to 0113. If a UK terrorist had been deployed to carry out this vicious attack on innocent civilians, she had every faith that together they could contribute to the war on terror, put a radicalised figure out of action and save the travelling public a lot of grief. She was ready to take whatever measures might prove necessary in order to secure a conviction, and so were they.

Following their row, Hank had gone for a walk. He'd been away a while and was fired up and ready for action when he returned. There was no bad mood, no hangover from their slanging match. Over the years they had worked together, their relationship had survived many a riled exchange. Neither mentioned the latest. It was forgotten already. They were close enough to ride out this blip.

Hopefully, the same could be said of her guv'nor.

Kate sent Hank off to liaise with Fraser Blue while she made a few calls, setting herself up for a full-on investigation. An email arrived from SAC Gabriele Torres that included no detail on the incident, merely a request that Kate make herself available to talk on the secure line, an encrypted video conference call.

Kate replied that she was both ready and waiting.

Steeling herself for a difficult conversation, she took a deep breath and sat up straight before the call connected.

She needed to be on her mettle now. If Torres detected any emotion in her voice, any hesitation or doubt in her ability to carry off a comprehensive investigation her end, her involvement with the US security service would be over before it had begun.

Introductions complete, Torres looked directly to camera, the two women checking each other out. Torres was of mixed race, older than Kate, with sharp eyes, soft features and dark, wavy hair, tied up. The sleeves of her cotton shirt were rolled up, a shoulder holster strapped to her chest. She wore a tiny gold cross around her neck but no wedding ring.

Who the hell had time?

Kate wished she'd made the time.

'Are you alone?' Torres asked.

'I am.'

'Then let's get to it. Parts of 0113's fuselage are now in our possession. Sadly, they're too small to determine cause. The search goes on. Based on available evidence, a mid-air explosion is the most likely scenario. There was no Mayday transmission from the cockpit and no one has yet claimed responsibility. As I said in my email, we're a long way from forensic examination, working on the assumption that a bomb may have been introduced to the flight at Heathrow. On that basis, are you willing to investigate undercover?'

'Absolutely.'

'It's a hot ticket, Kate. We need incriminating evidence. I'd like you to focus on the ground crew. How you handle that is your business. If you use your associate, get rid of his cell and use a burner.'

'I'll do the covert stuff myself. Hank's a big bloke, too big to hide.'

'Your call. Make sure you document everything where it can't be found. You trust your second-in-command?'

'With my life.'

'Let's hope it doesn't come to that.'

Kate received the warning loud and clear. 'Do you intend coming over?'

'Depends . . . if I do, we won't meet. You'll blend in. A US accent will raise suspicions. The last thing we want is to blow your cover and tip off the guys we need eyes on. You and your wingman have impressive résumés, the experience to deploy without drawing attention. Your chief tells me they don't come any better. I'm satisfied that you'll handle it your end.'

Kate didn't mention Bright's insistence that he needed one of his A Team back in the north.

Torres had already moved on.

She had a pronounced New York accent. Her delivery was clinical, conveying what she had to say with no hint of alarm or distress. She was persuasive, an agent with years of experience behind her, one who was used to commanding the attention of others. It was evident that she'd done her homework and knew more about Kate than she did about her.

Kate had organised many an undercover operation – and was up for the challenge – but it wasn't going to be easy. Since 9/11, US intelligence had upped their game, spending millions identifying those who would attack their citizens by listening to online chatter and infiltrating groups of suspects, collating information to share with world leaders across the globe. This recent incident had demonstrated that it wasn't enough. What they needed was detective legwork.

Torres was still talking. 'I'm putting together information on feeder flights. When, or should I say if, we locate more wreckage, we'll be able to pinpoint the seat of the explosion, identify exact cause and, if it turns out to be an IED, match it to a specific bomb-maker.'

'That's your best guess?'

'It's our only guess.'

'Then you must have an idea of who's responsible?'

Torres didn't even acknowledge that a question had been

asked. Every day of her working life, she dealt with the minutiae of investigations into air disasters like the one they were dealing with now. She had no intention of giving away more than was necessary.

In her head, Kate turned the pages of her own career. Right from the off, she'd developed a thirst for policing, accepting every challenge that presented itself, prepared to do whatever was asked of her. She'd learned how to handle herself if things got physical. And when she landed her present job as SIO in a Murder Investigation Team, working exclusively on major incidents, like Torres, she'd excelled at keeping secrets.

If she'd had any other boss than Bright, Kate would be tied to a desk, delegating from on high, but that wasn't a role that appealed to her. Like the special agent, she preferred to be hands-on with a solid and cohesive team behind her. There was a great deal of mutual respect between Kate and her guv'nor, but that wouldn't help her now. In London, she was out on a limb. Never had she imagined she'd be investigating mass murder, especially one involving Jo.

Never.

Kate would love to have her full team around her, to take charge and raise actions as she saw fit, rather than as dictated by Homeland Security. Though she may never meet Torres in person, Kate could tell a lot from what she could see of her American counterpart. She was alone, speaking from a self-contained office, rather than an open-plan area where she might be overheard. And then there was what she'd said or, more importantly, didn't say – her tone of voice, that steely look in her eyes, like she'd seen stuff any right-minded person would wish they hadn't.

Kate had read somewhere that a New Yorker used 60 per cent more words to convey the same information as someone from elsewhere in the US. That was simply not true of Torres. She made every word count and gave no extraneous detail, impressing the hell out of Kate.

There was a noise from the other end. Torres's gaze shifted to a point above her computer screen. Someone had entered the room. Kate couldn't see who it was, but the US agent lifted her arm to receive a sheet of paper from a visitor – a male hand appeared.

No words were exchanged.

Hearing the click of a closing door, Kate had no doubt that she was facing an agent respected by those under her command, the determination and grit to succeed in a world dominated by men. In that respect too, they had a lot in common, but while Torres had made all the right noises about Kate's vast and varied experience, the Northumbria DCI was under no illusion that she had to earn the American's trust. Only then would she be granted access to classified information.

Torres speed-read the document, then refocused on Kate, raising the possibility that a suicide bomber may have been on board and how easy it was to blow apart an airliner mid-flight: 'A relatively small quantity of explosive planted in the right place would do it,' she said.

'Small enough for ground personnel to get it through security?'

'We can't rule it out. In theory, it should never happen, but once luggage has been checked, it's all too easy to slip an explosive charge into a suitcase and then stash it in the hold.'

'Why focus your efforts here?' Kate asked. 'Couldn't the bomb have been planted on a feeder flight?'

'Unlikely.'

'But not impossible—'

'Passing explosives through more than one security device increases the risk of detection. Not all terrorists are sophisticated. Those that are have one thing in common. They're after maximum impact, high death rates, newspaper headlines. Rest assured, we have operatives in or on their way to every feeder airport. You're in the right place, and that's a huge responsibility, one that would normally fall to officers and agents engaged in counterterrorism.'

'So why not use them?'

'Because I need someone who can commit to this 24/7. With the threat level in the UK at an all-time high, they're knee-deep in other stuff, with hundreds of investigations open. Given that no one currently employed at Heathrow is on their watch list, we're working on the assumption that the person or persons responsible have slipped through the net.'

'A sleeper cell?'

'Formulated with the specific aim of carrying out this attack.'

'On a pre-arranged signal?'

'Exactly that.'

'Am I to report to SO15?'

'Directly to me.'

Kate wondered why Torres was bypassing Counter Terrorism Command. Maybe she was so high up, she had clearance to do her own thing. The majority of victims were US citizens. Homeland Security were the lead investigators.

Torres showed not a flicker of emotion as she warned Kate to be vigilant, sharing her reading of the situation, spelling out the dangers of pursuing the kind of people they were after and what she had in mind for Kate to do. 'Fanatics are prepared to die for their cause, which makes them unpredictable and dangerous. Those prepared to kill an unsuspecting public won't discriminate when it comes to law enforcers.'

'That's a given—'

'It bothers me that you'll be unarmed.'

It bothered Kate, too, though she kept that to herself.

'Do not underestimate their capability,' Torres said. 'Or mine. This is a two-way street, Kate. You'll be given every possible resource you need. The complexity of these attacks varies, but every incident provides new intelligence in the fight against terrorism. Be warned, these people are skilled in the art of duping security officials. As soon as loopholes are closed, they find new ways to get around them.'

It was mind-boggling to hear it spelled out.

Kate didn't think she'd ever fly again.

Torres misread the emotion. 'If you are in any doubt—'

'I'm not, but there's something you should know.' You didn't mess with women like Special Agent Torres. 'A close colleague of mine may have been on board 0113, a criminal profiler named Josephine Soulsby. She works for my unit in Northumbria—'

'If I didn't know that already, we wouldn't be having this conversation. If you're the detective I think you are, it'll make you more, not less, driven to help us. I'm counting on you.'

34

Later, Hank followed Kate to her car. She took off from the Casualty Bureau at a fast pace, relaying details of not one, but two, conference calls with Torres in the past couple of hours, including a well-worked-out strategy. 'An IED is looking more and more likely,' Kate said as they sped along the dual carriageway. 'Whoever planned this attack hasn't picked a random day, a random flight. Torres thinks this is another poke at the US. We're now working on the assumption that a malicious offender somehow bypassed explosive detection and X-ray machines and managed to secrete a bomb on board.'

'How is that possible?'

'I'm buggered if I know.'

Hank said, 'So where do we start?'

Kate changed down, flooring the accelerator. 'Torres is arranging an office for you at the airport. Whoever downed that plane planned his or her assault down to the last detail. She wants access to records of anyone on duty airside in the weeks leading up to the attack. If a baggage handler is our target, it's plausible that they might have been warned for breaches in the past.'

Hank wasn't buying it. 'A terrorist commander would use a clean skin, surely—'

'You'd think so, wouldn't you, yet how many times have we learned of an attack, only to find out later that a suspect was previously on an SO15 watch list?'

'Then surely Torres will be party to that intelligence.'

'We need to vet everyone, Hank.'

'What for?'

'Because I said so. Think about it. If we were investigating our own, we'd start with dirty cops—'

'Yeah, to cover our arses—'

'Hold that thought.'

Increasing her speed, she checked the road signs, ignoring the next slip road. Hank had no idea where they were heading and didn't ask. They weren't on the airport road, so he figured she was following orders and would fill him in when they reached their destination. For now, her focus remained firmly on airport personnel.

'We need to eliminate anyone who has come to negative attention. We'll be castigated for it if we don't and it turns out that one of them was responsible. We make no assumptions, Hank. Whoever we're after would've been told to keep their noses clean. A rule-breaker, however small, might have been too scared to own up to their handler in case it scuppered their plans.'

'Point taken.'

He studied Kate. She was on a roll, her mind on the job for the first time since they had driven south. Jo might be the reason they were there, but the case was bigger than one individual, no matter how large a hole her disappearance had left in Kate's heart. She hadn't mentioned Jo for the past few hours, but he'd noticed moments of darkness creeping up on her from time to time, interrupting her train of thought mid-conversation. He wondered if these waves of grief meant that she was slowly and painfully accepting that Jo was lost. Either way, the investigation had taken priority over all else.

Kate could bear the silence no longer. If Hank had any doubts she wanted to hear them. He'd gone very quiet. Taking her foot off the gas, she searched his face. He didn't react, just stared out of the front windscreen, a miserable expression. No matter how grave a situation they were dealing with – and they had dealt with many, albeit not one of mass murder – it was unlike him to shut down.

'Hank, if you have something to say, spit it out.'

'I don't.' He wound down the window.

An avoidance tactic? 'You sure? For a moment, I thought you'd dropped off. I need your full attention. I can't do this alone.'

'You don't have to.' He swivelled in his seat to face her. 'I'm in, Kate. I know what's required and I'm up for it, a hundred per cent . . .' He drew in a breath. 'I was thinking—'

'You usually do that out loud.'

'Would our target have had the bottle to sit tight? Surely they would have fled already.'

'Torres seems to think they're still around. If they were on the fly, the anti-terrorist branch would've passed on names and there would be a manhunt underway. I got the distinct impression that no one has a clue on ID, so you're probably right about a clean skin and, if that's the case, whoever did this could be planning another attack.'

'You think? Security will be tighter than ever now.'

'Yeah, but we have no idea how they got the explosives through or how, despite routine patrols, the sniffer dogs failed to detect them. We can't assume more aren't planned. In today's world, it's a leap of faith every time you step on an aircraft. We think we're safe, but how safe are we? There were nineteen hijackers involved in 9/11, on four separate aircraft.' She stressed the word nineteen. 'It's only a matter of time before terrorists try something equally outrageous. For all we know, the pilot or co-pilot are not who we think they are.'

'A suicide mission?'

'You tell me. They walk through security like they're God Almighty with four stripes on their epaulettes. Familiarity makes people lazy. How rigorously are their flight bags searched? Does anyone scrutinise their lanyards? Torres and her team are investigating all possibilities. We're a small cog in a very large wheel. Apart from Bright, Waverley and Blue, no one knows what we've been asked to do, and that's the way it stays. If we need assistance, we'll ask for it. We have a specific job to do. We stick to the role we've been given.'

'So, what's the plan?'

'Torres favours a covert op.'

'That's risky.' Hank narrowed his eyes. 'Don't suppose you mentioned that Bright has ordered one of us back to base, or that we've already been at Heathrow asking questions.'

'Not in the baggage shed we haven't.'

'I'll take that as a no then.'

'I'll talk to Bright.'

'You'd better do it soon. Actually, I'll do it. He'll be expecting me, not you.'

'No, leave it with me. If anyone is going to get it in the neck it should be me.'

35

Hank had suggested they flip a coin for the undercover job. Kate declined. This was one she wanted to take on herself. Staff turnover was huge in a place like Heathrow. Those who were supposed to be watchful couldn't possibly know everyone, and she didn't believe that every face was checked against a pass before ground crew were allowed in. Now she knew her remit, she needed to move fast. If anyone could get through who shouldn't be there, she wanted to know about it.

Hank was sulking. 'Undercover work is below your pay grade, isn't it?'

'When the stakes are this high, pay grade doesn't come into it.' Kate wondered if he wanted to keep her away from the baggage shed because he didn't trust her to lay off a suspect should she find one. He might have a point. 'I'll brass-neck it,' she said. 'Trust me, I'm good at this. No one will take any notice of me. From now on, I'm a daft sod who fled to London to escape an abusive partner, a man older than me.'

'Lush.' Hank raised a lecherous eyebrow. 'Didn't know you were into older men—'

She laughed. 'I'm not, so don't get any ideas.'

'You're not my type—'

'Nor you mine.'

'Hey! I'm not that much older.'

'Yeah, right.' Kate raised a smile. 'Anyway, I told Torres I'd do it. If I ran away from one bloke, I'd hardly be brave enough to mix with a terrorist organisation, would I? There's no reason anyone will get suspicious, assuming they buy my cover story. Besides, it'll keep my hand in. Don't fret, Hank. When I turn up for work, you won't even recognise me.'

'Kate, let me. These people are organised and ruthless.'

'I can handle myself.'

'And what will I be doing?'

'Interviewing. This is your opportunity to vet everyone face-to-face. Baggage handlers will be expecting to be questioned by police, in case they saw or heard anything dodgy in the days and weeks leading up to the attack. You'll be asking the same set of questions, over and over, in case they compare notes afterwards. No deviation. Torres sent a pro forma so you don't have to make one up. In fact, that sulky face you're wearing is perfect. If you could also act bored, your subjects will think you're a nobody doing the grunt work. Ask me, you're made for the role.'

They worked hard getting ready for the tasks that Torres had given them, Kate rehearsing her 'legend' as a Geordie runaway, Hank gathering the information he needed to interview staff in the baggage shed. While he was doing that, Kate took the opportunity to call Bright, explaining that her 2ic would not be returning as instructed.

He was livid.

Kate interrupted him in full flow. 'Phil, I don't want to argue—'

'Good, because I gave you a direct order. You don't get to choose which ones you obey, which ones you toss aside. I made myself perfectly clear, so if Hank fancies keeping his warrant card, he'd better be standing in my office by close of play with a begging bowl in his hand. Is that clear?'

'Torres needs us both.'

'Tough, I need you more.'

'We have dual roles here. How will it look if you pull us off now?'

He didn't answer.

'Believe it or not, your reputation matters to me. Mine I couldn't give a stuff about. Look, if Robbo needs help with his investigation up north, Hank and I will be on hand to offer support at every turn. We can work remotely. We have access to HOLMES and no intention of letting him cope with it alone.'

'That's big of you.'

'Have you ID'd the victim?' She was trying to deflect attention from her refusal to play ball and demonstrate that she was interested in what was happening on her home patch.

'We're working on it. He's a mess, Robbo couldn't make the ID. He said the guy looked like a businessman: posh suit, good shoes, expensive watch. We've acquired CCTV from the hospital to identify the men who delivered him to A&E and then left the scene. They told medics his name was Henry Ford, gave a dodgy address and date of birth. I have a bad feeling about this one, Kate.'

Kate fed this to Hank as she drove. It started to rain as she took a road signposted Hounslow, an area she'd never been to before. Traffic slowed to a crawl at a set of traffic lights. Once she got going again, she turned off at the T-junction heading for an address she'd committed to memory. Homeland Security had rented a one-bedroom crash pad for her in an area that was less than salubrious; part of her cover, should anyone follow her. Whoever Torres had sent to check out the property was experienced and had chosen well, a first-floor flat Kate could escape from if necessary, with a side window directly on to the flat garage roof.

Clocking it as she passed by, Kate nudged Hank with her elbow, flicking her eyes left. 'Take note of the green door. The first-floor window is mine.'

His eyebrows almost met in the middle. 'You're moving out?'

'So are you.'

'Great, I never liked the colour purple.' He checked out the house. 'Which window is mine?'

'You're not invited. You need to grab your stuff from the Premier Inn.' She reeled off an address. 'There's a room there for you.'

'Let me guess. It's a B&B with no bar.'

'Close.' She gave a wry smile. 'It's a section house with no bar.'

'You're kidding.'

There were no section houses left in the Northumbria force area, though he'd lived in one when he first joined the police. He'd often spoken about what went on there: the parties, the fights, the difficulties of young men struggling to cope. For most, it was their first experience of living away from home. His too.

'It'll be fun!' she said.

'It'll be gross. I can smell it from here.'

'It suits our purposes. My place is hardly the Ritz.'

'Yeah, but mine will be full of probationers.'

'Then you can pass on the benefit of your vast experience.'

'Do I have to?'

'I could always drop you at the airport.'

He let out a resigned sigh.

Kate drove on, turning left up a side street, then left again into the lane that ran behind her new rental so he could identify it from the rear. Despite his plummeting mood, Hank was taking notice as they cruised by, clocking the adjacent properties as well as her own. Kate went around again to be sure he'd seen enough, then doubled back, parking a few streets away outside a small café with few customers inside, telling him she fancied a coffee.

'In there?' He was unimpressed. 'This day just keeps on giving.'

She made no move to get out of the car. Secretly, she looked forward to getting her hands dirty in the baggage shed, but Hank required updating further. She handed over the keys to her vehicle. 'My car is now yours. Look after it. From now on,

I'm on the bus. Our only contact will be via text. Oh, and you need this . . .' She passed him her mobile phone. 'I have a new device. You're on your own, Hank.'

'How are you going to keep in touch with Robbo and Carmichael?'

'I'm not, you'll have to. Give me your phone.'

'What?'

'Give.'

He passed it over.

Accessing his address book, she entered a fictitious name and her new phone number, showed it to him, then handed it back. 'We have no contact whatsoever unless we have something important to share.'

'And if we do?'

'Your number is listed in my contacts as Andy O'Brien.' Hank approved. It was the name of a former Magpies defender he rated. Ignoring his silly grin, Kate continued: 'If you receive any calls from a number you don't recognise, you're a mechanic, not a footballer. You're my new fella and we'll communicate by text along those lines. A **Miss U** text from either of us means meet here as soon as we're able, or at The Sun around the corner if this place is shut. Text **Miss U lots** and we'll meet within the hour. **Miss U lots with a kiss** from me means send the cavalry . . . or get out of there if it comes from you.'

'Now you're worrying me.'

It worried her too, but Kate didn't voice her concern. Aware of the risks involved in any undercover operation, and the enormity of the task they were facing, the idea of a coffee no longer appealed. She had stuff to do and told him she'd rather push off than hang around. Asking him to flip the boot, she got out of the car. Hank followed suit, walking round to the rear of the car. Kate grabbed her kit and slammed the tailgate shut, hauling a large backpack onto one shoulder.

'All the details are in my Notes app, Hank. You clear on everything?'

He nodded. 'Miss you already.'

'Me too, now get out of here.'

36

Kate walked to her new digs alone and let herself in with a key hidden under a stone in the tiny front garden. As she approached the stairs, the front door opened behind her. She swung round to see who was there. The bloke who'd followed her in threw her a welcoming smile. He had long dark hair, great teeth, nice eyes. He was casually dressed: jeans, a windbreaker, a guitar slung over his back. He seemed as surprised to see her as she was to see him.

'Hi!' Leaning the guitar against the front door, he pulled off his scarf. 'I'm Michael.'

'Lou, nice to meet you.'

With no time for niceties, nor wish to get acquainted further, she told the truth: she was in a rush to get to work. Hitching her rucksack up onto her shoulder with two hands, she turned away, making for the stairs, leaving him affronted in the hallway. Before she reached them, he called after her.

'You the new tenant?'

She turned. 'Yeah, just off the train.'

'The flat will need airing. It's been empty for months. It'll be nice to have a neighbour.' He pointed at her rucksack. 'Need a hand? That looks heavy.'

'I can manage, thanks.'

'OK, holler if you need anything—'

The door to her flat opened directly into a grim living room that hadn't seen a lick of paint in years. On one wall, there was a black, faux-leather sofa with no armrests or cushions, a cheap coffee table in front of it, a grubby grey carpet on the floor. A TV sat in one corner, wires trailing to the nearest three-pin plug. Picking up the remote, she switched it on.

The picture wasn't great but she could catch the news and use the radio channels to make some noise.

There was nothing worse than silence.

Kate wandered aimlessly through the rest of the property, pushing open doors to the adjoining rooms. The bedroom was the saddest thing she'd ever seen. A queensize bed with a heavily stained mattress, a wonky lamp with no lightshade. Relieved to see a brand-new sleeping bag on the floor beside the radiator, she turned away. The bathroom had no shower. A single toothbrush lay abandoned in the sink that hadn't been cleaned when the property was vacated. Ditto the kit-chenette at the rear. Then and there, she decided she'd be eating out whenever she got the chance.

'Welcome home, Lou,' she said.

Her legend was simple: a northern lass who'd fled do-mestic violence and couldn't find work because her region was an unemployment wasteland now that shipbuilding and mining had disappeared. She didn't fancy a call centre, so she'd decided on a fresh start in the south. It was not only credible, it was perfectly reasonable that she'd head for one of the largest employers in the London Borough of Hillingdon where her non-existent female cousin lived – fifteen miles from the bright lights of central London.

Returning to the living room, she sat down heavily on the sofa, staring at the wall opposite. It was bare, save for lumps of Blu Tack that clung onto the torn edges of posters and photographs ripped down when the previous tenant left. It seemed he or she couldn't get out of there fast enough.

She could relate.

By comparison, Hank's place would feel like home.

The loneliness returned. It had hit her time and again all day – and not always when she was on her own. She'd done her best to hide it from Hank but it kept slamming into her when she least expected. He'd tried telling her that she was in denial, refusing to accept the inevitable. The more he hinted at it, the more she dug her heels in, and now she had to accept that he might have been right. It wasn't the fact that Jo hadn't been in touch. For her, that wasn't unusual. But there had been no bank transactions, and her phone had gone dead at the airport.

Kate felt sick to her stomach, the reality of the situation causing her untold pain. Slipping her mobile from her pocket with the intention of calling Tom or James only served to make matters worse. She couldn't do so on her new device, neither could she speak to her father. Another reason for him to hate her. She was now Lou Paige. Kate Daniels no longer existed. Her life was now in Hank's possession: her contacts and images; texts and emails; anything and everything that might ID her as a cop.

The mobile hit the table with a solid thump.

Kate couldn't write Jo out of her life yet. She still needed proof, one way or the other. Unanswered questions tugged at her heart: the discrepancy over Jo's hold luggage, the fact that two women didn't board the flight.

She willed one of them to be Jo.

Please, let her live.

Kate didn't know who she was praying to. Only that she was. Please let her live. The same words had spilled from her mouth when her mother was dying. If there was a God, he didn't listen then. Kate hoped the fucker was listening now.

She closed her eyes, mentally replaying the CCTV clip Carmichael had sent through, showing Jo walking away from the airport information desk, the tall guy following close behind. It was only a matter of time before Maxwell identified him. Hank would follow it up. Kate couldn't break cover. She'd given Torres assurances, and she had no intention of reneging on them.

I won't let you down, Gabriele.

Or you, Jo.

37

Having moved his gear from the Premier Inn, Hank grabbed a bite to eat at the section house before heading for Heathrow. As he approached the staff car park at Terminal 5, the barrier lifted allowing him in. Torres had thought of everything. Checking his watch as he got out of the car, he quickened his step, keen to get inside for his meeting with Somi Haq, Heathrow's Human Resources Manager. Briefed to provide him with the names of baggage handlers who had access to Flight 0113 – including those on duty the night before and details of any who'd been in trouble – she'd come in to take care of it herself.

She stood up to welcome him as he entered her office. 'DS Gormley, please sit down. I wish we were meeting under happier circumstances. I have everything you need right here.' She placed a slender, manicured hand on a pile of paperwork, then lifted it, removed the top sheet and held it up. 'This list contains the names of those who've been warned for breaches of protocol. I want you to know that we take these very seriously. We dismiss anyone whose actions threaten the security of the travelling public.'

'Have you fired anyone recently?'

'Not in the time parameters I was given, no. Nor has anyone gone sick, taken holiday or resigned – I checked.'

'That makes my job easier,' Hank said, 'although I may have to widen the timescale at some point.'

'Of course. The Airport Operations Manager has pledged full cooperation. I'll be on hand to assist you for as long as required.'

Hank thanked her with a half-smile. 'Have you taken on anyone new in the past few weeks?'

'One or two. Their names are highlighted. Staff who were on duty on Friday the seventeenth of October are also clearly marked.' This information was significant – the departure date for 0113. 'I've flagged them in my system. If anyone requests to take leave at short notice or disappears, you'll be notified immediately.'

'Thanks . . . I intend to stagger my interviews across each shift until all employees have been questioned, though I'd appreciate it if you would keep that to yourself.'

'Of course.'

They spent another hour together before Hank left for his office, a small box room overlooking the baggage shed. Somi explained that he'd been put there for three reasons: to facilitate a speedy flow of interviewees; to avoid staff having to leave the secure area; to expedite their return to work, causing minimum disruption to the workforce. If Hank was a betting man – which he wasn't – he thought there might be a fourth, a stipulation from Torres to watch over Kate.

Kate dressed in warm, dark kit, avoiding anything that would make her stand out. Before moving her belongings to Hounslow, she'd been through every pocket of her clothing to ensure that there was no receipt or clue to her real identity that might blow her cover.

The baggage shed was freezing, a huge corrugated iron structure, sectioned off and manned by workers of all nationalities. Having gone through the same brief induction process as any other staff member working behind the scenes, she'd got a sense of how closely staff were scrutinised as they entered the security identification display areas, and how they proved that they were legit. Agreeing to work a split shift, Kate had been given protective clothing, a security pass and a designated member of staff to tell her what to do. It wasn't rocket science. In no time she was hauling luggage like the rest of them.

The shed was busy, a constant flow of luggage arriving on a conveyor belt from feeder flights and directly from the check-in desks. As she worked, Kate thought about Torres. The special agent was convinced that someone here was either on the take, prepared to look the other way in exchange for cash, unaware that they were helping someone motivated by hate.

Kate wondered how Hank's preparations were going. Before starting his interviews, he'd have put together an overview of employees, seeking out those who'd drawn attention to themselves for the wrong reasons, sussing out any who'd been disciplined or found in sterile areas where they had no authority to be. Her priority was more straightforward: to identify suspects. It was a big ask, but one she was well placed to investigate as an insider. Her eyes scanned the baggage shed for anyone who looked nervous. As staff worked, they talked, to each other and to her. None seemed particularly interested in the northerner who'd arrived in the worst week possible, following an incident that had rocked the aviation industry around the world.

For the first time since he'd taken possession of Kate's police mobile, the device rang in Hank's breast pocket. Backing away from the entrance to the baggage shed, he found a quiet corner and pulled out the phone. Carmichael's name was on the home screen. She was already speaking as he lifted the device to his ear.

'Hello?' She seemed distracted. 'Sorry, Kate, false alarm. Thought I had good news for you, but I don't.'

'Lisa, it's me.'

'Is the boss there?'

'No, she's incommunicado. From now on, if you have anything for her, you'll have to go through me. I can't explain, so don't ask.' If Hank knew Lisa, she'd have worked out that Kate's lack of availability had something to do with the guy she was meeting in Windsor. 'She's busy, and so am I. That's all you need to know.'

'Yeah? There's absolutely nowt happening this end,' she said sarcastically. 'We have a murder victim no one has reported missing and no clue where to start. You pick your moments to be away, Sarge.'

Hank apologised.

With a new enquiry underway, the first few hours were critical. 'How's Robbo?'

'To be honest, he'd rather you weren't tying up resources.' Carmichael dropped her voice to a whisper. 'Why d'you think I'm calling from the locker room? Maxwell found the guy who was standing next to Jo at the information desk. You're right, he did follow her. She accessed one of the bars and he caught up with her at the counter. We can't be sure what was said but she looked a bit embarrassed when he approached.'

'She would. Kate overheard part of their conversation. Jo apparently told him to do one.'

'Doesn't sound like her.'

'Yeah, well she wasn't in the best frame of mind at the time. Can you get a lip-reader to take a look at the CCTV?'

'I could but there's no point. It's a dead end, Hank. Maxwell asked an immigration official if he could help ID the man as he passed through security. They came up with a match. The guy was a passenger on Jo's flight. He's not going to be answering any questions.'

38

Kate clocked Hank as he entered the baggage shed, a confident gait, a clipboard in one hand, a briefcase in the other. He unlocked the door to a small office, disappearing momentarily as it closed behind him. Seconds later, he appeared at the window, striking a formidable figure as he stood, arms folded, with a view over the workforce, a bored expression on his face.

His arrival had sparked an immediate reaction. All around, cages were rattling, literally and figuratively. Her new colleagues had stopped what they were doing, all eyes turned towards Hank's small office window, no one in any doubt that he was there to question them.

Hank appeared not to have noticed Kate, but she knew different. He'd have pegged her for sure and was avoiding eye contact, playing the role she'd given him, a Met detective who'd caught the thin end of the wedge, consigned to the grunt work for the foreseeable future. He was carrying out her instructions to the letter.

Deception cut both ways. It came as second nature to detectives trained in the art of subterfuge. Hank was no exception. He excelled at it. They had met during an undercover operation while working in the drug squad. Having received extensive instruction – and proved that they could withstand intense scrutiny if called upon to do so, scoring top marks in their psychological assessments – they were put to work, infiltrating an organisation prepared to flood the streets with chemicals so addictive that those stupid enough to use them would never fully recover. Passing themselves off as buyers was dangerous, but also thrilling. The sting had thwarted a serious and organised crime syndicate, resulting in long prison sentences.

Could they pull it off one more time?

They might be older, but they were no less hungry for a result.

Rolling her eyes at the young man standing by her side, Kate played dumb, asking him what the fuss was about, without the slightest hint that she was anything other than who she was pretending to be: Lou Paige, the latest recruit with no friends and even less of a clue as to what was causing such a stir among her distracted teammates.

'We'll be questioned,' he said. 'I suppose, from his perspective, we're all under suspicion.'

'Not me, surely!' Kate feigned outrage. 'I only started this morning.'

'Dunno.'

'Talk about bad timing.'

Grabbing more luggage, the guy examined the label and turned away. Kate resumed work, too. This one was in no mood for introductions and she didn't wish to appear too keen to make his acquaintance.

A few minutes later, Hank's door opened. He stood on the threshold, scanning the workers as a tannoy called out the first of many names, asking Pete Abraham to make himself available for interview, telling him where to go. Hank had chosen to work his way through his list alphabetically.

Positioning herself where she could see the interviewees going in and coming out of Hank's small office, Kate carried on working while keeping an eye on the door, noting the body language of those who were leaving and whether they struck up a conversation with anyone afterwards. Most looked unconcerned, a little sad perhaps, but that was only to be expected.

*

Kate was physically and emotionally exhausted when she finished her shift and made her way to Hounslow. The **Miss U lots** text arrived before she did, which meant that Hank would make his way to their rendezvous point within the hour. She replied. **Can't wait to see you**. Though she was desperate to soak her body in the bath – not necessarily the one in her new flat – she made straight for The Sun public house, ordered herself a large gin and sat down to wait.

It was an unremarkable pub, fairly popular with local people. Everyone seemed to know each other. Two young women caught her eye. They were sitting away from other customers, side by side, a cosy corner where they could chat over a glass of red without interruption. One of them reminded her of Jo, the way she paid attention to what the other was saying, as if she was the only person in the room, a private conversation that had a subtext Kate recognised instantly. The intensity between them was like a knife to the heart, triggering a reaction deep within her.

In a moment of heartbreak and sorrow, Kate resisted the urge to intervene. She wanted to tell them to hang onto what they had and not let their union slip away as she had done. What was she thinking, putting her job before Jo? She treasured her – just not enough. It had been a costly mistake to assume that she'd always be there. She wouldn't.

She wasn't.

Kate looked away as the pub door swung open, bringing with it a waft of cold air. Two men entered, Hank following them in. As always, he seemed pleased to see her. Her smile was forced. He'd seen the desperation in her eyes before she had time to hide it and gave her a moment to compose herself, grabbing a beer from the bar before walking towards her. Kate wondered if he'd texted out of necessity, or if she was merely a diversion from the section house. As it turned out, she wasn't.

'Can I get you another before I spill the beans?' he said. 'You look like you could use one.'

She shook her head. 'One more and I'll keel over.'

'Kate, what's wrong?'

'Nothing a hot soak in the tub won't fix.'

He wasn't fooled.

Straddling a bar stool, he took a swig of his pint, setting the glass on a beer mat advertising the gin she was drinking. 'Well,' he said, 'I hate to add to your woes but I had a call from Lisa. It's not good news. The man Jo spoke to at the airport was booked on the same flight to New York and is now on the "Missing Presumed Dead" list in Blue's office.'

'Maxwell found him?'

'Them,' Hank corrected her. 'They shared a drink, then went their separate ways. I checked in with Esposito. This guy she did remember. He was good-looking, charming too, or so she said. First at the gate, so presumably first to board. As Daisy Reynolds said, Jo was one of the last to board, so they weren't together. She hung back for some reason.'

'She always does. She can't be arsed to queue or wrestle with other passengers if she has a seat booked. She prefers to walk on when everyone else is settled. She'd have booked an aisle seat so as not to disturb anyone, too, I bet. I'd like to think that it saved her life, but as each day passes I have to face facts.'

It killed her to say it.

Words eluded Hank for a moment. 'Kate, there's still a chance.'

He was trying to lift her.

She loved him for it. 'There's a reason I can't accept that she's gone. If I let go, I may as well find myself a tall building.'

'Kate, don't. You're under a lot of stress. I get that, but you can't let it ruin your life.'

'That's just it. My life will never be the same without her in it.' Across the room, hands were finding each other – the slightest of touches. A demonstration of true love. 'See those women over there? We were like that once, couldn't take our eyes off each other for longer than a few seconds. Jo was the most wonderful person I ever met, Hank. How can I live with the fact that I failed her?'

39

The last few days had been agonising, every hour, every minute, every second having brought Kate nearer to the realisation that she'd never see Jo again. Hank's attempt to comfort her at the pub didn't help. Touching though it was, it felt like pity and she couldn't cope with that. She didn't feel worthy of his compassion — or anyone else's – and told him so. Against his advice, she'd bought a bottle of gin from the barman at The Sun, waved him off in her car and returned to her grotty flat with the intention of getting blotto.

Taking a chipped glass from the kitchen cupboard, the only one there, she'd poured herself a large drink and tuned the TV to a radio channel. The music soothed her as she cleaned and ran a hot bath. She'd just sunk her aching body in the water when A Great Big World came on the radio, the poignant lyrics of 'Say Something' floating in through the open door, the words moving her to tears as they had the first time she'd heard them. Back then, they had stirred her emotions. On this occasion the song echoed exactly what she was feeling, the words tugging at her heart. She would have followed Jo anywhere and was reluctantly giving up on her, regretting the fact that she couldn't get to her in time – physically or emotionally.

As drunk as she was when she finally made it to bed, Kate was too wired to sleep. She'd lain awake for hours, staring at shadows on the ceiling, blaming herself for pushing Jo too far, rerunning their life together: their first kiss; frequent holidays; theatre trips. Good times. But in the small hours, the memories had become darker: the disagreements; Jo's car accident resulting in partial memory loss interpreted by Bright as a way to avoid being questioned in connection with her ex-husband's murder; her subsequent arrest and remand in custody; the way Kate had fought tooth and nail to prove her innocence, putting her job on the line in the process; and finally, the horror of her flight to JFK being blown to bits over the Atlantic Ocean. Kate could only hope that every one of the passengers had died instantly, Jo along with them. To imagine anything else was too painful.

Next morning, feeling badly hungover and exhausted through lack of sleep as she got ready for another shift in the baggage shed, it took every ounce of resolve Kate possessed to report for duty. There were at least three hundred and sixteen reasons why she had no option but to continue what she'd started. Multiplying that figure by the extended families of flight crew, security staff and passengers from thirteen countries worldwide was unimaginable. Every single one of them deserved justice. If there was anything she could do to bring that closer, she would.

Nothing would deter her.

Nothing.

The name Lou Paige being transmitted loudly over the public address system made her look towards the window of Hank's office. Putting down the suitcase she was transporting to a cage bound for a flight due to take off within the hour, she checked in with her supervisor, then left the baggage floor for a chance to exchange information with Hank without having to wait for him to meet with her in Hounslow.

She'd not been idle but wanted his feedback first.

'It's interesting what you learn when you start asking questions,' Hank said. 'Already a picture is emerging. You were right. There's pilfering going on here. On what scale, I've yet to determine. People are tight-lipped. They want to keep their jobs. No one is prepared to admit to anything, certainly not to any knowledge of selling or cloning airside passes.'

'Why would they?'

'Exactly.'

Kate stared at the pro forma in front of him. From his position near the door, she was fairly sure he wasn't visible from the window. Facing away from it, she could talk freely, but she was taking no chances. 'Keep writing, Hank. We're under scrutiny. I can't stay long. Everyone knows I'm new in, so a nil return as far as you're concerned.'

He wrote her dodgy name on the sheet in front of him, then continued with his update. His contact in HR claimed that breaches involving security passes were usually a route to theft, not anything more serious. 'Assuming there was such a transaction, the person involved probably didn't know the intention of the buyer. I mean, why ask a question when you don't want to know the answer, when money is more important than anything else?'

'If anyone traded with someone motivated by terrorism it's a monstrous betrayal of trust on an unsuspecting travelling public,' Kate said, her tone bitter. 'Everyone who clocked on this morning was told that the Operations Manager has increased security. He's asking for vigilance. Well, it's a bit bloody late for that!'

A flash of anger hit its target.

Hank almost ducked.

Kate wasn't finished. 'Everything they do is supposed to be intelligence-led. And yet people are on the take, from taxis to hire cars to those working behind the scenes. If security have any idea what's going on, it seems to me that they're doing nothing to stamp it out. If they let people get away with the small things, it breeds contempt for the bigger things. According to Blue, they're losing millions and it's happening right in front of them.'

A nod from Hank. 'It's like trying to get toothpaste back in a tube—'

'You reckon?' She was being sarcastic.

Hank had allocated each interviewee a maximum of five minutes in order to get through as many as he could in the shortest possible time. He seemed distracted, as though he had something on his mind.

Kate was about to ask him to spit it out when he did.

'Does Torres really think we're still under threat?'

'I can't answer that. No one has yet claimed responsibility. She hinted at a new kid on the block, which makes our job a damned sight harder. Whoever we're looking for is not on any official watchlist.' Pulling up her sleeve, Kate consulted her arm where she'd scribbled down three separate times.

He was horrified. 'What the fuck is that?'

She gave him a pointed look. 'I could hardly take a notepad in without drawing attention to myself, could I? Your nine o'clock appointment I didn't like the look of.'

Consulting his list, he gave her the name of the corresponding interviewee. She wrote it next to the time on her arm, producing a great deal of anxiety in her 2ic. He had no need to warn her that she was taking a risk, but he did it anyway.

'Anyone else you're not happy about?'

'Yeah, your ten fifteen and ten forty-five.' He gave another two names, one of which he had to spell out for her. Another scribble on the underside of her left arm, then Kate pulled down her sleeve, before asking: 'How many more are there?'

'A shedload.' The pun was unintentional. 'I told all of them this is the start of a protracted enquiry and that they may be recalled.' He rotated his neck and flexed his shoulders. 'I'm knackered. It's so bloody hot in here.'

'Think yourself lucky, it's freezing in the shed. Muscles are aching where I didn't know I had any . . . and I'm dying for a cuppa.' She tapped her forearm. 'I'll feed this to Torres as soon as I get the chance.'

'When you have, wash it off.'

'Yes, Dad.' Her comment prompted her to ask him to call

the hospital and enquire about the patient. She pushed her chair away. 'I'm out of here.'

'No, don't get up.'

Kate was intrigued.

'You're not going to like this.'

'I can see that.'

Hank said, 'Whatever you do, promise me you won't react.'

She waited.

Reluctantly, he pushed a copy of the *Daily Mail* across his desk, open on page two, a half-page spread. Kate shook, clenching her hands as she read the print, unable to believe what she was seeing. Jo's smiling face stared at her from a photograph taken at a charity function they had both attended to support the work of a local hospice. Details of her life, family and job – including her role within Northumbria Police – the fact that she was once charged with her late husband's murder and released for lack of evidence, the whole shebang. At the bottom of the piece, a comment from Tom, a tribute to his mother that brought a lump to Kate's throat.

Kate felt the blood drain from her face. 'This has Blue's name all over it.'

A nod. 'He's getting at you for playing him.'

'It worked. Does the dozy knacker have any idea how dangerous this is?'

'No, but I do. You're exposed, Kate—'

'I'm exposed! You're a Geordie cop. What the fuck—'

'You need to tell Torres.'

'Let's not knee-jerk. Bright will go spare when he reads this. Waverley will be mincemeat and Blue will be out on his ear. Get in touch with Carmichael. Do it now. Tell her I want an internet search for any images of me and Jo together. If she can't find them, they don't exist. If she does, we have a real problem. You know what to do.'

40

Torres had made arrangements for the transfer of information, a designated hotel room where Kate's contact would meet with her whenever she deemed it necessary. Assuming she ever found who she was looking for, Kate knew that the prosecution of the perpetrators would be neither swift nor straightforward. It would take years of legal argument over jurisdiction, exactly what happened following the Lockerbie bombing. It took a decade to decide where to try Abdelbaset Al Megrahi and Al Amin Khalifa Fhimah, the Libyans claiming that they would not receive a fair trial in the US or UK. And finally, the case was heard in The Hague under Scottish law.

In Hounslow, Kate scrubbed the ink from her arms until they were red raw, changed her work clothes for a tracksuit and went for a run. After a day of heavy lifting, she felt better for it. She'd begun to slow her pace and was looking forward to her warm-down exercises – and another soak in the bath, this time without alcohol – when the road beside her was illuminated by headlights that didn't progress along the road as she expected. When they mirrored her stride and no vehicle sped past, it didn't take her long to realise that she was being followed.

Pulling up, she crouched down, a fake attempt to do up her shoelaces, offering the driver no choice but to cruise right by, hoping to catch his number.

The vehicle stopped.

Kate's heart almost followed suit. It was banging like a drum inside her chest, and not from exercise, the hairs on her neck pricking up, the sweat on her body beginning to freeze. She heard the engine idling, the door opening, then closing.

A pair of shiny shoes appeared on the pavement beside her. She looked up to find Detective Chief Superintendent Bright leaning against his selenite-grey Mercedes S-Class, a car she'd helped him choose.

'That's not funny, guv. You scared the shit out of me.' She knew him well enough to drop the formality of rank whenever they were alone but chose not to on this occasion. There had been so much angst between them lately, he seemed more like a 'guv' than a Phil, the man she admired so much. 'What the hell are you doing here?'

'Waiting for you.'

Kate stood up. 'How did you—'

'I run the CID, that's how.'

Anxiously, she peered along the street, scanning the cars on either side of the road, pavements too – fortunately, they were empty. She refocused on Bright. 'Are you trying to out me to the whole wide world, or have you come to have another go at me?'

He folded his arms, never taking his eyes off her. 'We need to talk.'

'And I need anonymity.'

'Then you're in luck. Carmichael says you're in the clear. There are no images of you and Jo together on the internet.'

'That's a relief.' She paused. 'I can't believe Torres told you where I was.'

'It was that or no deal,' he said.

'Yeah? She doesn't strike me as the type to negotiate.'

'Neither am I . . . except with you, apparently. If you think for one minute that I'd agree to your undercover deployment without knowing exactly where you'd be living, you're sadly mistaken. I don't give a toss about Torres, Homeland Security or the US President for that matter, but I do give a stuff about you, even if you make it impossible for me to like you sometimes.'

'Only sometimes?'

161

'OK, most of the time.' His face was set in a scowl.

Kate panicked.

He hadn't driven almost three hundred miles to trade insults. There was a reason he was there. She wondered if she was it; if he'd changed his mind about her involvement with Homeland Security, or if Torres had, egged on by Waverley. Had 'Gold' been stirring it, demanding a substitution with one of his own officers? He didn't need to discredit her in order to get his way. She'd done that all by herself. Bright had every right to pull her off the investigation and haul her arse north and Hank's along with it.

Let him try.

'If you're planning to order me back to base, you're wasting your breath as well as your petrol—'

He gave her hard eyes. 'Why would I give with one hand and take away with the other?'

'Beats me. I've given up second-guessing you. It makes my head hurt, so why don't you put me out of my misery and tell me why you're here before I freeze to death.'

'There's no mystery. I'm on my way to Hendon for a summit meeting . . .' His expression softened, a wry smile developing. 'Authorised Professional Practice, something *you're* not particularly good at and will bore the tits off me. As you were here, I came down early. Thought it was worth driving thirty miles to see my most bolshie DCI.'

'And your most successful,' she reminded him.

'That too . . . How are you holding up? I want the truth, not the well-rehearsed version.'

It was a daft question – one she had no intention of answering.

She tried not to get maudlin and hoped he'd do the same. Her emotions were all over the place. She was struggling. Anyone who cared to look would see that. Her mood swings were hard to cope with, for him and for Hank. Unqualified in self-diagnosis, she assumed this was part of a process she'd have to work through on her own.

Last night, she'd convinced herself that there was little chance of finding Jo alive, but where there was a flicker of hope, the slightest chance that she wasn't on that plane, Kate would hang onto it. She'd get angry if Bright suggested that she should face facts. They were similar in many ways but they often saw things differently. Ordinarily, Kate needed a body before she'd accept that there had been a death.

She simply wasn't ready for that.

The breeze on her damp skin made her feel cold and shivery. She rubbed at her upper arms, suddenly aware that she was standing with her guv'nor, dressed in Lycra in the middle of a hellhole, hair pinned untidily, sweaty after her run. Christ knows what she looked like. And she wasn't buying the Hendon visit as his reason for seeking her out.

'You said we need to talk, so talk.'

'Not here . . .' Laying a fatherly hand on her shoulder, Bright thumbed to her flat down the road. 'Go in and get dressed. I'll wait in the car.'

41

Kate didn't keep him waiting long; fifteen minutes, no more, before she opened the Mercedes door and climbed in, dressed more appropriately: warm kit, a hat to cover scruffy hair that needed a wash, no slap. At least her face was clean. She couldn't care less what she looked like and didn't intend hanging around long enough for him to notice her shoddy appearance. A quick drink – if that's what he had in mind – and she'd be away.

Despite telling him that she had work to be getting on with, he drove off like he knew where he was going, skirting High Point Village where Esposito lived, eventually arriving in Hayes fifteen minutes later at an inn called The Pheasant. There was a restaurant at the rear, the interior of which reminded her of one near her father's home in rural Northumberland. As she got out of the car, she wondered how he was doing and instantly felt guilty for not having contacted him.

At the rear entrance, Bright pushed open the door, standing aside to let her in.

Unless he happened to be in the Northumbria incident room, chasing a result she couldn't land quick enough for his liking, shouting her down for something or other in the privacy of his office at HQ, he was always the perfect gentleman, impeccably dressed, with a presence that drew the attention of everyone around him, including one female member of staff who greeted him with a smile as he approached the bar.

'Can I help you?'

'Yes, I have a table for two booked. The name is Wild.'

As the waitress consulted her electronic reservation book, Kate's mouth almost fell open. Her hackles were up and it showed. 'You . . . did what?'

'Oh, come on, Lou! I wanted to surprise you.'

He had. 'No, listen, I can't,' she said. 'I'm on early shift in the morning.'

'Nonsense. We need to talk and I've gone to a lot of trouble. You're not running out on me again.' Winking at the waitress, he ordered wine without consulting Kate. She bristled. Nothing to do with his choice, an Australian Grenache. After hanging one on last night, the thought of even a thimbleful of alcohol turned her stomach.

Sensing a tension developing between the new arrivals, the waitress grabbed a couple of menus off the counter and pointed to her left. She gave a nervous smile. 'Follow me, sir.'

Don't mind me, Kate thought, but didn't say.

They were led to an intimate table for two, away from other diners. She wondered if this was Bright's idea, pre-planned. Or, because they were obviously not on good terms, the waitress wanted to keep them away from other customers. He pulled out a chair. Kate sat down – a scowl on her face – taking a menu as it was held out to her, an impressive list that made her mouth water.

She hadn't eaten all day.

They waited for the waitress to return with the wine.

Pouring them each a glass, she made her getaway.

Kate wished she could follow suit. She leaned in, whispering through gritted teeth. 'Wild? My abusive ex? Are you serious?'

'What? You think I no longer have the skill?'

'Did I say that?'

'You didn't have to. Your face did it for you. Keep arguing, Lou. I'm supposed to be the monster you're running away from. In fact, if you could work in a tear or two, that would be bloody perfect.'

She glared at him.

Now they were inside, she noticed how drawn and pale he looked. She assumed it was because he'd been driving for hours without a break. She could tell he had more than that on his mind. He was biding his time, for what she didn't know.

The penny dropped – he had news from up north.

It didn't take him long to voice it. 'We have ID, Kate. Our victim is Yulian Nikolaev.'

'Jesus!' The name stunned her.

Nikolaev was a Russian drug lord, a self-made billionaire thanks to his drug-running operation. He was old school, brutal with it, prepared to kill anyone who got in his way, by any means. He'd murdered and tortured more people than most right-minded individuals could ever imagine, but the police had never been able to prove it. He had the best legal team money could buy. The opposition would simply disappear, never to be seen again. Witnesses too. He could run rings round law enforcement.

'How? Do you have a crime scene?'

'Doorstep shooting at his home. We have no leads and little chance of finding any.'

'Who would dare talk?'

'Precisely.'

'Is that why you're here, hoping to persuade me to return to Newcastle?'

'No, Robbo is doing a fine job. Besides, Torres seems to think she needs you more. I won't lie to you. I could do with Hank, but for now he's yours.'

Kate was overwhelmed. 'Thank you, Phil.'

He'd never know what it meant to have his support. She'd stepped out of line so often she'd lost count. Time and again he'd covered her arse, as he had with Waverley. Gold wasn't stupid. In lying for her, Bright had broken the invisible code of honour between senior officers, dropping himself in the shit, making himself look weak. He was nothing of the kind. Kate was off the hook, for now.

'I'll call Robbo.'

'He'd appreciate that.' Bright pointed at the menu. 'Shall we eat?'

A nod. Suddenly, Kate was hungry.

When they had finished their meal, Kate looked up to find Bright studying her. He could probably tell she was agitated, dwelling on her undercover deployment for Homeland Security, Nikolaev and Robbo, but mostly Jo. She was everything. Without her, what was there? Her guv'nor picked up his wine, on the verge of saying something, finally breaking the silence.

'Kate, I know you don't want to hear it—'

'Then don't say it. No words of comfort, from you or anyone, will make me feel any better.'

'Not now perhaps. It's too early in the process. You're too raw, but I want you to know that it won't always feel like this. You will get over it, eventually. It'll take time, but you have so much going for you—'

'Oh yeah?' She gave him the side-eye. 'Like what, exactly?'

'Like a close circle of friends, a good home, the job of your dreams—'

'Wasn't enough for you,' she snapped. 'Why should I be any different?'

'I was lucky to get a second chance. You will too.'

'I don't want a second chance, so stop right there! I mean it. Another word and I'll walk.'

Her comment had drawn the attention of other customers and members of staff; a few heads turned in their direction. Raising both hands, Bright fell silent. Kate stared at him. No wonder she'd lost it. He might as well have said what he was thinking, that Jo was fish-food. On the other hand, she could tell from his wounded expression that he was trying to help, not hurt her.

She apologised for biting his head off.

'No, you're right,' he said. 'I was out of order. It was a stupid thing to say. We should have gone to my hotel and had this conversation in private—'

'Or not had it at all.'

She knew he was trying to lift her, to remind her of the things that were once important. There was a time when she'd have given anything to get to the next rank and beyond, following in his footsteps. He'd groomed her to take over and that had driven her to hide who she really was. The sole reason for keeping her relationship with Jo a secret was blind ambition. Reaching her full potential seemed important then, but none of that mattered now.

None of it.

If Jo was gone, it had all been for nothing.

Kate dropped her head. In the past couple of years, she'd come to realise that her current role as Senior Investigating Officer in the MIT was where her talents lay. A step up would put her in a position that was purely administrative and she didn't want that. Even though the job and the responsibilities that came with it had come between them, Jo understood that Kate preferred to be hands-on, working with a great bunch of detectives who gelled as a team and looked after one another.

Jo felt it too . . .

On days off, they both missed the camaraderie within the office environment: Robbo's tales of his five-year-old son, brimming with hilarious questions; Carmichael and Brown's constant music debates; Maxwell's attempts at political correctness that fell woefully short of their target; Hank cracking them up with his friendly sarcasm. When Kate was at work, she valued Jo's unparalleled input as a criminal profiler, but it was their after-hours relationship that got her up in the morning.

The rest was meaningless.

'The team send their best,' Bright said quietly.

'I don't need their best. I have Hank. I have you.'

'Kate—'

'Don't you dare. Don't you *bloody* dare.' She turned away, looking out of the window, avoiding everyone around her. When she turned round, Bright was staring at her.

'I'm tired. What do you want, guv?'

'A straight answer would do for starters.' He dropped his voice to a whisper. 'I'm not pissing about here, Kate. Do you really think you're fit enough to investigate this plane crash?'

'Yes,' she snapped. 'And, coming from you, that sounds like a joke.'

'Except this is no laughing matter, is it? You were jumpy in the street—'

'So? You should try being a woman out in the dark sometime. It sucks.'

'It's unlike you, is all I'm saying—'

'How the hell would you know? You think because I'm a copper, trained to handle myself, I don't have the same concerns as any other female on the planet? Think again.'

'Kate, calm the fuck down. I'm worried about you, that's all. Didn't you ask me if I was fit for work when the roles were reversed? When Stella died, I seem to remember you telling me to ease up, seek professional help even.'

'And did you listen?'

'No, but—'

'There you go then. The roles aren't reversed. No partner died here, not until I say so. What would you have me do, Phil? Suck it up, go home and sit by the bedside of a sick man who can barely look at me and has taken twenty years to even tolerate the way I run my life? I'm on top of this, so either have me arrested for impersonating a police officer or back the hell off.'

Kate's jaw was rigid.

'All right, have it your own way, but don't come crying to me if you fall apart. Whatever you do for Torres, I expect you to support Robbo—'

'I said I would, didn't I?'

'Just so you know that you're no longer a spectator. You have the opportunity to collaborate on one of the most important and wide-ranging investigations you will ever come across. If this is the way you pay homage to Jo . . .' He lifted a hand, cutting off her attempt to interrupt. 'That's all well and good. As I told Torres, it makes your contribution all the more personal, but know this: you are in for the duration. There's no backing out later. So, if your answer is a categorical, no holds barred "yes" and you wish to continue with this madness, then make some noise and leave.'

'Fine!' Kate may have raised her voice, but this was no act for fellow diners. She meant it. Her chair scraped across the floor as she pushed it away from the table, grabbed her bag and stood up.

She couldn't wait to end their conversation.

Bright put on his best regretful face. 'Lou, don't do this.'

Taking out his wallet, he threw a bundle of notes on the table, flashing his cash for a reason, then hurried off after her. The businessman with money to burn and the woman with the fiery temper would be remembered if Kate had to prove she was who she said she was down the line.

42

Without access to her phone, Kate hadn't been able to call Robbo and find out how things were progressing at home. To do that, she'd have to retrieve the device from Hank. The sooner the better. If he'd spoken to Carmichael, Robbo probably knew the score by now. On second thoughts, she didn't think so. He'd have been in touch if he had.

Kate began her shift at six a.m. As she worked, she continued to watch the baggage handlers she had concerns about, their names firmly imprinted on her memory, though no longer visible on her forearm. At every opportunity they gathered in a huddle, casting an occasional glance in Hank's direction, keeping an eye on him as he ushered others into his office for interview. More importantly, from her perspective, if anyone official arrived, the three under observation would quickly separate. Had they conspired to bring down 0113?

One of them looked over.

She turned away, hauling another bag off the conveyor belt, the constant stream of luggage passing through the strip curtain setting in motion a memory. Having disembarked from a flight from Reykjavik to Edinburgh, she and Jo had been first to arrive in baggage reclaim when Kate spotted a lone bag going round and round on the carousel. After three revolutions, other passengers began arriving, small children among them. One or two became nervous as they looked on. Kate had called security and the hall was cleared, dog handlers arriving soon after to examine the suspicious item. A false alarm as it turned out, a weary passenger from an earlier flight having left the airport without collecting the bag.

Kate picked up yet another suitcase, this one wrapped in cellophane. In her peripheral vision, someone caught her eye. She knew furtive criminal activity when she saw it. The guy may as well have been waving a red flag. A Metropolitan Police Technical Support Unit had rigged up extra CCTV, but the bastard Kate was watching obviously knew where the cameras were.

How he'd found out was anyone's guess.

Withdrawing behind a pillar, she continued to observe him. He looked over his shoulder surreptitiously, using a master key to unlock an expensive-looking case. He rifled through it, took out something small and shoved it in his jacket pocket. The thought that he could just as easily have put something in made Kate want to rip his head off. As he relocked the case and moved on to the next, Kate took out her phone and pressed record.

She'd bank this.

Before her lunch break, Kate sent Hank a **Miss U lots** text. They rendezvoused at the café in Hounslow twenty minutes later, Kate explaining why she'd summoned him, making it her priority to share the news of Nikolaev's murder, stressing the need for him to keep in constant contact with Robbo in the Northumbria incident room. Hank was as worried as she was when she divulged the victim's name. Whoever had taken Nikolaev out would now be a target.

A turf war back home was all they needed.

Next, she showed Hank the short video she'd taken of the thief in the baggage shed, copying it to him, then deleting it from her phone. For evidential purposes, she shouldn't do it, but had no other choice in case she was caught with it in her possession. 'Whatever security measures are in place, they're not good enough. He's dodgy, and systematic.'

'What about the other three you queried?'

'I've watched them like a hawk.' She paused. 'They all speak English as well as we do and yet they're using a foreign language. One of them has a West Country accent. He's IC1 male, so it begs the question, where did he learn it? Obviously,

I can't tell what they're saying but I'll sure as hell find out. Wearing a wire is risky, but I need a listening device in there.' She checked her watch. 'I've got to run. You know what to do.'

43

As a detective of longstanding, Hank had learned to overlook a small offence in order to uncover a much larger one. Knowledge was power. He identified the offender Kate had seen from his personnel record as Thomas (Tommy) Patterson, forty-two years of age, married with three kids, living in Stanwell, a place Hank had never heard of. According to Somi Haq in HR, he'd been given a verbal warning for not pulling his weight and another for swearing at a female supervisor. He'd regret it if he had a go at Kate.

When she gave Hank the nod at the end of her shift, he locked his office, trailing Patterson from the terminal building to the staff car park, catching up with him as he blipped the locks of an old Audi with his key fob, the vehicle winking at him as he opened the door.

'Mr Patterson? Can I have a word?'

Startled, the guy swung round, his left elbow resting on the top of the car door. Hank had no need to identify himself. The man knew who he was from their earlier interview: a DS from the Casualty Bureau, or so he thought, a copper throwing his weight around.

Patterson looked like he was going to leg it. Let him try. He was red-faced, overweight, a beer-belly obscuring his waistband, legs like tree trunks. He wouldn't get far. Hank might be a big bugger but he was lightning fast. A rugby tackle would take him down.

'You and I need a chat,' he said.

'We had a chat.'

'We need another.'

Patterson was a Londoner, born and bred. Hank could tell by his attitude that this wasn't the first time he'd been questioned by the law for wrongdoing, though he'd gone through the normal CRB checks before gaining employment at Heathrow. He'd worked at the airport for several years and was probably due a review. Hank made a mental note to nudge Somi Haq.

'What's your problem?' Patterson asked.

'My "problem" is you weren't entirely honest with me during your interview. It seems you left a few details out—'

'So, recall me . . .' He was getting ready to climb in and drive away. 'I'm on earlies tomorrow.'

Hank stepped forward, an iron grip preventing the car door from closing. 'I'd rather do it now.'

'I'm not talking to you out here. I'm in a hurry, mate. Need to collect my lad from footy training—'

'He might be waiting a while.'

'He's thirteen!'

'Make a call by all means. I hate to come between father and son, but you're going nowhere until I say so. Do you really want your colleagues to see you hauled in for a second interview? They might form the impression that you're under suspicion. Won't win you any friends, given the reason I'm here, will it?'

Patterson didn't respond.

Hank continued: 'When we spoke yesterday, you said you were aware of things going missing in the baggage shed, not that you were responsible.'

'Fuck off!'

'That I can do – in exchange for information.'

Nervously, Patterson scanned the car park. Their conversation had not gone unnoticed. He turned back, facing his accuser. 'What information?'

'First things first.' Hank took out his phone, showed Patterson the video Kate had taken in the loading bay, the one in which he played a starring role. 'Stunning quality, don't you think?' It clearly showed him using a master key to rifle through a number of suitcases. 'Not so cocky now, are you? Hiding the key behind the pipe was clever. It wouldn't do to be found with it in your possession. Let me guess, spot searches aren't as regular as they used to be. No one has the time these days, especially now. If I was to search you – and you know I have grounds – I'm betting I'd find something that doesn't belong in your pocket.'

'I want my brief.'

'All in good time.'

'I'm saying bugger all till he gets here.'

'Relax, Tommy. I'm not interested in your petty thieving. When I've got what I want, you can continue on your merry way. As I said, I want information. We both know what I mean by that.'

Patterson was sweating now, avoiding the looks of other baggage handlers as they made their way to their vehicles. He pushed his hands deep into the pockets of his donkey jacket. 'S'pose I could give you five minutes.'

'That's very sensible.'

'And if I give you a name, then what?'

'Let's see how good your info is first, eh? For all I know you're a generous man who lent his ID to the wrong person in exchange for cash . . . someone with a bomb timed to go off over the Atlantic . . .' Sucking breath in through his teeth, Hank shook his head, a grave expression on his face. 'Conspiring to commit mass murder would send you down for life. Your kid'll have to find his own way home from footy training until he's about forty, forty-five. Start talking.'

'You're taking the piss, right?'

'I can assure you, I'm deadly serious.'

'No, look, you're barking up the wrong tree. God's 'onest, I had fuck all to do with that crash. What do you take me for? I'm a dad, not a terrorist. There were kids on that flight.'

Hank let him sweat.

'This is bullshit! I swear, you got the wrong geezer. If there's anyone in that line you need to speak to, it's Bakr. He's crazy, and so is his brother. It wouldn't surprise me if they were both Al-fucking-Qaeda. It's not me you want, it's them. I said the same thing to my missus when that plane went down. Bet they were laughing their cocks off. I hate working with them.'

Patterson was scared, too lazy to run, or so Hank thought. Except he did run, bolting towards the exit gate. Hank took off after him, lunging for him, felling him. The runner crashed to the ground, squealing as he hit the deck. He scrambled to get away, but Hank managed to get a purchase on one leg. Patterson kicked out with the other, catching the detective sergeant full in the face, stunning him, bloodying his nose. Throwing himself forward, Hank grabbed hold of him a second time. There was no comparison in size. Hank was too much for him. Patterson was overpowered in seconds.

Trying to focus, Hank wiped blood and snot from his face, wincing as he stood up, the arm around Patterson's neck applying gentle pressure, limiting his air supply. Hank tasted blood as it ran down the back of his throat. He swung Patterson round, eyeballed him. 'You know what? If you'd been a bog-standard tea leaf, I might've let you get away with your thieving in exchange for useful information. Don't suppose the airport pays much. The problem is, you're not only a thief, you're a foul-mouthed racist.' He held up his phone. 'This video is going to come in handy. By the way, I make a cracking witness. You're nicked, mate.'

'You said you'd look the other way.'

'I lied.'

44

Kate met with her contact in the designated hotel room as per Torres's instructions. The man was about forty: clean-shaven, shorter than her at five ten, with dark, wavy hair, cut short. He introduced himself as Agent Garcia – no forename – then immediately requested her mobile in order to set her up with a covert listening device that would transmit conversations directly from the baggage shed, which would be monitored round the clock, by him or someone like him.

Kate looked on as he got to work.

In the UK and the US, there were regulations governing the use of such devices. Eavesdropping on private conversations was frowned upon, but security and safety were paramount. Kate agreed with the sentiment. Those who sought to destroy lives had no right to privacy. If the three men she was interested in turned out to be innocent, that was unfortunate.

The idea rankled, but only slightly . . .

Innocent until proven guilty had always been her watchword, but when it came to major disasters across international boundaries, no individual was above suspicion. Having lost flight crew and witnessed the devastating fallout of what was being regarded by most commentators as a deliberate terrorist attack, honest workers would understand that law enforcement agencies were trying to save lives. That was her take on it. Under the circumstances – and with the potential of a second attack – she couldn't see it any other way.

Garcia stood up. 'Your cell is done, ma'am.'

'Great.' She was about to tell him to drop the formality and call her Kate, but decided against it. He may only be aware of her cover name: Lou Paige. The fewer people that knew who she really was, the better.

He handed over her mobile. 'You want to talk to Torres now?'

A nod. 'You've met her?'

'Yes, ma'am. I've had the pleasure.'

He turned away, killing the conversation dead. No offence was meant and none was taken. Kate knew the score. Garcia was closed off, disinterested in continuing the dialogue. He'd respond if she needed help, that was a given. He wouldn't speak, smile or engage, unless she had intelligence to pass on. Her security and safety was his sole consideration.

Slipping her phone into her pocket, Kate wandered over to the window, looking down over a leafy park, still mulling this over in her mind. Garcia didn't want to get to know her, find out that her father was sick or discover the nature of her relationship with someone she might have lost on board Flight 0113. He wanted to do his job. Period.

That suited her – she was in no mood for small talk.

Years of experience had taught her identical traits. It was enough to know that they were unified in the fight for justice. It was the same in her home force. If she called in a firearms team, she might never have clapped eyes on them, but knew that they would be on the same page when they arrived. That was why centralised training was important. It could be said of any department, the Casualty Bureau included. They worked in a uniform way, regardless of location, so that when resources were sent – 'mutual aid' as it was called – two disparate groups could merge seamlessly into one, a common goal uniting them. This was also true higher up the chain of command. From the top down they should, in theory, fit like a glove. Technology had followed suit. HOLMES was a quick and effective computerised tool providing access to information. You couldn't, nor should you, bastardise the system in order for it to work for a local force. It was a national resource, capable of handling major incidents and major disasters with the added benefit of being able to record data from the likes of Interpol.

'Ma'am?'

Garcia's voice cut into her thoughts. Kate turned from the window. He stood up, a nod to the chair he'd vacated, or more accurately to the monitor on the desk in front of it.

'Special Agent Torres is online.'

Moving to the desk, Kate sat down to talk to her US contact face-to-face, the same arrangement as before where they could talk in confidence. Torres had no further information to give in terms of wreckage recovery; either that or she was keeping it to herself. She looked weary, as Kate was feeling.

'How's it going your end?' Torres asked.

She didn't know the half of it.

Kate never mentioned helping Robbo with the investigation into Nikolaev's death. Torres would drop her like a stone if she did. Instead she filled her in on Hank's arrest of Patterson. 'Bakr, the guy he pointed the finger at, isn't one of the three suspicious characters I've been observing. According to my 2ic, he's a friendly, hard-working family man with an unblemished personnel record. Then again,' she warned, 'he hasn't been at Heathrow long and fits the profile of a clean skin.'

'He's not known to MI5?'

'No, I checked.'

Slipping on a pair of tortoiseshell specs, Torres asked for Bakr's full name, date of birth and last known address, scribbling the details down as Kate read them out. The agent's gaze dropped. Kate could hear her typing. Torres studied the screen, then looked up. 'He's not on my system either. Keep on it. We'll check him out, along with the other three you mentioned. Good luck your end. If you need anything, Garcia has your six.' The screen went dead.

45

With a stony expression on his face, Hank lifted his cup, eyeing the man sitting opposite. Euan Chadwick was around fifty years of age, grey-haired, with a five o'clock shadow and dark circles under his eyes. The detective sergeant was about to add to them. This wasn't a friendly ten-minute break with a fellow professional, it was a head-to-head exchange. Serious complaints were on the agenda with a senior security official whose job it was to police the airport and keep the public safe.

Hank hadn't even got to the good bit yet.

'I arrested Tommy Patterson for thieving,' he said. 'He'll be charged with that, and the added offences of resisting arrest and assaulting police.'

'That looks painful.' Chadwick was pointing at Hank's facial injuries.

'It is. The bastard nearly broke my nose.'

'You can prove theft?'

'Conclusively. He was seen with a universal master key, capable of opening checked bags without passengers being present or ever knowing anyone had been inside. I have a video to prove it. He's savvy enough to identify the locks he can gain access to, so not a full set of keys, only one, though officers are currently searching his home to see what else he has in his possession. He's been cautioned for arguing with a supervisor but has never been stopped by one. At the very least, that's shoddy security practice. Doesn't that concern you?'

Chadwick shifted uncomfortably in his seat. 'It does, but I can assure you that the key will not have come from us.'

'You sure about that? This guy helps himself whenever the fancy takes him.'

'Can I see it? The key, I mean.'

Hank shook his head. 'It's gone off for forensic examination. And it is one of yours. I checked in with Customs when I retrieved it.'

Chadwick took a deep breath. 'I don't know what to say.'

Hank showed him the video Kate had taken in the baggage shed, zooming in as far as he was able to show Patterson with the key in question.

The security official's expression darkened. 'Looks like one of ours.'

'I told you it was.'

'You live in Newcastle, Hank?'

'Yeah, why d'you ask?'

'Heathrow is the size of a small city. We try very hard to stay on top of breaches like this. I'm not making excuses. Believe me, if I could offer up a defence to cover myself I would. What you have to realise is that as soon as these keys were made, a new system in place, there were those looking to have them mass-produced in order to make money.'

'No lock is pick-resistant.'

'That's exactly it. BMWs are hard to steal, mate. Porsches even harder, but not for a clever criminal. Profit and ingenuity go hand in hand.'

Hank couldn't argue with that statement – criminals of the type they were discussing weren't called 'organised' by accident – but he did it anyway. 'With respect, that's no comparison. Car theft is a criminal offence, of course, but we're talking about the means and the opportunity to cause mass murder. It's hardly the same thing.'

'Was there anything else?' Chadwick asked. 'I hate to push you out, but I'm busy.'

'As it happens, so am I. This morning, I arrested another baggage handler who walked through security with an old pass, when a new one was issued less than three weeks ago, a replacement for one that was supposedly lost. He didn't have the new one on his person and couldn't explain where it is now. How can that happen? Surely you delete old ID when you issue a new one?'

'That's the rule.'

'Well, clearly someone can't read. Listen, it happens in my own organisation, I get that. I don't want to make waves or tell you how to do your job, but you need to get on top of this, Euan. There are hundreds of lives at stake here. This is not a minor security blunder, it's a fucking disgrace.'

'Don't I know it.' Chadwick looked away.

Hank almost felt sorry for the guy. 'It's not you I have a problem with. It's the casual way in which some of your lot seem to approach their jobs that's pissing me off, as if a breach of security is a foregone conclusion, something to be tolerated, rather than prevented. It's depressing.'

'Are we done?'

'Not quite.'

Hank had been thinking about Kate a lot since she'd gone undercover. She was still hanging onto hope, wanting to believe that Jo was still breathing. Until she knew, either way, she was stuck in limbo. Not knowing was destroying her. He wanted to end her misery and, with her back turned, he had the time and space to make enquiries on his own initiative, even though the likely outcome was not one she hoped he might find.

Chadwick might help, if Hank played his cards right.

Reining in his frustration, he asked: 'Mind if I run a scenario by you in relation to Flight 0113?'

'Sure. It might not feel like it, but we're all on the same side here.'

'One of Northumbria's criminal profilers was booked to fly, a connecting flight from the north-east.'

'That's tough. I didn't know.'

'Her name was Jo Soulsby.' Hank cleared his throat. 'Her

sons are past themselves – as we all are. Anyway, I know this is a long shot, but I have reason to believe that she was in two minds about travelling.'

'Then she'd have been in touch, surely.'

'You'd have thought so.'

Chadwick's expression screamed: *she's gone, mate. Let it go.*

Hank held his gaze, half expecting to be told that he was deluding himself. He wasn't. Kate was doing that all by herself. Hank kept her name out of it. Until she came to her senses, he'd push on and ask his questions. 'Humour me for a few moments longer. I arrived the morning the plane went down and questioned ground crew. When I caught up with Adriana Esposito, she wasn't very forthcoming. She told me that a couple of passengers didn't board but was unable to ID our profiler as one of them.'

'Why did you think she would?'

'We questioned her very soon after. I was hoping she'd remember.' Hank paused. 'I understand that my colleague was one of the last to pass through the gate. I gather there was a delay, and then a mad rush to get everyone on board so the pilot didn't lose his slot. Understandable, but I was told by someone else that as the final two female passengers entered the tunnel, one of them threw a bit of a wobbler – a fear of flying, according to my source. Apparently, the other went to her aid because she was hyperventilating. Jo has no flight phobia but she is definitely the type to help another passenger in distress.' Hank took a breather. 'This is purely conjecture but I wonder if, in that moment of hesitation, my colleague changed her mind about travelling. If that *was* the case and she'd cleared security, she'd have been escorted landside with the woman who was ill—'

'Can I stop you there for a second?' Chadwick looked decidedly uncomfortable, like he knew something Hank didn't and wasn't sure how to put it into words. 'You've been given a bum steer, mate.'

'What do you mean?'

'Only one passenger didn't board.'

'Are you sure?'

A nod.

Accessing his keyboard, Chadwick began typing. 'Esposito reported a potential medical risk. It was touch and go whether they would allow the sick passenger on. Those scared of flying can cause anxiety to others if they lose control.' His eyes flicked to the screen in front of him. 'In this case, they passed her as fit to travel, but she decided against. One of my team was dispatched to escort her landside.'

Hank swallowed the bile in his throat. The chance of Jo not travelling had just been cut by 50 per cent. 'You wouldn't happen to know the name of the passenger escorted landside, would you?'

'Aren't you Casualty Bureau?'

Hank needed that name. 'Yeah, but I'm not Met Police. I'm an outsider, which means I'm a thick Geordie who pulled the grunt work, interviewing workers in the baggage shed. I'm not allowed out until I'm done.' He failed to mention that he already was.

A beat of time.

'You didn't hear this from me.' Chadwick sat forward, pulling his computer keyboard closer.

Hank was unable to see what he typed into his system. He was now the one hyperventilating, still reeling from the disclosure that only one woman on the manifest didn't board. For Kate's sake, he hoped that the name the security manager was searching for would be Jo's. Over his shoulder, a printer spewed out a sheet of A4, including a woman's name and address, together with the scan of a cancelled boarding card, timed and dated after 0113 took to the skies.

46

Before Hank passed on the identity of the woman who didn't travel, he arranged to meet someone from Air Traffic Control to corroborate the information. His name was Chris Mahoney, a mild-mannered man with a mop of grey hair and pewter-rimmed specs to match. Calm and trustworthy were the two adjectives that passed through the detective's head as they took a seat in a tiny side office. The desk was ordered, much like Kate's adjoining the major incident room at her Newcastle base. Mahoney either hated clutter or believed, as Kate did, that a ship-shape desk was halfway to a tidy mind.

He'd already done his homework.

Lifting an A4 sheet from his desk, Mahoney handed it to Hank, a sheepish look on his face. The reason for that became immediately apparent as the detective scanned the document. Many lines of the text had been redacted from the transcript of the flight log.

'That's it?'

'The part I'm authorised to share,' Mahoney said. 'I can't impress on you how confidential it is. You'll appreciate why I can only supply you with this section of the dialogue. To give you any more at this stage of the investigation would be inappropriate.'

A nod from Hank.

Mahoney's department were in the thick of it. Anyone with a connection to Flight 0113 would be questioned at length. It was his duty to safeguard the information in his possession. If it fell into the wrong hands he'd be for the high jump. It would do untold damage to the investigation currently being put together by aviation authorities on both sides of the Atlantic. The intercourse between the captain and first officer

– before and after the plane left the ground – would form part of a top level and far-reaching criminal investigation should it turn out to be terrorist-related. All indications were heading in that direction.

Hank reread the document, immediately noticing that the delay was confirmed in a conversation between British pilot Matthew Wilkins and the control tower. Tapping the report, he said: 'This will go no further.' The medical risk Chadwick had talked about was now confirmed.

As he left Heathrow, Hank sent a text: **There's nowt on TV. Fancy a pint?**

A reply: **Ten, fifteen minutes suit?**

Perfect.

Kate wouldn't question why he wanted to see her. She'd be making the assumption that he'd got through his list of interviewees, that there was news of Nikolaev from Northumbria MIT, that he was missing her company or was merely thirsty. If his life depended on it, he'd never turn down the opportunity to sink a pint of John Smith's.

On his way to the pub, Hank was at his wit's end. How would he break the news when every sentence he formulated in his head was guaranteed to fell her in a way that no other had? However hard it would be, he'd decided to get it over with and stick with her tomorrow when they were both off duty.

As her 2ic, Hank was conflicted. He had a dual role: supporter and protector to a boss who was in a state, mired in the kind of trouble that could seriously damage her reputation, in the middle of an undercover assignment. His first thought was to contact Bright and beg him to pull her out. That would be the sensible option. But ratting on Kate to their guv'nor would be the ultimate betrayal, not to mention a potential career-ending fuck-up.

Kate had always kept her personal struggles to herself.

She'd lived in the hinterland between happy and sad, until she discovered a love she never imagined was for her, one that felt right. And yet she'd allowed her job to dominate her time. Long hours. Harrowing cases. Her appointment as SIO taking up much of her life. Consequently, she was never as close to Jo as she should've been.

Hank had been there, too, with Julie.

He understood.

Policing provided both detectives with structure where there were clear lines, boundaries and the security they needed. While Hank had put his own house in order, Kate's private life remained a tangle of uncertainty. Relationships outside of work had been formed, but the office environment allowed for them to be kept at arm's length. That suited her perfectly. Having built a wall around herself, it was hard to let Jo pull it down . . .

And now it was too late to reconsider her options.

Hank's thoughts swung wildly between paradoxical arguments: the need to look out for her and his duty to safeguard a high-level potential terrorist investigation. He knew which way it would go if Bright got a whiff of this. After Stella's death, he was a man who understood loss, but he'd make the right decision and withdraw his support, leaving Torres with no choice but to take Kate off the case. With Jo gone, if they pulled her out now – and they would if she was on the brink of compromising an undercover op – it would curtail her autonomy and take away the one thing she had left to live for.

And now Hank was about to throw her under a bus.

47

Hank's smile was forced as he entered the pub, the door swinging shut behind him. Kate was waiting, leaning with her back against the bar. She looked dreadful, having ignored his advice to take care of herself. Since arriving in the capital, she'd averaged around three hours' sleep a night. Everything she'd eaten, she'd thrown up. In a matter of days, her clothes were too big, flecks of grey appearing in her hair. She turned forty-six months ago and had told him that the last time she caught her reflection in a mirror, she hardly recognised herself. Tomorrow she'd be worse.

'What are you having?' she asked.

'The usual.' He needed Dutch courage to ease the way.

She ordered the drinks and pointed to a table in the corner.

'Mind sitting out?' He couldn't risk talking to her in a public place. 'I need some air.'

They moved to the pub's beer garden. It was empty, but then Hank knew that, having checked it out before going inside. They sat down in the covered area, out of the wind. He was on edge, but she seemed not to notice, merely asked about the injury to his face.

He explained about his scrap with Patterson in Heathrow's staff car park, a delaying tactic while he replayed his conversations with Chadwick and Mahoney in his head. He hadn't told a soul that all hope of finding Jo was in the wind. Kate had to be the first to know. It was killing him to be the death messenger. He didn't want the job and would have done anything to get out of it, but under the circumstances, who else was there?

Do it! Get it over with.

Now she noticed his anxiety. 'Hank? What is it?'

He hesitated, sickened by the reaction he might get. He imagined tears, a right hook even. It wouldn't be the first time a grieving loved one had taken a swing at him. News like this destroyed people. Some didn't recover.

Kate never would.

He took a deep breath. 'It's not good—'

'I can see that,' she said.

'I'm so sorry, but I now have conclusive proof that Jo was on that plane.'

Kate froze. Of all the things Hank might have said, she hadn't expected him to confirm her worst fears. A week ago, by no stretch of the imagination was she in a happy place; her father was gravely ill, Jo had taken off for JFK without her, but her murder case was solved and the rest could be fixed. She thought that her life was going one way and, in the blink of an eye, everything changed.

'That's impossible.' She shook her head. 'It's too early for proof—'

'Don't do this, Kate. Why would I tell you if I wasn't sure?'

She glared at him, heart beating faster.

'There's no doubt,' Hank added. 'I met with Euan Chadwick, the security manager, before I left Heathrow. He told me that only one woman missed the flight, not two as we'd been led to believe. It was a medical issue, confirmed by the transmission between pilot and ground crew before take-off—'

'How does that change anything? Do you *ever* listen? I told you she'd be last to board. You need to stop jumping to conclusions.' Kate refused to accept his word, guilt that she'd let her relationship with Jo slide driving her point of view. She simply couldn't give up on her now. To do so would mean acknowledging that the ghost of a chance to put things right was beyond reach.

'I've had enough,' Hank said. 'However unpalatable, you need to own this and move on. I realise how hard that is for you, and how you don't want to accept it, but I can't help that. A woman took ill before boarding. She was cleared to fly, then changed her mind and was escorted landside by security.'

'I want the fucking proof!'

Hank lost it then. 'You want it? Well, here it is.'

He stood up, took something from his pocket and threw it down on the table. Kate felt her face crumple as she read it. It was a cancelled boarding card, clear-cut evidence that a woman called Elaine Hayes had been taken landside, not Jo.

Suddenly, a light came on in Kate's head. Seeing Hank so distraught and angry was gut-wrenching, but she wasn't finished yet. Appreciation of his point of view didn't equal concurrence. Far from resigned to Jo's fate, she challenged him on the subject. 'Did you actually see the woman being escorted landside?'

'No.'

'Why not?'

'Because it would necessitate looking through hours of CCTV—'

Kate shot him a black look. 'You have something more important to do?' She ignored his wounded expression. 'So, instead, you decided to rush over here and feed me this garbage?' There was more than a hint of sarcasm to her voice.

'Fuck's sake, Kate, I only found out an hour ago.'

'Then until I've had eyes on that woman, *nothing* has changed.' She stood up, began pacing the garden, before turning to face him. 'You need to get your arse to Heathrow and secure that footage right now.'

The word 'ostrich' sprang to mind. Hank's head was pounding. The evidence was overwhelming and yet Kate was refuting it. On her game, rather than overwhelmed by grief, she wouldn't have. He was running out of ideas, patience and empathy. Suddenly the notion of a return to the North-East to help Robbo find Nikolaev's killer didn't sound so bad, but he had to get it through her thick head that this really was the end of the road. He understood her anguish, of course – she'd played a big part in Jo's departure from the UK and felt guilty for it – but what was done was done.

'Well?' She wouldn't let it go. 'What are you waiting for?'

'No,' he said. 'We're going to end this now.'

'Excuse me?' Her eyes were like saucers. 'In case you're in any doubt, that wasn't a request.'

A mobile – his or hers – vibrated in his back pocket. He took out both phones. Her device was showing a missed call from Carmichael. When Kate showed no enthusiasm for calling her back, Hank did it for her. What Lisa told him was impossible.

48

Hank wiped his face with his hand. Having gone ten rounds with Kate, he was beginning to feel punchy, struggling to process the information Carmichael had passed on. He took a long pull on his pint, a glance at Kate, she at him, a smouldering, simmering rage passing between them. He eyed the cancelled boarding card still in her hand, then walked away, turning his back on her.

'Say again, Lisa.'

Unaware of unfolding events in London, Carmichael sounded upbeat. 'I said, I just had a tip-off from Jo's service provider.'

'Yeah, I heard that bit.'

'Can you raise Kate and let her know?'

'She's with me now . . .' Hank turned to look at her. Kate was staring at him, rigid and grossly unhappy. No tears. Wishing she'd let go, he went back to his call. 'Switched on for how long?'

'Just a few minutes.'

'What of it?'

'"What of it?" Are you for real?'

'Means nowt, Lisa.'

'That's hardly the reaction I was expecting, Sarge. Are you OK? Is Kate?'

'Yes, no. There's stuff happening this end. I'll fill you in later. Before you go, I need a chat with Robbo about Nikolaev.' It was a heavy hint that the conversation was over.

'He's not in,' Carmichael said.

'Where is he?'

There was a pause, as if she was scanning the incident room to make sure. 'I don't know, to be honest. We're flat out this end but very excited by the news from EE, more than you appear to be.' Carmichael gave Hank more detail, including where Jo's mobile had been switched on, and the number it had been used to call. The longer she talked, the more worried he became. Given the boarding card still in Kate's hand, what Lisa was telling him made no sense. He was searching for an explanation and didn't find one.

'I don't want to raise expectations—'

'Neither should you.' Hank chose not to elaborate.

'Kate will be ecstatic when she hears the news though, won't she?'

Sidestepping her enthusiasm, he said: 'Tell Robbo I'll call him later.'

Hanging up, he walked back to Kate, asking her to sit down and finish her drink. He knew that when he shared Carmichael's news, Kate would go off on one, despite conclusive proof to the contrary.

She didn't disappoint. Hope once again took a stranglehold. Her eyes were on fire, desolation replaced by optimism.

Worrying.

'The phone alert is meaningless . . .' Hank said. 'You said yourself that her mobile was probably stolen. Some arsehole could be messing with it.'

'Her device is password-protected.'

'Yeah, and we all know how secure that is, don't we?' It was a valid comment even if she didn't want to hear it.

'When was the phone switched on?'

'At three fifteen in the OX20 postcode.'

'Oxford?'

'Woodstock.'

'Jesus!' Kate felt like she might throw up. 'Jo booked a hotel there once. Another cancelled trip when I was called out to a crime scene before we were due to travel. This isn't over yet. Not by any stretch of the imagination.'

'You're talking bollocks.' Hank had to dissuade her from this madness. 'You know perfectly well how these things work. Steal a phone, discover the ID of its owner, pretend to find it, then hand it over for financial reward. Given the evidence on that boarding card, that's the only explanation.'

'Now who's using the evidence to fit their point of view?'

'I'm not. You asked for proof and now you have it. Kate, our lives are stored on our devices. We're prepared to pay to find them when they're lost. The thieving bastard probably pressed the last number redial to find out who it belonged to so he or she could make their play.'

'Who did it call, Hank?'

He didn't want to answer. The results of triangulation had thrown him. Carmichael was probably still wondering why such a monumental breakthrough hadn't hit the mark. Ordinarily he'd have been praising her for a job well done. Coming on the back of Chadwick's revelation, he hadn't. He hung up without thanking her. He was still trying to put the pieces together, assuming he could get a word in edgeways.

'Well?' Kate said.

He had to tell her. 'North Tyneside Hospital, a call lasting a few seconds only.'

'Would that be the same hospital where my old man is still a patient? I rest my case.'

Smug didn't suit her. It never had. Kate was desperate, willing to believe her own hype, clinging onto anything and everything that suited her. Unhealthy. For someone so logical, she was beyond reason. Never in his wildest had Hank imagined her reaching a state of such weirdness. 'Lisa checked in with the hospital,' he said, in a last-ditch attempt to win Kate over. He had to find a way. 'No one could remember the call or the caller, whether male or female. They don't log all enquiries.'

'She's alive, Hank.' Kate stood up. 'What are the chances of a thief ringing that number from a place Jo loves, one that I happen to know is on her wish list?'

Hank had no answer to that. He had to concede she had a point.

She gestured with her hand. 'Gimme the car keys. We need to get going. I think I know where Jo went today.'

'Kate, we can't—'

'We can and we will, or I'll go alone.' Another hand gesture. 'Keys! Hand them over. I'll grab an overnight bag and we'll call at the section house to collect your stuff. That way, we can travel tonight and get an early start in the morning.'

An arc of light took Hank's attention. Two men emerged from the pub, loitering in the doorway, lighting their cigarettes. They were out of earshot. Still, he lowered his voice. 'What if Torres tries to contact you?'

'She won't. We're state zero.'

'She might. You're undercover.'

Checking her phone, Kate looked up and said: 'It's an hour away, M4, M25, M40. We'll be there and back before she knows we're gone.'

'We don't even know what we're looking for.'

'You might not. I do. If I'm wrong, I'll work it out. If Torres gets in touch, I won't answer.'

'And if she calls me? What will I tell her?'

'Make something up.' She took in his exasperation. 'And, if you're uncomfortable lying for me, tell her the truth. I don't give a fat rat's arse any more.'

49

Reluctantly, Hank handed over her keys. They left the pub without seeing their drinks off. There was no changing Kate's mind. God knows, he'd tried reasoning with her. She was on a mission . . . again. Her rebelliousness had landed them both in hot water more than once, but where she led, he followed. Until she'd exhausted all possibilities, she wouldn't rest. Although he didn't voice his opinion, Hank thought that going off-piste during an undercover operation was bordering on suicidal. If Torres found out, Kate could kiss goodbye to the most high-profile investigation she'd ever work on.

It bothered him that everyone at base was now rooting for Jo, unaware that he had unequivocal proof that she was gone for good. Kate had forbidden him from contacting them. Investigating the call from Jo's phone was her sole focus. The rest could wait.

What was the harm? Hank thought. They had twenty-four hours to kill. Given that they were leaving the area, at least he would have the opportunity to keep tabs on her and cover her back so she didn't blow her cover. Already, Kate was in the zone, concentrating on the road ahead, a very different woman now that Carmichael had stuck her oar in. He couldn't help but admire Kate's ability to keep the faith, however misguided, and decided to let her follow her nose until she met a dead end, then support her afterwards.

As the miles flew by, she shared her plans to make enquiries at Blenheim Palace, the Duke of Marlborough's ancestral home.

'Why there?' He couldn't imagine.

'It was on Jo's bucket list, a stone's throw from Woodstock.' She grinned at him, the weirdness continuing. 'If her phone was switched on, pound to a penny that's where she was when she made the call.'

'*If* she made the call.'

'She made it.'

Crossing his arms, Hank wound his neck in, his thoughts turning to Jo. Offender profiling for the MIT had only been part of her job. The rest of the time she'd spent at the Regional Psychology Service, diagnosing and treating people whose mental health was skewed in some way, offering them alternatives to medication through psychotherapy. A few days ago, he'd been prepared to believe that she'd recognised this in herself since the breakdown of her relationship with Kate and was trying to heal herself through meditation or by taking spiritual guidance, but not now. She might disengage at times of stress, curl up and read a book, but any more than a few days of turning her back on the world was a stretch to anyone in their right mind. Unless she'd taken a temporary vow of silence, surely she'd have turned on a TV, picked up a newspaper or called her kids. When he pointed out that she'd done none of those things, Kate bit his head off.

He yawned, exhausted with the whole affair.

Acting on a single phone call lasting twenty-seven seconds, Kate's self-deception had returned. Even though he didn't share the view that her destiny wasn't quite as bleak as it was yesterday, she seemed to have regained good karma without the need to stop talking. She was making his head ache.

'I'm knackered and ravenous,' he said. 'Mind if we grab some food?'

'I'll pull over at the next services. I need a map, and I'm hungry too.'

He smiled for two reasons. One: were maps even a thing these days? Two: for the first time since they had arrived in the south of England, it seemed that Kate had an appetite. By the time they pulled over, he'd booked a Travelodge five miles from Woodstock where they would spend the night.

After their meal in the service station, Hank leaned back in his chair, slipping Kate's mobile from his pocket, sliding it across the table. 'Here, you'll need this tomorrow.'

'Ta . . .' Kate scooped it up. 'Nudge me to give it back when we return to London.'

'Fiona left a few texts,' he said.

'Any from my old man?'

'No, sorry.'

'Why? I'm not.' She was. 'What about emails?'

'There are a few, all work-related.'

She tapped her phone. 'Anything on here that needs my attention?'

'Depends—'

Kate licked cream from her upper lip. 'On what?'

He crossed his arms. 'Are we talking professional or personal?'

'What the hell does that mean?'

'Nothing.'

'Doesn't look like nothing.' Kate lowered her fork. He had something on his mind she wasn't certain she wanted to hear. 'Will you stop talking in code? Either make a statement or ask a bloody question. Which is it to be? I won't bite.'

'You might.'

'Well, give us a clue. I'm not a mind reader.'

'Professional, one of us needs to speak to Robbo ASAP. I think it would be better coming from you. He might think I have an axe to grind. Personal, why do you keep in touch with Fiona Fielding?'

'She's a mate. Why wouldn't I?' Kate narrowed her eyes. 'Have you been reading my texts?'

'No!'

Kate relaxed. Fiona got a bit racy occasionally. 'Hank, I have one judgemental dinosaur in my life already. I don't need, nor do I want, another.' When he didn't respond, she carried on.

'What is it about my relationship with her that bothers you so much?' She knew the answer even before she'd asked the question. His feelings for Jo ran deep. Consequently, he saw Fiona as a threat to her happiness. He'd never understood the complicated triangle, because he'd chosen not to.

Bored with the conversation, and minus an answer, Kate got to her feet, keen to crack on, but he wouldn't let it go as they wandered to her car, his gob going the whole time. 'Fiona's a free agent. Fair enough, I'm a bloke, I get that. You had a fling. I get that too, but why keep it going?'

'Quit while you're ahead, Hank. You're beginning to piss me off.' Kate stopped walking. 'You've made up your mind that Jo is history, so now you want to play the blame game. Isn't that what all this is about?' She didn't pause for breath. 'You're wrong if you think Fiona got in the way of my relationship with Jo. So now we've ruled her out, do you want to start on me?' A pause. 'Has it *ever* occurred to you that I might not be to blame for everything that went wrong between us? Can I help it if the job takes precedence? Can you?'

He didn't answer.

Kate said, 'It wasn't only work that stopped me sharing everything with Jo. She was pulling me one way, my old man the other. I didn't know what to do, Hank. Fiona was different, the only one who didn't put me under pressure. You can't pick people up and discard them at will. No matter what the future holds, she's important to me. I'll always care for her and we'll probably never lose touch, so get over it. For the record, she's not at fault here. When Jo and I were together, she steered clear. I saw her when I wanted to. *Want* being the operative word.'

'Why?'

'Because she's fucking irresistible.'

Hank didn't raise a smile. 'And lonely, don't forget lonely. She wants you at any cost. You're blind if you can't see it—'

'Well, she can have me now, can't she? Even if Jo is alive, she's not interested in continuing our relationship.' Kate threw him her car keys. 'Now drive!' Her good humour over supper had vanished.

50

At the Travelodge, Kate rang North Tyneside Hospital. Her father was doing well, was out of intensive care and on a general ward. It was too late to wake him. Kate punched in Fiona Fielding's number for the hell of it. The greeting she received was warm and friendly, a stark contrast to the ear-bashing she'd received from Hank earlier. There was no awkwardness, no prying. There were few women who could maintain a sense of humour in the face of such tragedy and not sound like they were trying to fill a vacancy. In a race for Kate's affections, Fiona would lose. Not only did she know it, she'd accepted it without argument, something that Hank never understood.

The artist had been good for Kate, her liberal attitude and love of life rubbing off whenever they were together. If she was in the UK, they'd arrange dinner and meet up. If she was on the other side of the world, exhibiting her artwork, she sent postcards; code for a rendezvous when she was in town and Kate was at a loose end.

It felt so right, and yet so wrong . . .

Kate had a bundle of the postcards in a drawer at home.

Hearing Fiona's voice, thinking about her, lifted Kate from the gloom that had dominated the past week. She wasn't – and never had been – in the market for a new girlfriend. Their relationship was what it was: a shoulder to cry on initially; the development of a deep and meaningful friendship that had taken them both by surprise.

Kate didn't mention that Jo might be alive, kicking around in Oxford.

She wouldn't, not until she was sure.

They said their goodbyes, then Kate called Robbo,

apologising for the late hour, offering help should he need it, without making it sound like she didn't think he was up to the job.

'How's it going?' she said.

'From the outset there was little to go on,' he said. 'Nikolaev was shot on his doorstep by a high-powered rifle at long range, surrounded by his bodyguards. Two heavies rushed him to hospital but he was in a bad way. The minute he was pronounced dead, they scarpered.'

'Yeah, Bright told me. They've not been seen since?'

'No, but we've nailed their vehicle as it pulled up at A&E. It's difficult to tell if anyone else was inside. We also have stills and video footage of them entering the hospital. According to SOCA, we're looking for two men, both Russian: Vasily Zhuk, thought to be Nikolaev's head of security, and Alexei Dobrynin, his personal protection officer. They didn't do a very good job.'

Kate was pleased to hear that the Serious Organised Crime Agency were sharing intel. 'If either of them saw the shooter they'll be as keen to find him as we are,' she said. 'Any idea what type of weapon was used?'

'High-powered rifle. That's all we have.'

'Let me know if that changes.'

'You've seen the crime scene photographs?'

'Yeah, that's quite a pile.' Nikolaev's home was a fine mansion house with south-facing views over the Ingram Valley, a property surrounded by heather-clad moorland. 'Do you know where the weapon was fired from?'

'We're working on it, Kate. The property is sealed off, flanked by trees on either side, providing cover for anyone lying in wait.'

'Anything incriminating inside?'

'No.'

'Figures. If you want to run anything by me, get in touch.'

'Appreciate the call, guv.'

Blenheim Palace was bathed in autumn sunshine, the grounds extending to over two thousand acres. Kate had seen pictures of the World Heritage Site, but no image could match the reality of seeing the monument up close. It was as huge as it was glorious. Without taking her eyes off it, she slipped her phone from her pocket and called the incident room. The phone was picked up immediately. DC Carmichael was on the ball, as always.

'Lisa, it's me.' Kate wasted no time. 'What's the position with Jo's Santander account?'

'No transactions of any kind, guv. I'm receiving hourly updates from the bank. Great news about the phone though, eh?'

'Absolutely. I'm checking it out now.'

'Do you think . . . what I mean is—'

'I know what you mean, Lisa. There's no news yet.' Kate didn't mention that Hank had written Jo off on the say-so of Chadwick, Heathrow's security manager, or that they had argued over it. 'I'll update you when I can.'

'Where are you?'

'Incommunicado.'

'Understood. Is Hank with you?'

'Yeah, he is, but since when do I need a babysitter?'

Carmichael laughed. 'He's your dad, isn't he?'

Kate turned. Hank was walking away. 'Don't ever let him hear you say that, Lisa. Not until you outrank him – and you will if I have anything to do with it – then you can call him whatever the hell you like.'

A chuckle from Carmichael didn't match the tone of her voice when she spoke. She was worried. 'The team send their best. We're hanging in here, all hoping . . .' She left the sentence unfinished.

'Keep the faith,' Kate said. 'Say hi from me and let me know if there's any news.'

Hanging up, she scanned the crowds for Hank. He was seated on a bench, head down, reading the information leaflet handed to him through the car window as they arrived. He hadn't paid an entry fee, just showed his warrant card. Official police business. No one queried it.

He looked up as she closed in. 'Any joy?'

A sombre shake of the head. 'Jo hasn't used her bank account, but that means very little in the scheme of things. She may still have chosen not to fly.'

'Kate, if Jo hasn't used her bank account—'

'Don't go there, Hank.'

'It wouldn't be smart to get your hopes up—'

'If you don't want to be here, say the word.'

He stopped trying to convince her that she was on a hiding to nothing. It would only end in another row. They both knew it. He held up the leaflet, telling her that to go over the place properly, they needed more boots on the ground, even though he knew perfectly well that they were on their own.

'Where do you propose we start searching this particular haystack?'

'I don't know, is the truthful answer . . .' She sat down, reading over his shoulder, then took the leaflet from him. On the front were images of the house and grounds, but it was the advisory strip at the bottom, offering an annual pass for the price of one entry, that piqued her interest. 'Unless . . .' She met his gaze. 'I have an idea. Come with me.'

51

Hank followed Kate to a ticket kiosk in the East Courtyard. When she got to the front of the queue, she asked to see whoever was in charge. The girl behind the counter politely asked why. On seeing Kate's warrant card, she eyed Hank, then made a call, asking the detectives to wait. Someone was on their way.

A few minutes later, a woman arrived, dark hair, worn loose, a friendly face. 'I'm Helen Dean. How can I help?'

'Pleased to meet you, Ms Dean. I'm Detective Chief Inspector Kate Daniels. This is my colleague, DS Hank Gormley.'

'Please, call me Helen.' Intrigued, she moved away from queuing customers who were earwigging on their conversation. 'People always get nervous when the police turn up, not that it happens often, you understand. Most people who come here are lovely. Is there a problem?'

'No,' Kate said. 'But I'd like some information and I'm hoping you might be able to provide it.'

'What do you need to know?'

'I understand that it's possible to convert an entry ticket to an annual pass for free, one with no limit on entry.'

'Yes, that's correct, so long as you have a receipt.' Helen pointed towards the kiosk. 'You can do that here or online within fourteen days if you prefer.' She stared into the middle distance. 'As you can see for yourselves, the estate is extensive. It's impossible to see it all on one visit.'

Having studied the visitor map and read the information leaflet while she waited in the queue, Kate understood why multiple trips to Blenheim might be necessary. The house, she imagined, was capable of handling only so many visitors at a time. It would be crammed most days, the state rooms in particular. Then there were the pleasure gardens, the various exhibitions, the Capability Brown landscaped gardens, the maze, all within walking distance. The list of interesting places to see went on and on.

She smiled at Helen. 'I could spend a fortnight here.'

The woman nodded. 'I've been here for twelve months and I've yet to see it all. Many people spend their whole annual leave here, especially our international visitors. They adore the grandeur of the palace. Their fascination with British aristocracy is never-ending. The Brits, on the other hand, can take it or leave it.'

'How exactly is the transfer done?'

'Sorry? I'm not following.'

From the look of him, neither was Hank.

Kate explained: 'I assume those taking up the offer of annual membership receive some kind of photo ID to ensure that memberships are not passed around randomly.' She could draw parallels with Heathrow.

'Exactly that,' Helen said. 'They're all logged, timed and dated.'

Hank had already caught up, though Kate could see from his expression that he still thought she was crazy. His lack of enthusiasm was beginning to irritate her. Ignoring his negativity, she refocused on Helen. If Jo had exchanged her ticket for a yearly pass, she'd done it since 18 October, possibly as recently as yesterday when her mobile was activated, not before Flight 0113 went down.

'Helen, if I were to give you a name, how soon could you search your database?'

'I could do it right away if that would suit.' She glanced at the busy kiosk. 'Actually, I can access it remotely from my office.' She swept a hand out. 'It's this way.' She threw Hank a half-smile. 'There's room for you too, if you'd like to join us.'

Hank made a move.

Kate didn't.

In her peripheral vision, she'd spotted a woman who was going through the upgrade process, having her photograph taken at the kiosk. She was issued with an annual pass straight away. As she walked towards them, she smiled.

Kate asked if she might examine it.

After a brief inspection of the lanyard around Helen's neck, the woman handed the ID card to Kate. It was similar to her police ID, only white where hers was blue. The size and material of a credit card, it had a gold image of Blenheim Palace at the top, the name of the adult pass-holder, a long series of letters and numbers, an expiry date of 23 October 2015, a barcode at the bottom, terms and conditions on the reverse side.

'Thanks, that's very kind.' Kate returned the pass. 'Have a lovely day.'

Helen Dean's office was situated behind the Visitor Centre where the Queen Pool was visible through the window, a far cry from the detectives' Wallsend base where any kind of view was non-existent. Kate was drawn to look outside. She imagined Jo wandering the grounds, loving it, even on her own. It was simply stunning. Not too busy either, despite the fair weather, which would suit Jo perfectly. She'd hate crowds.

The detectives accepted the offer of coffee, declining anything to go with it. Helen's assistant left the room to fetch it, then all three sat down. While they waited for their refreshments to arrive, Kate pinched a pad from Helen's desk, writing down the parameters for her search, itching to get going.

Helen logged on to her computer, loaded the page and was about to enter the search criteria, when the coffee arrived. The assistant handed them out then made herself scarce, closing the door behind her so they wouldn't be disturbed.

Helen looked over her right shoulder. 'What name am I looking for?'

Kate sat forward, on the edge of her chair. 'Josephine Soulsby.'

'Middle name?'

'None.'

Hank avoided eye contact with Kate as Helen's fingers flew over the keys. She pressed enter, waited a moment, then more typing. She swivelled the screen so that the detectives could see the negative result, shaking her head at the same time. 'As you can see, there have been no recent applications with that name.'

'Damn.' Kate's head went down, figuratively rather than literally, her hopes plummeting. She'd pinned them to this one lead. She was about to get up, when Hank spoke out.

'Try Josephine Stephens.' He explained that Jo was a widow.

Helen repeated the action.

It was worth a punt, but Kate didn't think it would lead anywhere. While Jo's sons, Tom and James, were born during her marriage to Alan Stephens, their mother had reverted to her maiden name when she separated from her philandering ex-husband, who'd since been shot dead in his Quayside apartment overlooking the River Tyne. Jo's official documents and bank accounts were all in her maiden name, a detail Hank was aware of.

Still, he was trying to show support.

Kate appreciated that.

The expression on Helen's face when she turned to face them was answer enough. 'Nothing recent, sorry.' She thought for a moment, then resumed typing, studying a list that popped up on screen. She shook her head. 'No joy . . . I've now searched the whole database. We have a number of members with the two surnames you gave me, but none matching the forename Jo or Josephine, and there are no recent applications. Could it have been completed online at an earlier time?'

'Unlikely,' Kate said. 'She wasn't intending to come here when she set off from home.'

'Where is home?'

'The outskirts of Newcastle.'

Helen asked for the full address and postcode.

Kate gave it. Seconds later, her worst fears were realised – another nil return. She couldn't get out of there fast enough. She stood up, extending a hand to Helen, thanking her for her time. Hiding her bitter disappointment, Kate left the office with a bleeding heart. Hank's haystack had grown. The chances of finding the needle contained therein was zero.

Hank caught up with her outside. Kate was a mess, as expected, standing with her back to the warm palace wall, looking to the horizon, a wistful expression on her face, as if she might spot Jo walking across the extensive South Lawn. He didn't say anything, just placed a gentle hand on her shoulder and gave it a squeeze. What could you say to someone hell-bent on an impossible quest? Kate was so sad, so blinded by love, she stonewalled every counter-argument he put forward, unable to recognise her obsession.

She took off.

Where she was heading was anyone's guess. Hank hoped that she'd make for the car and stop buggering about. The fresh air might do her good. He soon realised that this was no ordinary walk in the park; it was a fast-paced charge. She was on a deadline, due at Heathrow by morning. If she didn't make it, Torres, Waverley and Bright would be queuing up to show her the door. Before they reached the car, she pulled up, turning to face him, signalling her intention to keep on with her search, whether he liked it or not.

He didn't.

Not only was he out of breath, he was bereft of ideas, unable to stop her futile search for a dead woman.

'Will you cheer up?' she barked. 'She's around here somewhere.'

'Kate, you heard Helen. There's no proof that—'

'Yet. There's no proof yet.' She met his gaze defiantly. 'I accept that Jo didn't convert her ticket, but you saw the queue at the kiosk. If it was that bad yesterday, she might not have bothered. It doesn't mean she wasn't here.' She paused. 'Are you going to help me find the evidence, or stand around with your hands in your pockets, moaning like a rookie on a first assignment because it didn't fall in your lap without you lifting a finger? You're a detective. Try acting like one.'

'Know what? I'm beginning to think that you're a sadist as well as a masochist.'

At last, a smile . . .

It didn't linger. Kate was on point, except he didn't think she actually had one. She was her own worst enemy, unable or unwilling to extricate herself from the guilt she was feeling, fighting with everyone who got in her way, including him.

It was driving him mad.

Sensing his irritation, she climbed down, apologising for having disrespected him. 'Hank, I went too far. It was unfair and uncalled for. There's not a polis alive I'd rather have by my side. All I'm asking is that you stop giving me grief. I promise I'll drop this if we don't find her today.'

'You said that out loud. You've never kept a promise in your life!'

Wounded, she stepped away.

He'd touched a nerve.

Kate was well aware that she was pushing him in a direction he didn't want to go, but he might as well have said: *isn't that why we're here, because you let people down?*

Like her, a moment ago, he was wishing he could take it back. 'Kate, I didn't mean—'

'No, you're right. I deserved that. I have broken promises. God knows I'm paying for it, but this is one I intend to keep.'

'Honestly?'

She gave a three-finger salute. 'Scouts' honour. Twenty-four hours, that's all I'm asking.'

'You're the boss.'

Hank was hoping, praying, that once she returned to London and immersed herself in work, she'd be so engrossed in the fight against terrorism, she'd forget this nonsense and keep that promise.

There was more chance of him making Chief Constable by midnight.

52

It began to rain as they left Blenheim, heading for the nearest pub, Hank in the driving seat. Having skipped breakfast, they were both ready to eat. There was no selection involved. They stopped at the first place they came to, the smell of good grub hitting them as soon as they walked in.

It would do nicely.

Having cleared the air, they were in a better frame of mind as they approached the bar. Kate ordered burger and chips, mayo rather than tomato ketchup. Unheard of. She needed to bulk up. Keen to do the opposite, Hank opted for a plough-man's, billed as a speciality, with local pickle, a favourite among the clientele according to the menu.

The barman asked where they were sitting.

'Can we have that table near the fire?' Kate pointed it out. 'And can I grab some water to take with me? Actually, give it to my colleague.' She caught Hank's eye. 'I'll meet you over there. I left my laptop in the car.'

'I'll get it.' He was out the door before she could argue.

Her mobile rang as she took the water and two glasses to the table, keen to plan her next move. By the time she sat down, the ringing tone had stopped. The device lit up as she took it from her pocket, a text arriving, a number not in her contacts. She stared at the message for a long time:

Word is the fat man is throwing his weight around. Might be able to help with that.

Kate was instantly on alert.

Her eyes made the pub door, looking for Hank, wondering what was keeping him. Did this have something to do with the racist he'd locked up at Heathrow yesterday? Was it a warning to back off?

A second text arrived:

It's Brian – aye, that one!

The accompanying emoji sent her pulse racing. A tiny flag . . . a Scottish flag. Her hands shook as she poured herself a glass of water, unable to believe what she was seeing. She read the texts again to make sure she wasn't hallucinating.

She wasn't . . .

There was no doubt in her mind who'd initiated the communication.

Brian Allen was the most brazen and inventive criminal she'd ever come across, a legend in his time, not a person she ever thought she'd see or hear from again. In his day, the one-time Glaswegian gangster had made a fortune out of other people's misery through organised crime. Although Strathclyde Police – now part of Police Scotland – had never been able to prove it, it was strongly suspected that, together with his cohort, Brian had killed a rival gang leader, Dougie O'Kane, in 1993. A wreath sent to taunt the O'Kane family had a message pinned to the front: *We done it.*

Such was the audacity of Brian Allen.

Five or six years later, he'd fled the city with his family. Reinventing himself in Newcastle didn't last. He later left the country. Police thought he'd gone soft, run away to save his skin, but that wasn't the case. He'd done it to protect Theresa, the love of his life and mother of his children, from those who would seek revenge for the killing of O'Kane. Just as Kate was jeopardising her job to find her soulmate.

The circumstances were different, but she could relate.

All she knew about Brian scrolled through her head.

In 2005 he'd faked his own death; so far as the world and his widow were concerned, he'd suffered a heart attack while on a golfing holiday in Spain. For the next seven years he remained out of sight, but then his sons, John and Terry, were tortured to death within hours of one another on Kate's patch, all the evidence pointing to O'Kane's sons, Craig and Finn. When the investigation led Kate to Glasgow, she found Finn O'Kane strapped to the front of a four-by-four, squashed like a fly against a wall, a handprint deliberately placed on the windscreen identifying Brian as the culprit.

An eye for an eye.

No one had seen it coming, including Kate. Newcastle cops, young and old, admired the guy, but not for rising from the grave to take revenge on the O'Kane boys. He'd done much more than that, saving the life of a much-loved detective, the one who'd just walked back into the pub.

53

Hank sauntered across the bar, pushing back wet hair, her laptop under his arm. For a split second, Kate wondered if he'd been standing there, watching her. If he'd seen her face drop, he didn't show it. As he sat down, she could smell smoke on his clothing, which explained why he'd been gone so long. She wasn't the only one under stress and keeping secrets.

Unaware that she was drowning in a case she'd rather forget, he placed the laptop on the table in front of her. Paralysed, her thoughts all over the place, Kate could only stare at it, unable to shake the image of Brian Allen from her head.

Might be able to help with that.

What exactly did he mean?

Taking a sip of water, she wondered what he was up to. The implication was clear. Whatever it was involved Heathrow. If he had information to give, it would be incumbent upon her to act on it immediately. She was conflicted. If she showed Hank the text, he'd haul her arse to London to report the matter to Torres. Aware of her promise to abandon their search for Jo by the end of the day, Kate kept it to herself, but still it played on her mind.

Hank eyed the laptop. 'Aren't you going to open it?'

'What?'

'The clock is ticking,' he warned.

'I thought we'd eat first,' was all she could think of to say.

His focal point was the pub's serving hatch. 'How long can it take to cook a burger and throw some cheese on a plate?'

'Be patient, they're busy.' Her tone was overly sharp.

Hank was bemused by it. 'You OK? Your hands are shaking.'

'Low blood sugar,' she lied. 'I'll be fine when I've eaten.' She didn't dare look at him.

He pointed at her laptop. 'Well, get a wriggle on while we wait.'

Kate played along, pulling it towards her, opening the lid, only half concentrating. What did Brian want? A fugitive on the run from British and Spanish police wouldn't show himself for nothing. With that thought lingering, with Hank breathing down her neck, she began googling nearby hotels. With time running out, she had to push on and find Jo.

Jo had always been the one who booked their holidays. She was prescriptive when it came to a crash pad. Kate could almost hear her voice: *too corporate* – she hated impersonal; *too near a main road* – she liked peace and quiet; *not enough outside space; no pool* – she loved to swim. Sharing her thoughts with Hank brought out the worst in him.

'That'll cut down the options considerably.' His sarcasm was cutting. 'There must be hundreds of hotels around here.' He pointed at the screen. 'What about that one?'

'She'd wouldn't stay there.'

'Why not?'

'Discount chains are not her style. She's a hotel snob. Put it this way, she knows what she likes.' Kate's voice broke as she said it.

He climbed down.

Their food arrived, the burger first. Kate had lost her appetite after reading Brian's text. She hadn't thought of much else in the past few minutes. She couldn't deal with this now . . . but deal with it she must. If he had information to share, she had a duty to locate him and report to Torres, despite the fact that it would raise awkward questions for her. The first thing the special agent would ask was how a fugitive from justice had her personal number. Apart from Kate, only Hank knew the answer to that.

She closed her laptop as the waiter placed Hank's lunch in front of him.

'Call that a ploughman's?' he said loudly. 'If you gave that to a ploughman where I come from, he'd kick your arse.'

Kate didn't laugh, though other customers were grinning at the hilarious Geordie sitting next to her. 'Take no notice,' she told the embarrassed waiter, pushing her plate towards Hank, pulling his towards her. His humour hadn't lifted her, nor did it take her focus off Brian Allen.

They were on the move. Kate made a few calls from the car, crossing hotel names off her shortlist as each one ruled itself out. Having drawn a blank, they had spent a while in nearby towns and villages she thought might attract Jo, calling in to one or two hotels that didn't exactly match the criteria, two in the medieval market town of Burford on the River Windrush – The Bay Tree and The Lamb.

No joy.

The sun came out as they resumed their search, the improvement in the weather failing to lift Kate's spirits as Hank drove on. She was running out of patience, running out of ideas, painfully aware that he was humouring her, for all the right reasons.

Putting on her sunglasses, she opened up her laptop, conscious that she might have missed a hotel on her first run-through. Having lost concentration due to Brian's text, she continued to scroll down on the loaded page. Her interest was taken by only one, the Old Swan and Minster Mill, a quintessential country 'Wolds' inn tucked away off a B-road – about fifteen miles from Oxford, a city Jo loved.

'Definitely a contender,' she said under her breath.

'What is?' Hank took his foot off the gas.

She looked at him, a half-smile developing. 'Ever heard of The Old Swan in Harrogate?'

'No, and we're not driving to Yorkshire—'

'I'm not asking you to.'

'Good, because we don't have time.'

'Will you let me finish? The Old Swan is where Agatha

218

Christie was found after she famously went missing, an event that triggered a manhunt in the 1920s.'

'Is there a point to this, or have you completely lost your marbles?'

'There is if you shut up and listen. Jo loves crime fiction. It would tickle her to think that she was doing the same, escaping to a hideaway where she could be alone, be herself.' She tapped her laptop. 'There's a hotel here of a similar name that happens to fit the bill. Their website offers pre-booked tickets to Blenheim Palace.'

'Yeah, along with the other eleven million hotels and B&Bs around here.'

'You're such a cynic.' Kate pointed to the front windscreen. 'Keep driving, we're on the right road, minutes away.'

54

Those few minutes were the longest Kate could ever recall. Brian was in her head. There and then, she decided she'd have to meet with him, for no other reason than to find out what he knew. If she didn't find him first, he would sure as hell find her, which could blow her cover – and she wasn't having that. His voice arrived in her head, a flashback from the only time she'd met him: *you were following me, when all the time, I was following you.*

Kate's eyes found the wing mirror, wondering if he was following her now. She was surveillance savvy, but then so was he. To do it effectively required resources, human and vehicular – both of which Brian would have in spades. His personnel would know when to keep their distance, when to hand over to another driver. Every car behind was potentially a tail. She didn't mention this to Hank.

There was only one way in to the Old Swan and Minster Mill, not the easiest place to find, a sharp left turn onto a leafy lane that took them back on themselves, down a hill, then right across a bridge, past a cricket pavilion. The hotel was split in two, The Old Swan on the right, The Minster Mill on the left, bathed in autumn sunshine. Spotting a sign for reception, Hank indicated left and turned in, parking directly opposite a path leading to the hotel's main entrance. For some reason, Kate was more interested in the car that turned the other way. Or maybe it was the pretty houses with thatched roofs that had drawn her eye.

As they got out of her vehicle, Hank sensed her anxiety. She'd pinned her hopes on a phone call lasting a few seconds and her personal knowledge of Jo. Fair enough, he could handle that. It was good police work, what they did every day of their working lives, albeit to find offenders. Tracking their movements. Visiting old haunts. Gathering insight from the people who knew them best.

As nervous as she appeared to be, he was feeling it too. He opened the gate, standing aside to let her pass, the blood draining from her face.

She didn't look at him.

Crunch time had arrived.

Kate was running out of options, running out of time.

He followed her up the narrow path and into the ancient building. Kate peered into a vaulted sitting room, tapestry-hung, with a minstrels' gallery above, where guests were enjoying the charm and ambience of the place, chatting over coffee or a glass of wine. She didn't say anything, just carried on around the corner to the check-in desk.

The girl behind the counter was busy with other customers, a group of Americans, one of whom wanted a cab to Oxford University where his son was a senior research fellow at Jesus College.

Hank rolled his eyes at Kate.

She looked ready to deck the Yank.

She'd have to get in the queue.

A few minutes more of his verbal diarrhoea and she'd had enough. 'You know what to do,' she told him. 'I'll take a look around.'

Kate walked out into the sunshine. Slipping her sunglasses back on, she turned right through the main gates, the Windrush on her left. On the river bank, a young couple were sharing a bottle of wine, the fast-flowing river in front of them. They paid her no heed as she passed by. Ahead, a block-paved pedestrianised road, fringed with plants, inaccessible to all but service vehicles cutting through the accommodation blocks, old and quaint, on either side. A sign pointing to the spa and fitness rooms.

Kate followed the path.

About halfway along, she saw movement and heard laughter. A middle-aged couple were playing croquet on the lawn. A happy scene. Her eyes moved past them to the vista beyond: weeping willows, pretty bridges, a domed summerhouse, the thatched roof of a tennis pavilion and a wild-flower meadow, the sound of water as it bubbled over rocks providing the perfect soundtrack. The place was idyllic, enchanting and tranquil.

It had Jo's name written all over it.

Kate would give anything to spend some serious time here with her. A quick look over her shoulder. No sign of Hank. For a moment, she stood frozen to the spot, unable to go on or back, fearful that he'd been right all along. That she'd been chasing a dream that would end with flowers floating in the Atlantic Ocean above a crash site.

Kate checked the spa: no Jo.

She could hardly breathe.

Get a grip.

A text came in from Torres: **Call me**.

Kate ignored it.

Setting off again, she crossed one of the bridges, then turned, heading back towards the hotel, expecting to see Hank walking towards her, hopes fading fast. He was nowhere to be seen, proof if it were needed that he'd lucked out and was avoiding her. She sat down under a portico, taking a moment to compose herself. Her heart nearly stopped as a door to one of the riverside rooms opened onto the balcony, a woman, tall and slim, with blonde hair, emerging. In the sunshine, she sat down and opened up her newspaper.

It wasn't Jo.

55

Hank's absence was a bad omen. Still no word from him: no call, no text, no comforting arm around her shoulder. Had the news been affirmative – had he found Jo as a registered guest – Kate would have known by now. Maybe he couldn't face telling her. It didn't mean that Jo wasn't in the Cotswolds somewhere – Kate clung onto that slim hope – but time had beaten her.

The search had finally run its course.

Deep down, Kate was forced to acknowledge that she may have been wrong all along: sight of that boarding card had broken her heart, sealing Jo's fate; only one female passenger hadn't boarded and her name was Elaine Hayes. Jo hadn't been in touch – and while that wasn't unusual, for all the reasons Kate had shared with Hank, the national coverage of the missing plane worried her.

What could Hank say that he hadn't already said?

Even if Jo was found, what had it all been for?

They were over long before now.

Alone in the garden, Kate was overcome by exhaustion. She'd played her hand, going against everything she believed in, falling out with everyone along the way, chasing a dream that may never have existed. She only had herself to blame for how she was feeling. The sense of loss was crushing.

Kate's life would never be the same without Jo in it. Every time she closed her eyes, she saw her face. Out of respect for her and all the victims of 0113, Kate had made a promise she intended to keep. She'd return to the capital to find those responsible if it took the rest of her life to do it.

If Brian Allen offered help, she'd take it.

Rules wouldn't stand in her way.

Kate would never love Jo more than she did right this minute. Scenes of their time together pushed their way into her thoughts, not the arguments or the secrecy that had blown them apart, but the joy of finding one another, the closeness that neither of them had experienced before. On so many occasions, Kate had imagined finding her, rehearsing what she'd say, how she'd beg for forgiveness – as she had so often – how things would be different from now on. In her head, she'd pictured Jo's reaction, that unique smile lighting up her face, no need for recriminations, a first kiss as they fell into an embrace.

Destiny was cruel sometimes.

A few minutes later, the blonde sitting outside her riverside room put down her newspaper. A smile, not for Kate, but for someone out of her eyeline. Kate stood up to get a better view, then bolted along the river bank, injuring her leg as she leapt over a fire pit on someone's patio, yelping in pain, ripping open her hand as she fell against a low stone wall. By the time she'd limped to the last room of the accommodation block, the door was shut.

Kate knocked – no reply.

She tried the handle.

It wasn't locked.

Hesitating before pushing open the door, Kate arrived in a pleasant room, no sign of its occupant, only the smell of her perfume, gym kit discarded on the bed. Her eyes found the en suite, her ears the sound of a running shower. She held her breath for a second, two, three . . . the tap was turned off . . . four seconds, five.

The sliding door opened.

Jo's eyes widened when she caught sight of her uninvited guest.

She was stunned to find Kate standing there.

That made two of them.

An awkward moment when neither woman spoke.

It was Jo who broke the deadlock. 'Kate, how on earth did you find me?'

Hearing her voice, Kate was instantly unglued, as speechless as she was distraught, a confusion of emotions taking her breath away. Deliriously happy on the one hand, confused on the other, an overwhelming mixture of relief and anger competing for space in her head. Unable to meet those pale blue eyes, she flipped out, the speech she'd rehearsed so carefully deserting her, stumbling over the only words she could find, disjointed as they came out . . .

'I'm a detective. It's what I do.' Her practical persona took over. Putting Jo's sons out of their misery was the only thing that mattered. 'Ring the kids. Do it . . . now!'

'What? Why? Are they OK?'

'Depends how you define OK. I take it you've not seen the news?'

'No, it's full of shit—'

'Yeah, it's *your* shit it's full of.'

Kate picked up the remote, turning on the TV. Although the presenter was talking about a high school shooting in the States – five dead, including the shooter – headlines that had dominated every news channel all week were moving in a continuous stream across the bottom of the screen. Jo was speechless. For a moment there was silence, her eyes fixed to the set. It seemed to take forever for her to process what she was viewing, a moment more to look at Kate, a horrified expression.

'Jesus! I didn't know, I swear.'

'Save it for Tom and James. They think you've perished on that fucking plane.'

Jo rushed over to the desk by the window. Scooping up her mobile, she turned it on and rang home. There were tears, apologies, a promise that she'd be home tomorrow that Kate found hard to witness. She could only imagine the reaction at the other end.

Jo hung up. 'Kate, I'm so sorry. When I changed my plans—'

'I don't want your fucking excuses. I've been out of my mind.'

'You think I haven't? You know I . . .' Jo's gaze dropped to the floor where Kate was standing. 'Kate, you're bleeding.'

She didn't know how true that was.

Kate looked down at the pale carpet, spotted with blood from a deep gash on the palm of her hand. She was so numb she couldn't even feel it. She raised her head. 'You are something else, you know that? When I think of the all the times you've accused me of being selfish—'

'Don't yell at me. How was I to know? I'm not a clairvoyant. I tried—' A sharp rap on the door stopped her mid-flow. She went to answer it, leaving Kate standing there, blood dripping through her fingers.

Kate was half expecting a pissed-off fellow guest telling them to keep it down.

Hank pointed at her as he crossed the threshold. 'You are fucking priceless!'

'And you're out of order, so keep it shut.'

Jo stepped towards Kate, arms extended.

Kate recoiled. 'Don't touch me.'

Hank did all the things she should have done. Kind words. A hug. Jo was limp in his arms. From over her shoulder, he glared at Kate. They'd had their differences, but she'd never seen him this wound up, this grossed out by her behaviour. His disapproval hit its target: *you don't help yourself.*

Kate was too distraught to care what either of them thought of her.

An incoming text from Torres, this one more impatient than the last:

I'm waiting.

'We've got to go.' Kate pocketed her phone. 'We don't have time for this.'

'Then make time,' Hank said.

'We're leaving.' Kate raised her mobile.

'Not until you apologise.'

'Can't you stay?' Jo said.

Kate gave an unequivocal, 'No.'

'I'll pack then. The least you can do is give me a lift home.'

The subtext wasn't lost on Kate. 'We're not heading north.'

'Where are you going?'

'I can't tell you.' It wasn't a lie. 'We've got a job on.'

'You've always got a job on.' Regretting the words as soon as they were out of her mouth, Jo shut her eyes, then opened them again. 'I'm sorry . . . Kate, I didn't mean that.'

'Didn't you?'

Hank intervened before it got ugly. 'She's right, we can't tell you what it is even if—'

'I can speak for myself,' Kate said.

She was back in work mode, with things to tell him she couldn't say in front of a material witness. Jo was the only passenger booked on 0113 who was alive to tell the tale. She didn't know it yet, but her evidence could prove crucial in a trial further down the line. 'Hank will take your statement, then we must leave. You need to tell him everything about your decision not to travel, including how you were escorted landside and how you came to be in possession of someone else's boarding card. I'll let him explain.'

She turned to leave.

'Kate, wait!' Jo's eyes were pleading. 'If I've given you grief, I promise it was unintentional. Can you honestly say the same? You didn't abandon a holiday, you abandoned me. My hands are up. I overreacted, but then so did you. I offered to fly home. You knocked me back.'

'She did what?' Hank gave Kate the side-eye.

Jo wasn't finished, not even close. 'Kate, you're not the only one with feelings here. Assuming you even have any. Look at you. You're an empty shell. Is it any wonder I needed some distance between us?'

'You didn't get far—'

'Because of you! Because if I'd boarded that plane, there was no turning back.' There was a long, painful pause. Jo held up a hand. 'Fine, you can't say I didn't try. I hope your job makes you happy for the rest of your life, because I sure as hell couldn't.'

Kate gave Hank the nod. 'Make it quick, say your goodbyes and meet me at the car.'

56

Kate left through the patio door, tears pricking her eyes. Avoiding the fire pit that almost took her left leg off, she staggered to the car, got in the passenger side, physically and mentally in no fit state to drive. Jo was alive. Alive! That's all that mattered. Kate didn't have a clue why she'd reacted that way, why the sight of her had triggered such a vicious outburst, the pent-up emotion flooding out. It had been an exhausting day, the most traumatic of her life. Taking into account what she did for a living, that was going some.

Every part of her wanted to go back and tell Jo how much she was loved, but Kate couldn't generate enough energy to get out of the car. She didn't want to see Jo again until she'd calmed down. Kate believed her explanation. Pity she hadn't accepted it. Jo loved to be free, hated listening to the news. Who could blame her? Lately, it had all been bad, doing everyone's head in. The country was becoming desensitised to tragedy, terrorism in particular, the incidences of which were becoming more and more radical. Mass murder was no longer an infrequent occurrence.

Flight 0113 was the latest atrocity but it wouldn't be the last. Every other day a bomb went off resulting in horrendous loss of life somewhere in the world. Recently – and with increasing frequency – the target was European cities. It saddened Kate to think that the public viewed such events so dispassionately. After their initial shocked response, their interest in such appalling incidents tended to be short-lived – too painful a burden, in all probability. Post an 'RIP' tweet. Move on.

Superficial bullshit.

Whether it be a madman letting loose with a gun, or

refugees floating in the water having died trying to escape oppression, the majority of spectators responded by blinking away a tear and returning to work. Or, like Jo, turning their backs on the world and its problems whenever they got the chance. Kate felt guilty then. Jo had put her, her family and her work colleagues through a terrible ordeal, but she hadn't done it on purpose. She deserved a hug, not a verbal slap.

Hank gave Kate a black look as he walked round the front of the car ten minutes later. The door opened and he climbed in. 'Well played, boss. You *really* know how to make a girl feel wanted.'

'Shut up and drive!'

He started the car, a glance into the passenger seat. 'Why, Kate?'

'Because I said so.'

'I mean, why are you here and not in there?' He flicked his eyes towards the guest accommodation.

Kate had got that the first time round but had chosen to ignore it. She'd handled it badly. That was a given. She didn't need him to remind her. As he reversed out of their parking spot, then pulled forward, the nose of the car was pointing towards the block-paved drive. Jo was standing at the top where it disappeared round the bend, looking down on them. It was a pitiful sight, one that made Kate's heart break all over again.

'Kate . . .' Hank didn't pull away. 'She's past herself. Can't you stick around? I'll book a room, get a few hours' kip and pick you up at four. We'll still make it to Heathrow in time for your shift.'

'Not an option.'

'Why not?'

'Torres wants a meet.'

'Let her wait.'

'Yeah, that'll work.' She shook her head. 'I'll call Jo later, 'before you and I go our separate ways.'

'Can't you call Torres and explain about that?' He was pointing at her bleeding hand. 'Make something up. You're good at that. She's not equipped with a lie detector, is she? Even if she is, you'd pass. Tell her you fell over. That cut looks nasty. You need to get it stitched—'

'I've had worse shaving my legs. Now get going.'

Kate threw her personal mobile on the dash, insurance in case she walked off with it. As he reversed, Jo got smaller through the front windscreen. Avoiding her gaze, Kate opened the glove box, took out a medical wipe and cleaned the blood away. It stung as she struggled to stick the edges of her wound together with a bandaid. Pity she couldn't mend a broken heart with one.

The car idled at the junction to allow other traffic to pass behind them. Hank was in no hurry to leave. Kate didn't say anything. She knew what he was doing. His eyes were on Jo, hers on him. 'I can't believe you're leaving her like that,' he said. 'This was your last chance, Kate. You will never forgive yourself if you blow it.'

Slowly, he reversed.

Jo looked so unhappy. So lonely.

'Stop the car!'

He braked, then pulled forward.

Kate got out and hobbled a few yards up the road. Jo ran towards her, almost knocking her off her feet as they came together. They hung onto one another for what seemed like an eternity.

No words were exchanged.

None was needed.

Kate stepped away, held Jo at arm's length. 'You know I can't live without you, right? I love you . . . and so, as it happens, does the soppy sod in the car.'

'I love him too. You?' Jo waggled her hand from side to side. 'I'm not so sure about.'

'You owe him. He made me do it.'

'He's watching us.' Jo's laughter turned a tap on. A single tear left her right eye, dribbling down her cheek into the corner of her mouth. She moved closer, a whisper in Kate's ear.

Kate stepped away. 'Really?'

'Really. Now go to work.'

'I'll call you as soon as I'm able. It might be a while.'

'Go!'

A nod. A salty kiss. Now they had made their peace, Kate didn't want to leave, except she knew she must.

57

Hank drove past the cricket pitch, across the bridge and out onto the open road, leaving Minster Lovell behind. Scooping her mobile off the dash, Kate called Bright. They spoke for no longer than a few minutes. He didn't ask for details. He knew the who, but not where or even how she'd managed to locate Jo while working undercover for Torres. He offered to share the news with the Murder Investigation Team, but that was one job Kate wanted to take on herself. As soon as he hung up, she called Robbo. Her Northumbria squad had waited long enough. There was no doubt in her mind that every single member of her team had been rooting for Jo. For Kate too, now they knew that there was more to their relationship than profiler and SIO working within the same unit.

The ringing tone stopped and Robbo's voice hit her ear. 'Guv, how's it going?'

Kate expected to hear the usual background noise, but there was silence at the other end: no phones ringing, detective banter, the buzz of officers discussing the case they were currently investigating.

Kate checked her watch: almost five.

Had she interrupted an important briefing?

Was Robbo not at work?

'Is this a bad time?' she asked.

'No, go ahead.'

He sounded on edge, which made her wonder if Hank had been right about him. On the other hand, Bright had told her that he was 'a natural', but maybe that was to put her in her place, payback for abandoning her post. Technically, she was on leave, a fact that seemed to have passed him by.

She hoped that Robbo hadn't bitten off more than he could

chew. He was dealing with one of the biggest incidents in Northumbria's history and had been stressing over Jo. Every day since 0113 went down, he'd taken time out to send a text to Kate's mobile, a few kinds words, a virtual hug to let her know that he was in her corner should she feel the need to talk. He was good like that.

Time to put him out of his misery.

'Jo made it,' she said. 'Tell the squad—' Six words was all she got out before a roar went up at the other end, cutting off the need to say more. It made her heart swell to listen to the MIT celebrating. She imagined hands punching the air, fist bumps, pats on the back, a drink being hastily arranged for the end of their shift. Robbo must've lifted a thumb or put the phone on speaker, as Kate had done.

'Guv, we're all thrilled!'

'I heard.'

'Was Hank with you when you found her?'

Kate threw her 2ic a smile. 'There was a bit of hand-holding going on. You know how I hate to hurt his feelings.'

'Since when?' Hank raised his voice. 'Mate, don't listen to her. I'm beginning to resemble a punchbag.'

Robson laughed. 'You want me to call on Tom and James?'

'Not necessary,' Kate said. 'Jo has already spoken to them. They're not kids any more. I'd leave them be. She's heading north tomorrow. I'm sure she'll stay in touch. You might even find that phone of hers is switched on—'

'It is. Lisa just received an alert from EE.'

Now Kate understood the silence that prevailed when he picked up. He'd primed the team for news. It made sense of his nervousness. 'Why don't you give her a call?' she said. 'Ordinarily she'd fly, but on this occasion she'll probably opt for the train. I wouldn't tempt fate if it was me. She might appreciate a lift from the station.'

'I'll sort it,' he said.

'Anything I need to be aware of?

'Yes and no.'

'Anything new on Zhuk and Dobrynin?'

'No sight of them so far, but the drug squad tipped me off that they've had them under observation in the past. Apparently, on each occasion they were observed, the two approached Nikolaev's home from the east end of the property. They drove in, turned his vehicle around and pulled up to facilitate his exit or entry from the rear nearside passenger seat, directly outside his front door.'

'Good work! The bullet entered the right side of his head, yes?'

'Correct. There was blood spatter on the front door, more at the top of the steps where he fell. His crew must've thought there was a chance of survival or they would have dumped him in the lake.'

'He has a lake?'

'Kate, he has a private golf course.'

'We're in the wrong job, mate.'

Robbo laughed. 'If Nikolaev was leaving the house, our best guess is that the sniper took his position in the woods on the west side, the opposite if he was entering. The PoLSA team concentrated their efforts on these two locations.'

'Which was it?' Kate asked.

'Vegetation was disturbed in two locations in the woods on the west side of the house.'

'So Nikolaev was leaving?'

'Looks like it.'

'Did you call out the dog section?'

'I did. There were bike trails where they lost the scent. I can't say for sure it was the shooter but it looks that way.'

'OK, keep me posted.' Kate paused, thoughts of the Russian mafia bringing an image of Brian Allen into sharp focus. 'Before you go, has anyone been asking for me specifically?'

'Like who?'

'Anyone who didn't leave a name.'

'Not sure.'

'Ask around?'

'Consider it done.' Robbo rang off.

Hank moved into the outside lane. 'What was that all about?'

Kate lied. 'Just wondering if my old man had been in touch. He wouldn't want me knowing he cared, would he?' What she really wanted to know was if Brian Allen or one of his cohorts had been checking out her movements, and if her cover was blown. 'You may as well head home, Hank. Much as I love having you around, your interviews at Heathrow are over and I no longer need an escort. I'm in this up to my neck now. I couldn't turn my back on the investigation even if I wanted to, but feel free to ship out. The MIT could do with your expertise. I'm going to push on and help nail the bastards who took down that plane. It's the only thing that matters to me now.'

'I'm going nowhere,' Hank said.

58

Kate had been checking her wing mirror at regular intervals to ensure that no one was following. Having noticed her nervousness, and without saying anything, Hank turned the opposite direction to the one she was expecting, crossing the carriageway, going up a side street, then another and another, doing a reciprocal at a roundabout, then finding his way to the motorway via an alternative route, a counter-surveillance technique he excelled at.

An hour into their journey, having taken several detours off the main road and back on again, Kate asked him to pull off the M40 into the southbound Beaconsfield Services on the pretence that she needed a break. It was time to come clean, and she wanted him static when he received news that he would knock him sideways.

And still she checked the road behind . . .

A few cars followed them off the motorway. It was dark now. Kate was blinded by their headlights, unable to see registrations or faces of the drivers behind, though she was fairly confident they weren't being tailed. That text from Brian had made her jumpy on the way to Minster Lovell. Kate dismissed it from her mind. She was probably adding two and two, making five.

Or was she?

A text from Torres made her think twice:

> You around?
> Had a bit of an accident.
> Oh no! Tomorrow?
> I'll bring cake. ☺

Kate waited.

Torres didn't reply.

Kate didn't expect her to. The texts going back and forth were coded, innocent, one friend to another. If read by anyone else, they would sound like two mates keeping in touch. Bringing cake meant she had something for the special agent. Hank didn't ask who the texts were from. He probably assumed it was Jo. That suited Kate. With Jo now safe, she had one thing on her mind, something that hadn't occurred to her till now . . .

Was she being tailed by someone other than Brian?

Garcia had accessed her burner so they could eavesdrop on Heathrow baggage handlers. Were Homeland Security able to activate the listening device remotely, earwigging on her conversations with Hank? Kate didn't think so. It would necessitate a link to her voice memos or kick in during an active call. She hadn't made any or used the app on that phone, but it didn't mean the special agent hadn't attached a tracker as a safety measure in case she was in trouble and required extricating from danger. She wouldn't put it past the US security agency to have done this without telling her.

Two could play at that game.

Kate wasn't intending to get out of the car, but Hank was keen to stretch his legs and grab a coffee and a sandwich. His burger – although better than the ploughman's he'd originally ordered for lunch – was a distant memory. Besides, she had a reason of her own to alight from the vehicle. Walking to the rear, she lifted the tailgate, removing the axe she always carried in case of RTAs and other emergencies.

Hank joked. 'I'm sure they'll provide us with knives and forks.'

Kate laughed out loud.

He looked on as she crouched down between two cars, removed the SIM from her burner and used the heavy tool to destroy both card and phone. Job done, she discarded the debris in a bin, put the axe back in the boot and walked on, explaining her actions as they approached the service station.

'Well,' he said. 'I can honestly say that is the weirdest anti-surveillance technique I've ever witnessed.'

Once inside, Kate got serious. Accessing the text she'd received from Brian on her police mobile, she showed it to Hank as they waited in the cafeteria queue. He studied the content, but didn't respond until they were seated.

She could see he was shaken.

'Brian's right,' he said. 'We could do with all the help we can lay our hands on, but how does he know what we're up to? Looks like you're compromised—'

'I think you'll find that "fat man" refers to you, not me, Hank.'

'Fair enough, but how in hell's name does he think he can help us?'

'He's helped us before.'

'And I'd like to shake his hand for it, but not like this.'

'We'll see.'

'You're not taking the guy at his word, surely?'

'No, but neither am I turning down intelligence if he has something we can use.'

'Kate, you don't want to go there.'

'Why not? He's part of the criminal underbelly, which probably means he's more clued up than we are, especially down here. We're incomers with no snouts to turn to. No one we can put the bite on for information. Blue isn't likely to share, is he? Not after I spurned his advances and boned him for putting Jo's name in the papers to get at me. He's a walking, talking egomaniac – that's if he still has a job.'

'He doesn't, not in the Casualty Bureau. Following a few choice words from Bright, Waverley got rid.'

'Yeah, well, I hope he's on traffic duty.'

'He had two black eyes at his leaving do.'

'Outstanding! I prefer Brian any day.'

'He murdered the O'Kane brothers in cold blood.'

'Yeah, yeah. Tell me something I don't know.'

'Kate, you can't meet with him.'

'I can and I will.'

'Then be prepared to lock him up.'

She admonished him with her eyes. 'You don't want that any more than I do.'

'To be honest, no. But he's wanted on a double murder charge. Anyway, he's not the kind of guy who'd come out of hiding unless it was mutually beneficial. What does he want?'

'Let's ask him. He came out of the shadows to right a wrong, Hank. Imagine if someone tortured your lad to death. I'm not excusing his behaviour, but I do understand it – and so do you, deep down. Aren't you grateful?'

There, she'd said it.

They were going round and round in circles, getting nowhere fast. And still the old case rolled around in her head, a gangland war that had gone on for two decades, unfinished business that had led her to Spain on the trail of a man hell-bent on killing Brian Allen and coming off worse. She'd worked out that Craig O'Kane had gone there with the express intention of avenging his father's death and, more recently, that of his brother, Finn. And when Hank was chasing up a lead, Brian was the man who stepped out of the shadows to save his life.

She'd never forget that day . . .

Before leaving the UK, Kate had liaised with the head of the Serious Organised Crime Agency's European operations. Back in 2006 they'd enlisted the cooperation of the Spanish police in launching Operation Capturà on the Costa del Sol, and since then they'd been collaborating in an international effort to detain and prosecute fugitives living abroad. Kate had added Brian Allen and Craig O'Kane to their 'most wanted' list. The Spaniards were keen to dovetail with British law enforcement in much the same way as US SAC Torres was doing now.

Getting to her feet, Kate put on her coat, keen to press on. Hank followed her out of the service station, giving her the benefit of his advice as they wended their way through parked cars to reach their own.

'You're playing with fire, Kate.'

'I'm aware. We're not investigating one murder or two. Mass murder means we need to be smarter. Prepared for anything. The ends justify the means.'

'You're consulting with Torres, right?'

'When I have something for her, of course.' Kate stopped walking and turned to face him. 'She'll be shaking our hands if we pull this off, but let's get one thing straight: I intend using everything in my armoury to investigate 0113, including Brian Allen. Torres isn't the kind of agent who'll stand on ceremony. If Brian can provide the key, I'm happy to unlock the case. Torres wants results. That's her endgame. She won't give a shit as to how we go about it. She's more likely to pin a medal on a guy who'd saved a cop from certain death than shaft him. You may have reservations about meeting him. I have no such qualms. Are we clear?'

He gave a resigned nod.

'Want me to drive?' she said.

'No, I'm good. How's the hand?'

It hurt like hell. 'It's a scratch.'

They climbed into her car and drove off, merging with the motorway. Hank put his foot down, concentrating on the road. He went quiet. Kate had a feeling that he'd be thinking about Brian, rerunning the old case in his head. In Spain, things hadn't gone according to plan. In order to find Brian, she'd decided that they must find Craig O'Kane, the Glasgow gangster who'd evaded capture time and again. And when Hank came close, the unimaginable happened.

She cringed as a shot rang out in her head. Officer down. At the time, details were sketchy. The race to the Santa Lucia Hospital in Cartagena was the worst journey she'd ever taken, a Spanish police escort sweeping other road users out of the way. Sirens. Blue lights. No one would meet her eye or tell her if Hank was likely to survive. And then there was the guilt. The self-loathing. She'd sent Hank out alone that day. He'd come through it, just as her father and Jo had escaped death a week ago.

She texted Brian from her police mobile:

Let's talk. Where?

59

Hank left Kate's vehicle with words of advice echoing in his head, a warning from Kate: 'Unarmed, you're vulnerable.' Yeah, like he didn't know. He tried not to think of the what ifs and the maybes. He'd seen at first hand what Brian Allen was capable of, but figured that a man who'd saved him once had no reason to turn on him now. Kate thought so too, or she'd never have agreed to let them meet. Brian wanted something and was willing to trade information to get it.

Tommy Patterson, the guy Kate had videoed in the baggage shed, might be the mole. He'd been charged and released on bail. If he was one of Brian's associates, the thieving git might have spilled the beans on the not-so-overweight Geordie cop who'd been giving him grief.

Hank discounted that.

Brian would have no way of knowing that he was that cop, unless Patterson had captured his image while he was in and out of his cubby hole interviewing staff at Heathrow, over a hundred of them working in that particular section airside. It could equally have been Bakr, the guy Patterson hated with a passion, who was not among the three Kate had asked Torres to focus on.

Hank would find out soon enough.

He ducked under the chain-link fence someone had pulled back, a section big enough for him to crawl through. Using a torch to find his way around the abandoned industrial estate, he was expecting his progress to be fed in real time to the man he'd come to see.

Sensitive to spies, Hank could feel eyes watching him.

Cautiously, he peered into the disused building Brian had described to Kate in a text, stepping over junk put there to alert those inside to the unexpected arrival of anyone who might wander in unaware that it was being used as a rendezvous point. Despite what Kate had said, Hank had no misgivings about meeting Brian – it was *her* meeting him that the detective sergeant was keen to avoid. He'd begged her to find another way. She'd taken some convincing before finally accepting that, in order to remain undercover, she couldn't afford to show her hand. She'd be regretting that now, stressing in the car, wondering what was going on, considering her next move, deciding what she'd tell Torres – a woman she'd described to him in minute detail.

A good judge of character, Kate was probably right about her. Though Hank hadn't met or spoken to Torres personally, he'd come across a few special agents during a state visit by US President George W. Bush to Prime Minister Tony Blair's constituency in 2003, when Durham Constabulary, fearing protests against the Iraq War, drafted in Northumbria officers.

Hank knew the type . . .

No one needed to draw him a picture.

The smell of urine at the entrance to the building was overwhelming. Broken glass crunched under his feet as he stepped inside, swinging his torch left and right over rusting machinery, an oil-stained floor, a few rags, an old mattress, an abandoned shoe. The place had been used by someone to doss down for sure, but not recently. They were long gone, probably driven out by Brian's lackeys, warned not to return.

A slit of flickering light ahead, a door hanging off its hinges. Leading where, Hank didn't know, but he was in the right place. As he walked towards the light, he had no doubt that there would be a rear entrance – more than one in all probability – every eventuality covered, an easy escape route for Brian and his crew in case Kate remembered she was a police officer and sent in armed response to capture a fugitive she had a duty to arrest.

No chance . . .

The Glaswegian wasn't the only heavyweight in town.

As the door creaked open, Hank caught the whiff of an expensive cigar – Brian's trademark. His description had been circulated on an intelligence bulletin sent to every force in the UK a couple of years ago; an 'Armed & Extremely Dangerous – DO NOT Approach' tag attached. Backup was a prerequisite in apprehending men like him: the dog section, armed response and tactical support.

Having never seen the guy in real life, Hank wasn't sure if this was him or one of his entourage. The closer he got, the less doubt there was in his mind. This *was* Brian Allen. He'd changed his appearance somewhat, probably had a new life, most definitely a fresh ID. The glasses were new and he'd changed his hair. It was worn long and tied in a ponytail. If the situation hadn't been so serious, Hank might have cracked a joke about his Francis Rossi impression.

He loved Status Quo.

The place was a shitpit: old mattresses, empty spirit bottles, roach ends, hypodermics. Closer still, a fire made of old wooden crates burning on the concrete floor. No one but Brian was visible.

Hank didn't look up to the second floor.

The two men locked eyes. No words were exchanged. Hank was big. Brian was massive, almost a caricature of a Scottish gangster, hard eyes behind steel-framed specs, fit-looking for a man of his age. In his youth, one look from him would terrify the opposition.

For a second, Hank was in a Spanish hotel room, the tinny sound of a phone disturbing his sleep, Brian's voice in his ear: *move from that room, she dies . . . Stay put and she lives. Do we have a deal?*

He did . . .

Brian had been talking about Kate.

Pushing the past away, Hank greeted the Glaswegian with a modest tip of the head, taking a few steps forward, eyeing the gun held loosely in his hand. This was no poxy imitation, designed to put the fear of God into an unsuspecting public unable to tell the difference; it was the real deal, most definitely loaded. Having faced a lethal weapon before, the sight of the firearm made Hank's stomach churn. Gun-related crime was on the increase, especially in the capital, illegal firearms easy to come by if you knew where to source one. The black market was a growing industry, London topping the pole for firearms offences.

Brian remembered the day he'd intervened in an attempt on Hank Gormley's life. That scumbag O'Kane had shot him in full view of tourists forced to flee the scene. Hank had dropped like a stone, down and almost out, blood seeping from a chest wound, chaos all around: tourists going apeshit, screaming and running for their lives, their trip to foreign shores unforgettable in a way not described in their holiday brochures. When O'Kane raised his gun a second time and took aim, keen to finish the job, Brian had a call to make.

Had he not acted, O'Kane would have pulled the trigger. Job done, he'd have walked away unperturbed. That split-second decision was costly, forcing Brian to shift his operation from Spain. A brief 'adios amigos' telephone conversation with Hank in the middle of the night leading him to believe that the two shared the same dry sense of humour, that had they not been on opposing sides, they might even have been friends. The undying impression he took from the call was that Hank was cool in a crisis. And so it proved as he approached across the warehouse floor . . .

'Thanks to you, my wife still has a husband,' he said. 'I'd have brought some beers to celebrate, but you've already been crowned a hero on social media, probably the only time in your life you've received good press.'

'Aye, nearly bought me a fucking cape.'

Hank laughed. Copper or not, he liked Brian.

'How much did you see that day?' the Glaswegian asked.

'The wrong end of a gun barrel, O'Kane being dragged away. Didn't know if he'd been hit and dropped the gun, or if the gun had gone off as your guys bundled him into a car.'

'What did you tell Kate afterwards?'

'Not a lot. Didn't need to, it was all captured on CCTV. You think she gave a stuff about O'Kane? Whatever you were doing to him, she hoped it hurt like hell. What you did to *her*, she was less happy about. Waking a lady while she's sleeping, tying her up, that's not nice.'

'She doesn't scare easily, your guv'nor.'

She was terrified, but Hank wasn't about to stroke the ego of the man he was facing, much as he owed him. Kate had woken in the early hours to find Brian at the bottom of her bed, smoking a cigar. To ensure that he had her full attention, he'd secured her to the bedhead with heavy-duty cable ties, stark naked. She didn't argue on account of the fact that he was armed. Hank wondered if it was the same gun he was holding now.

Probably not.

Somehow, fuck knows how, this hardman had knowledge of Kate's association with Jo Soulsby, as well as the bad blood that existed between Kate and her old man, private stuff half the MIT weren't party to until very recently. It was leverage, should Brian ever need to use it. Now Hank came to think of it, he probably knew everything about his own family, too. All very worrying.

'How come you know so much about her?' he asked.

'Money talks.'

Hank couldn't argue with the cliché. There had been no smirk on Brian's face as he said it. The comment was a statement of fact. He was a businessman with an eye on the opposition, tactics employed by every successful commercial enterprise. Being part of the criminal fraternity didn't equal dim. Nikolaev's wealth was testament to that.

'Your DCI is gutsy,' Brian said, 'a mouth on her that would go down well at an Old Firm fixture.'

Hank couldn't help but smile at Brian's reference to the Celtic–Rangers rivalry, often characterised by violence, slanging matches and bad language between the opposing football fans. He'd have loved to have been a fly on the wall during *that* conversation.

'Didn't I say as much when we last spoke?' he said.

'Aye, you did, and you were right. She cracks me up, like Bright used to in the old days. He was a "shouty-mouth dynamo" too. Congrats, pal. You nailed her in three words.' Brian paused a moment, studying Hank. 'Would you really have traded places to save her skin?'

'In a heartbeat.'

'She must be quite a woman—'

'Worth saving . . . most days.'

'Well, if she'd have done her job, grabbed O'Kane and fucked off home, I wouldn't have been forced to intervene—'

'I'm not sure that's how she sees it.'

'She can please her arse. His death and your life was my gift to her—'

'Isn't it the case that you'd already made up your mind to finish him before he caught up with you? It was never going to end well, was it?'

'Careful, Hank. That sounds like a self-defence plea . . .' Brian held back the smile developing at the corner of his mouth. 'Makes you so sure it was me who did the business anyhow?'

'If it wasn't, you gave the order.'

'And I'd do it again. I told Kate where she could find O'Kane. That must count for something, even to the pigs. You need to work on your gratitude, pal.'

Hank was poker-faced. 'C'mon, Brian. I wasn't born yesterday. You had your reasons for killing O'Kane. What better way to do it than in the defence of a polis, right? A hero, I heard. I hope it plays well for you in court when the Spaniards catch up with you, because they will. Be honest, you did it to get us off your back, and took Kate's number as insurance—'

'Looks like I'm busted. What are you going to do about it?'

Hank raised both arms. 'Not a damned thing.'

'Thought not. Dereliction of duty is more Kate's bag than yours—'

'Fuck off! Unless you know something I don't, you didn't execute anyone on our patch. Police Scotland are investigating the murder of Finn O'Kane, and Craig is a matter for the Spanish authorities. Kate has enough on her plate without coming after you.'

'I stand corrected . . . Still, she kept her big mouth shut, and I'm ready to return the favour. Like I told her at the time, my snouts are loyal. The best. Because of them, I have something she desperately needs—'

'Not interested.'

'Why?'

'You threatened to kill her.'

'Isn't that a criminal offence?'

'Last I looked.'

'I was buying myself time, you divvi. I owe her. I'd never hurt her . . . unless I had to. There's a deal to be done here.'

Brian picked up a plank of wood and threw it on the fire, sending sparks flying across the dark warehouse. He pointed to a rusting, upturned barrel, a makeshift seat. 'Why don't you take the weight off while we have a wee chat?' He got up, approached Hank, handing him a cigar, offering a light to go with it: Mr Polite. 'You're meddling in my business, Hank. We could fall out over it.'

'What do you want, Brian?'

'A meeting with Kate . . . for old times' sake.'

'Nice try.' Hank shook his head, puffing out a cloud of

smoke, eyeballing the Glaswegian. 'That's never going to happen.'

'I think it is.'

'What's your plan? You give her something and she rolls over? You underestimate her.' Hank held Brian's gaze. 'And since when did you become a grass? I'd have thought that was beneath you.'

'Doesn't sit well, to be honest—'

'Anyhow, Kate can't help, sorry. She's up north—'

'Is she shite! You two are joined at the hip.'

Hank didn't respond.

Brian made him wait for the killer punch. 'I reckon she's at the Casualty Bureau, bawling her eyes out. No reflection on her. This plane crash must've fucked with her head, Jo Soulsby being on the passenger list. I know stuff that'll put your boss in the picture. Question is, will you deliver it, or do I have to go find her myself?' The implied threat didn't register in Hank's eyes, but Brian wasn't fooled. 'Do you really want to be the one withholding crucial information?' He paused. 'No, I didn't think so. She'll listen to you, so why don't you toddle off and talk to her while the offer is still on the table. If this is a goer, tell her to visit her favourite pub, sit by the pay phone and await instructions. She comes alone.'

60

In the fifteen minutes since Hank left to meet Brian, Kate had been sitting alone in the car, lights off, window open, eyes fixed on a derelict warehouse. As a diversion, she used her police mobile to call the hospital. Her father was making progress, out of bed and taking gentle exercise. Next she attempted to call Fiona to tell her that Jo had been located before she saw it in the press. Journalists would jump on a good news story once they realised that 0113 had a survivor, albeit not from the crash.

The phone went straight to voicemail.

Kate hesitated before leaving a brief message. Finally, she called Jo. There were so many things she wanted to say to her, but none came out of her mouth. She was worried sick, too concerned to discuss anything other than Hank's venture into uncharted territory in pursuit of information that might ID those who'd brought down the flight, killing everyone on board.

But first, a warning . . .

'Be careful,' Kate said. 'This call may be monitored.' Garcia hadn't had his mitts on this device, but Kate was taking no chances. She didn't mention who might be monitoring the call. Jo was very well aware that Kate had dropped everything to travel to the capital in search of her. And that, once there, she'd continue to offer assistance to whoever asked for it. It wasn't too much of a stretch to imagine that it was either the British Security Service or another high-profile group.

'Noted,' Jo said. 'Are you OK?'

Kate was definitely not OK.

Brian might be keen to trade, but he was still a wanted man looking at life imprisonment if captured by the police. It was a volatile situation, Kate in two minds whether to follow him into that warehouse. A trigger-happy associate might open fire at the slightest wrong move: a detective's hand slipped inside a breast pocket; a sudden noise in the background; the sight of one officer that might mean five, ten or twenty, tooled up and ready to use force.

'Kate, what's wrong?'

'I'm worried about Hank.'

'Why? You two haven't fallen out over me, have you?'

'He's gone to meet an informant.'

'So? He's done it a hundred times—'

'Yeah, but this one is unpredictable, with nothing left to lose.' It was a heavy hint that Jo was guaranteed to understand. She was a pro, as switched on as any detective Kate had ever known.

When she'd returned from Spain's Costa Blanca two years ago, shaken up by events over there, including Brian's part in it, Jo was the perfect sounding board. They had talked about him a lot, including the fact that he had 'nothing left to lose' and the guilt Kate was feeling over Hank's near-death experience. As a highly trained and respected psychologist, Jo had tapped into that immediately, using her expertise to help Kate over it, offering unconditional support, good judgement and opinions that made her feel better . . .

Marginally.

She couldn't repeat the process now, not over the phone, and had no doubt worked out who Hank had gone to meet.

Kate's focus was outside of the car. No sign of Hank.

'He hasn't come back,' she said.

'He can handle himself. Give him time. If there had been an alternative, there's no way you'd have sent him in alone—'

'I didn't. He volunteered.'

'There you go then. I assume he made a good case for keeping you out of it?'

'He did.'

'Then what other choice did you have? You need to learn to trust him, and while you're at it, trust your gut. As much as you might like to, you can't protect everyone on your team. Hank is an experienced copper, a smooth talker with a sensible head on his shoulders. He's doing the job he's paid for, because he thinks it's the right thing to do—'

'He's been gone fifteen minutes already.' Tuning Jo out, Kate raised her binoculars, focusing on the gap in the chain-link fence, then the surrounding area, looking for a tiny speck of light that might give away one of Brian's crew checking a mobile or lighting a cigarette. She detected no movement. All she could see was a malevolent darkness.

'Kate, are you there?'

'I wish I wasn't—'

'Understandable. You've had a stressful week.'

'So has he—'

'Granted, but he didn't think he'd lost a loved one, did he? You've been to hell and back. It'll take time to recover—'

'Yeah, time I don't have.'

Jo didn't reply.

Kate shut her eyes and took a deep breath. She was doing it again. The job came first. Always had, and would continue to do so. There wasn't a hope in hell of that changing. Of all the promises she'd made while Jo was missing, Kate was stuck in the same rut that had been pushing them apart for years. Whether their relationship could survive was still to be tested.

'I'm sorry.' It came out as a whisper. 'This is who I am—'

'I know, and I wouldn't have it any other way.'

'Liar. You deserve better.'

'Agreed, but I can't help myself. I want you. No one else will do.'

'Will you ever forgive me?'

'Don't be daft. I'm crazy about you, you know that.'

Her words made Kate want to weep. 'I'll make time for us when this case is over. We'll throw a private party, down a bottle of red and dance till dawn. How's that sound?'

'Like a lot of fun. In the meantime, promise me you'll think twice before making any important decisions. Don't jump, that's all I'm asking, unless it's absolutely necessary.' A beat of time. 'Look, I won't pretend I'm not self-interested. Of course I am, but if you step on Hank's toes, he won't thank you for it. Let him do this for you. You know he's good for it. Clandestine meetings can go horribly wrong. You could be signing his death warrant, and yours, if you knee-jerk now.'

61

Somewhere outside of the car, a door creaked open. Whoever had exited the building didn't move. The rusting corrugated warehouse was only about thirty yards away. There was no moon. Without night-vision equipment, Kate couldn't see well enough to make an ID, but as her eyes adjusted to the darkness and the figure moved closer, she recognised the gait of the man strolling towards her.

She could breathe again.

Yanking open the door, Hank climbed in, turned on the ignition and pulled away, explaining what had gone down inside as he drove. Kate listened attentively, occasionally checking her wing mirror. The road was so busy, it was impossible to tell if they were being followed, though the overwhelming feeling that she was under surveillance – that prickle at the base of her neck she'd experienced earlier in the day – was evaporating.

She asked him to drop her off in Hounslow, about a quarter of a mile west of where she needed to be, telling him he could skirt the busy town centre on his way to the section house, avoiding the Saturday-night crowd. With Brian Allen and his cronies around, and no communication device, Hank wasn't happy with her plan to walk the rest of the way.

She was fairly sure they hadn't been followed and told him so. She'd had her eyes glued to the slip road that led onto the motorway the whole time. For as long as it was visible in her wing mirror, only one car joined the M4 after them. If Brian and his crew were tailing them, they would have used half a dozen vehicles, maybe more, and would never have risked losing her. Then again, realistically, where could she go? The next exit off the motorway was miles away. If they were on her tail, knowing what car she was driving, there would be no rush. They could afford to give her a head start, then floor the accelerator in order to catch up.

It hadn't put Hank's mind at rest . . .

Hers either, now she'd thought it through.

Checking his wing mirror, Hank indicated, then changed lanes, insisting that he drop her off at her flat or very close by. 'Brian wasn't joking when he threatened to come after you if I didn't deliver his message.'

'Well, you have, so stop carping—'

'He doesn't know that, does he?'

'Bollocks! He knows we're tight and, by extension, will have worked out that you wouldn't keep something that important from me. He may be all sorts of things but he's not stupid. You think he didn't know that I was outside waiting for you? Did he try to drag me in there, kicking and screaming?'

'No, but—'

'But what? There can be only one reason for that, Hank. Think about it. Brian wants me to go to him willingly. He knows I won't play ball if he employs any strong-arm tactics. That's why he didn't touch a hair on your head, and why he won't make a move on me. It would be counter-productive.'

'If you think so.'

'I know so.'

Hank fell silent.

Kate eyed the Kevlar vest in the footwell. She'd insisted he wear it beneath his overcoat when he took off to meet the Glaswegian. It wouldn't have helped if he'd taken a head-shot. She shivered at the thought. There was little doubt that the rendezvous in the warehouse had disturbed Hank more than he was prepared to admit. It wasn't every day you came face-to-face with a gunman who also happened to be the guy who'd saved your life. It was bound to have been stressful, stirring up emotions and memories he'd worked hard to forget.

*

It was a chilly night, a slight breeze taking a degree or two off the temperature, a lot of people about as Kate made her way to her temporary digs. With Torres pushing for a meet, she had no choice but to take her request seriously, especially since she'd hinted at a possible lead herself. She wondered what was going on, if Homeland Security had caught a break their end and had new intelligence to share, or if there had been a significant development of a different kind, wind of a further terrorist strike on the horizon, perhaps. Kate couldn't imagine that those responsible for the atrocity of 0113 would dare attack a second time with heightened security in place – but people with a cause rarely let that bother them.

They had done it before; they could do it again.

Trying not to second-guess what might lay ahead, good or bad, she had decided to make her way to Garcia's hotel room after her half-shift in the morning. Not to turn up at work might raise a few eyebrows from management and crew when she was new in post, particularly when everyone was suspicious of everyone else.

Crossing the road, she called Jo from a public call box to tell her that Hank was safe and to say all the things she hadn't said from her car while waiting for him to emerge from the clandestine meeting with Brian. Exhaustion had caught up with her. She returned to her flat and slept well for the first time in a week.

62

Kate's shift in the baggage shed flew by. She'd kept an eye out for anything that looked suspicious and got as close as she dared to the three guys whose names she'd passed on to Torres. Without her burner, any dialogue she picked up was committed to memory, no longer overheard by Garcia in the safety of his hotel room. He'd be furious. Tough. Changing priorities at short notice wasn't unusual in their line of work. She couldn't risk exposing Brian before finding out what information he had to give.

She clocked off and left Heathrow, taking a bus to meet Garcia. He was stony-faced when he let her in, checking the corridor before closing the door and locking it.

No words were exchanged.

Fine – Kate wasn't there for a friendly chat.

He'd made it clear last time that their relationship was strictly business. She could only imagine that his negative mood was due to the fact that she hadn't recorded her shift in the baggage shed that morning. He was avoiding eye contact, his jaw set like the blade of an axe, similar to the one she'd used to smash her burner to smithereens. If he was waiting for an apology for that – or not jumping the minute he'd asked to see her – he wouldn't get one. Kate had been buying time, giving Hank the opportunity to carry out her instructions before taking on Torres.

Maybe the SAC had been bending Garcia's ear.

Kate swung round as the adjoining door opened. She wasn't expecting company and tried not to react, though internally her chin nearly hit the floor with a thump as the woman she'd been thinking about entered the room. Torres was around the same height as Kate, a little over six feet tall.

Unlike her colleague, her expression was inscrutable.

She eyeballed Garcia. 'Clear the room.'

She didn't have to ask twice.

He was gone in a flash.

Kate met the impenetrable gaze of the woman facing her, experienced enough to know that they were about to lock horns. Torres didn't invite her to sit, and never took her eyes off the Northumbria detective. It wasn't a glare. Glares required emotion. Torres had none. She had something on her mind she'd dole out when she was good and ready and not before. Temporarily off-guard, Kate's head was spinning, thoughts that swung wildly between what she'd been up to in the past twenty-four hours and the task conferred on her by Homeland Security. It occurred to her that Torres was waiting to hear the lift go down, Garcia along with it.

The elevator wasn't far away.

Summoning all the spirit she could muster, Kate eyed the shoulder holster strapped to Torres's, chest, a reminder of the difference between them and how dangerous a case they were dealing with. To be carrying in the UK required special dispensation, though the special agent would still be subject to the same legal provisos and protocols of any British firearms officer, carefully negotiated by the United States agency and the British government. Her gun was as much a part of her as her upper limbs.

To be unarmed, in any situation, was unthinkable.

Torres hadn't intended making a trip to London and had said as much. The fact that she had, Kate interpreted as suspicious. Either she'd identified a suspect from her own enquiries or the case had taken a different turn. Kate was intrigued, a gut feeling that Torres knew something she didn't, a million scenarios rushing through her head. Had US intelligence dried up, stalling the investigation into the fate of 0113?

Kate didn't ask a question she'd never get an answer to, but whatever was bothering the special agent, it required her help. Why else would Torres waste her time in the UK?

I won't let you down, Gabriele.

The eyes behind the tortoiseshell specs hadn't blinked. 'Let's get one thing clear, Detective . . .' Torres's accent seemed thicker than it had over the secure link. 'If you have a lead, I want it. If you have an informant, you disclose it.'

'That would normally be the case—'

'That is the case. Period. You have something for me?'

Kate returned her gaze, a moment's hesitation while she considered what was really going on here. Clearly, Torres had been talking to Garcia. Only yesterday, Kate had told her that she was bringing 'cake', a euphemism for new intelligence, but no names had been mentioned. By her calculation, it would have been around one thirty in New York then, time enough for the lead investigator to jump on a plane and get over here, but why would she travel three and a half thousand miles without specifics?

Kate relaxed . . .

She was in the driving seat, a fact that seemed to have passed her American counterpart by. Or had it? Torres stood in the centre of the room, a commanding presence, no visible signs of jet lag, which made Kate wonder if she'd been in the capital all along, perhaps working from the US Embassy. Kate had intended keeping her in the loop, but not before she'd had time to meet with Brian and investigate claims that might lead nowhere. If Torres had flown over to oversee the operation personally, it gave Kate pause for thought. Maybe Brian was holding a trump card after all.

'You were made.' Torres's mobile left her hand like a missile.

Kate caught it mid-air.

As the SAC waited, Kate tapped the screen, shocked and embarrassed to find a photograph of herself and Jo outside the hotel at Minster Lovell. They were talking, not kissing – thankfully.

Torres didn't stand on ceremony. 'Agent Garcia has the

ability to follow anyone who isn't taking note of who's behind, someone so keen to reach their destination that they only have eyes front. That's dangerous, the mistake of a third-grader.'

'You're right.' There was no point bluffing. Kate should have, would have, spotted Garcia if she hadn't been so distracted by thoughts of finding Jo. Failing to spot a tail made her look stupid. She'd been caught asleep on the job, and that wouldn't play well with the woman facing her.

Torres kept her voice level. 'Who is she?'

'Not my lead, if that's what you're thinking.'

'Name?'

'Jo Soulsby.'

Tipping her head on one side, Torres frowned. 'The British profiler?'

'Yeah, I found her . . . but then you already know that.' After the desperation of the past week, Kate couldn't believe she was saying that out loud. 'Last-minute change of plan. She's the luckiest woman alive.'

'Congratulations.'

Coming from Torres, the word was drawn out, a 'dj' where the 't' should've been. The special agent wasn't praising Kate's achievement in locating a member of the Northumbria team – a survivor of one of the worst atrocities in recent history; she was being disrespectful, a dig at the DCI for working off-book and failing to spot one man in a car – a rookie mistake she'd made a point of highlighting. Bearing in mind the hundreds of names that must have passed over Torres's desk in the past few days, she'd been quick to recall Jo's name.

Kate would have to be quicker, smarter. 'It seems you've had a wasted journey,' she said.

The eyes didn't flicker. 'Listen, I don't give a flying fuck about you or your girlfriend—'

'Good, because our relationship is none of your business.'

'I made it my business. Whatever the circumstances, there's no room for personal crusaders on my team—'

'Bullshit!' Kate said defiantly. Waverley had said the same thing to her, more or less. Bright, too, though he was her mentor – her guv'nor for as long as she'd been a police officer – so it didn't sting quite as much. 'You'd have done the same thing in my position—'

'What concerns me is your inability to focus solely on 0113.'

'My finding Jo has done nothing to compromise the case. I was state zero with time on my hands, and so was my 2ic. He was following orders.'

'Shame you weren't.'

Dropping her gaze, Kate used her forefinger to flick left and right through Torres's photographs. Had Garcia deployed a surveillance team there would have been more content there, hundreds of photographs taken in quick succession, not one or two. Looking up, Kate chanced her arm. 'Did Agent Garcia stop for grub in Minster Lovell? I see no evidence here of what Hank and I got up to afterwards. It seems we lost him at around the same time as I destroyed the burner you supplied. Next time you decide on surveillance, perhaps you'd have the courtesy of giving me a heads-up.'

Her flippancy had hit home.

Torres wasn't used to backchat. 'Where did you go afterwards?'

'To meet an informant.'

'Specifically.'

'I can't tell you that.'

'You mean you won't.'

'You're a busy woman. I was planning to make contact when I had something worth handing over. I haven't spoken to him myself. I sent Hank in to protect my cover. Like most of my informants, this one won't talk to anyone but me.'

'I have three hundred and sixteen reasons why that doesn't work for me, Detective. Apart from the fact that you and I should have carried out a risk assessment before Hank went in alone, I gave you a specific instruction, which you ignored.'

'I might have a foot in the door. Have you?'

For the first time since Kate entered the room, Torres looked away.

'I'm taking this forward with or without your say-so, Gabriele. You want me to quit so you don't have to fire me? Hey, if that would make things easier for you, say the word and I'm gone.'

'Who is he?' Torres knew she wouldn't get an answer.

The SAC would never divulge a source, any more than Kate would. Even so, she felt compelled to give her something. 'He's a man neither of us wants to mess with. He's underworld, organised, in it for the money, not motivated by cause. Over and above that, I can confirm that he's eluded the authorities for years. I have reason to believe that he can and will unlock the investigation into 0113. He wouldn't have shown his hand if that were not the case.'

Torres didn't respond right away.

She was deliberating, weighing up the pros and cons of using information from a UK felon, a balancing act for anyone in her position, making a judgement about Kate too, no doubt. Their endgame was to wrap up the case, using any means at their disposal, so what in God's name was the woman waiting for?

Kate gave her a nudge. 'Don't underestimate me, Gabriele, or my snout. On a scale of one to ten, he's a ten. His people live in the shadowy space between freedom and incarceration, doing what they do best without a thought for the consequences. Criminals are standing in line waiting for a chance to work for him. He has the means to shut an operation down, up sticks and move on.'

'What does he want in return?'

'I don't know. The chance to carry on without interference from law enforcement I'd imagine, to operate without us treading on his toes.' Kate shoved harder. 'Our presence is pissing him off. He'll disappear if you go cold on me. We have a job to do. We're wasting precious time here. Once this man is in the wind, any information he has will be gone and we'll never find him.'

'Oh, we'll find him.'

Kate crossed her arms, refusing to be cowed, a slight shake of the head. 'Take my word for it, you won't. And even if you did, you'd get sod all out of him. I know him. You don't. And don't ask how, because that's not something I can divulge either.'

'I want results.'

'You think I don't know that?' Kate's tone softened. 'I'd rather cut my heart out than let these ideological freaks get away with a single death. Trust me, if this guy runs, you're nowhere. I may not be Homeland Security, but I'm all you've got. Your call. Do you want this information or not?'

'You think you can get it?'

'I can try.'

Torres didn't answer.

'It could be a game-changer,' Kate pushed. 'So, let's stop playing who's-in-charge and get on with it, shall we? You're going to have to sit this one out. Give me twenty-four hours. What do you say?'

She had her.

264

63

Kate drew a breath of fresh air deep into her lungs as she walked out of the hotel, exhaling slowly, repeating twice more, relieved to have got through her face-to-face with Torres relatively unscathed. Slipping on her sunglasses against the glare of a low sun, the DCI took off in the direction of her flat, keen to hurry things along now she had backing from SAC Torres and a new burner in her pocket. Though she was good for this assignment, with the energy and commitment required to carry it off, Kate had mixed feelings about meeting Brian Allen.

Had Craig and Finn O'Kane not tortured his sons to death, trying to extract information about their father's whereabouts, she liked to think that Brian would have stayed dead and kept his hands clean. In the intervening years, there was every reason to believe that he'd left behind the thuggery that dominated his early life, but, in protecting himself from a rival gang hell-bent on payback, he'd proved that he was still capable of extreme violence. He couldn't afford to back down. It would have meant running away, and that was not his style.

Other than circumstantial evidence linking him to Craig O'Kane's death in Spain, Kate had no proof that Brian had taken the law into his own hands. No one had seen who'd taken the shot to stop O'Kane pulling the trigger on Hank. There were times when police officers were tempted to do nothing and let the bastards kill each other. If Kate was being honest, she was secretly proud of Brian for intervening to save the life of a cop.

She'd arranged to meet Hank in the small café in Hounslow at four o'clock to update him on progress. The argument with Torres meant her meeting had overrun and she was late arriving. He was waiting patiently, nursing a second cup of coffee, the remains of a sandwich on a plate in front of him, a newspaper spread out on the tabletop with the crossword puzzle half done.

He looked up as she approached.

'We're on.' She slumped down in the seat opposite, her back to the window, affording him a good view of the street behind her.

'Torres agreed?'

'Reluctantly and rather personally.'

Hank's eyes widened. 'She's *here*?'

'I suspect she's been here all along. It wasn't a walk in the park convincing her. Put it this way, I'm under no illusion as to what she thinks of me.' Kate eyed the street. 'There's a Ford Focus parked across the road.' She reeled off its registration number. 'A covert team, no doubt. Could be Brian's crew but I'm inclined to think it's Torres.'

'Does she think you were born yesterday?'

'She might. Garcia followed us to Minster Lovell and had the photos to prove it. Fortunately we lost him on the return journey or we'd be in deep shit now.'

'Smart move, boss.' He was referring to the murder of a certain mobile phone.

'Imagine if he'd walked in on you and Brian. It would have been like a gunfight at the O.K. Corral. Did you get the cash?'

'And your wheels.'

'Good.'

Reaching inside the breast pocket of his overcoat, Hank drew out a brown envelope and slid it her way. Inside was a wedge of notes and a set of keys. Anticipating the nod from Torres, however begrudgingly, Kate had already told Hank that if this came off she needed to dump any technology Homeland Security had given her, just as she'd got rid of her police mobile and laptop. Neither would be used during the next phase of her operation – for any purpose – not even for an internet search or to contact Northumbria MIT. Silence and stealth was required from now on. She'd been clear on that score.

'Any update from the Casualty Bureau?'

'Not much . . .' Hank had spent the morning there. 'Elaine Hayes's husband finally knows the truth. Having been told that she was ill at the airport and didn't travel, he was shocked when officers turned up at his door to tell him that she did. Poor bastard was devastated, demanding ID, under the impression that it was the press at his door, not the police.'

Kate understood his confusion. Prior to boarding 0113, Elaine had fainted, spilling the contents of her bag on the floor. Jo had scooped it up, inadvertently handing her the wrong boarding card. In the split second it took Elaine to recover, opting to continue with her journey, Jo elected not to and was escorted landside.

'He must have known when she failed to return home though, surely—'

Hank shook his head. 'They're in the middle of a divorce, no longer living together. He was planning on a reunion when she got back. Sound familiar?'

Kate shuddered.

'It could so easily have been Jo,' he said.

'Thank God it wasn't. Did you call her?'

A nod. 'I told her you'd be out of contact for the foreseeable. She sent a virtual hug.' Hank was buoyant now that his two favourite women were on speaking terms again. 'How are you going to play it with Brian?'

'By the book. He's so minted, I reckon he might own the industrial estate where the two of you met. I can't see him using it a second time. You're done, for now, Hank. Under no circumstances do you go anywhere near it. You and I will not speak again until I have what we want.'

'Be careful.'

A nod. 'If I'm followed, I'll abort.'

64

Kate waited in The Sun for three hours, her head in a magazine, an occasional glance at other customers, none of whom seemed to be paying her any attention. She'd almost given up hope when the phone rang, startling her. Taking the call, she listened carefully to the man on the other end. It wasn't Brian but one of his minions, a young man by the sounds of it. He gave her a location and very little detail, enough to get her from A to B. No doubt there would be a second clue when she got there.

The line went dead.

Checking her watch, Kate waited a few minutes, as instructed. Folding her newspaper, she zipped up her leathers, picking up her motorcycle helmet and gloves. She carried them wherever she went, in case she wanted to hire a bike for business or pleasure. Bypassing the WCs, she used the rear door to exit the pub.

A Yamaha FZ6 Fazer was parked outside, exactly where Hank had said it would be. Kate preferred two wheels over four any day. The machine – much like the one she had at home – had the acceleration and size to weave in and out of traffic, the ability to get her out of trouble . . .

She hoped.

Taking a deep breath, Kate swung her right leg over the machine, dropping her visor, inserting the ignition key before pulling on her gloves. She never made it. Hauled off the bike from behind, she was manhandled towards a four-by-four and bundled into the back seat, two heavies wearing balaclavas flanking her. A female was in the driving seat. As the doors slammed shut, the vehicle took off at speed.

*

Shoved in the back, Kate fell forward, landing hard on concrete flooring, splitting open the deep cut on her hand, her motorcycle helmet rolling away like a giant glossy white marble. Swearing at her attacker, her eyes quickly scanned the inside of the derelict building, smaller than the one Hank had described to her, a former garage by the looks of it. There were half a dozen inspection pits, evenly spaced in the centre. Some had been filled in. Those that remained open were like ready-made graves.

Oh God!

As Kate scrambled to get up, the guy stood on her injured hand, causing unimaginable pain. Pushing her down, he struck her with a fist that felt like a lump hammer as it connected with her forehead. Momentarily stunned, Kate saw double.

She wasn't expecting this.

If Hank had been present, outnumbered or not, there would have been a riot. Ordinarily, Kate could handle herself, but she felt vulnerable without him by her side, more so than she ever had before. Suspecting that her second Homeland Security burner would also be rigged with a tracking device, at her instruction Hank was on the move, leading SAC Torres on a wild goose chase. Garcia too, in all probability.

Without backup, Kate was screwed.

She almost lost consciousness as a second blow landed on the left side of her jaw, followed by a sharp kick in the ribs. Her attacker, a young thug with a shaved head and skull tattoo on the side of his neck, a recent scar on his left cheek, moved away. For a moment, she lay still, praying he wouldn't come back for more, questioning the wisdom of meeting Brian and his crew.

Across the disused garage, a figure appeared in profile, backlit by a streetlight she could see through the rear door on the south side of the building, his entry point. As the Glaswegian came into focus, Kate breathed a sigh of relief. Unless he'd had a personality transplant she'd be safe.

Brian eyed the motorcycle leathers hanging off her left shoulder, the trickle of blood she could feel snaking its way into her left ear.

Kate could see his outrage from ten metres away.

Helping her up, his focus switched to the thug who'd laid into her with no regard for the fact that she was a woman, let alone a copper he had a lot of time for. Maybe the young thug didn't know. Unlikely, Kate decided. He'd have been warned to be careful, not to say too much in front of her.

No one had spoken a word in the car.

The subject of Brian's attention didn't appear so cocky now. The satisfied look in his eyes when he was laying into her had been replaced with blind panic. The muscles in his face were taut, one eye twitching nervously. He looked like he wanted to leg it.

Instead, he froze.

He knew what was coming, and so did Kate.

She met Brian's gaze. 'Don't bother on my account,' she said.

Ignoring her, he tipped his head on one side, his jaw bunching as he moved towards the man with the skull tattoo. Within striking distance, he made him sweat a while, his words slow and deliberate . . .

'Did I fucking ask you to rough her up?'

'No, boss—'

'Did I ask you to speak?'

The guy shook his head. 'No, boss.'

'Then shut the fuck up!'

Kate recoiled as Brian hit the young guy full in the face with the butt end of his handgun, sending blood spurting in all directions, snapping his head around so violently it almost broke his neck. Poleaxed, the kid looked up, hands raised, an appeal for mercy.

'Up!' Brian yelled.

The kid did as he was told. Wiping his mouth on his jacket sleeve, he brought himself upright, offering a grovelling apology to Kate. Other than that, he remained shtum, accepting his punishment and Brian's word that his actions were unwarranted, no way to treat a lady. The Glaswegian had done what Kate would have liked to have done, only with less mess – a sharp kick in the balls, enough to satisfy her sense of justice for overstepping the mark.

Brian apologised to Kate.

'What for? That's what you do, isn't it?'

'He wasn't acting on my instruction.'

Brian shared an economy of language with Torres. He was dangerous if crossed, but also a clever man, bizarrely an honourable man, in the way that those who operated in the murky underworld often were. It made Kate wonder what he might have made of himself had he not been born into a criminal family, experiencing violent behaviour from the moment he drew breath. He'd spent the majority of his life looking over his shoulder.

Such a waste.

He gave what looked like a prearranged signal to clear the building, before lighting up a long, fat cigar. Kate waited for his men to make themselves scarce, her eyes on their boss as a door slammed shut behind them.

'The UK doesn't suit you,' she said. 'You're less tanned than when I last saw you—'

'You're better dressed.' Brian was enjoying himself.

Kate wasn't. 'You caught me at a bad time.'

Brian nodded to someone out of her eyeline.

A woman stepped from the shadows. Made-up, nice eyes, hard as nails, the driver of the four-by-four that had transported her from Hounslow. Tugging at Kate's motorcycle gear, she told the detective to get her kit off.

'Uh-uh, I don't think so.'

'Do it.'

'I never strip, unless asked nicely. Ask your boss.'

'Girls!' Brian puffed out a cloud of smoke. 'Play nice.'

'You heard the man,' the woman said. 'We need to know you're not wearing a wire.'

We?

Kate wondered if they were an item. It wouldn't surprise her. Though rough around the edges, Brian was the quintessential lovable rogue. His former girlfriend, Dr Maria Benitez – who'd helped him construct a new identity by faking a death certificate, and who'd supplied him with the insulin needed to keep him alive – was languishing in a Spanish jail. Other women he'd used as informants, discarded when they were no longer of use to him, were left broken by the experience.

'Why didn't you say so?' Kate unzipped her leather one-piece, allowing it to fall to the floor. She was damned if she was taking off her boots. It was freezing in there. She crossed her arms, grabbing the hem of her T-shirt, pulling it over her head, then held her arms out, allowing the woman to pat her down, though there was no need. Kate's bra and pants were too small to hide a postage stamp.

'You look like you're enjoying that,' Brian chuckled.

Covered in goosebumps, Kate threw him a dirty look. 'Yeah, I'm having a ball.'

'Word is, you need a new squeeze.' He pointed at his female associate. 'In case you were tempted, Stacy's spoken for.'

'She's all yours. Unlike you, I'm not into women half my age.' Kate locked eyes with Stacy, a made-up name. If it had been real, Brian would never have mentioned it. 'Do yourself a favour and ditch him before he ditches you.'

Ignoring the comment, Stacy confirmed that Kate was clean and left to join the others. Seconds later, a car started up outside and pulled away, leaving Kate alone with Brian.

65

Kate shrugged on her leathers, the fog in her head clearing. The Glaswegian didn't know that Jo was alive. Kate wanted to keep it that way. For the first time since she'd been thrust headlong into the building, she studied the man she'd come to see. His attempt at cool was a façade, the eyes behind the new specs tired and tormented, those of someone who'd stood on the edge of the abyss more times than he could count. He was broken, as she had been when she thought she'd lost Jo – only his sons had stayed dead. Giving up everything to protect them had all been for nothing.

She almost felt sorry for him.

Brian wasn't the only criminal she'd grown to like – some villains were charming, laugh-a-minute, protective of those they loved – but he was the only one she'd hate to see locked up for the rest of his days, an outcome she'd lose sleep over. Reasons to lie awake at night were queuing up. Top of that list was whether or not her cover had been blown, a thought that prompted a question.

'How come you knew I was in the area?'

'I didn't.' Lowering his cigar, Brian sat down, placing his gun on the wonky rusting arm of a swivel chair that hadn't been sat on for years. 'In my business, it pays to keep up with current affairs. Your girlfriend's name in the papers was a big fat clue. When one of my guys was arrested by someone whose name he had the presence of mind to remember, I knew you wouldn't be far away.'

'And that concerns you why? You asked for a face-to-face, but I'm not here so we can play catch-up.'

'Shame.'

'I asked you a question.'

'You're queering my pitch, Kate.'

'And you mine.' Sick of standing, Kate upturned a wooden crate and sat down facing him. 'I'm investigating mass murder. What's your excuse?'

He didn't answer.

'Look, I don't have time for this cloak-and-dagger shit, so why don't you tell me what you know and I'll be on my way. If your intel is any good, you have my word that we'll not look too closely at you and yours. But know this: next time we meet, I'll be fully clothed, and there'll be a warrant in my pocket with your name on it.'

Brian threw her a beaming smile.

Embarrassed, Kate looked away. He knew she didn't mean it. He'd saved Hank's life and she'd never forget it. Bright had once asked if she'd let Brian go when she trailed him to the Costa Blanca. She hadn't – and could never be accused of doing so: she was tied to a bedpost at the time he legged it. Recovering from a gunshot wound to the chest, Hank was barely able to walk.

Bright wouldn't let it go.

The end of that conversation echoed in her head now . . .

'You didn't try very hard to go after him.'

'Not my problem, guv. I was a guest of the Spanish and Police Scotland weren't shifting themselves, were they? As far as they were concerned, Brian was outside of their jurisdiction and, when arrested, would become the subject of an extradition row . . . if they could be arsed to fill in the paperwork.'

A villain Brian may be, but Kate felt she owed him a debt. That wasn't a good place to be if you were a police officer. Though Bright loved Hank like a brother, he was fifteen hundred miles away when he was shot. He had no bloody idea what it felt like to be so far from home with an officer down. She was thrilled when Brian took off, evading capture, a secret she'd take to her grave.

A smoking cigar landed on the dusty floor beside her feet,

regaining her attention. Kate ground it out with her boot. When she looked at Brian, his smile had gone. He sat forward, head down, elbows on his knees, hands clasped in front of him, a moment of quiet reflection. He seemed to be weighing up the pros and cons of an internal argument.

He raised his head. 'What would you say if I told you that you're looking in the wrong direction?'

'I'd say you couldn't possibly know that.'

'I know more than you think. This is terrorism, but not the kind motivated by faith, not even close.'

'Then let's hear it.'

A beat of time.

'Start talking, Brian, or I'm out of here.'

'If I were you, I'd give Bright a call. There's a nasty piece of work in your freezer up north with half his head missing.' Bright and Brian were well acquainted. When the two men knew each other, the head of CID was a rookie on the regional crime squad, Brian a young gang leader who'd taken over when his father died, two ambitious young men on opposite sides of the law.

All that was a lifetime ago.

'What are you on about?' Kate said.

'Don't insult me.'

She looked away.

Feigning ignorance hadn't fooled him. She knew he could only be referring to Yulian Nikolaev, whose violent death Robbo and her team were investigating, almost three hundred miles away at Northumbria's Central Area Command. According to Robbo, they weren't getting very far. No one wanted to speak up and risk becoming the next target of these violent gangsters.

Brian could see that she was struggling to make a connection. 'Trust me, you need to head home. You won't find the answers to your air disaster here. I read the papers. The Met haven't a clue. MI5 or Homeland Security either. You're in

275

pole position to earn yourself a leg-up.'

'I don't need a leg-up. And how do I know you're not playing me?'

'You'll have to take my word for it.'

'Your word?' Kate arched an eyebrow. 'You're cracking me up.'

'When have I ever lied to you?'

He hadn't, at least not that she knew of.

'I understand you being sceptical,' he said, 'but ask yourself why law enforcement have no fucking clue, and why no one has claimed responsibility. If this was an ideological terror attack, they would have. These bastards thrive on publicity, invoking fear at every opportunity. They get off on intimidation. Aside from that, there are easier and quicker ways of getting you out of my hair than feeding you false information.'

Kate eyed the nearest inspection pit, a gaping hole in the ground that sent a shiver down her spine. Given their history, she didn't believe that Brian would harm her, but you could never take chances with men like him. 'Forgive me for being dim,' she said, 'but I'm struggling to make a connection between unrelated events happening at either end of the country. None of what you've told me makes sense. You're saying the Northumbria case is linked to this plane falling out of the sky?'

'That's exactly what I'm saying.'

Kate was intrigued. 'Motivated by what, exactly?'

'Profit margins are falling in the drug-running business. The territory is overcrowded, everything up for grabs. Drug cartels have fallen out. They're flexing their muscles, reducing the competition, cancelling each other out.'

'Sounds like history repeating itself.'

He looked wounded. 'I *never* involved myself in drugs. I've seen what that shit does to people.'

Bright had once described him as the most audacious criminal he'd ever come across, but it seemed he was once again telling the truth. There was nothing on his record to suggest that he'd dabbled in illegal substances, hard or soft.

'I need names,' Kate said.

'I need to keep breathing.'

His comment shocked her. It was clear that he didn't want to get too involved. For the first time ever, she could see a vulnerability in his eyes. He was gaunt, pale and fallible, definitely under par. She wondered if he was ill due to his diabetic condition, or just slowing down with age. Her mind was racing. He'd given her a lead, but with no meat on the bones. How could the death of a man involved in trafficking huge quantities of drugs into the UK be the key to the fate of Flight 0113?

Brian gave her a nudge. 'In my world, if you fail to take a warning seriously, you pay the price. My sons are six foot under for that very reason. The O'Kanes weren't going to stop killing until they had finished what I started in 1993. You know that, right? Kill or be killed. That's the way it works. I was no threat to them, but they were too thick to recognise it. Their decision to go after my lads couldn't be ignored, but we are small fry compared to the people Nikolaev wasted before he was taken out.'

'You're saying this is tit for tat?'

'I agree it seems excessive—'

'Excessive?' She spat the word out. 'A catastrophe is what it is. You don't kill over three hundred innocent travellers to take out a rival gang.'

'Gang is too small a word, Kate. This is huge, a global feud between major players worth billions. They have no morals, and more money and fake passports than you and I could ever imagine.' He paused. 'I don't know the ins and outs, but there's a rumour that it – whatever *it* is – went horribly wrong. Not that the people you're after will give a shit. They're ruthless. Why do you think I'm telling you this?'

'I need more.'

'You're smart,' Brian said. 'You'll work it out.'

'With your help, perhaps. Without it, I'm pissing in the wind.'

'I've given you all I've got.'

'Bullshit! You can do better than that.'

'I can't, so you had better get to it. These people won't stop at Nikolaev. They'll decimate his crew.'

That worried Kate. It seemed Robbo was in the centre of a turf war. 'How do you know all this?'

'I have informants who keep me fed—'

'Who I accept will tell you stuff they'd never tell me, but then they must know the ID of the others involved.'

'No one is sharing names.'

'C'mon, Brian, you've come good before. I'll never be able to repay you as long as I draw breath, but I'm begging you to help me nail those responsible for downing that plane.'

'You want blood? Because if I dig too deep, that's exactly what you'll get – only it'll be mine you'll be covered in, along with your own and whoever else gets in the way. These guys aren't fucking about. Whether you choose to believe it or not, I've changed. I'm sick of the violence.'

'Oh yeah?' Her eyes were on his weapon.

'No, really, I'm too old for this.'

Kate believed him.

Robbed of his sons – whose only sin was to have been born into the wrong family – Brian was a shadow of his former self, a man who'd fled to Spain and stayed relatively crime free, until the O'Kanes murdered his offspring. A clean kill would have been one thing; torture was something else. The way Brian's sons had been made to suffer before the O'Kanes put them out of their misery had unleashed a monster intent on revenge.

'I no longer have the desire, nor the energy, to fight or run, Kate. If they get wind of the fact that I'm talking to you, they will kill me.' Picking up his firearm, Brian studied it a moment, turning it over and over in his hands, a pensive look on his face. When he lifted his head, he looked emotional and sad, fear reflected in his eyes. Raising his arm, he pointed the barrel at his head. Kate's mouth dropped open as he released the safety catch. Slowly, he squeezed the trigger.

66

Having trudged almost half a mile to the nearest main road, Kate tried to thumb a ride, but no one slowed for the six-foot biker they probably assumed was a man. Ten or fifteen minutes later, her luck finally turned. Flagging down a cab, with no money to pay for it, she climbed in, giving the driver the address of the hotel where she hoped agents Torres and Garcia would be waiting.

'You OK, luv?' The driver's worried eyes met Kate's in the rear-view mirror.

A nod was all she managed in reply. She wasn't his 'luv', and had too many things on her mind to engage in small talk.

She glanced out of the window, remembering the outward journey, a hessian bag pulled over her head, duct tape wrapped around her neck to keep it in place. Smoke mixed with the motion of the car and the stench of cheap aftershave made her nauseous as they sped along the road. Stacy never spoke, nor did the guys either side of Kate, though she sensed the tension coming off them, all three ignoring the fact that they had abducted a cop.

'Did you have an accident?' The driver again.

For a moment, Kate didn't understand why he was asking, then realised that she was dressed in motorcycle kit, a nasty cut on her hand, dried blood and what felt like a lump the size of St James's Park on her forehead. Lying was sometimes easier than telling the truth. 'Yeah, my bike's a write-off. I'm a police officer. Any chance I could borrow your phone?'

He looked uncertain. 'Can I see your ID?'

'Don't have it on me.'

'Then no can do. I've been robbed before, luv. Comes with

the territory. You should know that. I thought your lot were welded to their ID—'

'Lost my wallet. If you want paying, you'll have to ring someone for me. Pull over.'

The driver obliged. He did want paying.

Off by heart, Kate couldn't remember Hank's mobile number – it was on constant speed dial on her police mobile – so she reeled off her own, knowing he'd pick up any calls. He'd be going out of his mind, having not heard from her. When the cabbie lifted the phone to his ear, she added, 'Tell the guy who answers to bring cash and meet us at the address I gave you.'

Hank was waiting patiently on the pavement when they arrived. He looked stressed out as he settled her fare and helped her from the vehicle, all the while the driver yapping on, asking if she really was a cop, apologising for doubting her, advising Hank that he should take her to hospital and have her medically examined. He said he would, thanked the driver and slammed the rear door, watching the cab disappear into heavy traffic before turning to face Kate, his eyes homing in on her head wound.

'It's nothing,' she said.

'Yeah, I can see that.' He eyed her car, which he'd abandoned at the kerb, the door wide open. 'Get in, I'll drive you to A&E.'

'No need, I didn't come off the bike.'

'I know. I found it lying on its side, keys still in the ignition. What the hell happened?'

'They grabbed me as soon as I left the pub.'

'That's not what I meant. I'll kill that bastard if I ever set eyes on him again.'

'Brian didn't touch me—'

'Well someone sure as hell did.'

'Lock the car and come inside. We don't have time for this.'

In the hotel, Kate ignored the lift that would take her to Garcia's room on the third floor, as well as the sympathetic looks from hotel guests as she passed through reception, finding a quiet corner where she could sit and talk to her overwrought detective partner. Hank was still trying to convince her that she should get checked out by a medic. When she refused, he left her for a moment, returning with a bucket of ice, then proceeded to wrap some cubes in a napkin which he placed in her hand, instructing her to apply it to the goose egg on her forehead.

She did as he asked.

Hank returned to the bar to collect a large bottle of water and two glasses. He set them on the table, poured them both a drink and sat down. Kate drank hers in one go, then filled him in on her meeting with Brian. She told him everything: about the unprovoked assault by the guy with the skull tattoo, the revenge attack that followed, the information Brian had shared with her and the fact that he'd turned the gun on himself, the horrific way in which he'd chosen to end their conversation.

'What?' Hank didn't shock easily.

'It wasn't loaded,' she said, 'but for a moment, I thought . . .' She choked on the words as the scene replayed in her head, an involuntary shiver as a ghost walked over her skin. 'I really thought he was going to off himself right in front of me. The crazy sod knows how to make a point.'

'Which is?'

'He was demonstrating the fact that the people we're up against are extremely dangerous. He's also had enough. Losing his kids has had a profound effect on him. Don't get me wrong, he's no saint, but he's not the man he used to be. He's older and wiser. His gun is insurance, a threat to those who work for him, no more. He told me afterwards that it's never loaded these days.'

'And you believe him?'

'I do, as it happens. Just a feeling I had when I was with him. Assuming he hasn't fed us a load of bullshit, we should be grateful for the information he supplied. If Nikolaev's rival was on that plane, that puts a whole new spin on things. It could be our starting point.' When Hank asked if she intended alerting Bright, Kate shook her head. 'Not yet. Torres is our handler. We're acting as her field team. She's the one we need to convince to take the word of a man like Brian.'

67

On the floor outside Garcia's room there were signs that he had company, and that they had already eaten, two trays lying side by side, waiting to be cleared away by room service personnel. No alcohol, only sparkling water bottles, Kate noticed. She waited for a couple of guys to pass along the corridor before knocking gently on the door, the feeling of being under scrutiny through the spy hole arriving instantly.

Seconds later, the safety chain came off.

Garcia opened up, his gun strapped to his chest.

If Kate never saw another firearm in her lifetime it would suit her. She limped across the threshold, Hank following her in. The US special agents were visibly dismayed when they saw the state of her. She wasn't expecting and didn't want sympathy, nor did she get it. Meeting Brian Allen had been her idea. She wouldn't complain about it now.

Introductions complete, Garcia shook hands with Hank. There was no verbal welcome from Torres, nor any physical contact, merely a slight nod acknowledging the British detective sergeant's presence. Kate could tell that she was pissed at him for having set an anti-surveillance trail, ensuring that no one followed her to her clandestine rendezvous.

Had it not been so serious, Kate might have smiled.

Having told Kate that Garcia had the ability to follow anyone, Torres was affronted by the fact that Hank had done such a good job managing to lose not one, but two US special agents. If she raised the matter, Kate would defend him. She was proud of him. If the Americans had entered the disused garage tooled up while Tattoo Man was polishing his boots on Kate's ribs, there might've been a bloodbath.

The atmosphere in the room was like lead.

Using a remote, Garcia killed the TV, a CNN report of two shootings in Canada's capital city: one at Ottawa's National War Memorial, where a soldier on sentry duty had died from a gunshot wound; and a second attack inside the parliament building, where the sergeant-at-arms, a former mounted policeman, was being hailed a hero for shooting a suspect dead, a man with connections to radical Islamists, the incident occurring days after a terrorist incident in Quebec that killed two Canadian soldiers.

The world had gone mad.

Torres's attention was on Kate, more specifically on the state of her face. 'That motherfucker really worked you over. That's what you get when you put your trust in a convicted felon. You're lucky he didn't kill you—'

Again, Kate found herself defending Brian, telling Torres not to jump to conclusions, that her injuries weren't caused by the informant she'd gone to see. 'If it hadn't been for his intervention I'd have ended up a basket case,' she added. 'If you think I'm a mess, you should see the other guy.'

Ignoring her, Torres examined Kate's head, applying the gentlest of pressure to her left temple.

Kate yelped, pulling away.

'Hold still. Serves you right for going in single-crewed.'

'That's what I told her.' Hank said. 'She has selective hearing, but I don't suppose that's gone unnoticed. She refused a trip to A&E. Maybe you can talk some sense into her.'

Torres ignored him in favour of Kate. 'You look like you could use a stiff drink.'

A nod. 'It might dull the pain.'

A flick of the head from Torres sent Garcia to the minibar. He took out a Scotch miniature, poured it into a glass and handed it to Kate while his boss disappeared into the bathroom, returning a moment later with a first-aid kit to clean her wounds. When Torres was done, Hank replenished the ice pack he'd had the foresight to bring with him from the hotel bar, instructing her to keep it on.

Torres took Kate into the adjoining room, kindly supplying tracksuit bottoms and a clean vest she could change into, closing the door behind her as she left the room. The clothes were a good fit, cool and comfortable, much lighter than Kate's leathers, though they had afforded her a great level of protection from injury, as they were designed to do.

Kate checked out the bed.

Now she was in a place of safety, all she wanted to do was curl up and sleep, but she had work to do that couldn't wait. Her reflection was blurry in the mirror, a bruise quickly developing above and below her left brow. She felt pressure building behind her eye and her sight was not as it should be. Convincing herself that she was mildly concussed, that her symptoms would pass, and spurred on by a potential new lead, she rejoined the others.

Putting them in the picture didn't take long. The special agents listened intently without interrupting. When Kate had finished, she asked Garcia, 'Do you have the passenger manifest handy?'

'Yes, ma'am.'

'The name's Kate.'

'Yes, ma'am.'

'Suit yourself.' Kate thumbed in Hank's direction. 'You should hear what he calls me.' It was the first time she'd heard Torres laugh. The US machine had a sense of humour.

Torres's mood was improving. 'You guys seem tight.'

'Give it time,' Hank joked.

'You've worked together a while?'

'Years. If you look closely, you'll see the scars.' Hank moved a forefinger between the two agents. 'How about you?'

'We go back,' Torres said.

In a matter of minutes, Hank had managed to get more

out of their US counterparts than Kate had in days. Except, unlike Hank, she wasn't fooled. Torres's friendly banter was a front. Underneath the warm and fuzzy exterior lurked a cold and prickly heart.

Kate blinked, trying to clear the film that seemed to have fallen like a veil over her eyes. Special Agent Garcia was out of focus as she studied him. 'I want the names of anyone travelling to Heathrow on a feeder flight from Newcastle.'

'Yes, ma'am.'

Hank was staring at Kate, trying to read her.

Did she look as odd as she felt?

Could he see that she was struggling?

Looking away, she watched as Garcia moved to a desk beneath the window, opened up his laptop and logged on. With the others breathing down his neck, he hit the keys. Details of eight passengers popped up on screen: four adult males, three adult females, one child. The text dancing beneath each one made Kate feel dizzy. She drew up a seat, let out a heavy sigh and sat down beside Garcia. Apart from Jo, who they now knew didn't travel, none of the names meant anything to her.

A non-verbal consultation with Hank resulted in a shake of the head.

He was every bit as clueless.

Torres said, 'If the guy we're after is as high-profile as your informant led you to believe, and not some lowlife peddling illegal narcotics, he'll be travelling under a false passport, an assumed name. He'll look more like a Swiss banker than a drugs baron: smart suit, good shoes, the best money can buy.'

She instructed Garcia to bring up their images.

He resumed typing.

The special agent was lightning fast.

They loaded in grid formation, one child and three women on the top line, four men beneath. Directly to Jo's left was a young child with golden curls and the face of an angel: Jack Harper was five and a half years old. Kate felt sick. Seeing his name on a list was one thing; viewing his cherub-like photograph on Garcia's computer screen was something else. It brought the events of the past week into sharp relief. She hadn't forgotten that, for some, the heartache and pain, the hope and desperation, weren't over. There were two other Harpers on the list who she presumed were the boy's parents. Jack was the spitting image of his mother.

Unwell, tired and emotional, it made Kate want to bawl.

Sensing her unease, Torres placed a hand on her shoulder. 'She's worth stepping out of line for.'

'Given the current state I'm in, she may not say the same about me.' Kate swivelled in her seat, correcting Torres. 'You misread me. The focus of my attention wasn't Jo, it was Jack and his parents. I can't imagine what their extended family must be going through.'

Torres back-pedalled. 'Not so long ago, you were standing in their shoes. There's no one better placed to investigate this appalling act of violence than you. That's assuming you feel up to it. If you're in any doubt, say the word. I wouldn't want to take advantage.'

'And I wouldn't want you to take the credit.' There was a wry smile on Kate's face, but there was also some truth in what she had said, though she lied about how she felt physically. 'I'm fine, so can we all relax? The families of civilians and crew deserve our best efforts. We need to pool all the resources at our disposal. If this turns out to be a linked incident – and I believe it will – my Northumbria unit is at your disposal, Gabriele. They won't let you down and neither will we. Hank and I are in for the duration.'

'Try keeping us out,' Hank said.

Torres thanked him. 'I was hoping you'd say that.'

Garcia didn't exactly nod but Kate could tell he was in agreement. Of course he was – they both were – Torres had zilch until Brian stepped up. Kate had nailed the Ice Queen and her sidekick good and proper.

'My tip-off makes sense to you?' Kate threw it out there. She'd rather know than not.

Garcia said, 'Nothing our investigators recovered from the sea – not that there's much debris – leads us to believe that the bomb on board 0113 was terrorist-related in the true sense of the word.' He didn't elaborate, and Kate didn't ask.

'He's right,' Torres said. 'We're on the clock. Are you two happy to work on?'

'Any chance of room service?' Hank caught Kate's displeasure and added, 'What? I'm bloody starving!'

'Order the whole damned kitchen,' Torres said. 'It's on the US dollar.'

68

They made some calls, working on into the small hours of Monday morning: Torres and Garcia liaising independently with Homeland Security, information crossing the pond digitally, in both directions. Kate placed a call to Bright at three a.m., her lead too hot to wait till morning. As Torres had been quick to point out, they were facing a race against time to find as much evidence as possible before the rats returned to the sewer.

Groggy from sleep, Bright's voice sounded thick in his throat. It took a moment for him to make sense of what Kate was telling him. He gave her short shrift, rubbishing the new intelligence as ludicrous, his voice so loud that everyone in the London hotel room could hear him. Torres and Garcia stopped what they were doing and paid attention. Hank worked on, waking his contacts in the Northumbria drug squad, hoping they might be in a better mood. He was used to his guv'nor bending Kate's ear.

He was still at it. 'Are you saying that you have cast-iron proof that the incidents are linked?'

'Not yet, guv.'

'That's what I thought.'

'That doesn't mean it doesn't exist,' she reminded him.

'Oh yeah?' He muttered softly to Ellen to go back to sleep. 'Then let me put you in the picture, since you obviously have no idea what's going on up here. If you'd been liaising with Robbo, you'd know that nothing has come up that would suggest there's any connection whatsoever to 0113. Find the evidence. When you have it, call me.'

'Guv, I already discussed this with Homeland Security.

They're on board, prepared to accept that the lead I gave you is sound.'

'Are they? Well, according to the press, even their own, they don't know which way is up, so you can tell Torres that you work for me—'

'She can hear you, guv.'

'Then you've no need to tell her. I've made my decision. Until you can give me the rationale behind the course of action you're proposing, I'm not linking the two incidents on the say-so of a snout you've picked up on your travels, no matter how reliable you think he might be.'

Torres rolled her eyes.

If her head was aching less, Kate might have returned the gesture. She didn't. 'I trust my source, guv. The question is, do you trust me?'

'That's a loaded question if ever I heard one. Hold on a moment . . .' He whispered to his wife again: 'Who d'you think? And, as usual, she's not taking no for an answer. Go back to sleep. This won't take long . . .'

It might if he didn't listen.

He was on the move.

Kate imagined him hauling himself out of bed, leaving Ellen's side, moving out of the room, a click as the door closed behind him, walking barefoot down the stairs into the kitchen of his home, the scene of many difficult conversations she'd had with him over the years. Kate heard bottles rattle as he opened the fridge and closed it again, the hiss of a beer can being opened. Bright was a man of habit.

'Do you trust my intuition?' Kate said impatiently.

'Ordinarily.'

'Ordinarily?'

'You've had a tough week.'

He didn't know the half of it. 'We've come through worse. Weren't you the one who told Torres and Waverley that they were lucky to have me?'

'They are, but let's not pretend, eh? You didn't go down there to lend a hand out of altruism. We both know you went to find Jo and nothing else mattered. Not me, your position as SIO, your father. I could go on—'

'Point taken, but—'

'But nothing!' He raised his voice. 'You barged your way into the Casualty Bureau without authority. You disobeyed orders and dragged Hank into this with complete disregard for his family and his role within the MIT. Kate, you've got what you wanted. Jo is safe, and I'm very pleased to hear it, but you need to come home, take stock and use the leave you booked before you lose her a second time.'

Kate could feel her face burning. 'In the middle of this mess?'

She may as well have said, *that's never going to happen*.

Across the room, Hank ended his call. He knew what Bright was like but Garcia didn't. The special agent dropped his gaze, embarrassed that Kate was being ticked off so publicly. Not so Torres. She was listening intently; having no doubt mixed it with guys like Bright her whole working life, she could read the situation. Kate might be taking a verbal beating, but she was sticking it to her superior, unafraid to say her piece, committed to her point of view.

'Guv, Jo wouldn't want me to pull out now. You know she wouldn't. Together, we have a chance to contribute. I have reason to believe that this is not over yet. If my source is right, the killing won't stop here.'

'Then find me hard evidence.'

Kate was beginning to lose her temper, but he wouldn't listen if she tried to make out that her motivation in the early stages of the investigation into the fate of 0113 wasn't exactly as he'd described. 'OK, my hands are up. Our hearts rule our heads sometimes. Even yours.' She kept it general, no specific references. No need to spell it out.

'I called in a favour,' she said. 'And I'm not about to throw it in the faces of those who put me in a position where I might do some good. My lead makes sense. I'm begging you to run with it.'

'It might help if you told me who your snout is.'

69

Torres locked eyes with Kate, wondering what the British SIO would do next. Kate wasn't sure she knew. She asked Bright to hold on a second. Thinking time. Excusing herself, she moved into the next room for some privacy. She hadn't revealed the identity of her informant to Homeland Security personnel, and was damned if she'd do so now. In talking to her, Brian had put himself in mortal danger, earning himself anonymity. It was up to her to see to it that he received it. Bright, on the other hand, deserved to know the full story. Since she was a teenage rookie in uniform, he'd been so much more than her senior officer; he might be a difficult man on occasions, but she could and would trust him with her life.

Holding onto her ribcage, she eased herself gingerly onto the bed, every bone in her body aching, her sight still cloudy. Consulting a doctor would have to wait. Lying back against soft pillows, she yawned, almost yelping with the resulting pain in her jaw. 'Brian Allen is my source,' she said.

'*What*?' It came out like an explosion. 'Since when?'

'He made contact with me two days ago—'

'How in hell's name did he manage that?'

'Does it matter?'

'It does to me. Did you know he was in the UK?'

'No, what do you take me for?'

'Then how did he get your number?'

Steeling herself for another dressing down, Kate drew in a deep breath. There were times in her career when, for good reason – to protect his reputation rather than her own – she hadn't been entirely honest with her guv'nor. Sometimes he'd found her out and reprimanded her for it, other times not. But she was hoping that if she told the truth now, it might sway him to back her point of view.

Tell him . . .

Get it over with.

'Brian had access to my mobile when he confronted me in Spain.'

'What? For fuck's sake, Kate. Potentially, you've compromised every police officer in your contacts list as well as your private numbers and any communications you sent or received from the MIT while you were over there trying to locate him.'

'There's no evidence of that, Phil.' She used his first name, hoping his attitude would soften. 'I've not heard from him in two years. In Spain, he used the phone to get Hank's attention, to ensure that he wasn't followed. Five minutes later, he was gone, leaving it under the wheel arch of my hire car before making good his escape, as he said he would.'

'That was big of him. Why am I only hearing about this now?'

'I didn't withhold it deliberately, I swear. I was tied up, physically. Hardly in a position to argue or make demands.'

There was a long silence. 'OK, I'm listening. Have you had any personal contact with him since you were on the continent?'

'Not until last night, no. You'd have been the first to hear of it if I had.'

'Is that right?'

'Believe what you like. Do you want to hear what I've got to say or not?'

'I'm still here, aren't I?'

'Hank met with him first, but he wanted a face-to-face with me and wouldn't tell him anything. I think he did it to protect Hank. Brian told me that I was looking in the wrong direction, that I should liaise with you and look closer to home. He mentioned a nasty piece of work in the deep freeze with half his head missing, or words to that effect, obviously referring to Nikolaev. He said that the people who killed him are off-the-scale heavyweights.' Kate gave a brief summary, leaving out the fact that she'd been bundled into a car like a sack of shit and worked over by one of the Glaswegian's men. 'If you'd seen how spooked he was, you wouldn't doubt the validity of his claims. He sent his crew packing. The fact that he wasn't prepared to talk with any of them present spoke volumes.'

Torres eyed Kate as she walked through the door, a mixture of suspicion and respect from a special agent well versed in the craft of using informants from the criminal underworld. Penetrating and neutralising organised crime syndicates – on whatever scale – was never easy. It would be doubly difficult if Brian's information turned out to be accurate. A lever, however small, against top-level personnel in the drug-trafficking world was useful to law enforcement.

'Is your ball-busting chief onside?' Torres asked.

A nod from Kate. 'He is now.'

'Your source must be major league—'

'Yeah, and he's put himself in the firing line talking to me. I'll do anything to protect him, Gabriele.'

'We're on the same side.' It was a gentle nudge to divulge her source.

'It's not that I don't trust you.'

Torres said no more.

Kate was tempted to tell her why Bright had changed his mind so readily. She chose not to. If she slipped up and gave too much away, the SAC would look into it. If the roles were reversed, Kate would, too. It was in their DNA to get the low-down on anything connected to a case, including investigating the good guys, which Brian was on this occasion. If he got a whiff of outside interference, he'd go to ground. Kate would lose him. She couldn't afford that.

Despite what he'd said, he might have more to give.

Since Kate left the location of their rendezvous, she'd not heard from him. They had not parted on good terms. After his spectacular demonstration of what he'd face if discovered feeding her intelligence, she'd flown into a rage that came from deep within. She'd almost thrown up as he pulled the trigger, expecting the firing pin to move forward, forcing the bullet out of the barrel, blowing out his brains. On seeing her reaction, the bastard laughed out loud.

I didn't know you cared.

That was the problem.

70

Having transferred from Garcia's hotel suite to the offices of the FBI's legal attaché at the US Embassy in London, they were set up in a spacious incident room with all the equipment they required. As special agent in charge, Torres was right at home, as she might have been in any of the FBI's fifty-six field offices across the United States. Based on Brian's tip-off, they had been there exactly a week.

Working on the premise that Nikolaev's death was tit for tat, that he'd killed a rival and was then executed for it, British detectives and US agents worked in tandem, each and every passenger on board 0113 undergoing forensic scrutiny. Picking over the minutiae of their lives, including background, family and known associates, the process they were hoping would identify Nikolaev's target was slow, painstaking work. Day after long day, they had ploughed on, amassing a mountain of paperwork, ruling people out, digging deeper into others.

They had begun with the obvious: ten middle-aged males who, on the face of it, were legitimate businessmen, but whose passport information suggested they were either from, or had links with, areas where the trade in illegal narcotics was rife – South and Central America, Asia, Africa, Russia. Crime families were active in places like Mexico, Colombia, Brazil, Bolivia, Peru and Venezuela, controlling the heroin and cocaine trade, shipping large quantities and weapons via mules into the United States and elsewhere, polluting society, increasing addiction and drug-related deaths.

The US, too, had its fair share of these Mafia-type figures who all had one thing in common. If the top dog was taken out, the head of an organisation chopped off, figuratively or literally, there was always a lieutenant waiting in the wings, ready to step in and take their place. Those that were imprisoned, rather than killed by a rival, were well looked after inside, resuming control the minute they swaggered in through the prison gates.

This is what law enforcers were up against.

Kate's mobile rang: Robbo.

'Boss, apologies for not coming back to you before now. I just wanted to let you know that no one has been asking after you specifically. I've spoken to everyone in the office, police and civilians, even the front desk, in case they took a call they couldn't immediately transfer to the incident room—'

'It's not important now. Sorry, I should've cancelled my request – the narrative has changed, Robbo. I'm flat out here, and I know you are too.'

'Bright told me we have a credible lead, but wouldn't say where it came from.'

'Nobody needs to know where it came from, including you. Take it as read. The important thing is that we have a linked incident that's drug-related, possibly cartel-related. You said yourself, no one up north will talk. You need to find someone who will.'

The line was open but Robbo didn't respond. He was probably pissed off that she hadn't shared the name of her informant.

'Robbo?'

'I'm still here.'

Kate detected resentment in his voice. 'We're not freezing you out, mate. I need you on your toes. The people we're after prefer to solve their own problems. Nikolaev's death is part of that. His objective was to get rid of the competition. We still don't know who the competition is, but we have reason to believe that the head of a rival gang was on that plane.' She remembered that he was an old pal of a DS in the drug squad. What Pete Brady didn't know about the underworld wasn't worth knowing. 'Put the feelers out with Pete but give nothing away. Tap your informants. Call me if you find anything.'

'Will do.'

Time to bolster his flagging ego.

'This is your chance to shine, Robbo.'

'I won't let you down, boss.'

Kate disconnected, hoping he could handle an enquiry this wide-ranging. She couldn't help noticing that Hank's head was down. There were many foreign-sounding names on the passenger manifest. Before she took Robbo's call, Hank had intimated that most of the 0113 passengers would be innocent travellers in transit, merely passing through JFK en route to somewhere else. Garcia agreed, pointed out that New York had the largest foreign-born population of any city in the world. He was the son of a Portuguese immigrant who'd arrived in the US when he was a child; Torres of Italian descent, like Esposito, the woman they'd had dealings with in Heathrow.

The world was shrinking.

Across the room, Torres was on the phone, feet up on her desk, the epitome of cool, despite the fact that the person on other end was giving her a hard time. It brought to mind Kate's conversation with Bright. Internal politics was part of the job, something both women had to cope with. Kate was impressed with Torres' professionalism. The SAC had clout. Based on nothing more than the say-so of a man whose identity she still didn't know – and a few snippets of information that supported his theory from the MIT – she was trying to persuade a big cheese in Homeland Security that a preliminary criminal investigation, led by air accident investigators and UK police, rather than US special agents concerned with anti-terrorism, was the way to go.

So far, she was holding her own.

'Sir, as of this morning, the most senior detective from one of the largest police forces in the UK has officially linked 0113 to the murder of a billionaire in the north of England,' she said. 'The murder victim was Yulian Nikolaev, kingpin of a Russian drug-running syndicate. We have reason to believe that his successor may be getting ready to avenge his death. Let me be clear: at this stage I'm not asking for anyone to be stood down . . .'

Just as well, Kate thought, because MI5 weren't listening.

Two days ago, Bright had flown to London, briefing top officials, including the Home Secretary, on the possibility that 0113 might not have anything to do with terrorism. His suggestion that it was part of a war between rival factions in the murky underworld was met with ridicule. Kate hoped, prayed, that she'd discover the truth of it, handing him the evidence that would prove him right.

'No, I agree,' Torres said. 'It's too early to make that call, but I'm prepared to accept that Detective Chief Inspector Daniels has stumbled upon vital intelligence that will take us closer to a resolution. Yes, that is correct. To run an enquiry on the scale outlined, I'm under no illusion that we require as much technical expertise as we can lay our hands on, from wherever we can get it. Yes, sir, thank you . . . yes, I'll keep you updated as and when we have anything to report.'

Kate began to relax.

Torres hung up and threw down her pen. Cupping her hands behind her head, she took a breather. Though she remained convinced that the case was beginning to turn on its head, despite exhaustive enquiries on both sides of the Atlantic by Homeland Security agents and Northumbria detectives, things were not moving fast enough for her liking, or those of her superiors, a thought she verbalised in the strongest possible terms, frustration finally getting the better of someone normally so unflappable.

Her eyes were on Kate. 'I'm sticking my neck out here. We can't work in a vacuum. You need to lean on your contact.'

'Won't do any good,' Kate said. 'If he had an ID, he'd have passed it on.'

'It's been a while since you two spoke.'

Kate scooped her mobile off her desk, making out that she was checking the screen. Unbeknown to Torres, she'd called Brian several times, leaving messages to no avail. If she had a mind to, Kate could find their rendezvous, and knew the location of the warehouse where Brian met up with Hank, but she doubted it would yield results. If Brian was in danger, he was too clever to hide in a place he'd used before, a location where he might be found, by her or the people who might now be looking to kill him for speaking out.

'I'll make the call,' Kate said.

Torres hadn't picked up on her anxiety. 'Let's back up a second. If Nikolaev struck first, he'll have kept his hands clean, paying a hitman to do his dirty work for him. He or she might be the only one who knows the identity of his target.'

'Find the hitman, find the target,' Kate said.

'You make it sound so easy.' Garcia was being facetious, the first time he'd spoken up without being asked to. 'I'll make some calls, ma'am, but your shooter will be long gone, assuming he's still breathing. For all we know, Nikolaev's successor may have taken him out already. If he's also dead, we're screwed.'

'It would explain why Nikolaev's crew – the few we know of – are shitting themselves up north,' Hank said. 'With any luck, they'll off each other and we can all go home.'

Kate tried to lift them. 'Take a break, you two. We're good for this. If we can't find the hitman, we keep searching until we find the target, however long it takes. No one on that flight is in a hurry, and their families want this done right . . .' Her eyes found the giant aircraft-shaped seating plan pinned to the wall, complete with the names of passengers according to the seats they had booked. 'I won't rest until we crack this case.'

Torres glanced at Kate. 'What's the latest intel?'

'Northumbria MIT are flat out. Nikolaev's crew aren't about to implicate themselves in any criminal activity, much less the murder of a competitor, but according to the eyes and ears on the street, they're growing increasingly nervous, and not necessarily about us. They're hunkered down, expecting a further backlash.' Kate made a judgement call. 'Hank and I need to head home.'

71

They took the evening flight out of Heathrow, touching down in Newcastle ten minutes ahead of schedule at nine fifteen. It was pouring with rain, a chill in the air as they disembarked, not that either of them cared. Even walking across the tarmac towards the terminal building, the difference in air quality was noticeable. They were thrilled to be on home soil, a chance to review the investigation into Nikolaev's murder in case Robbo had missed anything.

As they waited to reclaim their kit from the carousel, Kate thought about her time in the baggage shed. On the face of it, her undercover assignment hadn't yielded much; a couple of arrests for pilfering, but flagging Patterson had ultimately led to Brian, who might yet prove to be instrumental in resolving the investigation into 0113.

He'd since gone cold on her.

Worrying.

As she stood there watching luggage of all shapes and sizes slide through the strip curtain, the scrum of passengers sharpening elbows waiting to collect it, fragments of their conversation replayed in her head: *What would you say if I told you that you're looking in the wrong direction? You need to head home. You won't find the answers to your air disaster here.* Well, in the short term, Kate was home.

What now?

That question prompted others. How would she go about investigating Brian's claims? Where would she begin to unravel the assassination of two high-profile figures, one a Russian citizen, the other as yet unidentified? Numbers of drug-related deaths in the US and UK were staggering, associated murders and sudden disappearances almost as bad.

The drug squad had been on the blower to Hank, pointing out that Nikolaev had outfought several rivals in a bid for domination. He was alleged to have amassed a fortune from his trafficking exploits. His crew would be looking to continue in this vein. These people were scum. The North-East had the highest mortality rate from drug misuse. If the likes of Nikolaev had their way, that situation would remain.

Then there was the 'other' problem . . .

Since the assault by Brian's young cohort, Kate had experienced a few memory issues. She'd not shared that with anyone, not even Hank, putting on the appearance that she was fully functional – a competent, seasoned professional going about her business – when it was far from the truth. All week, she'd had a sense that Brian had said more than she'd been able to recall, stuff she should've fed to Torres. That onerous thought brought with it a sense of foreboding and frustration, like she'd lost pieces of a jigsaw she was desperate to finish. Only when they were located would the complete picture emerge.

It wasn't the first time she'd felt like this. Finding missing fragments of information went with the territory – the only way was to trace, interview and eliminate suspects – but there was a fundamental difference between that and what Kate was experiencing now. She wasn't grasping at something she didn't know, but something she did.

In her peripheral vision, Hank wandered off.

Kate now wished she'd taken him with her when she went to meet Brian. Clichéd though it may be, two heads really were better than one. By nature, she was a practical person. If a problem presented itself, she felt compelled to solve it, even if it meant breaking protocol. In order to secure intelligence that might help Torres, she'd been forced to play by Brian's rules, and now she was off her game.

Coppers couldn't afford that luxury, but she'd allowed her emotions to cloud her judgement as she had when she was looking for Jo. Kate had to put that behind her now and move on with a complex case that demanded her full attention. It must take priority over all else – and still that missing jigsaw piece refused to surface. Shutting her eyes, she replayed her conversation with Brian, walking herself through it, as she would in a cognitive interview with a suspect. She saw it like a video game, transporting her to that disused garage, a smoking cigar, a dusty floor, the inspection pits and her anxiety over what might already have been buried in them, her fear that one wrong move might see her run out of road. She recalled her surprise when Brian talked of a global feud between major players and her gut reaction to it.

That was her sticking point . . .

Try as she might, she couldn't get past it.

'Kate?'

The monologue was still running. Then, at the precise moment that Hank called out to her a second time – louder now, in an attempt to gain her attention – the elusive information clicked into place, like a roulette ball coming to rest in a pocket bearing the same number as the square where her chips were placed.

An idea arrived instantaneously.

She swore under her breath.

'Too slow.' Hauling his bag onto his shoulder, Hank walked towards her, an exasperated expression on his face.

For a split second, Kate was confused. 'For what?'

'Your holdall. It's on the magic roundabout. It sailed right by. Didn't you see it?' He lifted a hand, fending off a reply. 'Oh, I get it. Grunt work, right?'

'Sorry, I was distracted.'

'You don't say.' He shook his head. 'Be honest, Kate. You've been out of it since we left London. What the hell's wrong with you?'

'Keep it down, Hank. You sound like a disgruntled husband and I've got the remains of a black eye. Not a good combination, is it?' Kate spied the holdall before it disappeared through the strip curtain again. 'There's no need to lose your rag, I'll get it next time round. If you're in such a hurry, get yourself away. Whatever you do, don't wait on my account.'

He did, impatiently, and not out of politeness.

Kate was famous for not paying attention when she was mulling over a problem. In such circumstances, her lack of focus wasn't unprecedented, but neither was it the action of someone dying to get home, as Hank was.

He stared at her. 'Go on then, tell me what's on your mind.'

'I just remembered something Brian told me. It completely slipped my mind.'

'Nothing ever slips your mind—'

'Yeah, well, I wasn't thinking straight, was I? Tattoo Man was busy rearranging my teeth.'

'So, tell me.'

'Brian heard a rumour that something had gone horribly wrong. I don't know what he meant by it. I'll have to ask him.'

72

The question remained: how, despite rigorous scrutiny at Heathrow, a bomb had managed to circumvent airport security to take out 0113? Kate chewed on this thorny question as she followed Hank from the baggage area, held up by dawdling parents with frazzled toddlers riding on luggage trolleys. Up ahead, one small boy took off, flying into the arms of his grandfather, his golden curls reminding Kate of Jack Harper, who'd never see his grandparents again.

The DCI swallowed the lump in her throat.

The sight of Julie and Ryan Gormley waiting at the barrier for Hank lifted her; a happy family reunion – smiles and hugs all round – as if Kate's 2ic was a hero returning from a long-running conflict overseas. Feeling like she too had been engaged in battle, Kate could relate. Battered and bruised from her encounter with Brian's yob – but with her memory throwing up an all-important missed beat – she couldn't wait to pick up the reins with the Murder Investigation Team.

Having been warned that she was heading home to the North-East, the squad had been fully briefed to expect her first thing in the morning. From now on, detectives from across the force would be working round the clock. As soon as she clapped eyes on Kate, Julie's mouth formed the letter O. She turned on her husband, giving him a piece of her mind for not having protected his 'other' wife. Some of the passengers who followed them out were looking very confused. Julie wasn't joking. She saw less of Hank than Kate did.

'Believe me, I tried,' Hank said in his defence.

'Not hard enough,' his wife said. 'Look at the state of her!'

'It's a bruise,' Kate said.

'Yeah, on your face, not his.' Julie held up her car keys. 'C'mon, we'll drop you at home.'

Not wanting to intrude on Hank's homecoming, Kate refused a lift, opting to take a cab to Holly Avenue where she lived, a short distance north of Newcastle in the leafy suburb of Jesmond, a fifteen-minute ride from the airport. She could have taken the Metro but couldn't be arsed to walk even the short distance from the station at the other end. She was exhausted, the emotional fallout of the past couple of weeks taking its toll.

She'd simply hit a wall.

As the taxi pulled to the kerb, Kate noticed two things: a light on inside the house and Jo's car parked directly opposite. This time Kate had money to pay the driver and couldn't get out of the cab fast enough.

As it sped off, she practically ran up the path to her front door.

Fumbling her key in the lock, she pushed it open, the smell of food, rich and meaty, and the sound of Mary Lambert 'She Keeps Me Warm' drifting out from the kitchen, the door of which stood ajar. The lyrics alone were enough to make her weep. They spoke of a woman not being able to change, even if she tried, even if she wanted to; a story Kate could identify with – and some.

Squeezing past her Yamaha motorcycle, Kate hung her coat on a peg, dumping her kit on the floor, ignoring a neat stack of mail on the table. Ruffling her hair as she moved along the hallway, she wondered how Jo had managed to get in when she no longer had a key. She'd given hers to Fiona on the eve of her trip to New York, a signal that her relationship with Kate had run its course.

Thankfully she hadn't travelled.

At the kitchen doorway, Kate lingered a moment, watching Jo stirring the contents of a pot on the stove with a wooden spoon. This was her favourite room in the house: all clean lines, modern appliances, bamboo blinds that gave the place an oriental feel, subdued lighting, downlights only. Licking a splodge of sauce from her left forefinger, she wiped her hand on the back of her skinny jeans and picked up a glass half full of red wine. Taking a sip, she replaced it on the counter. She turned, sensing that she was not alone.

As their eyes met, Jo's face lit up.

If Kate could bottle that moment as a keepsake, she would.

Leaning against the kitchen counter, Jo couldn't fail to see how choked Kate was to arrive home and find her cooking dinner. Homing in on Kate's black eye, an exaggerated frown appeared on Jo's face as she tried to lift Kate from her melancholy mood. 'Ouch!' she said. 'Either that hurt when you got it or you're still undercover and in disguise.'

Kate's laughter almost turned to tears. 'How did you—'

'I was in the incident room when word came in that you were on your way home. Bright charged in, briefed the team, cancelling all leave at short notice. No excuses—'

'Yeah, but he didn't mean yours.'

'I volunteered to assist.'

'For me?'

'You might have had something to do with it. I won't lie. It wasn't the only reason. Remember that paper I wrote on desensitisation to violence among those embroiled in gang culture? Bright actually read it. Hard to believe, I know . . . I gather he was quite impressed by it.'

'He should be,' Kate said. 'You're very impressive.'

Jo caught the compliment but made a crazy face. She hadn't always got along with Bright. Before his promotion to his current post as head of Northumbria CID, he was the Detective Superintendent in charge of the Murder Investigation Team, Kate's immediate boss. He'd been too quick to charge Jo with her late husband's murder, something he'd later come to regret. And now he thought she might assist in the investigation into Nikolaev's assassination.

Jo struck a casual pose, feet crossed at the ankles, the wine glass in her hand. But she seemed nervous around Kate, awkward now that they were finally alone.

'How did you get in?' Kate asked.

Jo threw her a smile. 'Lisa seemed to remember you asking Hank to collect some case papers you'd taken home to study and needed urgently. She said you'd told him to hang onto the spare key in case the same thing happened again. I rang Julie on the off-chance she might know where he kept it.'

'Ah, no wonder she was so keen to drop me here.' Kate smiled. 'She didn't, I took a taxi, but it was nice of her to offer. It seems that we have more than one Cupid in our lives, both with the surname Gormley.'

'You're OK with me being here? I mean, if—'

'Jo, I never want you to leave my sight again.'

They stood for a while, eyes meeting across the room. Having made the first move, Kate didn't know what to say or do next. She decided to play it by ear – she'd already taken too much for granted – but the urge to hold her was strong. She took a few steps forward and had just put her arms round Jo when her mobile rang, killing the moment.

'Sorry.' She stepped away, slipping the device from her pocket, briefly checking the screen. Declining the call, she put it away, another apology on the tip of her tongue she didn't get out quick enough.

'Anyone interesting?' Jo turned away, stirring the pot again.

With her eyes on Jo's back, Kate panicked, wondering if she thought the call had come from Fiona at the most inopportune moment, when they had so much to say to one another. She hadn't heard from Fiona since she'd left word that Jo was safe, over a week ago. Was she overthinking this, seeing something that wasn't there? No, she didn't think so. It was the look in Jo's eye before she turned away that sealed the need for an explanation . . .

'It was Lisa,' she said. 'I'll call her later.'

Jo swung round. 'Call her now.'

'I don't want to. Really, it can wait.'

'Kate, it's fine.'

There was an urgency in Jo's voice that baffled Kate.

Jo picked up a remote control, turning off the music, her expression darkening. 'Kate, you have to call Lisa. She knows I'm here waiting for you. Believe me, she'd rather die than interrupt us tonight.'

Kate made the call, lifting the phone to her ear.

Carmichael answered immediately. 'Guv, you need to come now.'

73

Jo drove Kate to Northern Area Command, known as Middle Earth to those who worked there, though today no one was laughing or using the nickname. The whole of Middle Engine Lane was taped off, a deposition site rather than a crime scene. As Kate approached, broken and stunned by the development, detectives and uniformed personnel standing immediately outside the police cordon parted to let her through. Their heads were bowed, grave expressions on their faces. Hank was already there, Carmichael too.

No words were spoken.

Acting Detective Inspector Paul Robson's body was lying face up in front of the main entrance, one arm extended. He'd been thrown from a fast-moving vehicle like a sack of garbage, shot several times at point-blank range, once through the head, taking four in the chest. Swallowing hard, Kate looked away, Brian's words entering her head: *You want blood? Because if I dig too deep, that's exactly what you'll get – only it'll be mine you'll be covered in, along with your own and whoever else gets in the way.*

Hank had his arm round Carmichael. She was visibly distressed, nodding a response to something he'd said, words of comfort from her supervision. In time, Hank would speak to each and every member of the team. No matter the circumstances, the MIT couldn't afford to crumble. He turned, walking towards Kate, a forlorn figure, as sad as he was incensed by yet another tragedy, this one too close to home.

Kate stared at her fallen colleague, lying in the middle of the road, covered in blood, hardly recognisable. Like a jumbled montage, memories of their time together scrolled through her head: the day she and Robbo had met, cases they had solved together, the difficult conversations over his gambling addiction, but mostly the laughs and camaraderie in and out of the office. The day his son was born, Kate remembered him running like a loon from the incident room having received the call that his wife had gone into labour. The joy of becoming a father to Callum, now five years old. Celebrations to wet the baby's head had been curtailed due to pressure of work, but Robbo had returned to lend a hand before his paternity leave was over. He'd invited Kate to be the child's godparent. Having lost her faith when her mother passed away, she'd declined.

Today, she was regretting that decision.

'He never stood a chance.' Bright's eyes burned with hatred as he turned to face Kate. 'This is a warning to stay away. Robbo had been asking around, hoping to find someone willing to talk about Nikolaev. Lisa said he looked upbeat when he left the incident room, heading off to meet an informant. Whoever he or she is, I want them found.'

'Yes, guv. We'll need to spend some money.'

'Do it. The budget is my problem.'

'Has anyone informed his family?'

'Not yet.' Bright checked his watch. 'I need to get over there.'

'No, guv. I'll take care of it.' Delivering the death message was a task every police officer dreaded, doubly so if it involved one of their own, but Kate was Robbo's SIO. It was her duty to speak to his widow. 'Guv, I'm sorry, I should've been here.' She broke off, leaving the rest of the sentence unsaid.

'This is not your fault,' Hank said, as he arrived at her shoulder. 'If I'd returned to base when the guv'nor asked me to—'

'Well, you didn't!' There was a hard edge to Bright's voice. 'So, don't start whingeing about it now. Man up or get the hell out of my face. That goes for you too, Kate. There's no time for recriminations, what ifs or maybes. You didn't follow orders and I didn't make you. We're all at fault here. I need your minds on the job, not halfway down the fucking motorway.'

'They will be, guv.'

'They had better be.'

Kate's eyes found Jo's. She was in the car, waiting. Kate refocused on her guv'nor. 'If Jo is willing, I'll take her with me. You know what Irene's like. There's zero chance of her accepting a Family Liaison Officer and her parents are in the South-West. It'll take them a while to get here, Robbo's parents not so long. Jo and Irene get on. She doesn't need a stranger in the house.'

A nod. 'Don't use Jo's vehicle. Keep it out of sight, away from the main road. That goes for everyone else, too.'

Bright glanced at the detectives standing around with their hands in their pockets, many of whom were state zero when they heard. Some had been summoned by the control room, others had arrived of their own volition, making themselves available for work. Like him, they were anticipating a long night.

'You want me to wait for the pathologist?' Hank asked.

'No, seal the street.' Bright looked up at the windows of Northern Area Command HQ where staff with horrified faces stared down from practically every window. 'Put the word out. If any fucker in this building shares an image of Robbo on social media, they will be sacked. Then I want you in the incident room to get the ball rolling.' He thumbed at the crowd. 'There's no better time to remind them why we do what we do. Kate, I'd like you back in an hour, sooner if you can manage it. Don't let me down.'

74

The street was quiet, not a soul about. Jo knew the drill, aware that when the spouse or parents of a serving police officer opens the door at a quarter to midnight, sees a traffic car parked outside and a DCI standing on the step, they tend to know. Irene Robson was no different. It was a scenario that most loved ones had imagined many times, praying that it would never happen, including Jo herself when Kate was late arriving home.

The light went out in Irene's eyes.

Without asking why Kate and Jo were there, she turned away, padding across wooden flooring in bare feet, leaving the door wide open. Kate entered the house first, Jo following her in. They had hardly spoken in the car. Jo would take no part in conveying the bad news. Her role was to be on hand to look after Irene for as long as required afterwards. Only then would she have time to pick Kate off the floor.

As they passed along the hallway, Kate glanced at Jo: *I can't do this.*

Jo sent a non-verbal reply: *Yes, you can.*

Could she, though? Kate wasn't sure for how much longer.

The last time they were in the house had been a social occasion – laughter, presents, balloons and alcohol, the whole squad invited to celebrate Robbo's thirtieth, a big party that spilled out into the rear yard where lanterns burned all night and Carmichael kept the music going with the help of her bestie, DC Andy Brown.

The atmosphere was very different tonight.

Irene was sitting on the edge of the settee when they entered the living room, her face turned towards the door, a ghostly white. Wearing striped pyjamas, her hair tangled and sweaty, she looked like a kid who'd woken from a nightmare, shivery and cold, except that for her the horror was real.

Jo had never been present in a situation like this, but there'd been too many occasions when Kate had returned home in the early hours, wrung out after delivering 'the knock', breaking the news that a family member had died in violent circumstances. This time it was personal, not only because she knew the victim and his family, but because she blamed herself, thinking that she should've been the one Nikolaev's men had made an example of. The one now en route to the city morgue.

Hopefully Irene didn't feel the same way.

The woman who didn't yet know she was a widow was probably hoping for a non-fatal accident, the traffic car to speed her to a local hospital to sit by her husband's bedside. Kate was about to disabuse her of that self-deception and take away all hope.

Irene beat her to it.

'Is it bad?' She didn't wait for a reply. Seeing the answer reflected in Kate's eyes, Irene dry-heaved, hand finding her mouth, unable to stem the wail waiting there. 'He didn't make it?'

As Kate sat down, the two women fell into an embrace, grieving for a husband and colleague, part of the same police family.

Seemingly unaware of Jo lingering uncomfortably in the doorway, Irene pulled away, still processing the information. 'What happened?' Her voice was barely audible. 'Tell me the truth, Kate. All of it. I want none of your bullshit.'

Kate remained calm. 'It wasn't accidental. He was murdered for doing his job.' To anyone else, coming out with that might sound brutal, but Irene was relatively young, a strong woman. The couple had married in their late teens, shortly before Robbo joined the police. A decade on, she knew the score and deserved to know the whole truth. Kate owed her that courtesy.

'How much do you know about what he was working on?'

'Everything, so now *you* tell me.' Irene's expression hardened, a plea to be kept in the loop. 'Please, Kate. I need to know. Tell me he didn't do anything stupid to get himself killed.'

'No, he loved you too much for that. He was doing his duty, following orders . . .' *Her* orders. 'He was trying to gather intelligence—'

'On that piece of shit gunned down in a home built and paid for with blood money?' Irene was angry now. 'That bastard deserved to die in the worst way possible. Rob didn't, though he knew the risks involved and that people could get hurt. I never imagined it would be him.'

Kate's heart went out to her.

Irene was right, of course. Who the hell cared about the scum who trafficked drugs for profit?

Kate had more to say, none of it good. 'It's too early to tell you much. We don't know for sure, but we think Robbo went out to meet an informant and was followed. He was shot, more than once—'

'An execution then?'

Kate's nod was almost imperceptible.

'You must have your suspicions—'

'Bright thinks it's a warning, and I agree with him. Every one of us is now a target, including you. I've arranged for a protection team to watch the house. They'll be here before I leave and Jo will stay with you until Robbo's parents get here. An officer has been dispatched to break the news. What about your parents? Would you like me to tell them?'

'No, I'll do it. This news will destroy them. I wouldn't lay that on you.'

The subsequent telephone call was hard to witness.

Kate gave Irene a hug as she returned to the sofa. 'Robbo

is irreplaceable to all of us,' she said. 'Bright and the team asked me to pass on their condolences. I want you to know that we'll all be working round the clock to find whoever did this. You're not alone, so if you need anything, any of you, please ask. In the meantime, it might be advisable for you and Callum to stay with your mum and dad for a while, or with your parents-in-law if you prefer. I can make the arrangements for you. Just say the word. Until we know exactly what we're dealing with, we're taking no chances.'

Irene thanked her for her honesty.

'I knew he was up against it, but . . .' Her words caught in her throat. 'Kate, he was so proud to have been given the chance to prove himself. Acting DI was unexpected, but when Bright asked him to stand in as SIO, it was a dream come true. He was worried about Jo, about you, too, but he saw it as a way to prove himself, to make amends for past mistakes.'

Kate was almost lost for words. 'No one held that against him, Irene—'

'I know, but it's down to you that he kicked his gambling habit. You will never know how grateful he was, as I am. We nearly lost our home – not that it matters now. I couldn't live here without him.' Irene wanted to talk and Kate let her. 'When Rob was in uniform, I worried every day that he'd get injured, especially if he was on nights, but when he joined the MIT as statement reader, he joked that the worst thing that could happen to him was a paper cut.' Her bravery dissolved into a sob. 'How the hell will I explain to Callum that his daddy is never coming home?'

75

Kate was on autopilot as she was driven at high speed back to base, the cityscape flashing by, life going on as normal outside the vehicle, a heavy atmosphere within. Her driver, a female traffic cop she knew well, didn't speak and neither did Kate. Every member of the force was grieving. With an officer down, what the fuck was there to say?

When Kate walked into the incident room her team were subdued. Given that she and Hank had found Jo, if tragedy hadn't overtaken them, there would have been cheers, everyone on their feet, greeting them. On the plane, Kate had imagined their homecoming, how great it would feel to be back where she belonged, ready to resume charge of her team, but the atmosphere around her was grim.

Hank looked up from his desk, a half-smile of encouragement. She'd promised him a few days off, but that was now a pipe dream. His wife and son would have to wait a while longer to celebrate and spend time with him. Under the circumstances, they would make that sacrifice.

Carmichael walked by looking ill.

Kate grabbed her arm. 'You OK?'

Despite her best efforts, the young DC lost it, a reaction to Robbo's death and seeing her boss in the office for the first time since she'd disappeared to London on a personal crusade.

Kate locked eyes with her. 'Lisa, I need you to be strong now. With your help, we'll get a result. If you can't do it for the team, do it for Robbo, Irene and Callum. This is about them now, not us. Take five, then I want you in here with your shit together.'

Carmichael gave a nod, wandering away in no particular

direction, totally lost and far too upset to respond. Seeing her head go down, Hank had a quiet word as she passed his desk. There had never been a more important time to lift morale – not only hers, but everyone else's. He got up and joined Kate, letting out a sigh as he arrived by her side.

'She's OK,' he said. 'Are you?'

Kate flicked her head towards the muddle of work stations occupied by their detective colleagues. 'The bigger question is, are they?'

'They all volunteered to stay on rather than pitch up first thing in the morning,' Hank said. 'I think that says it all, don't you?'

'Bright called. He's briefing the chief. He'll be here any minute. Before the madness takes over, call Julie. Warn her to lock the door, not to answer to anyone.'

'She's gone already. Her sister's place. First thing I did when I heard the news.'

'Good move. Irene will follow suit as soon as her parents arrive. They're flying up from Heathrow, ETA eight fifty. Send a car to pick them up.'

'Will do. Is Jo here?'

'No, she's with Irene.' Kate took in his anxiety. 'Armed unit on site, Hank. They're well protected.'

Reassured, he focused on something over her shoulder. 'Mr Happy, your six o'clock.'

Kate turned to find Bright heading in, the door to the incident room slamming shut behind him. A man on a mission with a scowl on his face, he had an A4 document under his arm. He didn't approach either of them. Never one to stand on ceremony, he could probably guess the state of Irene without the need to spell it out.

At 00.50 Bright took up position at the front of the room, a signal that a difficult briefing was about to begin. Phone calls were hastily ended, whispered conversations too, everyone keen to get it underway. There was important work to be done before anyone retired for the night.

Bright cleared his throat. 'I'd ask for a minute's silence to remember Robbo, except he'd want you out there looking into his death. There are other ways we can pay tribute to him, as a mate and a colleague, like apprehending the bastards who took him down. It won't be easy, given the individuals involved, but there is no better murder investigation team in the force to do it. I'm counting on each and every one of you to give it your best shot – and so is Irene.'

Kate had rarely seen her guv'nor so distressed. He was as deeply saddened by the loss of a young DS as any detective in the hushed room. Like the rest of them, he'd work tirelessly to bring about a result. A Detective Chief Superintendent wouldn't normally involve himself in an individual murder enquiry. He was the CID's commander-in-chief, a delegator, an overseer, but this time he intended to be hands-on.

What he said next didn't surprise her.

'From this point on, I'm the SIO, the face of this enquiry. No one else gets a mention in the press. In case you're in any doubt, I'm not pulling rank or grabbing headlines. My involvement has nothing to do with the fact that your guv'nor wasn't here when we began the enquiry into Nikolaev. It's because every one of you in this room and every member of your family could be under threat. DCI Daniels will act as my deputy.'

Kate didn't argue. There was little point. He was taking over for all the right reasons.

Bright nodded to Carmichael.

Using a remote control, she uploaded an image of Robbo lying dead on the street. You could hear a pin drop.

'Take a good look,' Bright said. 'Because if any of you make your mouth go about this investigation, you'll be pinning a target on your back. So keep your gobs shut. You tell no one that you are part of this enquiry – and that includes your loved ones. If you're out on the streets, protect your anonymity at all times. I know this will be difficult, but you'll be issued with business cards with no names, just a number. This is a linked incident, but I'm not remotely interested in Nikolaev. As far as I'm concerned he can rot in hell, but if we identify his killer, we'll find the person who took Robbo out.'

'Sir?' Maxwell's hand was up. 'Surely Nikolaev's men are responsible for this.'

'Theoretically,' Bright said. 'There's a turf war on our patch between rival factions. Robbo was caught in the middle of it. Our target could be on either side, so no jumping to conclusions. These are thugs, the like of which you've never come across. These evil bastards will rock you off without a second thought. They'll waste anyone who gets in their way, so be on your guard. Kate, as soon as Jo is free, I'd like to see her. Carry on.'

76

If Bright had been trying to put the frighteners on the MIT, he'd succeeded. He was doing it for their own good, trying to instil a sense that the team were not dealing with a straight-forward murder enquiry but one that would take on a life of its own. He was also putting the target on his own back rather than theirs.

Everyone in the incident room knew it.

'Let's not sugar-coat this,' Kate said. 'We're dealing with the execution of a serving police officer. This investigation isn't just personal for the team and the force, it's personal for the families of every single passenger on 0113. We have multiple victims. As the guv'nor said, we don't yet know who is re-sponsible, only that it involves a fight for supremacy. This has a cartel signature all over it. We believe that Nikolaev took out a major player whose ID has yet to be established. Others are working on that. Hank and I are here to get a handle on who's in charge following Nikolaev's death. The only way we do that is to lean on people.'

Detectives were jittery. Understandably so. Leaning on an informant was what had put Robbo on a cold slab in the morgue. No one was keen to follow, but it would be a neglect of duty if she didn't reinforce Bright's warning in the most graphic terms. The situation they were facing was all too real, not some Sunday-night TV cop show make-believe.

There was nothing entertaining here.

Pushing home the dangers might save lives.

'You're right to be anxious,' she continued. 'Most of us have never worked on an investigation of this nature, including me. The guv'nor has. He'll be on hand to share his insight. Each time these thugs are taken down, they regroup, more resourceful and brutal than ever. The guv'nor has seen officers followed, homes trashed, burned down even, families moved to safe houses in order to protect them. He learned a lot from the experience, and you will too. We've lost one colleague. Let's make sure we don't lose another.'

Kate paused, scanning the room.

'The people we're up against treat everything like a military operation, and that's what we'll be doing from now on. The good news is, we have assistance from American law enforcement. My contact in Homeland Security has put the DEA on alert.' Kate focused on Hank, his chance to pitch in, an opportunity for her to take a breather.

'They have clout we can only dream of,' he said. 'Thousands of agents and intelligence analysts who'll offer operational support. Through their domestic field and foreign offices, they have global reach, so while we sleep, others will work and vice versa. The investigation will have twenty-four-hour cover.'

'He's right,' Kate said. 'The Serious and Organised Crime Agency, surveillance teams, armed and technical support units, are all on standby. From this moment on, pubs are off limits. All service vehicles will be equipped with dashcams. Private cars are out, too. They're too easily traced. You've all been trained in counter-surveillance. Employ those techniques religiously. We need to close this down, mount a coordinated strike on any suspects we identify, but first we need to find them.'

Since she'd mentioned the Drug Enforcement Administration, a federal law agency that came under the US Department for Justice, she'd noticed the team change gear. Aware of the DEA's ability to track down and prosecute the big guns who perpetrated violence on an industrial scale, to seize and forfeit assets in an attempt to stop drug-trafficking, Kate no longer needed to raise the heads of the detectives facing her. They were on starter's orders, paying attention, note-taking, everyone prepared to do their bit in what she considered would develop into the fight of their lives, something she decided not to dwell on now.

She singled out Carmichael. 'Lisa, you were working closely with Robbo in the days leading up to his death. Walk us through what you know.'

77

It can't have been easy for a detective so young in service to brief the team on a high-profile murder investigation with the head of CID looking on at one o'clock in the morning, especially when she'd been on duty since seven a.m. and had lost a colleague. Lisa Carmichael rose to the challenge. 'We have no forensics on Nikolaev's killer,' she said. 'No witnesses either. It had all the hallmarks of a professional hit, probably someone from out of town.'

'That's all we need,' someone mumbled. 'A high-level enforcer on our patch.'

'Robbo said at the time that the easiest and best way to kill was from a distance.' Carmichael paused a moment. A slight wobble. 'Nikolaev's house is way off the beaten track, guv. We used ANPR to clock any suspicious vehicles on the main roads.'

As she talked, Bright caught Kate's eye from across the room. He'd not been winding her up when he told her that Robbo was on his game. It sounded like he'd done everything right.

'Who has the ANPR report?' Kate asked.

Maxwell's hand went up.

'Any joy?'

'There were a couple that fit the profile of the vehicles Nikolaev's crew use, one of which we've since ruled out. It belongs to a legitimate businessman who just happens to like privacy glass. The other fell off our radar when it turned off the A1 heading north. It's registered to an Edinburgh address but we've yet to trace its owner. I wouldn't hold your breath, guv. Nikolaev's crew would be using dodgy plates. I doubt it'll take us anywhere.'

Kate took in the sea of sombre faces crammed into the incident room. 'Look, you all need some kip, but the key to this is Robbo and what he was working on. That's what I'm after before you go home, then we'll regroup at first light. Lisa, carry on.'

'He was liaising with the drug squad,' Carmichael said. 'Trying to establish who in Nikolaev's crew might have stepped into a dead man's shoes. There were several candidates, but his alleged successor was his youngest son, Marat. He's our best bet.'

'Based on what?' Kate asked.

'Word on the street. He's lying low.'

'Yeah, probably directing operations from elsewhere,' Maxwell said.

'Do we have Robbo's mobile?' Kate asked.

A nod from Carmichael. 'I found it locked in his drawer.'

Kate eyed the only desk unoccupied, the words 'dead man's shoes' echoing in her head. Or maybe it was empty out of respect for a valued detective none of his peers had yet had time to grieve. She scanned their tired faces, thinking about her meeting with Brian and the measures she'd taken beforehand, ensuring she wasn't followed, ordering Hank to stay away. 'Am I the only one who thinks Robbo dumped his device because he went out to meet someone iffy and perceived a risk?'

'No, guv.' It was the first time DC Andy Brown had contributed. He pointed to a row of pegs on the wall by the door. 'His coat is here, too. His wallet and warrant card were in his breast pocket. It seems to me that he left them here for that very reason. It begs the question as to how his killer knew he was a copper when he wasn't carrying ID.'

Kate felt her stomach roll.

This is your chance to shine, mate.

'The last time I spoke to him, I asked him to talk to Pete Brady in the drug squad and tap his informants. Robbo hadn't fed back on either action. Either he was still in the process of intelligence-gathering or he'd made a connection he was keeping to himself. Which is it?'

No one spoke up.

Kate's eyes momentarily found the floor. Had Robbo pushed too hard, trying to impress? Had she? He was her responsibility. Hers. A heavy weight settled in her chest. She was struggling to breathe, guilt adding to her sense of loss. Clearing her throat, she looked up, refocusing on Carmichael, grateful that the after-effects of her mild concussion had now passed. 'Where's the mobile?'

'With technical support, guv. They'll have a report for you by morning.'

'I also want an audit trail of all enquiries Robbo was working on, a printout of the actions he took personal responsibility for, any internet and PNC searches he carried out. That might give us a clue as to what prompted him to leave the office and where he might have gone. If he was meeting an informant, I want him or her found. Lisa, first thing tomorrow find out if he carried out any vehicle checks. The rest of you, I want a minute-by-minute timeline of what he was doing in the last few days, specifically in the hours and minutes before he left the incident room last night.'

'He was in and out,' Andy said.

'And how did he seem?'

'Preoccupied.'

Kate was good at reading people. Right now, Carmichael was avoiding eye contact. She wondered if the thought of Andy going through Robbo's pockets had upset her and that she was trying not to let it show. 'Lisa? Did you have anything else you wanted to share before we wrap up for the night?'

She did, everyone could see it.

Finally, she spoke up. 'I promised Robbo I wouldn't say anything, guv.'

Kate locked onto her so she couldn't look away. 'He's dead,

Lisa. You don't get to decide what you do and don't disclose, so spit it out, right now!'

All eyes turned to Carmichael.

She was uptight, face flushed, eyes filling up, lips trembling. Whatever she was keeping to herself was causing her a great deal of anxiety. The silence in the room was heavy with expectation, the atmosphere like lead. There was no room for divided loyalties in police work. Kate had found that out the hard way.

Bright admonished her – the thousand-yard stare – encouraging her to tread gently.

The hell with that. Carmichael wasn't the only one grieving. With an officer down, sparing her feelings wasn't an option. Kate would push her if forced to. 'Lisa, you're tired and emotional, I get that. We're all crushed by Robbo's death and will miss him dreadfully. Some of us have worked with him for a very long time, but if you know something you haven't yet told us, you need to front up. Whatever it is will go no further than this room. You have my word.' A smile. 'You know I never break promises, right?'

Carmichael laughed, then cried.

She wasn't the only one. A couple of mature detectives were wiping their eyes. Andy got up and handed her a tissue. Carmichael pulled herself together, apologising for her loss of control and for not speaking up at the first opportunity.

'Robbo mentioned a woman he'd met at a casino. He wasn't gambling again, at least that's what he told me, but he was worried that the guv'nor might think he was and take him off the investigation. He didn't know how he'd explain that to Irene.' Carmichael paused. 'He seemed to think that this woman might have information. I don't know her name, only that she lives in Jesmond somewhere. I think he'd gone out to meet her.'

78

Kate stared out of the window at an empty car park. Practically every available pool car was in use so that detectives could flood the area and yet maintain a low profile in the search for the bodyguards who'd witnessed Nikolaev's murder. They couldn't afford to show the Northumbria Police insignia. Beyond the car park, on the sealed-off road outside Middle Earth, the forensic tent was visible, CSIs going about their business, a task that had resumed at dawn.

Kate turned away from the window, relieved that Irene and Callum Robson were now out of harm's way, along with many families of MIT detectives. They were hard at work, Kate and Hank providing the bridge between enquiries undertaken by the DEA in the United States and those carried out on home turf, law enforcement on both sides of the Atlantic doing their level best to disrupt drug-trafficking. Kate had also made use of Jo's expertise, putting together a profile on the type of offender they were hunting.

Her mobile rang: Robbo's old friend, Pete Brady from the drug squad returning her call.

She lifted the phone to her ear. 'Pete, what have you got for me?'

'Marat Nikolaev has just been spotted by two of my crew, guv. They have him under observation. What do you want them to do?'

'Tell them to sit tight while I get a surveillance team organised.'

'Seriously?' He sounded bitterly disappointed. 'He's worth a punt, surely. My guys are ready to bring him in. The street is rife with theories. Most reckon he offed his old man in order to take control of the family business.'

'I wouldn't put it past him. He may even have ordered Robbo's execution, but I have no evidence. Until I do, we sit tight. You know what he's like. If we bring him in, he'll run rings round us, or his brief will. Harassing the bereaved relative of a dead man, etcetera, etcetera. He'll be claiming compensation before he walks. I have no grounds for arrest yet. Don't worry, you have my word that he'll be under surveillance, day and night. With any luck, he might hook up with the witnesses we want to question. Text me his location and I'll send backup. The surveillance team will log his movements from now on.'

'You're the boss.'

Sometimes she wished she wasn't.

As she hung up, she heard the text ping into her phone and deployed a surveillance team immediately. The phone was still in her hand when SAC Torres called to pass on her condolences. Bright had informed her of Robbo's death. Her Homeland Security colleagues were still working their way through the 0113 passenger list with nil results against the world's 'Most Wanted', and Kate appreciated the call.

'It's slow-going,' Torres said.

As Kate listened, her mind wandered to the enquiries the MIT had been carrying out prior to her arrival on home soil. The day before Robbo died, someone had seen him talking to Eddie Veitch, a sergeant who worked in the front office. It worried her. The two had played poker together with other guys from the station. They had done so for years, a few laughs, a few beers, until Robbo's addiction got the better of him. Veitch claimed that the two had just been chatting, that he had no idea what Robbo was up to, and that's where they'd left it.

With Robbo dead, there was no reason for him to lie.

Torres requested an update on the woman Robbo had gone out to meet.

'Every woman in his address book has been spoken to,'

Kate said. 'They're mates, all of them. His wife confirmed it. In interview, they all checked out. The woman Carmichael referred to isn't there, but she found out that Robbo was checking a list of logistics companies on the morning of his death. It turns out that he used to have a 'lady friend' when he was gambling. They'd fallen out of contact – until the day he died.'

'You've spoken to her?'

'One of my team has. Robbo called her, out of the blue apparently.'

'Why would he do that when he was so overworked?'

'He wouldn't.'

'Be careful, Kate. She could be in cahoots with Nikolaev, someone trying to cultivate a copper who has or had a gambling problem, a detective they might consider malleable to their malign manipulations. That's how they operate. I mean no disrespect.'

'None taken. It's a fair point, given Robbo's history—'

'Except they didn't turn him, did they? He must've been quite a guy.'

Kate had no words as a wave of grief hit her.

Torres was intuitive, clever enough to know that the best way to help Kate over her temporary silence and get her on track was to give her something else to think about, preferably work. She asked, 'How's your timeline going?'

'It's coming together. No arrests yet. That'll change. Our targets may have gone to ground, but they can't lie low for ever. We have surveillance on one or two of their runners and, as of five minutes ago, Nikolaev's son, too. The team are making slow and steady progress. Robbo had been working hard. CCTV captured him entering our command HQ at around six o'clock on the night he was murdered. At five past the hour, he checked the PNC, our national computer database, accessing the vehicle index, a general search on Audi R8s registered locally.'

'Interesting. Did he find any?'

'Two. We're attaching significance to it. He didn't raise an action with our receiver to trace either of the owners. That's not how we normally do things, which suggests he wanted to check it out himself. I'm about to follow up on that now.'

'Take a SWAT team with you.'

'Not our style.'

Carmichael passed Kate a note: *I found her.*

Kate lifted a thumb, a big smiley thank you, an urgent tone to her voice as she returned to her call. 'Gabriele, I've got to run. I may have caught another break this end. I'll update you as soon as I know more.'

'Good luck.'

The line clicked. Torres was gone.

The woman's name was Anita Marr. She seemed to be legit, the MD of her own company that had been going for several years and was now worth a small fortune. She'd favoured a meeting out of town. Carmichael agreed, though she insisted on a location of her choosing, a good move on her part. Only Kate knew where it was. Unhappy about this, Jo collared Bright as soon as he arrived from HQ, voicing her concerns in the strongest possible terms, pointing out that Robbo might have been lured to his death by Marr.

Kate thought so too.

Given that the nature of Marr's business was logistics, managing the flow of goods from A to B, it was the perfect foil for a slick drug-trafficking operation. Supply and demand was the name of the game. Pushed for time, she interrupted Jo mid-sentence. 'What you're saying makes perfect sense, were it not for the fact that Lisa was the one who made contact, not the other way around.'

'Yeah, like Robbo, so forgive me if I'm not reassured.'

'Jo, calm down.'

'No, you need to listen to me. These people aren't stupid.

What makes you think that they didn't anticipate that Robbo might get in touch? Has it even occurred to you that he wasn't a random choice? That, in killing him, Nikolaev's men or whoever is responsible knew perfectly well that you'd analyse his lifestyle in minute detail and follow up on his contacts, especially the dodgy ones?' Jo turned her attention to Bright. 'Guv, this meeting could be a ploy to target more police.'

'Jo's right,' he said to Kate. 'You could be walking into a trap.'

Kate scanned her team.

Every MIT officer seemed to agree.

She was outnumbered.

Jo was staring at her. She'd said her piece, but it was unlike her to lose her temper. She didn't apologise for letting fly in front of everyone, an unprecedented public outburst that took them all by surprise, including their guv'nor and Kate herself. Jo was right to be cautious, Kate was well aware of it, but what happened next was a frustration she could do without. Detectives were stood down, the briefing delayed while arrangements were made.

Bright left the incident room without another word.

Kate followed him to his office, not bothering to knock as she walked in. 'Sir—' She rarely called him that. 'I can't wait around. I have a potential, possibly vital, lead.'

'Close the door on your way out,' he said.

'But—'

'You heard me. You can thank me later.'

'Fuck's sake!' It wasn't said under her breath. 'The witness is waiting to talk to me at a prearranged time and place. Marr sounded extremely nervous when Carmichael made contact. If I don't show, she'll be in the wind.'

Her plea was ignored.

Kate stormed out.

They didn't speak again until he summoned her and Hank to his office and gave them the go-ahead to leave Middle

Earth, much later than scheduled, wearing Kevlar vests beneath their overcoats at his instruction. The detectives were to be tailed by armed response, insurance against ambush. The last thing Bright said echoed in their heads as they left the building.

'You go after them, they'll come after you.'

79

'Well, that was fun.' Hank punched a Durham postcode into the satnav as they left Northern Area Command HQ. 'Jo obviously thinks this meeting is a bad idea. She might be right if we're late getting there. I can't see Marr hanging around for long, can you?' He checked his watch. 'You'll have to step on it, Kate. It's almost seven forty-five. We said we'd be there by eight.' He tapped the navigation screen. 'According to this, we have an ETA of eight fifteen.'

Flooring the accelerator, Kate checked the rear-view mirror, a smile developing as the car behind picked up speed. 'Relax, Hank. Jeff is our escort. They don't call him Shifty for nothing.'

Hank crossed his arms, watching the speedometer climb . . . seventy . . . eighty . . . ninety miles an hour. He liked nothing better than a fast ride. 'Don't worry about Jo,' he said. 'Carmichael is under orders to sit on her till we get back.'

'You don't think she's that stupid—'

'To follow us? Hardly. You'd give Lewis Hamilton a run for his money.'

Kate didn't laugh. 'You didn't tell her where we're going?'

''Course, I told her to bring her mates along too.'

'Sorry . . .' Changing down, she negotiated a roundabout at high speed, taking the slip road south. 'I shouldn't have asked.'

'No, you shouldn't.'

'Jo had no right—'

'She had every right. Didn't take you two long to start arguing, did it?'

'Not surprising. She's stressed to death.'

'And you're not?'

Kate deflected the question with one of her own. 'If we don't act, who will? I'm damned if I'll let these bastards slip away from us. I promised Irene that I'd hunt them down until they have no hiding place. We can't afford to lose momentum.'

The hotel was set back off a B-road. Carmichael had chosen well, one road in and out, no junctions, easily managed if there was a threat. Kate drove into the car park, relieved to see one of three vehicles registered to Marr's address parked up near the rear door, a new Land Rover Discovery with a 64 registration plate, practically brand new.

As the armed response vehicle pulled up in a location that gave him the best viewpoint, Shifty's voice filled the car: 'Hold your position while I recce the building, guv.'

'Make it quick, Jeff. If she spots you, she might leg it.'

'I would if I were her,' Hank said. 'He scares the hell out of me.'

A chuckle over the radio. 'I'll try not to frighten the lady.'

Shifty got out, scanning the fringes of the car park, the hedges and shrubbery. It was ominously quiet and, like all armed response personnel, he had a nose for danger. Satisfied that there was none, he walked towards the pub while his colleague remained in the car, checking the registration of two unidentified vehicles that had been reversed into spaces close to the main gate.

'You think Robbo was slipping?' Hank said, while they waited.

Remembering her chat with Veitch, Robbo's poker buddy, Kate said, 'Do you?'

'Once an addict, Kate.'

'You're such a cynic. You're wrong, Hank. Robbo was his old self. Once Irene knew he had a problem, she watched him like a hawk. The only nights he spent out of the house were ones when he was genuinely working late.'

'She couldn't possibly know that. How many of our lot

338

are screwing around, passing off their absence from home as work-related. It's the cover-all excuse, the oldest trick in the book.'

'True, except for one detail.' Kate grimaced. 'Irene and I had a pact. Whenever I asked him to stay on, I texted her.'

'Remind me never to have an affair.'

Kate grinned. 'It was for his own good.'

Moments later, Shifty emerged. A nod: all clear.

'That'll be her.' Hank peered into the bar through a double-glazed door with a good view of the room. He stood back, allowing Kate to step forward. A well-dressed brunette, more tanned than most Brits at this time of the year, was sitting alone, flicking through her mobile phone, a strand of hair flopping over her eyes.

Kate glanced over her shoulder at Hank. 'Did you work that out all by yourself?'

He laughed. Anita Marr was the only woman in the bar.

Kate was already disappearing through the door, making a beeline for Marr's table, conscious of him on her tail. The woman looked up as they approached, poker eyes, a blank facial expression. If she was angry because they were a few minutes late, she didn't show it. Apologising for keeping her waiting, Kate took care of the introductions, asking if she'd like a drink.

'Don't touch the stuff.'

'Hank will get us a coffee.'

He headed towards the bar. Despite the heat from a wood-burning stove, Kate kept her coat on for fear of exposing the Kevlar underneath. She sat down opposite Marr. The woman was around Robbo's age. Kate didn't know why, but she'd expected her to be older. 'Thanks for seeing us. We appreciate you taking the time to drive so far.'

'I wasn't given a choice. I'm only here because of what happened to Rob, I mean Paul.' She explained, 'I always knew him as Rob. I was stunned when I saw his photograph on TV. It really upset me.'

Hank arrived and sat down. 'The barman will bring them over.' He pointed at Marr's latté glass. 'I ordered you the same again. Is that OK?'

'Perfect, thank you.' Marr asked, 'Were you guys close to Rob?'

'As close as it gets,' Kate said.

'Then I'm sorry for you. He was a great bloke.'

'The best.' Hank meant it.

Even though Robbo had fallen from grace, the team had rallied round once they knew he had a problem. He was universally popular. Kate felt a tug somewhere deep inside her chest, but remained focused on her witness. 'How long had you known him?'

'We met about three years ago at a casino in town.'

'Which one?' There were several.

'The only one for serious gamblers: Providence. I find the rest a bit seedy. The Pro has a good vibe. Rob was new. Unsure of himself. Roulette was more his thing, but he used to watch me play poker and blackjack. I knew he was in trouble. I can spot a loser a mile away. I mean in the literal sense, not to be unkind. He was losing heavily, chasing his bets, a mug's game. It didn't take long to realise that he was unable to bankroll his addiction. He was very concerned that he might lose his family, his job, or both. I gather he very nearly did.'

Kate didn't confirm it. 'And you'd kept in touch?'

'No. Until Monday, we've not seen each other or spoken in almost two years.'

'You told DC Carmichael that he called you out of the blue.'

'That's right.'

'You didn't perhaps instigate the call via text?' She eyed Marr's phone. 'They're easily deleted.'

'No, I did not.' Marr slipped her device in her pocket, a hint that they would have to take her word for it. 'He wanted to meet but wouldn't tell me why. I asked him if he'd started gambling again and he said he'd explain when he saw me.'

'He didn't disclose the fact that he was a detective?'

'Not until we met the other day, though I had my suspicions.'

'Where did that meeting take place?'

'At my Jesmond office.'

The barman arrived with their coffee. As he set it down on the table, Marr thanked him, drawing her drink towards her. She was very polite, soft-spoken and articulate. Kate could see why Robbo would take to her. Momentarily, she wondered if they had ever been closer than betting pals, but then discounted the idea. He'd never cheat on Irene.

Marr was staring at Kate. 'Look, this is a bad idea. I don't want to get involved.'

'You are involved,' Kate said. 'You were the last person we know of to see him alive, which makes you a person of interest. What did he want?'

'Information.'

Hank said, 'Then it stands to reason he thought you had some to give.'

'It wasn't me he was interested in.'

'Oh?'

Replacing her coffee in its saucer, Marr leaned forward, dropping her voice. 'When Rob was frequenting the casino, there was a young couple throwing their cash around. They were new too. Not members, I know that much. They bribed their way in. Everyone has a price, right? The doormen are supposed to keep non-members out, but this bloke was personable and loaded. Right up their street. He was keen to strike up a relationship—'

'With you, or DS Robson?' Kate asked.

'Rob. I warned him off.'

'Why?'

Marr hesitated. 'I had a bad feeling about the guy and I didn't like his girlfriend. I walked in on her snorting cocaine in the toilets. The evil bitch saw me looking, put me up against the wall and told me to keep my mouth shut or she knew someone who'd slit my throat and make me disappear. She was off her face.'

Kate was intrigued. 'You believed her?'

'She was laughing when she said it.'

'And you told DS Robson?'

Marr's confirmation explained a lot. 'It didn't surprise him. He was like the rest of you, eyes everywhere, checking out who was coming and going. I thought he was nervous by nature, making sure he didn't come across someone he knew who might tell his wife what he was up to. He was a mess. But as time went on, I'd made up my mind that he was in your line of work. It made sense of his anxiety, the fact that he kept a low profile. I was the only one he had any dealings with.'

'It seems he had good taste.'

'Don't patronise me, Inspector. Not all gamblers are a lost cause. The difference between me and Rob was that I have a disposable income and know when to stop. Rob didn't. I also win more than I lose. Not many can say that. You're his boss, right? The one who got him to kick the habit, the one who paid his IOUs?'

Kate didn't admit or deny it.

Hank showed no reaction, but she could feel his laser eyes burning a hole in the side of her head, probably wondering how much it had cost her. Kate thought Marr was on the level, but maybe poker wasn't the only game she was good at. Now she'd started talking, they couldn't shut her up, another reason to be wary, but also a chance to move off the subject of what Kate had done to save one of her crew from imploding.

'You know Rob,' Marr said. 'He was intuitive, a man who trusted his instincts. He didn't need my warning to stay away from this guy and his girlfriend. He'd already clocked them as trouble. His gambling skills were crap but his radar was spot on.'

'And still you didn't ask what he did for a living? I find that hard to believe.'

'I'm telling the truth. Like I said, I had my suspicions. I figured he'd tell me if he wanted me to know. He might've been a liability from your point of view, but not from mine.'

'Describe this couple for me.'

'The guy was late twenties, early thirties. Impeccably dressed. Good shoes. Foreign, a very bad loser. A taker, too, asked a lot of questions but gave nothing of himself. He didn't give a name. We didn't ask – at least, I didn't.'

Kate was desperate to ask if he was Russian but couldn't lead the witness. 'Can you take a punt at nationality?'

Marr gave a shrug. 'Spanish, Portuguese, I'm not sure.'

The words South American popped into Kate's head. She was itching to know if Hank was thinking the same thing. She decided to bank it for later. When Marr told her that Robbo was more interested in the girl, it made perfect sense. He'd have been looking for a weak link. Leaning on a coke-head, someone he may have perceived as suffering a greater addiction than his own, probably hoping to get a handle on her boyfriend before making his move.

'And the woman?'

'Younger than him. A looker. Dark hair. Expensive kit. Articulate. I got the impression she was independently wealthy.'

'Is there anything more you can tell us about either of them?'

'Neither of them drank alcohol. Beyond gambling, it was the only thing we had in common.' Marr paused. 'The girl was a piece of work. She liked the high life, and worked the room in the casino at every opportunity. She had multiple relationships. Only hung out with monied, shady characters who, for some reason, were falling over themselves to gain her attention. I couldn't see the attraction myself.' Marr paused. 'I go every week and saw them often, together and with other escorts.'

'Have you seen them recently?'

'That's what Rob asked. He wanted to know if the pair were still around.'

'What did you tell him?'

'That the guy hadn't been in for a while, which was unusual. The last couple of times I saw him, he was on his own. I guessed they'd fallen out. He didn't always get his way with her. I saw them leave the club once . . .' She explained that the ladies' restroom overlooked the car park behind the casino. 'They were having a right go at one another and he was coming off worse. It surprised me. He didn't strike me as a man you'd cross. She drove off in a red Porsche leaving him to find his own way home. He was bloody furious when he walked back into the casino. Their relationship was a ticking bomb if ever I saw one.'

Bad choice of words, Kate thought.

Was Marr playing games?

'If this couple worried you so much, why did you not stay away from the casino?'

'Gambling is what I do. It's a big part of my life. I told you, the Pro is where I hang out. I have a lot of friends there. If there was any trouble, there are people on the premises trained to make it disappear.'

Kate let it ride.

She knew how difficult it was for Robbo to resist gambling, even though it was destroying his life, threatening his marriage, his job. It would be no different for a professional gambler like Marr. 'This meeting between you and DS Robson may be highly significant. Can you remember his exact words? What he asked you, what you said in return?'

Hank took notes as Kate walked Marr through the conversation. The gambler paused now and then to think. Kate imagined her at the gaming tables, taking her time to consider her options before placing her bets. She quit talking when the door to the bar opened, losing her cool momentarily, her eyes pinned to a big man approaching the counter.

The detectives watched as the barman greeted him.

The two seemed to be well acquainted. A local, perhaps. Relaxing, Kate refocused on her witness. Had she perceived a threat, or was she making out she had? Her recovery was instantaneous.

She was on track in seconds.

'Rob asked if I knew where he might find the girl. I asked him why he was interested. He wouldn't say. It was obvious that he was on an important assignment. I'd never seen him so animated, even when he was on a roll in the casino. Granted, that wasn't very often, but you know what I mean.' She looked away, then at Kate. 'I wish I hadn't told him now.'

Hank raised his pen from his notepad, looking up. 'Told him what?'

'That the woman scared me. They both did. When you gamble, you develop a sixth sense, an ability to read people, especially those that might flip. Rob was really keen to find them, so I told him what I knew.'

'Which was?' Kate asked.

'They hang out in Jesmond sometimes. My office looks down on to Osborne Road. I've seen them walk by once or twice, and drive by many times. I love my cars, so I tend to notice them. He drives an Audi R8. You don't see too many of them about.'

Again, Hank lifted his pen. 'Are you sure it was an R8?'

'Positive. I've seen it parked outside one of the residential properties close to my office, though not for a few weeks. I'm hoping the bitch moved out. I not only work in Jesmond, I live there. It's one thing running into them at the casino, but in Jesmond? That's a bit too close for comfort.'

For me too, Kate thought.

Marr's office was a stone's throw from her own front door, practically around the corner, except that she wasn't living there at the moment. For security reasons, on Bright's advice, she'd locked up her house and moved in with Jo; strength in numbers and moral support were important at times like these. Other than collapsing into the same bed, they had hardly seen each other, let alone had a decent conversation, but it was good to hold her while she slept.

Kate refocused on the witness. 'Where exactly was the R8 parked?'

'I don't know the house name or number, but it's her place, not his.'

'The road will do.' Kate needed specifics.

Marr gave one that Hank didn't bother writing down. It was a pivotal moment. The location rang a bell with both detectives, a road that Robbo had found on the PNC while looking for an R8. The detectives were a phone call away from a name and house number.

'You think I'm to blame, don't you, that I set Rob up?'

'Did you?' Kate asked.

'No . . .'

Kate took a photograph of Marat Nikolaev from her pocket. 'Have you ever seen this man?'

Marr's poker eyes hardened. She didn't answer.

Kate took it as a yes. 'With the same girl?'

'Maybe . . . I'm not sure.'

Marr was lying through her teeth. Hooking a forefinger round a stray hair, she raked it away from her forehead, embarrassed to have been found out. 'I've answered your questions, so now I have one for you. Tell me the truth, Inspector. Am I in danger?'

'Possibly.' They all were, though Kate didn't voice it.

'Can you protect me?'

'Depends . . .' Kate picked her moment. 'My DS was dead within hours of seeing you. After your meeting with him, who did you tell?'

80

Kate escorted Anita Marr to her vehicle, thanked her for her help and watched her drive away. The DCI was fairly sure she was on the level, but the jury would remain out until she'd completed her enquiries into the couple Robbo had been so keen to ID – assuming they even existed. When all was said and done, she only had Marr's word for it. Kate turned to find Hank standing behind her, hands in pockets, a wry smile on his face.

'What?' she said.

'Subtlety was never your strong suit, was it?'

'Strong suit? Are you having a laugh? I was testing her.'

'Robbo trusted her.'

'We *think* he trusted her,' she corrected him. 'And I'm fairly sure it led to his death, aren't you?'

Before he had a chance to answer, the armed response duo arrived.

Shifty lit a cigarette, offering the pack around. There were no takers. Now he'd shadowed Kate to her rendezvous, he was under the impression he'd be stood down. He had another thought coming. She needed his expertise and that of his colleague for a while longer. She checked the protocol for their continued involvement, then all four piled into their cars.

Hank took the wheel this time, heading towards Newcastle, freeing Kate to make a few calls en route. As she was not the SIO, she had to defer to Bright before taking further action. Going off-book to find Jo was one thing. She wouldn't risk doing it again. The guv'nor was the first person she called, this time interrupting him at a senior officer's strategy meeting he couldn't get out of.

'You're making a habit of this,' he said. 'However, on this occasion, you're forgiven. I'm glad you called. It gives me an excuse to leave.'

'Guv, I think we know who Robbo was going to see: the owner of an R8 purchased in London, a woman who now lives in Jesmond. With your permission, Hank and I are going straight there. If she's not in, we'll play it by ear. I'll get a warrant sorted in case we have any difficulties.'

'Armed support are still with you?'

'Yes, fully on board.'

'OK, I'll put a team of spotters in the area.'

Happy with her plan, he warned her to be careful.

Kate hung up, tapping on a second number, also on speed dial.

Carmichael picked up instantly.

'Lisa, the searches Robbo carried out on the vehicle database. I need the Jesmond address for the R8.'

Carmichael gave it. 'It's a rental, guv. I checked.'

Kate loved the way her young DC anticipated what was coming next, and told her so. If she hadn't found Marr first, Kate would have been chasing up the R8 herself. 'How many occupants in the flat?'

Carmichael hit her keyboard at full pelt, a match for Garcia any day – and some. It didn't take her long to find what she was after. 'One according to the electoral roll. Her name is Stephanie Jackson. Guv, my enquiries with the DVLA list two cars registered there. Makes you wonder what she does for a living to own an R8 and a Porsche.'

'Marr says she's loaded. Does Jackson have form?'

More keystrokes as Carmichael checked the PNC. 'One conviction for possession of Class A.'

'Figures.' They both knew that the rich were less likely to get busted for drugs.

'It wasn't much. Own use. She got off lightly. Sending an image through to your mobile.'

It arrived instantly and Kate confirmed receipt. Jackson was indeed a looker, just as Marr had described her. She asked Carmichael to do some digging into her background. 'Maybe her boyfriend registered the car to her address without her knowledge. If he's been in her flat, then so has his DNA. I want a CSI team on standby and an immediate warrant for her home. Whoever obtains it needs to meet me there ASAP.'

'It'll probably be me, boss. We're a bit thin on the ground here.'

'OK, the warrant is your priority. Ask Andy to do a check on Jackson. Bright is on his way in. He'll organise everything else.'

'Hank said that Jo was my priority.'

'She was, is . . .' Kate paused, a worried exchange with Hank. 'Where is she now?'

'Asleep in your office.'

'Make sure she stays that way. Tell the squad she's not to go home under any circumstances. Get Maxwell to sit on her if necessary.'

'Eurgh! Rather her than me.'

Kate laughed. Humour would get them through this.

81

Hank drove across the Tyne Bridge, taking the central motorway north, then east towards the target property. Kate was exhausted but also buzzing with anticipation. No organisation was foolproof. Like Robbo, she badly needed to find a link to Stephanie Jackson's 'foreign' associate, hoping that she'd collapse under pressure, prepared to drop him in the shit once she was informed that a police officer had been murdered, a thought Kate shared with her 2ic. 'Whether it'll take us anywhere is less certain.'

'Robbo's questioning of Marr played a part in his death, Kate. Jackson's boyfriend is the key—'

'I agree, but he doesn't sound like the type to testify against those higher up in the chain—'

'In an investigation this big? No chance. Besides, the CPS will never agree to immunity from prosecution, not with Robbo's blood on his hands, not to mention the victims of 0113—'

'No, but in exchange for credible intel they might show leniency when the case comes to court.'

'You think so?'

'No, you divvi! That's the line I'll be peddling all the same.'

'Good luck with that.' He turned left, minutes away from their destination. 'In or out of custody, a turncoat would be signing his own death warrant.'

'That's what I love about you, Hank. You look like you give a shit. Me? I'd gladly waste them all. These scumbags volunteer for what they do. Can I help it if their enemies have the ability to penetrate the walls of a high-security jail? Because that's exactly where they're heading, whether or not they help us crack this case. Their life expectancy is the least of my worries.'

Hank slowed, a head check in his rear-view mirror.

Kate was instantly on alert. A four-by-four was approaching at speed. Shifty took immediate action, straddling two lanes, ensuring that it couldn't overtake. Kate tensed, turning her body round to look out the rear window, eyeing the cars behind. The four-by-four behind the firearms team indicated, then turned off.

Shifty flashed his lights.

False alarm.

The radio crackled into life, one of the spotters reporting that his team were in position, awaiting further instructions. 'No sign of the R8, but the Porsche is parked across the road, ma'am. No lights or movement in the flat, front or rear. We're as convinced as we can be that the property is empty. The neighbouring house is illuminated.'

Carmichael responded. 'I have the warrant, boss. On my way.'

Kate pressed to transmit: '7824 to all units: two minutes out. Stand by.'

The street where Jackson lived was leafy and upmarket, a line of high-end motors parked on either side. Again, Kate used the radio: '7824 – on scene, hold your positions.' Deflated by the fact that the house appeared to be deserted – not so much as a tell-tale flicker from a candle or mobile phone – she asked Hank to drive by and park up a short distance from the property.

He carried out her instructions, as did armed response, pulling in behind.

'7824 – hold your positions and maintain radio silence.' Unclipping her seat belt, Kate said, 'Wait in the car, I won't be long.'

Hank reached for the door handle. 'Where you go, I go.'

'Not this time, Hank.'

'Kate—'

'Stay. Put.'

He did.

Climbing from the vehicle, Kate informed Shifty not to follow. He wasn't happy. She crossed the road, keeping as close as she could to the exterior of the three-storey Victorian terrace in case anyone was watching from Jackson's ground-floor flat. Tapping on the door of the adjoining property, she waited.

A middle-aged man answered, a stern expression. 'Yes, can I help you?'

'I hope so.' Kate threw him a wide smile which was not returned. 'I'm sorry to disturb you at such a late hour, but I've obviously got the wrong house. I'm looking for Steph Jackson . . .' She peered up and down the street, a finger to her lips, pretending to be clueless. 'I know she lives round here somewhere. I'm ashamed to say I was a bit tipsy last time I was here. I was *sure* this was the one. Sorry to have troubled you . . . Is it the one next door?'

'I wouldn't bother knocking,' the man grumbled. 'Unless the lights are on or the music is blasting, they're not in. I thought students were a pain, but Miss Jackson and her friend are ten times worse.'

Kate's giggle turned into an enquiry. 'Mind if I ask you something?'

'Yes, I mind.' He made a move to close the door.

'You said "they" . . .'

He was too polite to ignore her.

Kate made a begging face. 'I thought she'd thrown him out. Is he still living there?'

'No, but he's a frequent visitor.'

'Right. He gives me the creeps.'

'Well, at least we agree on something. Now sling your hook. I don't want the likes of you round here. My wife is very ill. She's had enough of the screaming and yelling. Do yourself a favour. Stay away from those two. They're trouble.'

'That's what I thought.' Kate held up ID. 'Sir, I misled you. I'm an undercover police officer.'

'About time.'

'Excuse me?' Kate was pleased that he hadn't insisted on a name and rank, since she wasn't at liberty to give him one.

'My wife and I witnessed a serious assault yesterday and now you turn up?' He checked the street nervously. 'You'd better come inside.'

With his back turned, Kate gave Hank the thumbs up, then stepped over the threshold. Without sight of her, there wasn't a hope in hell of him waiting in the car. The householder sat down in the living room and gave his name as William Rossiter. Kate explained that tracing Jackson was urgent.

'It's a bit late for that,' he said angrily. 'What we saw shook us up, I can tell you. We were extremely distressed by it. Miss Jackson's friend, if you could call him that, dragged her out of the front door by her hair, manhandled her into his car and drove away. I know the police are under pressure, but what does it take to get a rapid response these days?'

Kate understood his hostility and felt bad that 'her lot' had let him and Jackson down. Cuts in funding were failing the community they served. Anger boiled in her gut. If the police had turned up and lifted the man, Robbo might still be alive. She suspected Jackson would follow him to the morgue if they ever found her body. Had the foreigner seen Robbo leave? Had she called to warn him that police were asking questions?

A fatal mistake.

'So, you're pretty convinced they're not in there?'

'I'm certain of it.'

'Can you describe the layout of the flat for me, sir?'

'It's a mirror image of this one.'

Kate could see along the hallway. At the rear of the

property, there was a large breakfast room – an extension she assumed – a table, eight chairs and bi-fold doors leading to the garden. 'So, living room at the front, kitchen at the back, bedrooms and bathroom across the hallway?' She'd had a peek on her way in.

'Except I have three bedrooms upstairs and two above that, which Miss Jackson doesn't have.'

'That's really helpful. I'll get someone to come and take a statement from you. Sir, I have a warrant to search the premises next door, but there might be some noise going in, so apologies upfront for that. It won't last long. There's nothing for you or Mrs Rossiter to worry about. Please stay inside and lock the door when I leave.'

'Far be it from me to spoil your fun, but there's no need to kick the door down. You're obviously far too busy to deal with an urgent callout, let alone a compensation claim for damages. I'm the owner and landlord of the apartment next door. An official complaint to the Chief Constable will be on his desk by morning. I didn't like Miss Jackson, but she deserved protection.' Rossiter slipped a hand into his trouser pocket. He drew out a set of keys, removed one and handed it over. 'Help yourself. You'll find the eviction notice on the mat.'

82

The spotters remained outside to ensure that the house the firearms officers were about to enter wasn't under observation by those who might do them harm. Shifty went in first, followed by his colleague, shouts of 'Clear, clear' echoing through the ground-floor apartment as rooms were checked one by one.

Thirty seconds later, Kate and Hank were in.

Like Rossiter's home, the place was classy. No expense had been spared on furniture, art and decor, but there were signs of a struggle. An armchair was lying on its side, tipped over, a broken mirror on the floor, red wine splashed across the carpet, a glass lying on its side, a small amount of what looked like blood. Trailing wires suggested a hasty exit by someone who'd removed technology in a hurry, leaving chargers plugged into the wall sockets.

Hank said flatly, 'Must've been a hell of a fight.'

'A beating, you mean.' Kate scanned the room. 'Check out the bedroom.'

As he wandered away, Kate continued to look around, though she didn't touch anything. A forensic search of the premises was a job for others. Her priority now was to find Jackson, no easy task. If she'd spoken to Robbo, Kate suspected that she'd eat her words. She'd be the one with her throat cut, the one who'd been made to disappear, potentially another blind alley for the MIT.

Kate heard movement, a creaky floorboard she hoped was Rossiter making his way upstairs next door. The noise caused her to look up. What she saw explained a lot. She called out. 'Hank, get in here!'

He arrived in the room. 'No blood in there, Kate.'

'Take a look.' She pointed at loose wires dangling from the corners of the living room ceiling where CCTV had been ripped out. 'That's how they knew what Robbo looked like. All Jackson's boyfriend had to do was to lie in wait outside Middle Earth, follow and rock him off, then deliver his body back to us.'

There was a moment when neither detective spoke.

Kate's mobile rang, breaking the silence.

'It's Bright.' She put the phone on speaker so Hank could listen in. 'Go ahead, guv?'

They expected their SIO to ask how things were going, to find out if they had apprehended Jackson and were bringing her in for questioning, but he had something more important on his mind. 'Marr has been on the phone. Our man is at the casino.'

Those twelve words turned the investigation on its head. Bright instructed all units to switch to a secure channel – identifying the number – ensuring that all transmissions from this point on were reserved only for those involved in the operation. No other police units would be accepted into the conversation.

He disconnected.

Kate summoned Carmichael, telling her that crime scene investigators should make their way to Jackson's apartment and keep a low profile. They were not to enter until she had her target in custody. Any sign of forensic suits, in or near the property, might tip off their target before Kate got to the club.

'When, and only when, he's in custody are they to go in,' she repeated. 'Then I want them to tear it apart and report to me first thing in the morning.' She blew out a breath. 'I want a PNC marker for the R8 and Jackson and a low-loader for the Porsche for forensic examination. If she happens to turn up, which I very much doubt, she'll report the car stolen and we'll hear about it.'

'I'll make the call.'

'You happy to hold the fort here?'

'Yes, boss.'

'Really? You've got a face like a slapped arse.'

Carmichael wasn't scared to be left alone in the flat. Any sign of trouble and the spotters outside would move in, as would armed response. No; the reason her face was tripping her was because she was dying to be in on the action.

Kate changed her mind.

Carmichael might be useful, before and after police hit the casino. She loved undercover work. Able to blend in with the movers and shakers, Lisa could go in first, make contact with Marr and give them the heads-up on where exactly the target was in relation to the entrance. Once the cuffs were on, she could hang around afterwards and listen to the chat following his arrest, assuming Kate made one. Operation Phoenix was in full swing.

83

The dash into town took minutes, Northumbria officers flooding the area from all directions. On Carmichael's signal, they hit the casino mob-handed, arresting their target on suspicion of assault, a nod from Carmichael picking him out among his fellow gamblers, a clean strike. No injured personnel. No fuss. No fighting or shouting. Why should there be? These people had the finance to secure quality advice, the best legal teams money could buy. Mr Cool would be expecting bail in a matter of hours. Within no time, he'd be clocking up the Air Miles on his way to who knows where.

Well, Kate would see about that.

Taking him out the casino's rear entrance, they loaded the piece of shit into a van that had been backed up to facilitate a quick getaway, two firearms officers getting in with him. They were both covered up, so as not to be identified. Kate gave Hank instructions to take them somewhere other than Middle Earth. If they went there, every officer and civilian leaving the premises was vulnerable. There was every possibility that his ruthless cohorts could mount an attack with automatic weapons when they left work.

Take a SWAT team with you.

Torres would be loving this.

The undisclosed location was very close to the police armoury, a destination that would remain secret to all but a small team of trusted detectives. Each one had been vetted by Bright. All were trained in covert operations. As her watch ticked past midnight, Kate followed the armed convoy, confident that Bright would do this right. He'd had dealings with the IRA in the past and knew instinctively what they were up against.

He called her.

She could tell he too was in transit.

'Kate, I'm on my way to you. This guy is bad news. I want no one within a hundred yards of him who can't keep their mouths shut . . .' As if she needed reminding that lives might be lost should news of the arrest get out. 'Gotta go,' he said. 'I have a call waiting.' He disconnected.

Gates opened up ahead as the van approached, allowing them through. Kate followed them in. The van swung round in a wide arc, then reversed until it was almost touching an open door, at which point the suspect was bundled into the building and processed, all personal possessions removed: a Hublot watch worth the best part of thirty grand, a shedload of cash, a mobile phone that was sure to be a burner.

Kate allowed the suspect to sweat while she grabbed a sandwich. The meal Jo had made for her had been abandoned on the stove. If she was awake in Kate's office, she'd have heard the news and would be waiting for an update. With no time to take care of it, Kate sat down to work out an interview strategy. This was not going to be easy.

While she was preparing, her mobile rang: Torres.

Kate didn't answer. She needed her focus on Mr Cool.

A knock at the door. 'Come!'

Hank wandered in and sat down. 'What did I say? Once an addict.'

'Smart arse.' Kate smiled. 'It never occurred to me that the cocky bastard would return to the casino. Marr's tip-off has put us in the driving seat.'

Hank didn't respond.

She eyed the papers in his hand. 'Tell me that is good news.'

'Not really . . .' He threw a post-mortem report on her desk. 'As we thought, Robbo was shot four times in the chest, once in the back of the head. He was probably kneeling at the time. Bastards.'

Kate couldn't allow it to put her off her stride. 'Anything else?'

'Yeah, the vehicle he was thrown from and the R8 have both been found on fire.'

'Together?'

'It seems that our man has friends. Someone knows he's been lifted and they dumped the incriminating vehicles. Kate, it could be Marr. Maybe our suspect is expendable.'

'Fuck!' Kate exploded. 'Get Carmichael out of there. Now!'

'Calm down. An extraction is underway.'

Hank didn't often show his emotions – let alone fear – but on this occasion he did, despite what he'd just said. How could she calm down when all she could think of was the look of disappointment on Carmichael's face when she'd asked her to stay behind at Jackson's apartment, the fact that she'd allowed it to sway her decision to leave her there? Deploying her at the casino had placed her in grave danger.

'Christ!' Wanting to weep, Kate wiped her face with both hands. She couldn't lose Carmichael. She couldn't. 'Does the guv'nor know?'

'Who do you think is getting her out?'

'He's not. He's on his way here.'

'When he heard that the vehicles had been found, he diverted immediately.'

Kate remembered the call waiting. 'You should've told me, not him.'

'I'm telling you now. He's SIO in name only. This is your case and you have a credible suspect in custody.'

Hank's head went down.

Kate misread him. 'The vehicles are burned out?'

'Not totally. It's Guy Fawkes. The dash and splash were out in force. They happened to be driving by an allotment in the East End when they saw the flames. Thinking it was kids lighting a bonfire early, they went to investigate. They doused the vehicle and notified the control room.'

'Why?'

'They found what looked like bullet holes.' Hank looked away.

There was more . . . Kate sensed it.

She waited.

Hank added, 'Robbo's watch was found concealed beneath the flooring. He hid it there for us to find, Kate. He must've known it was never going to end well.'

84

The suspect was uncooperative. He'd refused to give a name on the grounds that he'd done nothing wrong and had waived his right to a solicitor. That didn't surprise Kate: unless he was being locked up for something and wasn't getting out, why would he bother? The smirk he was sporting slid off his face when she arrested him on suspicion of the murder of a police officer, Acting DI Paul Robson, and an additional offence, the abduction of Stephanie Jackson. She didn't mention that she had a credible witness.

Rossiter wouldn't live long if she did.

Her suspect chose to exercise his right to legal counsel then, a London brief she suspected was on the payroll of his employer, whoever that might be.

'As you wish.' Kate gathered up her papers. 'Make yourself comfortable. This may take a while. Me? I have all the time in the world. Detective Inspector Robson was one of mine. I look after my people in life and in death.'

'So did she.' His eyes were cold, full of anger and resentment.

She? Oh God!

Had Marr shafted them both? Kate didn't react, but she couldn't breathe. Couldn't wait to get out of there either. Wondering what the state of play was with Carmichael, it seemed to take an age to find the strength to stand. Pushing through the door, she stood against it, hyperventilating. Hank's face was chalky white. As they proceeded along the corridor, the double door ahead of them swung open.

Bright walked through it.

Kate stopped walking, lost for words.

Hank's hand closed around hers, a gentle squeeze.

362

'Carmichael's fine,' Bright said. 'More than fine . . . she won fifty quid.'

Kate laughed, then nearly wept, unable to suppress her relief.

Covering his face with his hands, Hank turned away, a moment to compose himself, not quick enough to hide his emotional reaction to the fact that Carmichael was safe and well. In all the years they had worked together, Kate had never ever seen him so overwhelmed by news, good or bad, not even when Robbo's body was tossed from a moving vehicle outside Middle Earth.

'You two look exhausted.' Bright spread his arms. 'C'mon, group hug.'

He sent them home. They'd have to wait till morning for the brief to arrive from the capital. The suspect refused a local one. Collecting Jo from Middle Earth, Kate hardly said a word until they arrived at her place, greeted by Nelson at the door. Kate gave the dog a pat, ruffling his coat, her mind on her suspect. She was stressing on how flimsy the evidence was against him. She was certain she'd be able to link him forensically to Jackson's flat – Rossiter had witnessed him dragging her out of there into the R8 and would make an excellent witness. Jackson hadn't been seen since – so no problem with the abduction allegation. That car and the van in which Robbo's watch had been found were driven to the allotment and set on fire within minutes of the arrest at the casino. Unless they found something more, Kate was on dodgy ground.

Was Marr that clever?

It was clear that Robbo trusted her. At her own admission, she'd identified him as vulnerable. Had she picked him out as someone she might cultivate? Had what she'd told Kate been part of a dangerous game? Was she now warning them off, demonstrating her supremacy? On the flip side, A TIE action – to Trace, Interview and Eliminate her – had found nothing to link her to the underworld. She'd also run a successful business for years.

If not Marr, then who had the suspect paid to tip off his crew?

Kate needed the answers to those questions and more. Unsure if she could summon the energy to do battle with a top London brief who would tear apart uncorroborated evidence, unable to think where something more substantial might come from, she fell into bed. Bright had found Carmichael. For now, that was all that mattered.

Kate slept badly, the face of Marr entering her dreams. It morphed into that of her suspect. They were tormenting her, laughing at her, images that faded away in slow motion, only to be replaced by one of Robbo and Irene, laughing at his birthday party, so very much in love. A lingering doubt woke Kate at four a.m., sweaty and unable to rest. Using her mobile's torch to light her way, she slid out from under the covers, a backward glance as she reached the bedroom door.

Jo was dead to the world, snuggled into her pillow, a strand of hair falling across one eye, her lips slightly parted, her chest rising and falling shallowly. The sight of her lying there was something Kate could never have imagined a couple of weeks ago. Sneaking down the stairs, she entered the kitchen, closing the door before turning on the light.

The floor tiles felt refreshingly cool beneath her feet.

Turning on the tap, she filled a glass with water, helping herself to a couple of Paracetamol. There was an A4 pad on the counter. Grabbing it and a pen, Kate took them to the table and sat down.

85

An hour later, and no further forward, Jo's arms enveloped Kate from behind, a kiss on the top of her head, a gentle nudge that she should return to bed and get some sleep before she resumed her interview with her suspect and his high-profile London brief. Wise words, but Kate couldn't rest. She stroked Jo's hand, a show of affection to let her know that she was grateful for the support.

Aware that she'd never get Kate back to bed, Jo made them a coffee, strong and black, then grabbed a chair and sat down. Pulling her dressing gown around her shoulders, tying the belt in a bow around her waist, her eyes found the scribbled notes spread out on the table, mostly questions Kate needed the answers to.

Jo looked at her. 'Does any of that make sense?'

'Not much . . .' Kate shared the nightmare that had kept her awake before she'd slipped out of bed, the fact that she felt woefully unprepared, dreading the day to come. 'Sorry, I tried not to wake you.' She tapped the notepad. 'I'm going round and round in circles here, to be honest.'

'I'm not surprised. Kate, you're pushing yourself too hard. Everyone has a limit, and I know you don't want to hear it, but I think you've reached yours. What is it that's bothering you, specifically I mean? I might be able to help.'

Yawning, Kate rubbed at her temples. 'Bright said that Lisa was with Marr when he walked into the casino, sharing a drink and a snack would you believe, two punters taking a break from the gaming tables. As soon as Lisa clocked him, she realised that it was time to go. Neither of them seemed concerned about Marr—'

'That's good, isn't it?'

'I don't know is the honest answer.'

The blinds were open but it was dark outside, the only light a hazy orange glow from a street lamp beyond Jo's rear yard. Something moved outside, so quick Kate didn't see what it was. It turned out to be nothing more than the neighbour's cat, but it had produced a moment of fear, prompting her to get up and check that the door was locked and bolted. Pulling down the blinds, she turned to face Jo, spooked but trying not to show it.

'Look, the less you know about this case, the better.'

'I should know.' Jo's tired eyes flashed a reprimand. 'Will you stop trying to protect me? I'm a professional, a fully paid-up member of the MIT, in case you'd conveniently forgotten. If you don't tell me, someone else will, so stop buggering about.'

Kate sat down, half an eye on the door. 'When I was about to leave the interview room, I told my suspect that Robbo was one of mine and that I look after my officers. He said, and I quote: "So did she". Note the word "did" past tense. I took it as a heavy hint that he'd been shafted by someone high up in his organisation – a woman – and that Marr had played me and cut him adrift. I may have miscalculated.'

'Slip of the tongue?'

'I doubt that. He was angry, for sure, but also sad. I think he meant someone else.'

'Like who?'

'What if he was talking about Nikolaev's victim, a woman on 0113, someone he looked up to and respected, the person whose death started all this killing?' Kate took in the wall clock. 'I have less than four hours before I resume interviewing.'

'Then we'd better get dressed.'

86

They took a cab to Middle Earth. In the incident room, Kate sat down at the first work station she came to, logging on with her warrant card. Before she'd left London, the DEA had provided her with a large folder containing information she hadn't had time to read, let alone digest. She asked Jo to fetch it from her office and start going through it while she accessed the passenger list.

The clock was ticking.

Collecting it, Jo sat down next to her, turning to the first page of the thick document, an index of all drug cartels and their personnel, living or dead, including the countries they hailed from, any significant arrests, indictments and periods in custody, the amount of violent murders they were thought to have been responsible for.

'These figures are mind-boggling,' she said. 'I'm not talking about the body count. The amounts of money these people rake in is unbelievable.'

'That's probably the tip of the iceberg. For every name in there, there'll be ten the DEA don't know about.' Kate glanced at the folder Jo was reading. The lowlifes listed had inspired many a book or film. It stuck in her craw to think that men and women who traded in other people's misery had been immortalised in this way.

'Exactly what am I looking for?' Jo asked.

'If my theory is correct—'

'You have a theory?' Jo gave a wry smile. 'Outstanding!'

'Don't take the piss. Torres and I may have missed a trick. It's not something I'm proud of. So far, we've been concentrating our efforts on men who either arrived on feeder flights from the North-East or who had some connection with areas associated with the drug trade.' She let the sentence hang, though the implication was clear.

Jo's smile turned to a grimace. 'Don't be so hard on yourself. Nine times out of ten, drug cartels *are* run by men. It's the same in any illegitimate economy. Historically, women have held auxiliary roles: cultivating crops, acting as mules, stashing drugs, street-level tasks – you could say the risky stuff that leads to imprisonment. I can't imagine that Homeland Security technicians won't have passed the images of all adults through facial recognition, regardless of gender—'

'Yes, but don't believe the hype. Artificial intelligence isn't all it's cracked up to be. Race and gender play their part in skewing the results. The darker the skin, the more the accuracy drops, particularly in women. We're white, so we'd have little chance of escape, but a woman of colour could probably sneak through at a push.'

'Back up, you've lost me.'

'It's complicated,' Kate explained. 'Our suspect is foreign, Hispanic or Portuguese, Marr said, but I did wonder if he might hail from Central or South America. That's where the DEA's focus is. Ninety-five per cent of drug imports reach the US via Mexican cartels. I suspect that our guy may be a lieutenant sent here about three years ago to muscle in on Nikolaev's drug-trafficking operation. If his boss was on that plane, he may even be the shooter who took Nikolaev out, though I can't prove it yet. If I'm right about this, we should concentrate our efforts on non-white females.'

Kate pulled the images of all non-white female passengers up on her computer screen, asking Jo to look at those listed on the DEA report. It was good to be working together again, as they had on many occasions in pursuit of the truth. They ploughed on for a good hour, Jo making occasional observations on the information she was reading, the sheer numbers of killings carried out by those who made their money from smuggling narcotics to major cities across the globe, the US being the largest consumer.

'Do you have a digital copy of this file?' she asked.

'Can't you read it?'

'Yeah, but I'd like to blow up the images. These are too small.'

Preoccupied with what she was doing, Kate pushed a laptop Jo's way. The profiler already knew the password.

'That's strange,' Kate said.

Jo looked up. 'What is?'

'There's a first-class female passenger here for whom there's no next of kin listed in Casualty Bureau records – suspicious, don't you think? She's not been reported missing either.' Kate was asking herself why. The passenger's name was Maria Alexander.

This needed looking into.

Kate stopped what she was doing and rang Bright. An early riser, he was up and eating, a fry-up, he said, guaranteed to last him all day. She had a feeling he was going to need it. 'Guv, I might be on to something. I know we are time-limited, but is there any possibility we can delay the interview with the man we have in custody?'

He didn't ask and she didn't offer any more detail.

'Where are you?'

'In the incident room.'

'And Jo?'

'With me.' She glanced at the floor. 'And we have a guard dog.'

Nelson wagged his tail. Bright and the rest of the team loved him. Jo often brought him to work. Kate was about to throw her a smile but she was otherwise engaged, staring at the image on Kate's computer, comparing it with one she'd found in the digital version of the DEA report, her eyes flicking between the two. Kate couldn't see the laptop screen – it was at an angle, turned away from her – but hope and intrigue reigned. Transfixed by the expression on Jo's face, she almost forgot that she was still on the phone when her guv'nor spoke again . . .

'What was it about "go home and get some kip" you two failed to understand?'

Jo didn't react, though she couldn't fail to hear him.

'Your breakfast is getting cold, guv.' Kate wanted him gone. 'Tell me, yes or no, can we delay the interview?'

'No, but keep working. I'm happy to pit my wits against your man's poncey legal counsel and buy you some time. I live with Ellen. She can argue for England, but I can still get the better of her.'

'Hey!' Ellen's voice made itself heard in the background.

'Ouch.' Bright laughed. 'I have an audible witness to that assault.'

Kate disconnected, emailing her interview notes to him, then reached out for the laptop, bringing two images side by side, zooming in on each in turn. The one on the left was a passport photo of the dead woman, Maria Alexander, a Kensington resident who, bizarrely, no one seemed interested in; the one on the right, an American police mugshot. There were differences – the subject had paid a lot of money to change her appearance – but there was no disputing her identity.

87

As their MIT colleagues drifted into work, Jo and Kate moved into the privacy of her office. With Bright busy interviewing their suspect at a secret location, he wouldn't need to commandeer her space. Time to do more digging. When they were finished, Kate sent three images to Torres: one of the unidentified suspect Kate had in custody; the passport photo of Alexander and the police mugshot Jo had found in the DEA's report, explaining the whys and wherefores of what they had found. Maria Alexander had been passing herself off as a legitimate businesswoman, though in reality she was one of the richest, most dangerous women in the world. Her real name was Maria Jiménez.

Minutes later, Torres arranged a conference call. This time, Garcia and Jo sat in, four minds preferable to two. Kate took care of the introductions and the meeting got underway.

Torres didn't often look rattled.

She did now.

Jiménez was a relation of the late Margarita Montoya, a Mexican drug trafficker whose cocaine distribution network once spanned the US; a woman alleged to have ordered multiple assassinations that ran into the hundreds while shipping cocaine from her home country to New York, Miami and New Orleans. Despite the notoriety of these two women on the other side of the world, Kate had never heard of either before today.

Kate told the Americans what she knew: 'According to the DEA report, Montoya groomed Jiménez to take over the organisation, but she was caught and locked up. In 2008, four years before Montoya's death, Jiménez was released from prison, more powerful than when she went in, thanks to corrupt law enforcement. Until she got on that doomed flight, she was very much alive and active.'

Jo had read that she'd settled in Venezuela, using it as a base for her operation, shipping cocaine through Mexico. She had several aliases, including Mujer Malvada (evil woman), and within her organisation was known as La Madonna Negra – the Black Madonna – and Kate passed that on. 'She married an Englishman, Terence Alexander, a male version of herself, an organised crime syndicate leader, someone with a legal team whose bill would make your eyes bleed. They lived the good life in Kensington, London and yet he never reported her missing. It seems my informant was right. These people are in a different league. Nikolaev picked a fight he couldn't possibly win.'

Torres, Garcia, Kate and Jo spent a lot of time discussing how an IED might have been secreted aboard 0113, whether in the hold or the cabin. In either scenario, given strict security procedures, enhanced state-of-the-art scanners and X-ray machines capable of screening for explosive chemicals, metals or radiological materials, any attempt to get one through represented a huge risk.

'No system is foolproof,' Torres said. 'Modern technologies can only go so far. You go clean through security and get dirty at the other end. Travellers are only scanned once.'

'An inside job?' Jo queried.

'It happens,' Garcia said.

'More wreckage is what we need—'

'Talking of wreckage,' Torres interrupted. 'If we find proof that the explosion occurred in the hold, I'll need you back at Heathrow and the search will go on.' She stopped talking as the door behind Kate and Jo was flung open.

Carmichael arrived in the room like she'd been shot from a cannon. She pulled up sharp, her face going red when she realised that Kate and Jo were in conference with Homeland Security personnel.

The expression on her face was one of horror.

Torres was staring at her from the screen.

Stifling a grin, Kate said: 'Special agents, meet Detective Constable Lisa Carmichael, who will undergo additional training on how to enter a room as soon as this call ends.'

Carmichael didn't know where to put herself. 'Sorry, guv. I was expecting the chief super.'

'Evidently. There's been a change of plan. He's with our suspect. Can you give us a moment?'

'I'll wait outside.'

'No need, we're done here.' Buoyed by a breakthrough in the case, Torres was keen to put the wheels in motion with the DEA to establish the identity of the man Kate had in custody. 'Congratulations, everyone. The Phoenix is rising.'

'It sure is!' Carmichael had come with good news.

Torres was intrigued. 'You have something to add before I go, Detective?'

'Yes, ma'am.'

Kate gave Carmichael the nod to proceed.

She spoke directly to Torres. 'Rubbing shoulders with Marr paid off. We won the jackpot, so to speak. We might not know our suspect's name yet, but forensics found minute traces of blood in the strap of his Hublot watch.'

'Do you have a match?' Kate asked.

'It's Robbo's, guv.'

'So it wasn't Marat Nikolaev as we first thought.'

'No . . .' This was a difficult conversation for Carmichael but she recovered quickly, her focus back on Torres. 'The even better news is, CSIs have finished their examination of Jackson's flat. My guv'nor asked them to take it apart and they have. In the living room, they found a burner phone hidden beneath the floorboards and lifted prints that match the man we currently have in custody. There's no match with our database, but perhaps there will be on yours. I'll send them to you in a moment, but you all need to see and hear this.'

Carmichael slid a thumb drive into Kate's computer and pressed play. Kate angled it so the special agents could view it, too. The video clip showed the interior of what resembled an old barn or storage facility, long abandoned by the looks of it. Rusting farm tools were propped up in the background. It had been filmed from the outside looking in, jagged glass visible around the edges of the window frame, every surface covered in dust, cobwebs and dead flies. The camera, obviously handheld, wobbled slightly as it zoomed in on two men engaged in an angry exchange.

Whoever was holding the device was breathing heavily enough for it to register.

The clip was shot from over the left shoulder of a well-built man who was facing away from the lens. Clearly this was not the lowlife Kate had in custody. His accent was unmistakably Russian. The other man's hands were tied together above his head by wire that bit into his wrists and was looped over an industrial hook, the type used for lifting heavy weights, suspending his body about two feet from the ground. Dripping blood had covered his face and clothing. He was pleading for his life . . .

On both sides of the Atlantic, detectives, special agents and criminal profiler collectively held their breath. They all knew what was coming. The standing man turned, a sinister sneer on his face as if playing to an audience. He spoke in Russian to someone who was out of shot, then threw his head back, laughing.

For Torres's benefit, Kate paused the tape, identifying him as Nikolaev's son, Marat – a man who had been, and, as far as she knew, was still under surveillance.

She pressed play . . .

On screen, Marat was clearly enjoying himself.

'You make mistake, Stu.' Marat spread his hands wide. 'Your name is short for stupid, no? You kill eeeeverybody on plane. My papa paid many bucks for good job, but you fuck up. He is dead because of you. How we blame Americans now?'

The hanging man was begging to be spared, mumbling about a faulty timer, trying to explain what went wrong.

'What kind of bomb-maker you are? You don't tell time too good.' Marat laughed again. 'As enforcer, is my job to punish.'

'Please, don't hurt me. I'm sorry about your father—'

'He was piece of shit. You think I care about him?' Marat pointed at his chest with both hands. 'I am big boss now.'

He screwed a silencer to his weapon.

Carmichael looked like she was about to vomit. Kate didn't feel too good herself. It was one thing turning up after the event of a violent death, but witnessing a life taken took things to another level. There were six thuds as Marat emptied his gun, five to the torso, one to the head. The bomb-maker's body jerked and swayed like a macabre puppet. The place, should they ever find it, was now a crime scene.

88

So many people had lost their lives on Flight 0113, a sudden and cataclysmic event that had sparked a wide-ranging investigation involving law enforcement across the globe. Many theories had been raised and discounted. Terrorism had led everyone down the wrong road, but Kate had lots of people to thank for their contribution in the battle against organised crime. Her guv'nor, Detective Chief Superintendent Philip Bright, was top of that list for having turned a blind eye to so many indiscretions; Hank, her 2ic, a close second for shadowing her and keeping her sane. There was her friend, Air Accident Investigator Rob Clark, who'd managed to circumvent red tape – when no one else could – so she could join the inner circle of top-level investigators. Kate had been proud to collaborate with Homeland Security's SAC Torres, Special Agent Garcia and their Homeland Security and DEA colleagues. She was proud of the Murder Investigation Team who had worked round the clock to bring about a resolution – such as it was – off-book in the case of Carmichael who, at one point, Kate feared might have been spirited away by underworld figures and executed. Then there was Brian Allen, without whom she'd have remained undercover in the baggage shed as Lou Paige with nothing to show for it.

The DEA were able to provide fingerprint identification and a name for the 'piece of shit' Bright had in custody. Raúl Rodríguez had coughed under interrogation – it was almost impossible to get blood out of a watch strap – but then he made the fatal mistake of offering the head of Northumbria CID a bribe that would make him a rich man if he buried the evidence. He was told in no uncertain terms that he was wasting his breath, that British coppers were different from those in Mexico, that they couldn't be bought. Rodríguez was charged with Robbo's murder and, on Rossiter's evidence, the abduction of Jackson, arguably now missing presumed dead. They hadn't managed to pin Yulian Nikolaev's murder on Rodríguez yet, but that still might come. It mattered not in the scheme of things. He'd go down for life, and that was good enough for Kate.

Marr's evidence had proven useful. She'd led detectives to Jackson. In turn, the burner CSIs recovered from her flash Jesmond apartment turned the investigation on its head, the video clip providing irrefutable evidence against Marat Nikolaev for the cold-blooded murder of an unknown man. As suspected, the offence had been filmed by Rodríguez as insurance and stashed at Jackson's place for retrieval and use when it suited him. Fortunately, he was arrested before that could happen, but what better way to get rid of an arch-enemy than to catch him in the act?

Kate suspected that Rodríguez had followed Marat, hoping it would lead him to the bomb-maker – both sides were gunning for him – and just happened upon the brutal murder taking place, saving him the bother of killing the man himself. Rodríguez would not admit it to police, but that was their take on it. In the absence of prints on the mobile, there was no evidence to suggest that Jackson handled or had any knowledge of it before her sudden disappearance.

It was clear from the dialogue on the clip that Marat Nikolaev had taken over his father's illegal drugs empire. Obvious too that his argument with the bomb-maker concerned the death of Maria Jiménez-Alexander and the subsequent backlash that had triggered a bitter turf war, and the death of his father, who he hated with a passion.

Enquiries revealed that Jiménez-Alexander had a regular

arrangement with a Heathrow worker to exchange her bag once she was through security with an identical one that contained money, jewellery and fake passports she knew wouldn't get through airport security. Having got wind of it, with or without his son's help, Yulian Nikolaev had paid the worker even more to substitute the bag for one containing an explosive device.

You go clean through security and get dirty at the other end.

Travellers are only scanned once.

Torres had summed it up perfectly.

Nikolaev's plan – that the detonation should not take place until after the plane touched down in the US, laying the blame elsewhere – was perfect but for one small matter: human error. The Heathrow worker claimed he knew nothing of what was contained in the bag he switched, but was now on remand facing trial for conspiracy to murder Jiménez-Alexander and, by extension, the manslaughter of three hundred and fifteen innocent civilians and crew en route to JFK.

These same charges were levelled against Marat Nikolaev when arrested by an armed response team within minutes of the video falling into possession of police, the clip providing conclusive proof that he'd also shot dead an unidentified male with the first name Stu, without blinking. As soon as Kate had viewed the footage, she'd ordered his immediate detention. He hadn't been 'big boss' for long, and would spend the rest of his natural life behind bars.

It saddened her to think that his father's plan had gone so horribly wrong and cost so many lives, leaving the bereaved families devastated and without closure. Kate hated loose ends and did her level best to answer all the questions raised during the life of an enquiry, large or small, but no resolution of a case was ever 100 per cent complete.

Examination of the surveillance log led her to conclude that Marat had murdered the bomb-maker prior to the team being deployed by her. Subsequently, neither the kill site nor his body had been found and Stephanie Jackson was still missing, presumed dead. Kate didn't think she'd ever find her body. She would try.

It was clear that Jackson had been playing both ends against the middle; Marr had seen her with Raúl Rodríguez and Marat Nikolaev on separate casino visits. Jackson had been dicing with death, vying for the affections of two ruthless men prepared to give her money and feed her cocaine addiction.

She was probably the one who ended up with her throat cut . . .

She'd never bother Marr again.

In the days following the take-down of these two drug lords, over two hundred officers from Northumbria and neighbouring forces had rounded up as many of their cohorts as they could find, seizing hundreds of thousands of British pounds and foreign currencies, an armoury of weapons and huge quantities of drugs. The seizures had the potential to save many lives. Kate liked to think that, in a small way, it would balance out those taken on Flight 0113. In the US, the wheels of justice were also turning, with arrests in New York and other US cities, a joint report being painstakingly prepared by British Police, Homeland Security and the DEA for the United States Attorney General.

The case would run and run. In time, Marat Nikolaev would be interviewed by the American authorities, though Bright was keen that he should be tried in the UK. And yes, he wanted Kate, Hank and Northumbria Police to take the credit, not the Metropolitan Police Gold Commander, Waverley, Homeland Security or the FBI. The US would almost certainly demand that British authorities surrender him for trial, US citizens making up the majority of those who'd lost their lives. It had taken over twelve years to reach a verdict in the Lockerbie disaster, the costs running into millions. Kate hoped that the wealth of evidence against Marat would speed the process this time around.

She wondered what Brian was up to, believing that there was some good in even the most audacious villain. This one had proved her right so many times, saving Hank and providing intelligence that she'd never have uncovered without his help. Jo had tapped into Kate's ambivalence towards him. The profiler was understandably wary. She had mixed feelings towards him, too. Though, unlike Kate, she hadn't seen his sons' bodies – or what was left of them – after they were brutally tortured to death by a rival gang. It was far from pretty. Brian was wrong to exact revenge and take the law into his own hands. But Kate knew, deep down, that if they had been *her* offspring – or Jo's – she'd have been tempted to do exactly the same, morally reprehensible though it may seem to some.

89

Robbo's burial was hard to take, hundreds of mourners turning out to pay their respects along with a guard of honour. Unexpectedly, Irene brought Callum along to see his daddy sent in a special box to heaven, his uniform hat atop the casket, surrounded by floral tributes from family, friends and colleagues dressed in full uniform. The sight of that child holding hands with his mum nearly broke Kate's heart. The fact that his father had died in the line of duty while taking her place as SIO she'd have to learn to live with.

A posthumous award would come later.

Afterwards, Kate had gone to see her father, taking Jo and her sons along, a statement of intent he could never have imagined and wasn't expecting. For once, he seemed pleased to see her. He was home and doing well; his attitude towards her had softened considerably. Finally, he could see how much it meant to his daughter to have a family around her, Jo especially. Better get used to it. She had no plans to leave and there was no way Kate would allow history to repeat itself.

At Kate's place later, Tom and James stayed for a quick drink, then left Kate and Jo alone, making an excuse that they had other plans. It was rubbish, of course, but neither woman made much effort to prevent them from leaving. If Kate had learned anything while investigating 0113, it was that she must make adjustments and see more of Jo.

She'd asked Jo to move in and she'd accepted.

Jo was sitting opposite her now, eyes sparkling, a glass of celebratory fizz lifted to lips that Kate found hard not to focus on. They were both ready to make allowances others might see as sacrifices. To do that, Kate would shed the person trapped inside her body for so long, the one who'd been bullied into submission by a senior officer, Atkins, her shift sergeant back when she was a rookie. They might now be the same rank, both DCIs, but he'd caused untold damage to her happiness. She used to think she couldn't change that, though this past couple of weeks had taught her that it was up to her, and no one else, to ensure that he didn't win. Like many of the people she'd come across during this tragic case, Kate had hidden her true identity, compartmentalising her life, being true to no one, least of all herself. She'd allowed Atkins to rule her life for the last time.

The mobile in her pocket vibrated. It was Torres. Jo got up to refill her glass, leaving Kate to take the call. Though not in any detail, Torres now knew about Brian and was less conflicted than Kate. In fact, she wished him well, hoping he'd live the rest of his days on the right side of a cell door.

A lot of people had him to thank for resolving the investigation into 0113.

Ending her call with Torres, Kate called him. When he'd saved Hank from certain death, for obvious reasons there was no commendation for him. 'That'll be the case this time around,' she said. 'Though you should know that my US contact would, and I'm quoting her now, "pin a purple heart on you if she could", and so would I.'

'Kate, I got what I wanted, thanks to you.'

'Which was? You never did tell me the real reason you involved yourself in this case. You can handle yourself, I get that, but Jiménez-Alexander, Rodríguez, Marat and Yulian Nikolaev are off the scale. Why on earth did you take that risk?'

There was a heavy pause.

'Theresa was on that flight,' he said finally.

'What?' Kate was genuinely shocked to hear it.

Brian was talking about his wife, the woman who believed that he'd died in Spain all those years ago when he fled Newcastle, faking his death in order to keep her safe. Last

Kate heard, she was living with his former right-hand man, a heavy called Arthur Ross McKenzie. He'd not only taken over Brian's UK operation, but his wife too. Brian's resurrection hadn't brought her back.

'I'm so sorry,' Kate said.

'Don't be, I lost her a long time ago.'

'McKenzie called you?'

'The minute the plane went down. If you have any sympathy, send him a bunch of flowers, hen. Theresa and I never did get divorced, so if you've come to your senses and hopped on the right bus, now she's gone I'm available, if you're interested.'

Kate wasn't fooled by his humour. She left the kitchen before Jo noticed her sadness. She was worried about her friendly fugitive, remembering his antics when they met on the outskirts of London, the gun aimed at his head. Was he contemplating a replay?

For the first time in his life, Brian had nothing to live for.

As she entered the hallway, Kate bent down to scoop up a pile of letters from the floor and others that Jo had placed in a neat pile on the table, having let herself in the night Kate arrived home from the south. They were mostly utility bills but, as she sifted through them, she came across one whose handwriting she recognised. It had a London postmark dated Friday, 17 October, the day Jo had been due to fly to New York. Moving into the living room, Kate sat down on the sofa, cross-legged. She tore open the letter, a single sheet of good writing paper with a watermark, the script beautifully written in fountain pen.

Hello Kate,

I'm writing this from Heathrow. I was in such a state before I left, I didn't even know what I was doing. I'm not sure what I said to Fiona, but I figured that I might have gone too far, returning the key to your ~~heart~~ front door.

I'm sorry, I didn't mean to hurt you.

I'm so relieved to hear that your old man survived his op – has he cracked a smile yet? Anyway, I thought I'd write you a letter, rather than call. A text didn't seem right somehow.

You sounded very emotional on the phone. Understandable. You're up against it, at home and in the office, I know that now. Too bad I didn't recognise it sooner. I made a mistake and I'm truly sorry. I hope you're not blaming yourself.

I'm just as much at fault.

When I responded to the callout over the airport tannoy, I knew it was you. I was thrilled, until you told me that it was a work issue and not an excuse to stop this nonsense and return home, but it wasn't to be. It was only when I realised that you were trying to save a life that the guilt kicked in. I feel terrible now. If you managed to do that, or even if you didn't, I know you'll have given it your best shot, as you always do.

I'm so proud of you.

I hope the case went well and you now have your shit together. Hopefully, you're basking in the glory of closing the investigation. If nothing else, you're good at that!

You're good at other stuff too, but I won't go there. ☺

I feel totally lost without you, Kate. I wanted you to know that I'm not going to New York. I need some space, but not in the US without you by my side. I'll find somewhere else to lick my wounds until you're ready to talk to me. I'd have come home if you'd asked me to. The fact that you didn't, spoke volumes. I can't imagine how angry you must be.

What am I saying?

You must be climbing the walls.

Not sure how long I'll be away but, having stamped my feet over our fucked-up relationship, it might be good to put some distance between us for a while. It'll give us both time to cool off and think of what we're about to throw away. Who knows, we might even come to our senses.

Kate, I adore you. If my luck is in, maybe one day you'll realise just how much. I know one thing: if I was ever in danger, I can think of no one I'd rather have looking out for me than you. Not that it matters now. It was my choice to end it. I don't expect you to understand my point of view, let alone forgive and forget. See, you don't hold the monopoly on bad judgement in the love department.

I'm desperately sad right now but I hope we can get through this and give it one last chance. I hear acting like grown-ups is all the rage!

Please think about it.

I do love you,

Jo x

Kate lost it then, big blobs of tears pouring from her eyes. The case had taken its toll on her from the moment she left Newcastle on a mission to find Jo. The list of her experiences seemed endless: informing Tom and James that their mother may never be coming home; barging her way into the Casualty Bureau without authority; disobeying her guv'nor; risking her job and Hank's; meeting secretly with a fugitive from justice; finding Jo, then losing Robbo; giving Irene the death message; attending the funeral today when Acting Detective Inspector Paul Robson booked off for the last time. All these things had come at a price, awakening emotions in Kate she never knew she had.

She'd argued relentlessly, angry with almost everyone: her father, Bright, Waverley, Blue, Esposito, Torres and Jo. Hank, too, on several occasions, though he'd stuck with her throughout, helping keep the dream alive. Had she not been so impetuous, running off to London in search of Jo the minute she heard the news, Kate would have received the letter and saved herself untold agony.

It had all been too much . . .

The letter, the tipping point.

When Kate looked up, Jo was standing in the doorway.

She walked towards Kate and sat down, eyeing the sheet of writing paper in a shaky hand. 'You look like you could use a hug.'

They embraced. 'Why didn't you tell me?' Kate whispered, still holding her.

Jo pulled away. 'I tried . . . twice. As I recall, you were biting my head off at the time.' She gave a shrug. 'I could say it slipped my mind since, but that would be a lie. It's a love letter addressed to you, and a criminal offence to tamper with the Royal Mail.' She made a crazy face. 'Do you know nothing?'

Kate laughed.

Jo bit her lip, a playful expression. 'There's another one here if you're interested.' She took something from the back pocket of her jeans and passed it over – a postcard from Paris. She looked on, watching Kate blush as she read it, then said: 'I'm not entirely sure that one was intended for my eyes.'

Kate grinned. 'That's what you get when you burgle some-one's home.'

'I had a key—'

'But no permission to use it.' Kate held up the card. 'I'm sorry—'

'You can't knock a girl for having good taste. Your postie must love these. I saw you had a few more stuffed in the kitchen drawer. Fiona's good with words, isn't she?' Jo laughed. 'What? Don't look at me like that! I had to have something to do while I waited. Couldn't help myself, guv'nor.'

'Does it bother you?'

'Not unless you're about to give me the brush-off.'

Kate stopped grinning. 'Actually, I do have something to tell you.'

'You slept with her.' Jo spread her hands. 'Can I help it if I can read between the lines?'

'Be serious . . . What I'm making such a hash of affects us both. A proposal. I haven't made my mind up whether or not to accept it. It's a big step, one I don't think I'm ready for.' Seeing that the comment had knocked Jo sideways, Kate put her out of her misery. 'Agent Torres offered me a job in New York, a chance to see the investigation through to the bitter end, if I'm up for it.'

'That's huge. Congratulations!' Jo was crestfallen, trying to hide it.

Kate stroked her right thumb across Jo's left cheek. 'Would you come with me?'

A beaming smile. 'When do we leave?'

'We don't. I just needed to know that you would if I asked you to.'

'You turned it down? Why?'

Kate kept a straight face. 'I'd have thought it was obvious – there's no way I could leave Hank.'

Acknowledgements

Rarely have I been so keen to deliver a book as I was this time around. *Without A Trace* has been a long time coming, and Team Orion are very excited to publish it. I have my brilliant editor, Francesca Pathak, to thank for accepting that Kate Daniels has waited long enough for another outing.

There are others to thank for their contribution: Alainna Hadjigeorgiou, Lynsey Sutherland, Tomás Almeida and copy editor Anne O'Brien, who is nothing short of a magician. Also, everyone who has supported me over the years: fellow writers, readers, bloggers, booksellers and librarians, all at A. M. Heath Literary Agency – you are the best.

A decade ago, agent Oli Munson plucked an aspiring writer from nowhere, believed in her and gave her the chance to realise a dream of being published. That writer was me. From the moment we began working together, he's had my back, understanding why I felt compelled to create the character of Kate. His vision for the series matched my own from the outset. Words cannot express enough gratitude.

A big high five to family Hannah: Paul, Kate, Max and Frankie; Chris, Jodie, Daisy and Finn, whose love and support I value above all else. And finally, Mo, to whom this book is dedicated. In her, I have the perfect muse, professional collaborator and life partner. If you look close enough, she appears in every line of this book, for good reason – without her, Kate Daniels would not exist.

Credits

Mari Hannah and Orion Fiction would like to thank everyone at Orion who worked on the publication of *Without A Trace* in the UK.

Editorial
Francesca Pathak
Lucy Frederick

Copy editor
Anne O'Brien

Proofreader
Jenny Page

Audio
Paul Stark
Amber Bates

Contracts
Anne Goddard
Paul Bulos
Jake Alderson

Design
Debbie Holmes
Tomás Almeida
Joanna Ridley
Nick May

Editorial Management
Charlie Panayiotou
Jane Hughes
Alice Davis

Finance
Jasdip Nandra
Afeera Ahmed
Elizabeth Beaumont
Sue Baker

Marketing
Lynsey Sutherland
Lucy Cameron

Sales
Jen Wilson
Esther Waters
Victoria Laws
Rachael Hum
Ellie Kyrke-Smith
Frances Doyle
Georgina Cutler

STONE & OLIVER SERIES

THE LOST

Alex arrives home from holiday to find that her ten-year-old son Daniel has disappeared. It's the first case together for Northumbria CID officers David Stone and Frankie Oliver. But as the investigation unfolds, they realise the family's betrayal goes deeper than anyone suspected. This isn't just a missing persons case. Stone and Oliver are hunting a killer.

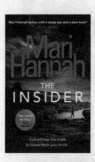

THE INSIDER

When the body of a young woman is found by a Northumberland railway line, it's a baptism of fire for detective duo DCI David Stone and DS Frankie Oliver. The case is tough by anyone's standards, but Stone is convinced that there's a leak in his team — someone is giving the killer a head start on the investigation. These women are being targeted for a reason. And the next target is close to home...

THE SCANDAL

When *Herald* court reporter, Chris Adams, is found stabbed to death in Newcastle with no eyewitnesses, the MIT are stumped. Adams was working on a scoop that would make his name. But what was the story he was investigating? And who was trying to cover it up? When a link to a missing woman is uncovered, the investigation turns on its head. The exposé has put more than Adams' life in danger. And it's not over yet.

Help us make the next generation of readers

We – both author and publisher – hope you enjoyed this book. We believe that you can become a reader at any time in your life, but we'd love your help to give the next generation a head start.

Did you know that 9% of children don't have a book of their own in their home, rising to 13% in disadvantaged families*? We'd like to try to change that by asking you to consider the role you could play in helping to build readers of the future.

We'd love you to think of sharing, borrowing, reading, buying or talking about a book with a child in your life and spreading the love of reading. We want to make sure the next generation continue to have access to books, wherever they come from.

And if you would like to consider donating to charities that help fund literacy projects, find out more at www.literacytrust.org.uk and www.booktrust.org.uk.

Thank you.

As reported by the National Literacy Trust